Praise for Rob

Munich

"The Munich conference has had many histories, but in *Munich*, Robert Harris gives the events their best fictional treatment yet."
—*The Christian Science Monitor*

"An intelligent thriller . . . with exacting attention to historical detail. The novel's power lies in the conflict between our hindsight and the characters' all-too-believable hopes and fears."
—*The Times* (London), Best Historical Fiction of the Year

"An entertaining mix of diplomacy and derring-do. . . . History buffs should find it exhilarating."   —*Richmond-Times Dispatch*

"Another thrilling historical novel from Robert Harris."
—*The Guardian*

"Harris has built a career upon painstakingly researched what-if stories centered on World War II, and with *Munich*, he weaves fiction into the fabric of history without even the tiniest hint of a seam. This is a fine addition to a fine writer's oeuvre."
—*BookPage*

"Thumbs up. Harris fashions an absorbing tale."
—*Metro* (London)

"Gripping. . . . Harris is a marvelously compelling storyteller. . . . A historical novel, a novel of ideas, and a gripping thriller."
—*The Scotsman*

Robert Harris
Munich

Robert Harris is the bestselling author of fourteen novels: the Cicero Trilogy—*Imperium, Lustrum,* and *Dictator*— *Fatherland, Enigma, Archangel, Pompeii, The Ghost, The Fear Index, An Officer and a Spy,* which won four prizes including the Walter Scott Prize for Historical Fiction, *Conclave, Munich, The Second Sleep,* and *V2.* Several of his books have been adapted into films, including *The Ghost.* His work has been translated into thirty-seven languages. He lives in West Berkshire with his wife, Gill Hornby. .

www.robert-harris.com
Twitter: @ Robert___Harris
Facebook.com/RobertHarrisAuthor

Also by Robert Harris

Munich

Munich

Robert Harris

Vintage Books
A Division of Penguin Random House LLC
New York

TO MATILDA

FIRST VINTAGE BOOKS MOVIE TIE-IN EDITION,
JANUARY 2022

Library of Congress Control Number: 2017959856

Vintage Books Trade Paperback ISBN: 978-0-525-43643-0
Vintage Books MTI ISBN: 978-0-593-46867-8
eBook ISBN: 978-0-525-52027-6

Map copyright © 2017 by Gemma Fowlie
Eagle illustrations © Naci Yavuz/Dreamtime
Book design by Betty Lew

www.vintagebooks.com

Printed in the United States of America
10 9 8 7 6 5 4 3 2 1

We should always be aware that what now liest
in the past once lay in the future.

—F. W. MAITLAND, HISTORIAN (1850–1906)

We ought to have gone to war in 1938 . . .
September 1938 would have been the most
favourable date.

—ADOLF HITLER, FEBRUARY 1945

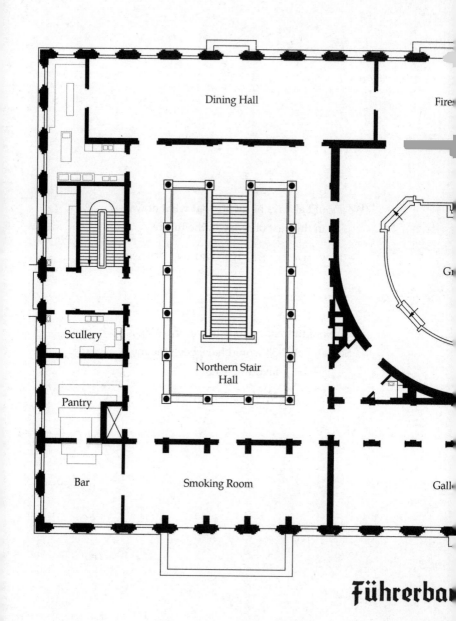

Dining Hall

Fire

G

Scullery

Northern Stair
Hall

Pantry

Bar

Smoking Room

Gall

Führerba

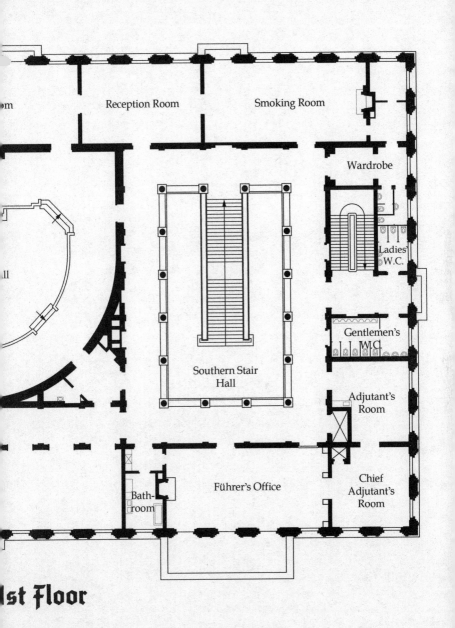

Reception Room

Smoking Room

om

Wardrobe

ll

Ladies'
W.C.

Southern Stair
Hall

Gentlemen's
W.C.

Adjutant's
Room

Führer's Office

Chief
Adjutant's
Room

Bath-
room

1st Floor

Day One

Shortly before one o'clock on the afternoon of Tuesday, 27 September 1938, Mr. Hugh Legat of His Majesty's Diplomatic Service was shown to his table beside one of the floor-to-ceiling windows of the Ritz Restaurant in London, ordered a half-bottle of 1921 Dom Pérignon he could not afford, folded his copy of *The Times* to page 17, and began to read for the third time the speech that had been delivered the night before in Berlin's Sportpalast by Adolf Hitler.

HERR HITLER'S SPEECH

FINAL WORD TO PRAGUE

PEACE OR WAR?

Occasionally Legat glanced across the dining room to check the entrance. Perhaps it was his imagination but it seemed that the guests and even the waiters moving back and forth across the carpet between the dusky pink upholstered chairs were unusually subdued. There was no laughter. Soundlessly beyond the thick plate glass, forty or fifty workmen, some stripped to the waist in the humid weather, were digging slit trenches in Green Park.

There should remain no doubt for the whole world at this time that it is not one man, or one leader, who speaks but the whole German people. I know that in this hour the whole people—millions strong—agree with every one of my words (Heil).

He had listened to it on the BBC as it was delivered. Metallic, remorseless, threatening, self-pitying, boastful—impressive in its horrible way—it had been punctuated by the thumps of Hitler's hand pounding the podium and by the roar of fifteen thousand voices shouting their approval. The noise was inhuman, unearthly. It had seemed to well up from some black subterranean river and pour out of the loudspeaker.

I am grateful to Mr. Chamberlain for all his efforts, and I have assured him that the German people want nothing but peace. I have further assured him, and I emphasise it now, that when this problem is solved, Germany has no more territorial problems in Europe.

Legat took out his fountain pen and underlined the passage, and then did the same with another, earlier reference to the Anglo-German Naval Agreement:

Such an agreement is only morally justified if both nations promise one another solemnly never to wage war against one another again. Germany has this will. Let us all hope that those who are of the same conviction will gain the upper hand among the British people.

He put aside the paper and checked his pocket watch. It was characteristic of him not to carry the time on his wrist like most men of his age but rather on the end of a chain. He was only twenty-eight yet seemed older—his face pale, his manner grave, his suit dark. He had made the reservation a fortnight ago, before the crisis had blown up. Now he felt guilty. He would give her another five minutes; then he would have to leave.

It was a quarter-past when he glimpsed her reflection between the flowers in the wall of gilded mirrors. She was standing on the edge of the restaurant, practically on tiptoe, peering around blankly, her long white neck extended, her chin tilted upwards. He studied her for a few more moments as if she were a stranger and wondered what on earth he would make of her if she were not his wife. "A striking figure"—that was the sort of thing people said of her. "Not pretty, exactly." "No, but handsome." "Pamela's what one calls a *thoroughbred."* "Yes, tremendous breeding—and entirely out of poor Hugh's league . . ." (This latter he had overheard at the party to celebrate their engagement.) He raised his hand. He stood. Finally, she noticed him, smiled and waved and moved towards him, cutting quickly between the tables in her tight skirt and tailored silk jacket, leaving a wake of turned heads.

She kissed him firmly on the mouth. She was slightly out of breath. "Sorry, sorry, sorry . . ."

"It doesn't matter. I've only just arrived." Over the past twelve months he had learned not to ask where she had been. As well as her handbag she was carrying a small cardboard box. She placed it on the table in front of him and pulled off her gloves.

"I thought we agreed no presents?" He lifted the lid. A black rubber skull, a metal snout and the vacant glassy eye sockets of a gas mask stared back up at him. He recoiled.

"I took the children for a fitting. Apparently, I'm to put theirs on first. That will test one's maternal devotion, don't you think?" She lit a cigarette. "Could I have a drink? I'm parched."

He signalled to the waiter.

"Only a half-bottle?"

"I have to work this afternoon."

"Of course you do! I wasn't sure you'd even show."

"I ought not to have done, to be honest. I tried to call but you weren't at home."

"Well, now you know where I was. A perfectly innocent explanation." She smiled and leaned towards him. They clinked glasses. "Happy anniversary, darling."

In the park, the workmen swung their picks.

She ordered quickly, without even looking at the menu: no starter, Dover sole off the bone, green salad. Legat handed back his menu and said he'd have the same. He couldn't think about food, couldn't rid his mind of the image of his children wearing gas masks. John was three, Diana two. All that cautioning of them not to run too fast, to wrap up warm, not to suck on toys or crayons because you never knew where they might have been. He put the box under the table and pushed it out of sight with his foot.

"Were they very frightened?"

"Of course not. They thought the whole thing was a game."

"Do you know, sometimes I feel exactly that? Even if you see the telegrams it's difficult not to think it's all just some ghastly joke. A week ago it looked as though it had all been fixed. Then Hitler changed his mind."

"What will happen now?"

"Who can say? Possibly nothing." He felt he should try to sound optimistic. "They're still talking in Berlin—at least they were when I left the office."

"And if they stop talking, when will it start?"

He showed her the headline in *The Times* and shrugged. "I suppose tomorrow."

"Really? As soon as that?"

"He says he'll cross the Czech border on Saturday. Our military experts reckon it will take him three days to get his tanks and artillery in position. That means he'll have to mobilise tomorrow." He tossed the paper back on the table and drank some champagne; it tasted like acid in his mouth. "I tell you what—let's change the subject."

From his jacket pocket he produced a ring box.

"Oh, Hugh!"

"It will be too big," he warned her.

"Oh, but it's charming!" She slipped the ring onto her finger, held up her hand and turned it back and forth beneath the chandelier so that the blue stone glinted in the light. "You are a wonder. I thought we hadn't any money?"

"We haven't. It was my mother's."

He had been afraid she might think him cheap, but to his surprise she reached her hand across the table and laid it on his. "You are sweet." Her skin was cool. Her slim forefinger stroked his wrist.

"I wish we could take a room," he said suddenly, "and stay in bed all afternoon. Forget about Hitler. Forget about the children."

"Well, why don't you see if you can arrange it? We're here. What's to stop us?" She held his gaze with her large grey-blue eyes and he saw, with a sudden insight that caught him in his throat, that she was only saying it because she knew it would never happen.

Behind him a man coughed politely. "Mr. Legat?"

Pamela took away her hand. He turned to find the maître d', palms pressed together as in prayer, grave with self-importance.

"Yes?"

"Number Ten Downing Street are on the line for you, sir." He was careful to say it just loudly enough for the neighbouring tables to hear.

"Hell!" Legat stood and threw down his napkin. "Will you excuse me? I'll have to take it."

"I understand. You go and save the world." She waved him on his way. "We can have lunch any time." She started packing her things into her handbag.

"Just give me a minute." There was a pleading edge to his voice. "We really have to talk."

"Go."

He hovered for a moment, conscious of the nearby diners staring at him. "Do wait," he said. He assumed what he hoped was a neutral expression and followed the maître d' out of the restaurant and into the lobby.

"I thought you'd like some privacy, sir." The maître d' opened a door to a small office. On the desk was a telephone, the handset beside it.

"Thank you." He picked up the receiver and waited until the door had closed before he spoke. "Legat."

"Sorry, Hugh." He recognised the voice of Cecil Syers, one of his colleagues in the Private Office. "I'm afraid you're going to have to come back right away. It's about to get rather hectic. Cleverly is asking for you."

"Has something happened?"

There was a hesitation at the other end. The private secretaries were told always to assume the operator was listening in. "It looks as though the talking's over. Our man is flying home."

"Understood. I'm on my way."

He replaced the receiver on its cradle. For a moment he stood paralysed. Was this what History felt like? Germany would attack Czechoslovakia. France would declare war on Germany. Britain would support France. His children would wear gas masks. The diners at the Ritz would abandon their white linen tablecloths to crouch in slit trenches in Green Park. It was all too much to grasp.

He opened the door and hurried back across the lobby into the restaurant. But such was the efficiency of the Ritz's staff that their table was already cleared.

In Piccadilly there was not a taxi to be had. He danced back and forth in the gutter, vainly waving his rolled-up newspaper at every passing cab. Finally, he gave up, rounded the corner into St. James's Street and set off down the hill. From time to time he glanced across the road in the hope he might see his wife. Where had she gone in such a hurry? If she was walking straight home to Westminster, this was the direction she would have to take. Best not to think of it; best never to think of it. Already he was sweating in the unseasonable heat. Beneath his old-fashioned three-piece suit, he could feel his shirt sticking to his back. Yet the sky was dull, threatening a rain that somehow never came, and all along Pall Mall, behind the tall windows of the great London clubs—the Royal Automobile, the Reform, the Athenaeum—the chandeliers glittered in the humid gloom.

He did not slacken his pace until he reached the top of the steps leading down from Carlton House Terrace to St. James's Park. Here he found his path blocked by a silent crowd of twenty watching what looked like a small airship rising slowly behind the Houses of Parliament. It ascended past the spire of Big Ben, an oddly beautiful sight—majestic, surreal. In the distance he could make out half a dozen others in the sky south of the Thames—tiny silver torpedoes, some already thousands of feet high.

The man beside him murmured, "I suppose you could say the balloon's gone up."

Legat glanced at him. He remembered his father using exactly the same expression when he was home on leave during the Great War. He had to go back to France *because the balloon had gone up.* To Hugh's six-year-old ears it had sounded as if he was going off to a party. It was the last time he had seen him.

He edged his way around the spectators, trotted down the three wide flights of steps, across the Mall and into Horse Guards Road. And here, in the centre of the sandy expanse of the parade ground, in the half-hour since he left, something else had happened. A pair of anti-aircraft guns had appeared. Soldiers were unloading sandbags from a flatbed lorry, working quickly as if they feared the Luftwaffe might appear at any moment, passing them from hand to hand along a human chain. A half-built wall of sandbags surrounded a searchlight battery. A gunner furiously turned a wheel; one of the barrels swung around and elevated until it was almost perpendicular.

Legat took out a large white cotton handkerchief and wiped his face. It would not do to turn up red-faced and perspiring. If there was one sin that was frowned upon above all others in the Private Office, it was appearing to be in a flap.

He climbed the steps into the narrow, shadowed, soot-blackened cutting of Downing Street. On the pavement opposite Number 10, a group of reporters turned their heads to follow his arrival. A photographer raised his camera, but when he saw it was no one of importance he lowered it again. Legat nodded to the policeman, who rapped once, hard, with the knocker. The door opened as if of its own volition. He stepped inside.

It was four months since he had been seconded from the Foreign Office to work in Number 10 yet each time he felt the same sensation: as if he were entering some gentlemen's club that was no longer fashionable—the black-and-white-tiled lobby, the walls of Pompeiian red, the brass lantern, the grandfather clock ticking its leisurely heartbeat, the cast-iron umbrella stand with its solitary black umbrella. Somewhere in the depths of the building a telephone rang. The doorkeeper wished Legat a good afternoon and returned to his leather coachman's seat and his copy of the *Evening Standard*.

In the wide passageway leading to the back of the building Legat paused and checked himself in the mirror. He straightened his tie and smoothed down his hair with both hands; he braced his shoulders; turned. Ahead of him was the Cabinet Room, its panelled door closed. To his left, the office used by Sir Horace Wilson, also closed. To his right, the corridor that led to the offices of the Prime Minister's private secretaries. The Georgian house exuded an air of imperturbable calm.

Miss Watson, with whom he shared the smallest office, was bent over her desk, exactly as he had left her, walled in by piles of folders. Only the top of her grey head was visible. She had begun her career as a typist when Lloyd George was Prime Minister. He was said to have chased the Downing Street girls around the Cabinet table. It was hard to imagine him chasing Miss Watson. Her responsibility was preparing answers for Parliamentary questions. She peered at Legat over her barricade of papers. "Cleverly has been in looking for you."

"Is he with the PM?"

"No, he's in his office. The PM's in the Cabinet Room with the Big Three."

Legat made a noise that was between a sigh and a groan. Halfway along the corridor, he stuck his head into Syers's office. "All right, Cecil, how much trouble am I in?"

Syers swung round in his chair. He was a small man, seven years

Legat's senior, constantly and irrepressibly and often irritatingly amused. He wore the same college tie as Legat. "I'm afraid you picked rather the wrong day for a romantic lunch, old fellow." His voice dropped sympathetically. "I hope she didn't take it badly."

Once, in a weak moment, Legat had hinted to Syers of his difficulties at home. He had regretted it ever since. "Not at all. Things are on an even keel. What happened in Berlin?"

"Apparently it degenerated into one of Herr Hitler's tirades." Syers pretended to strike the arm of his chair. "'Ich werde die Tschechen zerschlagen!'"

"Oh, good grief. 'I will smash the Czechs!'"

A military voice called along the corridor, "Ah, Legat, there you are!"

Syers mouthed, "Good luck." Legat stepped backwards and turned to confront the long, moustached face of Osmund Somers Cleverly, universally known, for reasons unexplained, as Oscar. The Prime Minister's Principal Private Secretary crooked a finger. Legat followed him into his office.

"I must say I'm disappointed in you, Legat, and more than a little surprised." Cleverly was older than the rest of them, had been a soldier by profession before the war. "Lunch at the Ritz in the middle of an international crisis? It may be the way things are done in the Foreign Office; it's not how we do them here."

"I apologise, sir. It won't happen again."

"You have no explanation?"

"It's my wedding anniversary. I couldn't get hold of my wife to cancel the table."

Cleverly stared at him for a few seconds longer. He did not bother to hide his suspicions of these brilliant young men from the Treasury and the Foreign Office who had never served in uniform. "There are times when one's family has to take a back seat; now is such a time." The Principal Private Secretary sat behind his desk and switched on a lamp. This part of the house faced north across the Downing Street garden. The unpruned trees that screened it from Horse Guards Parade cast the ground floor in a perpetual twilight. "Has Syers filled you in?"

"Yes, sir. I gather the talks have broken down."

"Hitler has announced his intention to mobilise at two o'clock tomorrow afternoon. I'm afraid all hell is about to break loose. Sir Horace should be back to report to the PM by five. The PM will broadcast to the nation at eight. I'd like you to deal with the BBC. They are to set up their apparatus in the Cabinet Room."

"Yes, sir."

"There will have to be a full Cabinet meeting at some stage, probably after the broadcast, therefore the BBC engineers will need to clear out quickly. The PM will also be seeing the Dominion High Commissioners. The Chiefs of Staff are due to arrive any minute—take them in to the PM as soon as they all get here. And I shall need you to take a note of the meeting so that the PM can brief the Cabinet."

"Yes, sir."

"Parliament is being recalled, as you know. He intends to make a statement to the House on the crisis tomorrow afternoon. Have all the relevant minutes and telegrams for the past two weeks arranged for him in chronological order."

"Yes, sir."

"I am afraid you will probably have to stay overnight." The phantom of a smile played beneath Cleverly's moustache. He reminded Legat of a muscular Christian games master at a minor public school. "It's a pity it's your anniversary, but it can't be helped. I'm sure your wife will understand. You can sleep in the duty clerk's room on the third floor."

"Is that all?"

"That is all—for now."

Cleverly put on his spectacles and began studying a document. Legat walked back to his office and sat down heavily at his desk. He opened a drawer, took out a pot of ink and dipped in his pen. He was not used to being reprimanded. Damn Cleverly, he thought. His hand shook slightly, rattling his nib against the glass edge of the pot. Miss Watson sighed but did not look up. He reached into the wire basket on the left of his desk and took out a folder of telegrams recently arrived from the Foreign Office. Before he could untie the pink ribbon, Sergeant Wren, the Downing Street messenger, appeared in the doorway. As usual he was out of breath; he had lost a leg in the war.

"The Chief of the Imperial General Staff is here, sir."

Legat followed him as he limped down the passage towards the lobby. In the distance under the brass lantern stood Viscount Gort reading a telegram, his polished brown boots planted wide apart. A glamorous figure—an aristocrat, a war hero, a holder of the Victoria Cross—Gort seemed oblivious to the clerks and secretaries and typists who had suddenly discovered pressing reasons to cross the lobby in order to catch a glimpse of him. The front door opened on a cascade of flashes from the photographers' cameras, out of which stepped Air Chief Marshal Newall, followed seconds later by the towering figure of the First Sea Lord, Admiral Backhouse.

Legat said, "If you would kindly come with me, gentlemen . . ."

As he led them into the interior he heard Gort say, "Is Duff coming?" and Backhouse reply, "No, the PM thinks he leaks to Winston."

"Would you mind waiting here for a moment . . . ?"

The Cabinet Room was soundproofed by double doors. He opened the outer and knocked gently on the inner.

The Prime Minister was seated with his back to the door. Facing him across the centre of the long table were Halifax, the Foreign Secretary; Simon, the Chancellor of the Exchequer; and the Home Secretary, Hoare. All three looked up to see who had come in. The room was in absolute silence apart from the ticking of the clock.

Legat said, "Excuse me, Prime Minister. The Chiefs of Staff are here."

Chamberlain did not turn. His hands were on the table, spread wide on either side of him, as if he were about to push back his chair. His forefingers slowly tapped the polished surface. Eventually, in his precise, slightly old-maidish voice, he said, "Very well. Let us meet again when Horace returns. We'll hear what more he has to say then."

The ministers gathered up their papers—awkwardly in the case of Halifax, whose withered left arm hung uselessly at his side—and rose to their feet without saying a word. They were men in their fifties or sixties, the "Big Three," in the prime of their power—bulked by their dignity beyond their physical size. Legat stood aside to let them pass—"like a trio of pall-bearers in search of their coffin" was how he described them afterwards to Syers. He heard them greet the service chiefs waiting outside—hushed, grim voices. He said quietly, "Would you like me to show in the Chiefs of Staff now, Prime Minister?"

Still Chamberlain did not turn to look at him. He was staring at the opposite wall. His corvine profile was hard, stubborn; belligerent even. Eventually he said, distractedly, "Yes, of course. Yes, bring them in."

Legat stationed himself at the far end of the Cabinet table, close to the Doric pillars that supported the ceiling. The bookcases showed the spines of brown leather-bound statutes and silvery blue editions of Hansard. The Chiefs of Staff placed their caps on the side table by the door and took the seats vacated by the ministers. Gort, as the senior officer, occupied the central position. They opened their briefcases and spread out their papers. All three lit cigarettes.

Legat glanced across at the mantel clock above the fireplace behind the Prime Minister's head. He dipped his nib into the nearby inkstand. On a foolscap sheet he wrote, *PM & CoS. 2:05 p.m.*

Chamberlain cleared his throat. "Well, gentlemen, I'm afraid the situation has deteriorated. We had hoped for—and the Czech Government had agreed to—the orderly transfer of the Sudeten territory to Germany, subject to a plebiscite. Unfortunately, Herr Hitler announced last night he was not prepared to wait even so much as a week longer, and will invade on Saturday. Sir Horace Wilson saw him this morning and warned him privately but very firmly that if France fulfils her treaty obligations to Czechoslovakia—which we still have every reason to believe she will—then we shall be obliged to support France." The Prime Minister put on his spectacles and picked up a telegram. "After his customary ranting and raving, Herr Hitler responded, according to our Ambassador in Berlin, in the following terms: 'If France and England strike, let them do so. It is a matter of complete indifference to me. I am prepared for every eventuality. I can only take note of the position. It is Tuesday today, and by next Monday we shall all be at war.'"

Chamberlain put down the telegram and took a sip of water. Legat's pen ran rapidly across the heavy paper: *PM—latest from Berlin—breakdown of talks—violent reaction by Herr Hitler—"Next week we will be at war—"*

"I shall of course continue my efforts to find a peaceful solution if one exists—although it's hard at the moment to see what more can be done. But in the meantime, I fear we must prepare for the worst."

Gort looked at each of his colleagues. "Prime Minister, we have drawn up a memorandum. It summarises our collective view of the military situation. Perhaps I might read out our conclusion?"

Chamberlain nodded.

"'It is our opinion that no pressure that Great Britain and France can bring to bear, either by sea, on land, or in the air, could prevent Germany from overrunning Bohemia and from inflicting a decisive defeat on Czechoslovakia. The restoration of Czechoslovakia's lost integrity could only be achieved by the defeat of Germany and as the outcome of a prolonged struggle, which from the outset must assume the character of an unlimited war.'"

Nobody spoke. Legat was acutely conscious of the scratching of his nib. Suddenly it sounded absurdly loud.

Eventually Chamberlain said, "This is the nightmare I have always dreaded. It's as if we've learned nothing from the last war and we are reliving August 1914. One by one the countries of the world will be dragged in—and for what? We've already told the Czechs that once we've won, their nation in its present form cannot continue to exist. The three and a half million Sudeten Germans must have the right of self-determination. Therefore the separation of the Sudetenland from Germany will not even be an allied war aim. So for what would we be fighting?"

"For the rule of law?" suggested Gort.

"For the rule of law. Indeed. And if it comes to it, we shall. But by God, I wish we could find some other way of upholding it!" The Prime Minister briefly touched his hand to his forehead. His old-fashioned winged collar drew attention to his sinewy neck. His face was grey with exhaustion. But with an effort he recovered his usual businesslike manner. "What practical steps now need to be taken?"

Gort said, "We shall send two divisions to France immediately, as we have already agreed, to demonstrate our solidarity. They can be in position within three weeks and ready to fight eighteen days after that. But General Gamelin has made it quite clear the French have no intention of mounting anything more than token raids on Germany until next summer. Frankly, I doubt they'll even do that. They'll stay behind the Maginot Line."

Newall added, "They're waiting until we arrive in greater strength."

"And is the Air Force ready?"

Newall was sitting up very straight—a thin-faced man, skeletal almost, with a small grey moustache. "I have to say this comes at the worst possible time for us, Prime Minister. On paper, we have twenty-six squadrons available for home defence, but only six have modern aircraft. One has Spitfires. The other five have Hurricanes."

"But they are ready to fight?"

"Some are."

"Some?"

"I'm afraid there is a technical problem with the guns on the Hurricanes, Prime Minister—they freeze above fifteen thousand feet."

"What's that you're saying?" Chamberlain leaned forward as if he had not heard correctly.

"We're working on a solution, but it may take some time."

"No, what you are actually *saying*, Air Marshal, is that we have spent one and a half thousand million pounds on rearmament, the bulk of it on the air, and when it comes to it our warplanes don't work."

"Our planning has always been predicated on there being no conflict with Germany before 1939 at the earliest."

The Prime Minister turned his attention back to the Chief of the Imperial General Staff. "Lord Gort? Can't the Army shoot down most of the attacking aircraft from the ground?"

"I'm afraid we're in a similar position to the Air Chief Marshal, Prime Minister. We only have about a third of the number of guns we believe are necessary to defend London, and most of those are obsolete relics from the last war. We are equally short of searchlights. We have no ranging or communication equipment . . . We were also counting on another year to prepare."

Halfway through his answer Chamberlain seemed to have stopped listening. He had put on his spectacles again and was sorting through his papers. The atmosphere in the room had become uncomfortable.

Legat continued writing calmly, smoothing the awkward facts into bureaucratic prose—*PM expressed concern at adequacy of home air defence*—but the orderly mechanism of his mind was disturbed. Once again, he couldn't escape the image of his children in gas masks.

Chamberlain had found what he was looking for. "The Joint Intelligence Committee estimates there will be one hundred and fifty thousand casualties in London by the end of the first week of bombing. Six hundred thousand by the end of two months."

"That's unlikely to happen immediately. We assume that to begin with, the Germans will direct their principal bombing force against the Czechs."

"And when the Czechs have been defeated—then what?"

"Then we don't know. We should certainly use the time available to take precautions, and start evacuating London tomorrow."

"And how prepared is the Navy?"

The First Sea Lord was a striking presence, a good head taller than anyone else in the room. His grizzled skull was bald, his face deeply scoured, as if it had been exposed to the elements too long. "We have some shortages of escort vessels and minesweepers. Our capital ships require fuelling and arming; some of the crews are on leave. We shall need to announce mobilisation as quickly as possible."

"When would you need to do that, to be operational by the first of October?"

"Today."

Chamberlain sat back in his chair. His forefingers tapped the table. "Of course that would mean we would mobilise before the Germans."

"Partially mobilise, Prime Minister. And there is something else to be said for it: it would have the effect of showing Hitler we aren't bluffing—that if it comes to it, we are prepared to fight. It might even make him think twice."

"It might. Or it might push him into war. Remember, I have stared into that man's eyes on two occasions now, and in my judgement, if there is one thing he cannot tolerate, it is losing face."

"But surely if we're going to fight it's important he should be left in no doubt of that fact? It would be a tragedy if he interpreted your courageous visits and your sincere efforts for peace as a sign of weakness. Wasn't that the mistake the Germans made in 1914? They thought we weren't serious."

Chamberlain folded his arms and stared at the table. Legat couldn't tell whether the gesture meant he had rejected the suggestion or was considering it. Shrewd of Backhouse to flatter him, he thought. The PM had few obvious weaknesses but strangely for such a shy man his besetting vice was vanity. The seconds ticked by. Finally, he looked up at Backhouse and nodded. "Very well. Mobilise."

The First Sea Lord stubbed out his cigarette and stuffed his papers into his briefcase. "I'd better get back to the Admiralty."

The others rose with him, grateful to escape.

Chamberlain called up to them, "I would like you to hold your-selves in readiness to brief senior ministers later today. In the mean-time, we should avoid doing or saying anything that contributes to a mood of public panic, or forces Hitler into a position from which he cannot back down, even at the eleventh hour."

After the Chiefs of Staff had gone, Chamberlain let out a long sigh and rested his head in his hand. Glancing sideways, he seemed to notice Legat for the first time. "Were you making a note of all of that?"

"Yes, Prime Minister."

"Destroy it."

2

In Wilhelmstrasse, in the heart of the government sector of Berlin, in the sprawling three-storey nineteenth-century building that housed the German Foreign Ministry, Paul von Hartmann was contemplating a telegram that had come in overnight from London.

CONFIDENTIAL   LONDON 26 SEPTEMBER 1938

IN THE NAME OF OUR OLD FRIENDSHIP AND OUR COMMON DESIRE FOR PEACE BETWEEN OUR PEOPLES I DO URGE YOUR EXCELLENCY TO USE YOUR INFLUENCE TO POSTPONE THE DECISIVE MOVEMENT OF OCTOBER FIRST TO A LATER DATE THAT TIME MAY BE GIVEN TO ALLAY PRESENT PASSIONS AND PROVIDE OPPORTUNITIES FOR REACHING ADJUSTMENT OF DETAILS

ROTHERMERE
FOURTEEN STRATTON HOUSE PICCADILLY LONDON

Hartmann lit a cigarette and considered what sort of response was required. In the seven months since Ribbentrop had taken over as Foreign Minister he had been called upon many times to translate incoming messages from English into German and then to draft replies in the Minister's name. At first he had adopted the traditional, formal, neutral tone of a professional diplomat. But many of these early efforts had been rejected as insufficiently National Socialist; some had even been returned to him by SS-Sturmbannführer Sauer of Ribbentrop's staff, with a thick black line scrawled through them.

He had been forced to recognise that if his career was to prosper a certain adjustment of style would be necessary. Gradually therefore he had trained himself to mimic the Minister's bombastic manner and radical world view, and it was in this spirit that he set to work answering the owner of the *Daily Mail*, his pen scraping and stabbing at the paper as he worked himself into a state of faux-outrage. His concluding paragraph in particular struck him as masterly:

The idea that because of the Sudeten problem, which is completely secondary to England, peace might be destroyed between our two peoples, seems to me madness and a crime against humanity. Germany has pursued an honest policy of understanding with England. It desires peace and friendship with England. But when foreign Bolshevist influences have come to the fore in English politics, Germany must be prepared for every eventuality. The responsibility before the world for such a crime would not fall to Germany—as you, my dear Lord Rothermere, know better than anyone.

He blew on the ink. Really, with Ribbentrop one could not lay it on too thick.

Hartmann lit another cigarette. He started again from the beginning, making small corrections here and there, squinting at the paper through his smoke. His eyes were a striking shade of violet, and slightly hooded. His forehead was high; his hairline, even at the age of twenty-nine, had already receded almost to his crown. His mouth was wide and voluptuous, his nose strong—it was a mobile and expressive face: compelling, unusual, almost ugly. And yet his genius was for making men and women love him.

He was about to place his draft in the basket to be sent to the typists when he heard a noise. Or perhaps it would be more accurate to say that he *felt* a noise. It seemed to travel through the soles of his shoes and up the legs of his chair. The pages in his hands shook. The rumble intensified, became a roar, and for a ludicrous moment he wondered if the city was experiencing an earthquake. But then his ear picked out the distinctive note of heavy engines revving and the clank of metal tracks. The two men with whom he shared the office, von Nostitz and von Rantzau, glanced at one another and frowned. They got to their feet and went over to the window. Hartmann joined them.

A column of drab, olive-green armoured vehicles was trundling south down Wilhelmstrasse from the direction of the Unter den Linden—artillery half-tracks, panzers on the backs of tank transporters, heavy guns towed by trucks and by teams of horses. Hartmann craned his neck. It went on for as far as he could see: a full motorised division to judge by the length of it.

Von Nostitz, who was older than Hartmann and one grade higher, said, "My God, is it already starting?"

Hartmann went back to his desk, picked up his telephone and dialled an extension. He had to cover his left ear with his hand to shut out the noise. A metallic voice at the other end said: "Kordt."

"It's Paul. What's happening?"

"Meet me downstairs." Kordt rang off.

Hartmann took his hat from the stand. Von Nostitz said mockingly, "Are you going to join up?"

"No, obviously I'm going outside to cheer our gallant Wehrmacht."

He hurried along the high gloomy corridor, down the central staircase and through the double doors. A short flight of steps, blue-carpeted in the centre and flanked by a pair of stone sphinxes, led to the entrance hall. To Hartmann's surprise the lobby was deserted, even though the air itself seemed to be vibrating with the noise from outside. Kordt joined him a minute later, his briefcase wedged under his arm. He had taken off his spectacles and was breathing on the lenses, polishing them on the thick end of his tie. Together they went out into the street.

Only a handful of Foreign Ministry staff had gathered on the pavement to watch. Across the road, of course, it was a different story: in the Propaganda Ministry they were practically hanging out of the windows. The sky was overcast, yearning to rain—Hartmann felt a drop of moisture on his cheek. Kordt took him by the arm and together they walked in the same direction as the column. A score of red-white-and-black swastika banners hung motionless above their heads. They gave the grey stone facade of the ministry a festive air. But it was striking how few people were lingering on the street. Nobody was waving or cheering; mostly they had their heads down, or were staring fixedly ahead. Hartmann wondered what had gone wrong. Normally the Party stage-managed these things much better.

Kordt had yet to speak. The Rhinelander was taking quick, nervous steps. About two-thirds of the way down the length of the building he steered them into an unused entrance. The heavy wooden door was permanently barred; the porch offered privacy from prying eyes. Not that there was much to see: just the head of the Foreign Minister's Private Office—a harmless, bespectacled, clerkish figure—and a tall young *Legationsekretär*, holding an impromptu meeting.

Kordt clasped his briefcase to his chest, undid the catch and drew out a typewritten document. He gave it to Hartmann. Six pages, typed in the extra-large characters the Führer preferred, to spare his far-seeing eyes whenever he had to deal with bureaucratic trivia. It was an account of his meeting that morning with Sir Horace Wilson, written up by the Foreign Ministry's chief interpreter, Dr. Schmidt. Couched in the blandest official language, Hartmann could nevertheless visualise what it described as vividly as if it were a scene in a novel.

The obsequious Wilson had congratulated the Führer on the warm reception of his speech at the Sportpalast the previous evening (as if anything else was possible), had thanked him for his kind references to Prime Minister Chamberlain, and at one point had asked the others present—Ribbentrop, together with Ambassador Henderson and First Secretary Kirkpatrick of the British Embassy—to step out of the room briefly so that he could assure Hitler in private, man to man, that London would continue to put pressure on the Czechs. (Schmidt had even recorded his words in his original English: *I will still try to make those Czechos sensible.*) But none of that could disguise the central fact of the encounter: that Wilson had had the temerity to read out a prepared statement declaring that in the event of hostilities the British would support the French, and had then asked the Führer to repeat back what he had just told him, to be sure there was no misunderstanding! Little wonder Hitler had lost his temper and told Wilson he didn't care what the French or British did, that he had spent billions preparing for war, and if war was what they wanted, then war was what they would get.

Hartmann thought it was like watching an unarmed passerby trying to persuade a madman to hand over his gun.

"So it will be war after all."

He returned the document to Kordt, who locked it back in his briefcase.

"That appears to be the case. Half an hour after the meeting ended"—Kordt nodded towards the armoured column—"the Führer ordered this. It's no accident it's driving straight past the British Embassy."

The noise of the engines split the warm air. Hartmann could taste the dust and the sweetness of the fuel on his tongue. He had to shout over the noise. "Who are they? Where are they from?"

"Witzleben's men from the Berlin garrison, heading to the Czech frontier."

Behind his back Hartmann clenched his fist. At last! He felt a rush of anticipation. "So now, you must agree, there is no alternative, yes? We must act?"

Kordt nodded slowly. "I feel like I'm going to be sick." Suddenly he put a warning hand on Hartmann's arm. A policeman was walking towards them, his truncheon drawn.

"Gentlemen! Good afternoon! The Führer is on the balcony." He gestured with his truncheon further along the street. His manner was respectful, encouraging. He was not telling them what to do, merely alerting them to an historic opportunity.

Kordt said, "Thank you, officer."

The two diplomats stepped back into the street.

The Reich Chancellery stood next to the Foreign Ministry. Across the road, in Wilhelmplatz, a small crowd had gathered in the broad expanse of the square. This was unquestionably a Party claque; some even wore swastika armbands. From time to time, a ragged shout of *"Heil!"* went up, and arms were raised in salute. The men in the armoured column swivelled their heads eyes right, and saluted. Young men mostly—far younger than Hartmann. He was close enough to see their expressions: amazement, wonder, pride. Beyond the high black iron railings of the Reich Chancellery was a court-yard; above the main entrance to the building, a balcony; on the balcony the unmistakable lone figure—brown jacket, brown cap, left hand clutching the buckle of his black belt, the right arm occasion-ally flashing out, robotic in its absolute steadiness: palm flat, fingers extended. He couldn't have been more than fifty metres away.

Kordt saluted and muttered, *"Heil Hitler."* Hartmann did the same.

Once it was past the Chancellery, the column accelerated south towards Blücherplatz.

Hartmann said, "How many people would you say have turned out to watch?"

Kordt scanned the few groups of spectators. "I'd say no more than two hundred."

"He won't like that."

"No, he won't. For once I do believe the regime has made a mis-take. The Führer was so flattered by Chamberlain's visits, he let Goeb-bels tell the media to go to town. The German people thought they were going to get peace. Now they're told they're going to get war after all, and they don't like it."

"So when are we going to act? Surely this has to be the time?"

"Oster wants us to meet tonight. A new place: Number Nine Goethe Strasse, in Lichterfelde."

"Lichterfelde? Why does he want us to meet all the way out there?"

"Who knows? Arrive as close to ten as you can. It's going to be a busy evening."

Kordt clasped Hartmann's shoulder briefly then walked away. Hartmann stood for a while longer, his eyes trained on the figure on the balcony. Security was astonishingly light—a couple of policemen at the entrance to the courtyard, two SS men on the door. There would be more inside, but even so ... Of course, once war was declared it would be a different matter. Then they would never get anywhere near him.

After a couple more minutes the figure on the balcony seemed to have had enough. He dropped his arm, peered up and down Wilhelmstrasse like the manager of a theatre appraising the disappointing size of the night's audience, turned his back and stepped through the curtains into the Chancellery. The door closed.

Hartmann took off his hat and flattened his thinning hair, then pulled down the brim once more and walked back thoughtfully in the direction of his office.

3

At 6 p.m. precisely, the tolling of Big Ben carried into Number 10 through the open windows.

As if on cue, Miss Watson stood, collected her hat and coat, wished Legat a crisp "Good evening" and left the office carrying one of the Prime Minister's red dispatch boxes filled to the brim with her carefully annotated files. The recall of Parliament for an emergency debate on the Czech crisis had put an end to her leisurely summer. Legat knew she would now bicycle, as she always did, down White-hall to the Palace of Westminster, leave her ancient machine in New Place Yard, and walk up a private staircase to the Prime Minister's office, which lay across the corridor behind the Speaker's chair. There she would meet Mr. Chamberlain's Parliamentary Private Sec-retary, Lord Dunglass, upon whom she had an obvious and unre-quited crush, in order to discuss answers for PM's written questions.

This was Legat's chance.

He closed the door, sat at his desk, picked up the telephone and called the switchboard. He tried to make his tone casual. "Good eve-ning. Legat here. Could you please put me through to this number: Victoria 7472?"

From the instant the meeting with the Chiefs of Staff had ended until that very moment, Legat had been fully occupied. Now at last he laid his notes down on the desk. Trained since childhood for the gladiatorial combat of the examination hall—school, scholarship, Oxford finals, Foreign Office entrance—he had written on one side of the paper only, to avoid smudging the ink. *PM expressed concern at adequacy of home air defence . . .* Quickly, he turned the foolscap sheets over, so that the blank side was uppermost. As ordered, he would destroy them. But not quite yet. Something was preventing him. He could not say precisely what—an odd sense of propriety, perhaps. All afternoon, as he had ferried in successive visitors to see the Prime Minister and compiled the documents the PM needed for his speech to Parliament, he had felt himself privy to the real truth. This was the information upon which government policy would be decided: one might almost say nothing else much mattered in comparison. Diplomacy, morality, law, obligation—what did these weigh in the scales against military strength? An RAF squadron, if he remembered correctly, consisted of twenty planes. So at high altitude there were only twenty modern fighters with working guns to defend the entire country.

"Putting you through now, sir."

There was a click as the connection was made, followed by the long double-purr of the number ringing. She answered far quicker than he had expected, and brightly: "Victoria 7472."

"Pamela, it's me."

"Oh, hello, Hugh."

She sounded surprised, and possibly also disappointed. He said, "Listen, I can't speak for long, so please concentrate on what I'm about to say. I want you to pack a week's worth of clothes and get the garage to drive you and the children to your parents' right away."

"But it's six o'clock."

"They'll still be open."

"Why do we have to go in such a rush? What's happened?"

"Nothing. Nothing yet, anyway. I just want to know you're somewhere safe."

"It sounds rather panicky. I hate people who panic."

He tightened his grip on the receiver. "But I'm afraid people *are* going to panic, darling." He glanced at the door; someone was walking past; their footsteps seemed to stop. He lowered his voice but spoke with greater urgency. "By later tonight it may be very hard to get out of London. You need to go now, while the roads are still clear." She started to object. "Don't argue with me, Pamela. Will you just, for once, do something I bloody well ask?"

There was a pause. She said quietly, "And what about you?"

"I have to stay here overnight. I'll try to call you later. I have to go now. You will do this? You promise me?"

"Yes, all right, if you insist." He could hear one of the children in the background. She hushed them: "Quiet, I'm talking to your father." And then to him: "Do you want me to bring you an overnight bag?"

"No, don't worry. I'll try to slip out at some point. You concentrate on getting out of London."

"I love you—you do know that?"

"I know."

She waited. He knew he ought to say something back but he couldn't find the words. There was a clatter as she hung up, and then all he could hear was the dialling tone.

Someone knocked on the door.

"Just a moment." He folded his notes from the Chiefs of Staff meeting in half, and then in half again, and slipped them into his inside pocket.

In the corridor was Wren, the messenger. Legat wondered if he had been listening. But all he said was, "The BBC have arrived."

For the first time since the crisis started, there was a large crowd in Downing Street. They had gathered quietly near the photographers on the opposite side of the street to Number 10. What seemed to have attracted their attention most was a large dark-green van with the BBC's coat of arms and OUTSIDE BROADCAST painted on its sides in gold lettering. It was parked just to the left of the front door. A pair of technicians was feeding cables from the back of the van, across the pavement, and through one of the sash windows.

Legat stood on the doorstep arguing with the young engineer, whose name was Wood. "I'm sorry, but I'm afraid it's just not possible."

"Why not?" Wood wore a V-necked pullover under a brown corduroy suit.

"Because the Prime Minister will be holding meetings in the Cabinet Room until half-past seven."

"Can't he hold them somewhere else?"

"Don't be absurd."

"Well, in that case, couldn't we do the broadcast from a different room?"

"No, he wishes to address the British people from the heart of government, and that is the Cabinet Room."

"Well, look—we're on the air at eight and it's gone six now. What if the equipment fails because we haven't tested it properly?"

"You'll have half an hour at the very least, and if I can get you any more time, I shall—"

He broke off. Behind Wood's shoulder, a black Austin 10 was turning from Whitehall into Downing Street. The driver had switched on the headlamps in the early-evening gloom and was edging forward slowly to avoid hitting some of the onlookers who had spilled off the pavement into the road. The newsreel cameramen recognised the passenger before Legat did. The brilliance of their arc lights briefly blinded him. He raised his hand to shield his eyes. He muttered, "Excuse me" to Wood, and stepped down onto the pavement. As the car drew to a halt he opened the rear door.

Hunched down in his seat, Sir Horace Wilson had an umbrella between his knees and a briefcase cradled on his lap. He gave Legat a weak smile and slid out of the car. On the step of Number 10 he turned for an instant, his expression lugubrious and non-committal. The flashbulbs popped. He scuttled inside, like some nocturnal animal allergic to light, ignoring his companion who was emerging from the other side of the car. He advanced towards Legat, hand outstretched. "Colonel Mason-MacFarlane. Military attaché, Berlin."

The policeman saluted.

In the entrance hall, Wilson was already shedding his overcoat and hat. The Prime Minister's Special Adviser was a slight, almost emaciated figure, with a long nose and pendulous ears. Legat had never found him less than polite, even on occasions slyly charming—the sort of reserved senior colleague he feared might one day unburden himself of confidences one would prefer not to hear. He had made his reputation at the Ministry of Labour dealing with trade union leaders. The thought that he had come straight from delivering an ultimatum to Adolf Hitler was bizarre. Nevertheless, the Prime Minister considered him indispensable. He placed his rolled umbrella carefully into the stand next to his master's and turned to Legat. "Where's the PM?"

"He's in his study, Sir Horace, working on his broadcast for tonight. Everyone else is in the Cabinet Room."

Wilson set off confidently towards the back of the building. He beckoned to Mason-MacFarlane to follow him. "I want you to brief the PM as soon as possible," he said, and added over his shoulder to Legat, "Would you be kind enough to tell the PM I'm back?"

He threw open the doors to the Cabinet Room and marched in. Legat had a glimpse of dark suits and gold braid, of strained faces and of coiling blue clouds of cigarette smoke suspended in the dusky light, and then the door was closed again.

He walked down the corridor, past Cleverly's office, and Syers's, and his own, to the main staircase. He ascended past black-and-white etchings and photographs of every Prime Minister since Walpole. By the time he reached the landing the house had metamorphosed from gentlemen's club into a grand country mansion, mysteriously deposited in central London, with sofas and oil paintings and high Georgian sash windows. The vista of empty reception rooms was quiet and deserted; beneath the thick carpet the floorboards creaked. He felt like an intruder. He knocked lightly on the door to the Prime Minister's study. A familiar voice said, "Come."

The room was large and light. The Prime Minister was sitting with his back to the window, bent over his desk, writing with his right hand, a cigar burning in his left. An array of pens and pencils and ink pots stood on a little rack in front of him, alongside a pipe and a tobacco jar; apart from these, and his ashtray and a leather-bound blotter, the big desk was bare. Legat had never seen a man look lonelier.

"Sir Horace Wilson has returned, Prime Minister. He's waiting to see you downstairs."

As usual, Chamberlain did not look up. "Thank you. Would you mind holding on for a moment?" He paused to suck on his cigar and then continued to write. Wreaths of smoke hung around his grey head. Legat stepped over the threshold. In four months he had never had a proper conversation with the Prime Minister. On several occasions, minutes he had submitted overnight had come back the following morning with expressions of gratitude written in the margins in red ink—"*A first-rate analysis*"; "*Clearly worked-out and well-expressed, thank you, NC*"—and he had found himself more touched by these schoolmasterly words of praise than by any amount of the usual politician's bonhomie. But he had never been addressed by name—not even by his surname, as Syers usually was, let alone by his Christian name, which was a distinction reserved for Cleverly alone.

The minutes passed. Surreptitiously Legat took out his watch and checked it. Eventually, the PM finished writing. He replaced his pen in the rack, balanced his cigar on the edge of the ashtray and gathered together the sheets of paper. He squared them and held them up. "Would you be so good as to have these typed?"

"Of course." Legat walked over and took the pages; there were about a dozen.

"You're an Oxford man, I suppose?"

"Yes, Prime Minister."

"You have a turn of phrase, I've noticed. Perhaps you would read it through? If you find there are passages that need amplifying, feel free to make suggestions. I have so much else on my mind. I worry that somehow it does not *flow*."

He pushed back his chair, retrieved his cigar and stood. The sudden movement seemed to make him dizzy. He placed his hand on the desk to steady himself, then headed for the door.

On the landing, Mrs. Chamberlain was waiting. She looked as if she had already dressed for dinner in some sort of velvety gown. She was a decade younger than the Prime Minister: kind, vague, bosomy, softly stout, she reminded Legat of his mother-in-law, another Anglo-Irish county girl said to have been a beauty in her youth. Legat hung back. She said something quietly to her husband and to his amazement he saw the Prime Minister briefly take her hand and kiss her on the lips. "I can't stop now, Annie. We'll talk later." As Legat passed her it looked to him as if she had been crying.

He followed Chamberlain down the stairs, noticing the narrow sloping shoulders, the silvery hair curling slightly where it was cut short at the back, the surprisingly powerful hand brushing lightly along the banister rail with the half-smoked cigar still wedged between the second and third fingers. He was a Victorian figure. His portrait on the staircase ought to be halfway up rather than at the top. When they reached the Private Office corridor, the Prime Minister said, "Please bring me the speech as soon as you can." He walked on past Legat's office, patting his pockets until he found his box of matches. At the entrance to the Cabinet Room he stopped and relit his cigar, then opened the doors and disappeared inside.

Legat sat at his desk. The Prime Minister's handwriting was unexpectedly flowery, theatrical even. It hinted at a more passionate persona beneath the carapace of rectitude. As for the speech itself, he did not care for it. There was too much of the first person singular for his taste: *I was flying backwards and forwards across Europe . . . I have done all that one man can do . . . I shall not give up the hope of a peaceful solution . . . I am a man of peace to the depths of my soul . . .* In his ostentatiously modest way, he thought, Chamberlain was as egocentric as Hitler: he always conflated the national interest with himself.

He made a few changes here and there, corrected some of the grammar, added a line announcing the mobilisation of the Navy which the PM seemed to have forgotten, and took the text downstairs.

As he descended to the Garden Room the atmosphere of the house changed again. Now it was like going belowdecks on a luxury liner. Oil paintings and bookcases and calm gave way to low ceilings, bare walls, stale air, heat and the incessant racket of more than a dozen Imperial typewriters clattering away at a rate of eighty words per minute. Even with the doors open to the garden it felt oppressive. Thousands of letters a day had been pouring into Number 10 from members of the public ever since the crisis began. Sacks of unopened mail were piled in the narrow passage. It was getting close to seven o'clock. Legat explained to the supervisor the urgency of his mission and was led over to a young woman seated at a desk in the corner.

"Joan here is our fastest. Joan, dear, you'll have to stop whatever it is you're doing, and type up the Prime Minister's broadcast for Mr. Legat."

Joan pressed a lever on the end of her typewriter carriage and pulled out the half-finished document. "How many copies?" Her voice was "smart," cut-glass. She might have been a friend of Pamela's.

He perched on the edge of her desk. "Three. Can you decipher his writing?"

"Yes, but it'll be quicker if you dictate it." She wound the paper and carbons into place and waited for him to start.

"'Tomorrow, Parliament is going to meet and I shall be making a full statement of the events that have led up to the present anxious and critical situation . . .'"

He took out his fountain pen. "Sorry: it ought to be 'the events *which* have led . . .'" He marked the change on the original and carried on. "'How horrible, fantastic, incredible it is that we should be digging trenches and trying on gas masks here because of a quarrel in a faraway country between people of whom we know nothing . . .'"

He frowned. She stopped typing and looked up at him. She was sweating slightly beneath her makeup. There was a tiny line of moisture above her upper lip, and a patch of dampness on the back of her blouse. He noticed for the first time that she was pretty.

She said irritably, "Is there something wrong?"

"Only that phrase—I'm not sure about it."

"Why?"

"It sounds perhaps rather dismissive."

"He's right though, isn't he? That's what most people think. What's it got to do with us if one lot of Germans wants to join another lot of Germans?" She rattled her fingers impatiently on the keys. "Come on, Mr. Legat—you're not the Prime Minister, you know."

He laughed, despite himself. "That's true—thank God! All right, let's carry on."

It took her about fifteen minutes. When they reached the end she unwound the final page, arranged the three copies in order and fixed them together with paperclips. He inspected the top copy. It was flawless. "How many words is that, would you say?"

"About a thousand."

"So it should take him about eight minutes to deliver." He stood. "Thank you."

"You're welcome." As he moved away she called after him, "I'll be listening."

By the time he reached the door she was already typing something else.

Legat hurried back upstairs and along the Private Office corridor. As he approached the Cabinet Room, Cleverly appeared. He seemed to have been lurking outside the nearby lavatory. "What happened to your minute of the PM's meeting with the Chiefs of Staff?"

Legat felt his face colour slightly. "The PM decided he didn't want the meeting recorded."

"Then what are you carrying there?"

"The speech for his broadcast tonight. He asked me to bring it to him as soon as it was typed."

"All right. Good." Cleverly held out his hand. "I'll take it from here." Reluctantly Legat handed over the pages. "Why don't you go and see what the BBC are up to?"

Cleverly let himself into the Cabinet Room. The door closed. Legat stared at the painted white panels. Power depended on being in the room when the decisions were taken. Few understood that rule better than the Principal Private Secretary. Legat felt obscurely humiliated.

Suddenly the door reopened. The bottom part of Cleverly's face was twisted into a ghastly rictus-smile. "Apparently he wants you."

A dozen men, including the Prime Minister, were seated around the table. Legat took them in at a glance: the service chiefs, the Big Three, the Dominions Secretary and the Minister for Defence Co-ordination, plus Horace Wilson and the Permanent Under-Secretary at the Foreign Office, Sir Alexander Cadogan. They were listening to the military attaché, Colonel Mason-MacFarlane.

"So the very strong impression I received from my visit to Prague yesterday is that Czech military morale is poor . . ." His delivery was clipped but fluent. He seemed to be enjoying his moment on stage.

The Prime Minister noticed Legat standing in the doorway and gestured with a nod of his head that he should come and sit next to him, in the seat to his right usually reserved for the Cabinet Secretary. He was already reading through the speech, running his pen down the page, occasionally underlining a word. He gave the impression that he was only half-listening to the colonel.

". . . Until last year, the Czech General Staff had planned on countering a German attack from two directions—from the north via Silesia, and from the west via Bavaria. But the incorporation of Austria into the Reich has extended their border with Germany to the south by almost two hundred miles, and that threatens to turn their defences. The Czechs may fight, but will the Slovaks? Also,

Prague itself is hopelessly under-defended against bombing by the Luftwaffe."

Wilson, who was sitting on the other side of the Prime Minister, cut in. "I saw General Göring last night and he was confident the German Army would overrun the Czechs not in weeks but in days. 'And Prague will be bombed to rubble'—those were his very words."

There was a snort from Cadogan on the opposite side of the table. "It's obviously in Göring's interests to present the Czechs as a push-over. The fact remains the Czechs have a large army and strong defensive fortifications. They might well hold out for months."

"Except, as you've just heard, that's not Colonel Mason-MacFarlane's view."

"With respect, Horace, what does he know about it?" Cadogan was a small, usually taciturn man. But Legat could see he was de-fending the prerogatives of the Foreign Office like a bantam cock.

"With equal respect, Alec, he has actually *been* there, unlike the rest of us."

The Prime Minister put down his pen. "Thank you very much for coming all the way from Berlin to see us, Colonel. It has been most useful. I know we all wish you a safe trip back to Germany."

"Thank you, Prime Minister."

When the door had closed, Chamberlain said, "I asked Sir Hor-ace to bring the colonel back to London with him and report to us directly because this seems to me a crucial point." He looked around the table. "Suppose the Czechs were to collapse before the end of October: how would we convince the British public the war was worth continuing through the winter? We would be asking them to make the most tremendous sacrifices—and to achieve what, pre-cisely? We have already conceded that the Sudeten Germans should never have been transferred to a Czech-dominated state in the first place."

Halifax said, "That is certainly the position of the Dominions. They have made it absolutely clear to us today that their people won't stand for a war on such a narrow issue. America won't come in. The Irish will be neutral. One does begin to wonder where we shall find any allies."

Cadogan said, "There are always the Russians, of course. We keep forgetting they also have a treaty with the Czechs."

A murmur of unease went round the table. The Prime Minister said, "The last time I looked at the map, Alec, there wasn't a common border between the Soviet Union and Czechoslovakia. The only way they could intervene would be by invading either Poland or Romania. In that event they would both enter the war on the side of Germany. And really, even putting aside the facts of geography—to have Stalin, of all people, as our ally in a crusade to uphold international law! The notion is grotesque."

Gort said, "The strategic nightmare is that this becomes a world war, and we end up having to fight Germany in Europe, Italy in the Mediterranean and Japan in the Far East. In that event, I have to say, in my view, the very existence of the Empire will be in grave jeopardy."

Wilson said, "We are drifting into the most appalling mess, and it seems to me there is only one way out. I have drafted a telegram telling the Czechs that in our opinion they should accept Herr Hitler's terms before his deadline of two o'clock tomorrow—withdraw from the Sudetenland and let him occupy the territory. It's the only sure way for us to avoid being entangled in a war that could quickly grow to enormous proportions."

Halifax said, "But what if they refuse?"

"They won't, in my judgement. And if they do, then at least the United Kingdom would no longer be under any moral obligation to get involved. We would have done our best."

There was a silence.

The Prime Minister said, "It does at least have the merit of simplicity."

Halifax and Cadogan exchanged glances. Both began to shake their heads—Halifax slowly, Cadogan with some vigour. "No, Prime

Minister, that would make us effectively the Germans' accomplices. Our standing in the world would collapse, and the Empire with it."

"And what about France?" added Halifax. "We would put them in an intolerable position."

Wilson said, "They should have thought about that before they gave a guarantee to Czechoslovakia without consulting us."

"Oh, for goodness' sake!" Cadogan raised his voice. "This isn't an industrial dispute, Horace. We can't allow France to fight Germany alone."

Wilson was unfazed. "But surely Lord Gort has just told us France has no intention of fighting? Apart from the odd raid, they will stay behind the Maginot Line until the summer."

The service chiefs started talking all at once. Legat saw the Prime Minister glance over at the clock above the mantelpiece, then return his attention to his speech. Without his controlling authority, the meeting quickly disintegrated into a hubbub of separate conversations. One had to admire his powers of concentration. He was in his seventieth year, yet he kept on going, like the grandfather clock in the hall—*tick, tick, tick . . .*

Through the high windows the light had begun to fade. The time reached seven-thirty. Legat decided he ought to say something. "Prime Minister," he whispered, "I'm afraid the BBC will need to come in now to set up their equipment."

Chamberlain nodded. He glanced around the table and said quietly, "Gentlemen?" Immediately the voices fell silent. "I am afraid we shall have to leave matters there for now. The situation is obviously as grave as it could be. We now have less than twenty hours before the Germans' ultimatum expires. Foreign Secretary, perhaps you and I could talk a little more about this question of a telegram to the Czech Government? Horace, we'll go into your office. Alec, you'd better come too. Thank you all."

———

Wilson's office adjoined the Cabinet Room and was linked to it directly by its own door. Often, when the Prime Minister was working alone at the long coffin-shaped table, the door was left open so that Wilson could wander in and out at will. In the press, he was written up as Chamberlain's Svengali but in Legat's observation that was to underrate the PM's dominance: Wilson was more like a supremely useful servant. He glided silently around Downing Street keeping an eye on the machinery of government in the manner of a store detective. Several times when he had been working at his own desk he had felt a presence and had turned to find Wilson quietly observing him from the doorway. His face would be expressionless at first; then would come that sly unnerving smile.

The BBC engineers unspooled cables across the carpet and set up the microphone at the far end of the Cabinet table close to the pillars. It was suspended from a metal stand: an object large and cylindrical, tapering to a point at the back, like the sawn-off end of an artillery shell. Beside it was a loudspeaker and various other mysterious pieces of equipment. Syers and Cleverly came in to watch. Syers said, "The BBC have asked if they can also make a live broadcast of the PM's statement to Parliament tomorrow."

Cleverly said, "That's not a matter for us."

"I know. It would obviously set a precedent. I've referred them to the Chief Whip."

At five minutes to eight, the Prime Minister emerged from Wilson's office, followed by Halifax and Cadogan. Wilson was the last to appear. He looked irritated. Legat guessed he must have had a further argument with Cadogan. That was Wilson's other great usefulness—to act as a surrogate for his chief. The Prime Minister could use him to test out ideas, and then could sit back and observe what happened without having to expose his own views and risk his authority.

Chamberlain took his seat behind the microphone and spread out his speech. His hands were shaking. One of the pages fell to the floor and he had to bend stiffly to retrieve it. He muttered, "I'm wobbling about all over the place." He asked for a glass of water. Legat poured one from the jug in the centre of the table. In his anxiety he over-filled it. Beads of water stood out on the polished surface.

The BBC engineer asked them all to sit at the other end of the room. Outside over the garden and Horse Guards Parade darkness had fallen.

Big Ben chimed eight o'clock.

The announcer's voice came over the loudspeaker. "This is London. In a moment, you will hear the Prime Minister, the Right Honourable Neville Chamberlain, speaking from Number Ten Downing Street. His speech will be heard all over the Empire, throughout the continent of America, and in a large number of foreign countries. Mr. Chamberlain."

Beside the microphone, a green light glowed. The Prime Minister adjusted his cuffs and picked up his speech.

"I want to say a few words to you, men and women of Britain and the Empire, and perhaps to others as well . . ."

He enunciated each syllable carefully. His tone was euphonious, melancholy; as inspiring as a dirge.

"How horrible, fantastic, incredible it is that we should be digging trenches and trying on gas masks here because of a quarrel in a faraway country between people of whom we know nothing. It seems still more impossible that a quarrel which has already been settled in principle should be the subject of war. I can well understand the reasons why the Czech Government have felt unable to accept the terms which have been put before them in the German memorandum . . ."

Legat glanced across the table at Cadogan. He was nodding in agreement.

"Yet I believe after my talks with Herr Hitler that, if only time were allowed, it ought to be possible for the arrangements for transferring the territory that the Czech Government has agreed to give to Germany to be settled by agreement under conditions which would assure fair treatment to the population concerned. After my visits to Germany I have realised vividly how Herr Hitler feels that he must champion other Germans. He

told me privately, and last night he repeated publicly, that after this Sudeten German question is settled, that is the end of Germany's territorial claims in Europe . . ."

Cadogan winced at Halifax but the Foreign Secretary stared ahead. His long, pale, pious, crafty face was motionless. In the Foreign Office they called him "the Holy Fox."

"I shall not give up the hope of a peaceful solution, or abandon my efforts for peace, as long as any chance for peace remains. I would not hesitate to pay even a third visit to Germany if I thought it would do any good . . ."

Now it was Wilson who was nodding.

"Meanwhile there are certain things we can and shall do at home. Volunteers are still wanted for air-raid precautions, for fire brigade and police services, and for the Territorial units. Do not be alarmed if you hear of men being called up to man the anti-aircraft defences or ships. These are only precautionary measures such as a government must take in times like this . . ."

Legat waited for the line announcing the mobilisation of the Navy. It did not come. The Prime Minister had cut it. Instead he had inserted a new paragraph.

"However much we may sympathise with a small nation confronted by a big and powerful neighbour, we cannot in all circumstances undertake to involve the whole British Empire in war simply on her account. If we have to fight it must be on larger issues than that . . .

"If I were convinced that any nation had made up its mind to dominate the world by fear of its force, I should feel that it must be resisted. Under such a domination, life for people who believe in liberty would not be worth living. But war is a fearful thing, and we must be very clear, before we embark on it, that it is really the great issues that are at stake, and that the call to risk everything in their defence, when all the consequences are weighed, is irresistible.

"For the present I ask you to await as calmly as you can the events of the next few days. As long as war has not begun, there is always hope that it may be prevented, and you know that I am going to work for peace to the last moment. Good night."

The green light went out.

Chamberlain exhaled a long breath and slumped back in his chair.

Wilson was the first on his feet. He walked towards the Prime Minister, softly applauding. "That really was superb, if I may say so. Not one stumble or hesitation."

Legat had never seen the Prime Minister's grin before. It bared a neat row of yellowish-grey teeth. He looked almost boyish in his pleasure at being praised. "Was it really all right?"

Halifax said, "The tone was perfect, Prime Minister."

"Thank you, Edward. Thank you, everyone." He included Legat along with the BBC engineers in this general benediction. "I always find the trick, when I'm speaking on the wireless, is to try to imagine I'm talking just to one person, sitting in their armchair—intimately, as a friend. That was harder to do tonight, of course, knowing I was also having to talk to a second person, sitting in the shadows of the room." He took a sip of water. "Herr Hitler."

4

The civil servant in charge of the German Foreign Ministry, State Secretary Ernst von Weizsäcker, had announced that he wished to have a German translation of the Prime Minister's speech in his hands within thirty minutes of its delivery. He had entrusted the responsibility to Paul von Hartmann.

High up in the Radio Monitoring Room in the eaves of the Wilhelmstrasse building, beneath the huge array of radio aerials that sprouted from the roof, Hartmann had duly assembled a three-woman team. First, a stenographer took down Chamberlain's words in English (no easy task, since by the time the BBC's signal reached Berlin it had lost much of its strength and the Prime Minister's ethereal voice, fading in and out of the clouds of static, was often difficult to make out). As soon as each page of shorthand was filled, a second secretary typed up the notes in English, triple-spaced. Hartmann wrote down his translation beneath the lines of English text and passed the pages one by one to a third secretary, who typed up the finished German version.

Wie schrecklich, fantastisch, unglaublich ist es . . .

His pen moved rapidly over the cheap paper, the brown ink bleeding slightly into the coarse weave.

Ten minutes after Chamberlain had finished speaking the job was done.

The typist tore the last page from her machine. Hartmann grabbed it, slipped the speech into a cardboard folder, kissed the top of her head, and strode out of the room, pursued by relieved laughter. The instant he was in the corridor his smile disappeared. As he walked towards Weizsäcker's office he flicked back and forth between the pages of the speech with increasing dismay. The tone was far too wary and conciliatory—thin stuff, mere audio-ectoplasm. Where was the threat, the ultimatum? Why hadn't Chamberlain repeated in public that evening what his emissary had told Hitler in private that morning—that if France went to the aid of Czechoslovakia, Britain would support France?

He descended the stairs to the ground floor, knocked on the door of Weizsäcker's outer office and went straight in without waiting for a reply. The room was large and high-ceilinged, overlooking the park that ran along the back of the Ministry. It was lit by a vast and elaborate chandelier. In the darkened windows, beyond the reflection of the electric lightbulbs, it was still just possible to make out the shapes of the trees against the evening sky. The junior secretaries had all gone home, their typewriters shrouded for the night like the cages of sleeping birds. Seated alone in the office, at her desk beside the central window, was Weizsäcker's senior secretary. She had a cigarette between her scarlet lips and a letter in either hand and was looking from one document to the other, frowning.

"Good evening, my dear Frau Winter."

"Good evening, Herr von Hartmann." She bowed her head with equal formality, as if he had paid her a great compliment.

"Is he in?"

"He's with the Minister in the Chancellery."

"Ah." Hartmann was taken aback. "In that case what should I do with Chamberlain's speech?"

"He said you were to take it round to him immediately. Wait," she called after him as he turned to go, "what is that on your face?"

He stood obediently under the chandelier as she inspected his cheek. Her hair and fingers smelled of perfume and cigarette smoke. He could see strands of grey in her dark curls. He wondered how old she was. Forty-five? Old enough, anyway, to have had a husband who had died in the war. "Ink!" she murmured disapprovingly. "*Brown* ink. Really, Herr von Hartmann, you cannot enter the Chancellery looking like that. What if you bump into the Führer?" She drew a white handkerchief from her sleeve, moistened the corner with her tongue and dabbed gently at his cheek. She stepped back to inspect the result. "Better. I'll telephone to say that you're on your way."

Outside, the night was still warm. The prewar street lamps along Wilhelmstrasse, set far apart, offered little isolated pools of illumination in the darkness. Hardly anyone was about. In the middle of the street a cleaner was shovelling up piles of horse shit left behind after the parade. The only noise was the scrape of his spade on the asphalt. Hartmann clutched the folder and walked quickly along the facade of the ministry until it gave onto the railings of the Reich Chancellery. One of the big iron gates was open. A Mercedes was driving out. The policeman saluted. Hartmann couldn't see who was in the back. As the car headed off in the direction of the Anhalter Bahnhof, he gave his name and department to the policeman and was waved through without a word.

Lights were on in the windows all around the courtyard: here, finally, was a sense of activity, crisis. Beneath the canopied main entrance one of the SS sentries carrying a machine gun asked to see his papers, then nodded him permission to enter the reception hall, where two more SS guards were standing, armed with pistols. Yet again he showed his pass and announced that he had come to see State Secretary von Weizsäcker. He was asked to wait. One of the sentries went over to a telephone on a table against the far wall. Hartmann made a mental note: two policemen on the gate, four SS-Schütze here, and at least another three he could see in the guardroom.

A minute passed. Suddenly the large double doors opened and a uniformed SS adjutant strode in. His heels clicked and his arm shot out in the Hitler salute, as precise and immaculate as a clockwork soldier. Hartmann returned the obligatory greeting. *"Heil Hitler."*

"Follow me, please."

They passed through the double doors and across an endless

tract of Persian carpet. The room smelled of the Kaiser's time: sun-faded old fabric, dust and beeswax. One could imagine Bismarck stamping across it. Watched by another SS guard—what was that: the eighth?—Hartmann followed the adjutant up a marble staircase, past Gobelin tapestries, to the second-floor landing, through a pair of doors and into what he realised, with an accelerating pulse, must be the Führer's private apartment.

The adjutant said, "May I have that? Wait, please." He took the folder, knocked quietly at the nearest door and slipped inside. For a moment before it closed Hartmann heard voices, then the mur-mured conversation was cut off. He glanced around. The room was surprisingly modern, tasteful even—decent paintings, small tables with lamps and bowls of freshly cut flowers, a rug on a polished wooden floor, simple chairs. He was not sure whether he should sit or not. He decided not.

Time went on. At one point a handsome woman in a starched white blouse carrying a pile of papers entered the meeting and left almost immediately, empty-handed. Eventually, after a quarter of an hour, the door opened again and a sleek silver-haired man in his mid-fifties emerged, a Nazi Party badge in his lapel. This was Baron Ernst von Weizsäcker, although in the spirit of these egalitarian days he had dispensed with his title at roughly the same time he had acquired the badge. He gave Hartmann an envelope. "Thank you for waiting, Hartmann. This is the Führer's reply to Chamber-lain. Please take it immediately to the British Embassy and give it to either Sir Nevile Henderson or Mr. Kirkpatrick personally." He leaned forward and added confidingly, "Draw their attention to the final sentence. Tell them it's in direct response to tonight's broad-cast." And then, more quietly, "Tell them it wasn't easy."

"Weizsäcker!" Hartmann recognised Ribbentrop's peremptory voice calling from the room. The barest hint of a grimace flicked across the State Secretary's smooth features, and then he was gone.

———

The British Embassy was less than a five-minute walk away at the northern end of Wilhelmstrasse, just beyond the Foreign Ministry. As Hartmann waited for the police sentry to open the Chancellery gate he examined the envelope. It was addressed, in Weizsäcker's hand, to *His Excellency Sir Nevile Henderson, Ambassador of Great Britain;* it was unsealed.

"Good night, sir." The policeman saluted.

"Good night."

Hartmann walked a little way up the wide street, past the silent darkened windows of the Foreign Ministry, and then casually—so casually that if anyone had been watching him they would have thought his behaviour entirely natural—he turned into the main entrance. The night porter recognised him. He mounted the carpeted steps between the stone sphinxes, hesitated, then turned left into the deserted corridor. His footsteps echoed off the stone floor, the lime-green plastered walls, the vaulted ceiling. On either side the doors were closed. About halfway down was a lavatory. He let himself in and turned on the light. His reflection in the mirror above the washbasins appalled him—stooped, furtive: in every respect suspicious. He wasn't really cut out for this sort of business. He went into one of the cubicles, locked the door and sat on the edge of the toilet.

Dear Mr. Chamberlain,
I have in the course of conversations once more informed Sir Horace
Wilson of my final attitude . . .

There were perhaps seven paragraphs, some of them long. The gist of it was belligerent: that the Czechs were stalling for time, that their objections to immediate German occupation of the Sudetenland were contrived, and that Prague was working to achieve "a general warlike conflagration." The final sentence, of which Weizsäcker was so proud, did not strike him as offering much hope for peace:

I must leave it to your judgement whether, in view of these facts, you consider that you should continue your efforts, for which I once more sincerely thank you, of bringing the government in Prague to reason at the very last hour.

The typed letter was signed with a scrawled *Adolf Hitler.*

He reached von Weizsäcker's office just as Frau Winter was locking up to go home. She was wearing a fashionable wide-brimmed hat. She stared at him in surprise. "Herr Hartmann? The State Secretary is still at the Chancellery."

"I know. I hate to ask you this—I wouldn't if it wasn't important."

"What?"

"Can you copy this, quickly?"

He showed her the letter with its signature. Her eyes widened. She glanced up and down the corridor, then turned and unlocked the door and switched on the light.

It took her fifteen minutes. He kept a lookout in the corridor. She didn't say anything except towards the end. "He seems determined to have a war." She said it matter-of-factly, without looking round from her typewriter.

"Yes—and the English are equally determined to avoid one, more's the pity."

"There." She pulled the last page out of her typewriter. "Go."

The corridor was still empty. He walked back briskly the way he had come and had just reached the top of the last flight of steps leading down to the lobby when he noticed a figure in a black SS uniform heading across the marble floor towards him. Sturmbannführer Sauer of Ribbentrop's private office had his head down and for an instant Hartmann considered turning round but then Sauer glanced up and recognised him. He frowned in surprise.

"Hartmann . . . ?" He was about the same age, with a blank face from which most of the colour seemed to have been drained—white-blond hair, pale skin, pale blue eyes.

For want of a better response, Hartmann flung out his arm. *"Heil Hitler!"*

Sauer responded automatically: *"Heil Hitler!"* But then he peered at him. "Aren't you supposed to be at the British Embassy?"

"I'm on my way now." Hartmann descended the last few steps and hurried towards the main entrance.

Sauer shouted after him, "For God's sake, Hartmann, get a move on! The future of the Reich is at stake—"

Hartmann was already in the street and striding away from the building. He had a premonition of Sauer running up behind him—challenging him, drawing his pistol, ordering him to turn out his pockets, discovering his notebook. But then he told himself to calm down. He was a Third Secretary in the English Department, responsible among other duties for translation. For him to have a copy of an official letter to the British Prime Minister—a letter that would, in any case, be in London in less than an hour—was hardly treason. He could talk his way out of it. He could talk his way out of almost anything.

He climbed the five deeply worn stone steps to the entrance of the British Embassy. The interior of the large portico was lit by a single gloomy lamp. The iron doors were locked. He rang the bell and heard it chime somewhere in the building. The sound died away. Such silence! Across the road, even the Adlon, the most fashionable of all Berlin's great hotels, was quiet. It was as if the entire city had gone to ground. Eventually he heard bolts being drawn back and a lock turning. A young man poked his head around the door.

Hartmann said, in English, "I have an urgent message from the Reich Chancellery which I must give either to the Ambassador or the First Secretary in person."

"Of course. We've been expecting you."

Hartmann followed him inside and up a second flight of steps to an imposing reception hall, two storeys high, with an oval glass roof. It had been built in the last century by a famous railway tycoon who had gone bankrupt soon afterwards. The air of opulent bad taste was all-pervasive. Not one but two grand staircases with porcelain balustrades rose and curled around the opposing walls and met in the middle. Nimbly descending the left-hand flight, sideways-on, like Fred Astaire, was a tall, slim, dandyish figure in a dinner jacket with a red carnation in his buttonhole. He was smoking a cigarette in a jade holder.

"Good evening—Herr Hartmann, is it?"

"Good evening, Your Excellency. Yes, it is. I have the Führer's reply to the Prime Minister."

"Wonderful."

The British Ambassador took the envelope, quickly pulled out the three typewritten pages and started reading them where he stood. His eyes flickered rapidly back and forth. His elongated face with its drooping moustache, already melancholy in repose, seemed to grow even longer. He grunted under his breath. When he had finished he sighed, clamped his cigarette holder back between his teeth and gazed at the skylight. His cigarette smoke was fragrant, Turkish.

Hartmann said, "The State Secretary wanted you to take particular note of the last sentence, Sir Nevile. He said to tell you it hadn't been easy."

Henderson looked again at the last page. "Not much of a straw to clutch at, but I suppose it's something." He gave the letter to his young aide. "Translate it and telegraph it to London immediately, will you, please? No need for cipher."

He insisted on showing Hartmann to the door. His manners were as exquisite as his clothes. He was rumoured to be a lover of Prince Paul of Yugoslavia. He had once turned up at the Chancellery wearing a crimson pullover under his pale grey suit: Hitler was said to have gone on about it for days afterwards. What were the British thinking of, Hartmann wondered, sending such a man to deal with the Nazis?

At the door he shook Hartmann's hand. "Tell Baron von Weizsäcker I appreciate his efforts." He stared along Wilhelmstrasse. "Extraordinary to think we may be out of here by the end of the week. I can't say I shall be entirely sorry."

He took a final draw of his cigarette, then pinched it delicately between his thumb and forefinger, extracted it from his holder and flicked it away to disintegrate on the pavement in a cascade of orange sparks.

The Legats lived in a small rented terraced house in North Street, Westminster, that had been found for them by Legat's then-superior in the Foreign Office Central Department, Ralph Wigram, who lived with his wife and son at the top of the same road. Its advantage was its proximity to the office: Wigram expected his juniors to work hard and Legat could be at his desk within ten minutes of leaving his front door. Its disadvantages were almost too numerous to list and stemmed chiefly from the fact that it was more than two hundred years old. Apart from the installation of electricity little seemed to have been done to it in all that time. The Thames was barely a hundred yards away; the water table was high. Dampness rose from the ground to meet the rain that trickled from the roof. Furniture had to be artfully arranged to hide the patches of blackish-green mould. The kitchen was prewar. And yet Pamela loved it. Lady Colefax lived in the same street and in the summer held candlelit dinner parties on the pavement to which the Legats were invited. It was absurd: he only earned £300 a year. Although they had been obliged to sublet the basement to help pay the rent, they still maintained a precarious access to the tiny garden by means of a rickety set of steps from the drawing-room window; Legat had improvised a makeshift lift using a rope and laundry basket to lower the children to play.

It was to this once-romantic but now essentially impracticable domestic arrangement—symbolic, Legat had come to think, of the general state of his marriage—that he found himself hurrying less than an hour after the Prime Minister had finished his broadcast, in order to pack an overnight bag.

His path took him, as it always did, past the Wigrams' house at the top of the street. Most of the flat-fronted houses were blackened by soot, their facades brightened by the occasional window box full of geraniums. Number 4, however, looked blind and abandoned. Behind the small Georgian windowpanes, the white-panelled shutters had been closed for months. He wished suddenly, with a longing that was almost palpable, that Wigram might still be inside. For it was Wigram, more than anyone, who had predicted this crisis— obsessively predicted it, if the truth were told, so that even Legat, who had loved him, had thought him half-mad on the subject of Hitler. He could call him to mind in an instant—the urgent blue eyes, the fair moustache, the thin taut mouth. But even more than the visual memory, he could *hear* him, limping along the corridor towards the third secretaries' room—first one heavy footstep and then the sound of his left leg being dragged along behind it, his stick tapping out a warning of his approach—and always the same subject on his lips: Hitler, Hitler, Hitler. When the Germans had reoccupied the Rhineland in 1936, Wigram had asked to see the Prime Minister, Stanley Baldwin, and had warned him that in his opinion this was the Allies' last chance to stop the Nazis. The PM had replied that if there was only one chance in a hundred that an ultimatum might lead to war, he could not risk it: the country would not stand for another conflict so soon after the last one. Wigram had come home to North Street in despair and had broken down in front of his wife: "Wait now for bombs on this little house." Nine months later, he had been found dead in his bathroom aged forty-six—whether by his own hand or by some complication of the polio that had crippled him for the past decade, nobody seemed to know.

Oh, Ralph, thought Legat, poor dear cracked Ralph, you saw it all.

He let himself into his house and turned on the light. Out of habit he called a greeting and waited for a reply. But he could see that they had all gone, and in a hurry by the look of it. The silk jacket Pamela had worn at lunch was draped over the finial at the foot of the banisters. John's tricycle lay on its side and blocked the passageway. He righted it. The stairs cracked and creaked beneath his feet. The wood was rotting. The neighbours complained about the moisture coming through the party wall. And yet Pamela somehow had contrived to make the place chic—a profusion of Persian rugs and crimson damask curtains, peacock and ostrich feathers, beads and antique lace. She had an eye, no doubt about it: Lady Colefax herself had said so. One night she had filled the house with scented candles and made it into a fairyland. But the next morning the smell of damp was back.

He went into their bedroom. Even though the lamp was broken, there was just sufficient light from the landing for him to see what he was doing. Her discarded clothes were heaped up on the bed and strewn across the floor. He had to step over her underwear to reach the bathroom. He packed his razor, shaving brush, soap, toothbrush and tooth powder into his sponge bag and returned to the bedroom in search of a shirt. A car was driving slowly down North Street. He could tell by the whine of its engine that it was in a low gear. The glow of its headlights lit up the ceiling, projecting an outline of the window frame across the opposite wall; the dark lines swung like the shadow on a sundial. Legat paused with his shirt in his hand and listened. The car seemed to have stopped outside with its engine running. He moved over to the window.

It was a small car—two doors, the passenger's open. He heard a clatter downstairs. A moment later a figure in a hat and a dark coat moved smartly away from the house, folded itself back into the car and pulled the door shut.

Legat was across the bedroom in two strides. He took the stairs three or four at a time, collided with the tricycle and almost fell fulllength. By the time he opened the front door, the car was just rounding the corner into Great Peter Street. For a second or two he gazed after it, recovering his breath, then stooped to retrieve the envelope from the doormat. The stationery was heavy, official-looking: legal perhaps? His name was misspelt: *Leggatt.* He carried it into the sitting room and sat down on the sofa. He worked his finger under the flap and carefully tore it open. He didn't pull the document out immediately. Instead he parted the envelope with two fingers and peered inside. It was his way of preparing himself for bad financial news. He could just make out the typed heading:

Berlin Mai. 30. 1938
OKW No. 42/38. g. Kdos. Chefsache (Streng geheim, Militär) L I

Within ten minutes he was on his way back to the office. Everywhere he looked he detected signs of anxiety—a ruby necklace of taillights stretching all the way down Marsham Street to the petrol station where motorists were queuing for fuel; a hymn being sung in the open air within the cobbled precincts of Westminster Abbey as part of a candlelit vigil for peace; the silver flare of the newsreel cameras on the blackened walls of Downing Street silhouetting the dark silent mass of the crowd.

He was late. He had to squeeze his way through to get to Number 10, his overnight bag lifted high above his head. "Excuse me . . . excuse me . . ." But the moment he was inside he saw that his effort had been wasted. The ground floor was deserted. The ministers had already gone through for the 9:30 p.m. meeting of the Cabinet.

Cleverly was not in his office. Legat stood for a moment in the corridor and wondered what he should do. He found Syers seated at his desk, smoking a cigarette and staring out of the window. Syers glanced at his reflection in the glass.

"Hullo, Hugh."

"Where's Cleverly?"

"In the Cabinet Room, standing by in case they decide to send Horace's telegram to the Czechs."

"Is Cadogan in with them?"

"I haven't seen him." Syers turned round. "You sound a bit overwrought. Are you all right?"

"Perfectly." Legat hoisted his bag to show him. "Just slipped back home to get some things."

He left before Syers could ask him anything else. In his office he opened his bag and took out the envelope. It seemed treasonous simply to have brought it into the building, dangerous to be caught in possession of it. He ought to pass it up the chain of command, get it out of his hands as soon as possible.

By a quarter to ten he was crossing Downing Street, pushing his way more urgently now past the throngs of spectators. He went through the big iron gate on the opposite side of the road and into the vast quadrangle of ministerial buildings. In each the lights were burning: the Colonial Office in the bottom left-hand corner, the Home Office in the top left, the Indian Office top right, and immediately next to him, up a flight of steps, the Foreign Office. The night porter gave him a nod.

The corridor was grand and lofty in the Victorian imperial style, its extravagance calculated to awe those visitors whose misfortune it was not to be born British. The Permanent Under-Secretary's room was on the ground-floor corner, overlooking Downing Street on one side and Horse Guards Road on the other. (Proximity being the index of power, it was a matter of pride to the Foreign Office that their PUS could be sitting opposite the Prime Minister in the Cabinet Room within ninety seconds of being summoned.)

Miss Marchant, the senior secretary on duty, was alone in the outer office. She normally worked upstairs for Cadogan's short-sighted deputy, Orme Sargent, universally known as "Moley."

Legat was slightly out of breath. "I need to see Sir Alexander. It's very urgent."

"I'm afraid he's too busy to see anyone."

"Please tell him it is a matter of the gravest national importance."

The cliché, like the watch chain and the old-fashioned dark suit, seemed to come naturally to him. He planted his feet apart. Breathless and junior though he was, he would not be shifted. Miss Marchant blinked at him in surprise, hesitated, then rose and tapped softly on the PUS's door. She put her head into the distant room. He could only just hear her: "Mr. Legat is asking to see you." A pause. "He says it's extremely important." Another pause. "Yes, I think you should." From the interior came a distinct growl.

She stood aside to let him through. As he passed he gave her a look of such gratitude she blushed.

The hugeness of the room—the ceiling must have been twenty feet high at least—emphasised the smallness of Sir Alexander. He was seated not at his desk but at the conference table. The surface was almost entirely covered by paper in various colours—white for minutes and telegrams, pale blue for drafts, mauve for dispatches, aquamarine for Cabinet papers, interspersed occasionally by brown foolscap files tied with pink ribbon. The Permanent Under-Secretary wore a pair of round-lensed tortoiseshell glasses, over the top of which he peered at Legat with an expression of some irritation. "Yes?"

"I'm sorry to disturb you, Sir Alexander, but I thought you ought to see this at once."

"Oh, God, now what?" Cadogan reached out, took the five typewritten pages, glanced at the first line—

Auf Anordnung des Obersten Befehlshabers der Wehrmacht.

—frowned, then flicked through to the last—

gez. ADOLF HITLER
Für die Richtigkeit der Abschrift:
ZEITZLER, Oberstleutnant des Generalstabs

—and Legat had the satisfaction of seeing him sit bolt upright in his chair.

The document was a directive from Hitler: *War on Two Fronts with Main Effort in the South-east, Strategic Concentration "Green."*

"Where on earth did you get this?"

"It was put through my letterbox at home about thirty minutes ago."

"By whom?"

"I didn't see them. A man in a car. Two men, actually."

"And there was no message?"

"None."

Cadogan cleared a space on the table, laid the document in front of him and bent his disproportionately large head over it. He read with intense concentration, his fists pressed to his temples. His German was good: he had been in charge of the embassy in Vienna in the summer of 1914 when Archduke Franz Ferdinand was assassinated.

It is essential to create a situation within the first two or three days which demonstrates to enemy states which wish to intervene the hopelessness of the Czech military position . . .

  The army formations capable of rapid employment must force the frontier fortifications with speed and energy, and must break very boldly into Czechoslovakia in the certainty that the bulk of the mobile army will be brought up with all possible speed . . .

  The main strength of the Luftwaffe is to be employed for a surprise attack against Czechoslovakia. The frontier is to be crossed by aircraft at the same time as it is crossed by the first units of the Army . . .

As he finished each page, Cadogan turned it over and placed it neatly to his right. When he reached the end of the document, he squared the pages. "Extraordinary," he murmured. "I suppose the first question we have to ask ourselves is whether it's genuine."

"It certainly seems it to me."

"I agree." The Permanent Under-Secretary inspected the top page again. "So this was drawn up on the thirtieth of May." He ran his finger under the German, translating: " '*It is my unalterable decision to smash Czechoslovakia by military action in the near future . . .*' That certainly *sounds* like Hitler. In fact, it's almost word for word what he said to Horace Wilson this morning." He sat back. "So if we work on the assumption it's genuine, which I think we may, the next questions that arise are essentially threefold: *who* gave it to us, *why* did they give it to us, and more particularly—why did they give it to *you*?"

Once again, Legat experienced a peculiar sensation of guilt, as if, merely by possessing the document, his loyalty had been compromised. He preferred not to think where it might have come from. "I'm afraid I can't answer any of those."

"As far as the matter of who gave it to us is concerned, we know there certainly *is* some sort of opposition to Hitler. Several opponents of the regime have been in contact with us over the summer, claiming they would be willing to overthrow the Nazis if we were to guarantee to stand firm over Czechoslovakia. I can't say they're a very coherent group—a few disaffected diplomats and some aristocrats who want to restore the monarchy. This is the first time we've actually received anything specific from them—not that it tells us much that we don't already know. Hitler wants to destroy Czechoslovakia, and he wants to do it quickly—hardly news." He took off his spectacles and sucked on the stem. He studied Legat with detachment. "When were you last in Germany?"

"Six years ago."

"Have you kept in touch with anyone over there?"

"No." It at least had the merit of being true.

"You were in Vienna, as I recall, after your first attachment to the Central Department—is that right?"

"Yes, sir, from 'thirty-five to 'thirty-seven."

"Friends there?"

"Not especially. We had a small child and my wife was pregnant with our second. We tended to keep to ourselves."

"What about the German Embassy in London—do you know any of the staff here?"

"No, not really."

"Then I don't understand. How would the Germans even be aware that you work in Number Ten?"

Legat shrugged. "My wife, perhaps? She's in the gossip columns occasionally. Sometimes my name's dragged in." Only the other week, the *Daily Express*—he blushed with shame at the memory— had run an item about one of Lady Colefax's parties, describing him as "among the Foreign Office's brightest young stars, now assisting the PM."

"The '*gossip columns*'?" The Permanent Under-Secretary repeated the term with distaste, as if it were something unspeakable that needed to be handled with a pair of tongs. "What on earth might they be?" Legat couldn't tell whether or not he was joking. But before he attempted to answer, there was a knock at the door. "Come!"

Miss Marchant was carrying a folder. "A telegram from Berlin has just come in."

"About time!" Cadogan practically snatched it from her hand. "I've been waiting for this all evening." Once again he laid the document on the table and lowered his large head over it, reading so intently he seemed almost to fall into the page. He muttered under his breath. "Bugger . . . bugger . . . *bugger!*" Since the crisis had started he had never left the office before midnight. Legat wondered how he stood the strain. After a while he looked up. "This is the latest from Hitler. The PM needs to see it straight away. Are you going back to Number Ten?"

"Yes, sir."

Cadogan replaced the telegram in the folder and gave it to him. "As far as the other business is concerned, I'll put it into the system, see what our people make of it. I'm sure they'll want to talk to you tomorrow. Give the matter some thought. Try to work out who's behind it."

"Yes, sir."

Cadogan reached for another file.

According to the Cabinet minutes, telegram 545 from Berlin (*Letter from the Reichschancellor to the Prime Minister*) was handed to Chamberlain a little after 10 p.m. The Cabinet table was full: twenty ministers in all, not counting Horace Wilson—who was attending in his capacity as Special Adviser to report on his meeting with Hitler—and the Cabinet Secretary, Edward Bridges, a bespectacled donnish figure whose father had been Poet Laureate. Most were smoking. One of the big sash windows overlooking the garden had been opened in an attempt to disperse the fug of cigars and pipes and cigarettes. A warm night breeze occasionally fluttered the papers that were spread around the table and strewn across the carpet.

Lord Halifax was speaking when Legat entered. He moved discreetly to the Prime Minister's side and laid the telegram in front of him. Chamberlain, who was listening to the Foreign Secretary, glanced at it, nodded in acknowledgement, and gestured with a slight inclination of his head that Legat should go and sit with the other officials in the row of chairs that lined the wall at the far end of the room. Two were occupied by note-takers from the Cabinet Office, both scribbling away, the third by Cleverly. His chin was on his chest, his arms and legs crossed, his right foot twitching slightly. He looked around gloomily as Legat slipped into the seat next to him, leaned sideways and whispered, "What was that?"

"The reply from Hitler."

"What does it say?"

"I'm afraid I didn't look."

"That was remiss of you. Let's hope it's good news. I'm afraid the poor PM's having rather a sticky time of it."

Legat had a clear sideways view of Chamberlain. He had put on his spectacles and was reading Hitler's letter. He couldn't see the Foreign Secretary, who was sitting opposite the PM, but his voice was unmistakable, with its rolling r's and its tone of confident moral authority, as if he were speaking from some invisible pulpit.

". . . and therefore with considerable regret I fear I cannot, in good conscience, support the Prime Minister on this particular matter. I would feel great difficulty in sending the telegram as drafted by Sir Horace. To tell the Czechs to hand over their territory at once, under the threat of force, would amount in my opinion to complete capitulation."

He paused to take a sip of water. There was a perceptible tightening in the atmosphere around the table. The Holy Fox had broken cover! A couple of ministers actually leaned in to make sure they were hearing correctly.

"I quite understand," Halifax went on, "that if we don't send Sir Horace's telegram, the consequences may be grievous for many millions of people, including our own. It may make war certain. But we simply cannot urge the Czechs to do what we believe to be wrong. Nor do I think the House of Commons will accept it. Finally—and this to me is the crux of the matter—we cannot offer the Czechs any firm guarantee that the German Army will content themselves with stopping at the borders of the Sudetenland and will not go on to occupy the entire country."

All eyes turned to Chamberlain. In profile, the bushy grey eyebrows and moustache seemed to bristle; the hawk's-beak nose tilted up in defiance. He did not like to be contradicted. Legat wondered if he might lose his temper. It was not something he had witnessed. On the rare occasions it did occur, it was said to be spectacular. Instead the Prime Minister said coldly, "The Foreign Secretary has just given us powerful and perhaps even convincing arguments against my proposal, although it does seem to me to be the last real chance we have." He looked around at the faces of his ministers. "But if that is the general view of colleagues . . ." He left an expectant pause, like an auctioneer hoping for a final bid. Nobody spoke. "If that is the general view," he repeated, and now his voice was harsh in defeat, "I am prepared to leave it at that." He looked at Horace Wilson. "The telegram will not be sent."

A collective shifting in seats and adjustment of papers ensued—the sound of peaceable men girding themselves reluctantly for war. The Prime Minister's voice cut through the murmur. He was not done yet.

"Before we proceed further, I should inform the Cabinet that I have just received a reply from Herr Hitler. I believe it might be useful if I were to read it to you now."

Several of his more sycophantic ministers—Maugham, the Lord Chancellor; "Shakes" Morrison of Agriculture—said, "Yes," and, "Absolutely."

The Prime Minister picked up the telegram. " 'Dear Mr. Chamberlain, I have in the course of conversations once more informed Sir Horace Wilson, who brought me your letter of the twenty-sixth of September, of my final attitude . . .' "

It was disconcerting to hear Hitler's demands coming out of Chamberlain's mouth. It made them sound quite reasonable. After all, why should the Czech Government object to the immediate occupation of territory which they had already conceded in principle should be transferred to Germany? " 'This represents no more than a security measure which is intended to guarantee a quick and smooth achievement of the final settlement.' " When they complained about the loss of their border fortifications, surely the world could see they were only stalling for time? " 'If one were to wait for the entry into force of the final settlement in which Czechoslovakia had completed new fortifications in the territory that remained to her, it would doubtless take months and years.' " And so it went on. It was almost as if Hitler had been given a seat at the Cabinet table to make his case. At the end, the Prime Minister took off his spectacles. "Well, that is obviously very carefully drafted and will require more time to analyse, but it doesn't leave me entirely without hope."

Duff Cooper, the First Lord of the Admiralty, piped up at once. "On the contrary, Prime Minister, he hasn't conceded a single point!" He was a raffish figure who always exuded, even in midmorning, a vague late-night whiff of whisky and cigars and the perfume of other men's wives. His face was flushed. Legat couldn't tell whether it was anger or if he had been drinking.

"That may be true," said Halifax, "but it's noticeable he hasn't entirely slammed the door, either. He does conclude by inviting the Prime Minister to continue his efforts for peace."

"Yes, but only in the most lukewarm manner: 'I leave it to you to *decide if it's worth carrying on.'* He obviously doesn't mean it for a moment. He's just trying to shift the blame for his aggression onto the Czechs."

"Well, that is not without significance in itself. It suggests that even Hitler feels he can't entirely ignore world opinion. It may give you something to work on, Prime Minister."

Now see how the Holy Fox doubles his tracks, thought Legat—one minute for war and the next for peace . . .

Chamberlain said, "Thank you, Foreign Secretary." His tone was chilly; clearly he had not forgiven him. "You all know my convictions. I intend to go on working for peace until the last possible moment." He glanced over his shoulder at the clock. "Time is drawing on. I need to prepare my statement to Parliament tomorrow. Obviously I shall have to go further than I did in my broadcast this evening. The House will need to be informed of our warning to Hitler this morning. I suggest we agree collectively on the form of words I should use." He caught Legat's eye and beckoned him over. In a quiet voice he said, "Would you be so good as to find me a copy of Hitler's speech from last night? Bring it to me after Cabinet."

The only version of Hitler's speech that Legat could lay his hands on was the one published in that morning's *Times*. He sat at his desk with his own copy and smoothed the pages flat with his palms. Already it seemed an age since he was sitting reading it in the Ritz, waiting for Pamela to arrive. He suddenly remembered he had promised to call her in the country. He eyed the telephone. It was probably too late now. The children would both be in bed, and doubtless Pamela would have drunk one cocktail too many and had a row with her parents. The awfulness of the day overwhelmed him: the abandoned lunch, the workmen in Green Park, the barrage balloons rising over the Thames, the gas masks for his children, the car pulling away from the kerb in North Street . . . And tomorrow would be worse. Tomorrow the Germans would mobilise and he would be questioned by the Secret Intelligence Service. He would not be able to deflect them as easily as he had Cadogan. They would have his file.

He heard voices. It sounded as though the Cabinet meeting was over. He stood and crossed to the door. The ministers were emerging into the corridor. Normally after Cabinet there was some laughter, a little back-slapping, even an occasional argument. There was none of that tonight. Apart from a couple of hushed conversations, most of the politicians put their heads down and hurried out of Number 10 alone. He watched the tall solitary figure of Halifax put on his bowler hat and collect his umbrella from the stand. Through the open door came the now-familiar cold white flickering and shouted questions.

Legat waited until he judged the Prime Minister must be alone, then entered the Cabinet Room. It was deserted. The litter and the overwhelming smell of stale tobacco smoke reminded him of a railway station waiting room. To his right, the door to Cleverly's office was half-open. He could hear the Secretary to the Cabinet and the Principal Private Secretary conferring. To his left, the door to Horace Wilson's room was closed. He knocked and heard Wilson call out for him to come in.

Wilson was at a side table, squirting soda from a siphon into two tumblers of what looked like brandy. The Prime Minister was sprawled back in an armchair, legs outstretched, arms dangling over the sides. His eyes were closed. He opened them as Legat approached.

"I'm afraid I could only find the speech in *The Times*, Prime Minister."

"That's all right. That's where I read it. God!"

With a groan of exhaustion, he hauled himself from the depths of the armchair. His legs moved stiffly. He took the newspaper, placed it open at the speech on Wilson's desk, extracted his spectacles from his breast pocket and began looking up and down the columns of newsprint. His mouth hung open slightly. Wilson came over from the side table and politely showed Legat the tumbler. Legat shook his head. "No, thank you, Sir Horace." Wilson placed it next to the Prime Minister. He looked at Legat and raised his eyebrows slightly. There was something almost shocking in the complicity of it—the suggestion that they were both having to humour the old man.

The Prime Minister said, "This is it: *'We have never found a single Great Power in Europe with a man at its head who has as much understanding for the distress of our people as my great friend Benito Mussolini. We shall never forget what he has done in this time, or the attitude of the Italian people. If similar distress should ever befall Italy, I shall go to the German people and ask them to do for the Italians what the Italians have done for us.'"* He pushed the paper across the desk for Wilson to look at. He picked up the tumbler and took a sip. "Do you see what I mean?"

"I do."

"Hitler plainly isn't going to listen to me, but he might well listen to Musso." He sat at the desk, took a sheet of Number 10 notepaper and dipped a pen in the inkwell. He paused to take another drink, gazed ahead in thought, then started to write. After a while, he said to Legat, without looking up, "I want you to take this to the Foreign Office cipher room right away and have them telegraph it immediately to Lord Perth at the embassy in Rome."

"Yes, Prime Minister."

Wilson said, "If you're writing to the Ambassador, don't you think you ought to tell the Foreign Office?"

"Damn the Foreign Office." The Prime Minister blotted the wet ink. He turned and smiled up at Legat. "Please forget you heard that last remark." He held out the letter. "And when you've done that we'll get to work on my speech to Parliament."

A minute later, Legat was hurrying back across Downing Street towards the Foreign Office. The road was clear. The crowds had gone. Thick cloud over London obscured the stars and moon. An hour remained until midnight.

The lights were still switched on in Potsdamer Platz, looming war or no. The dome of the Haus Vaterland, with its UFA-cinema and its giant café, was lit by traceries of four thousand electric bulbs. Opposite it, an illuminated billboard showed a movie star with glistening jet-black hair, his face at least ten metres high, smoking a Makedon cigarette—"*Perfekt!*"

Hartmann waited for a tram to pass, then strolled across the street to the Bahnhof Wannsee. Five minutes later he was aboard one of the suburban electric trains, rattling southwest into the night. He could not entirely throw off the sensation that he was being followed, even though his carriage—he had chosen to ride in the last one—was empty apart from a pair of drunks and an SA man reading the *Völkischer Beobachter.* The drunks got off at Schöneberg, bowing to him elaborately as they left, and then it was only him and the stormtrooper. The city lights dwindled. Great areas of darkness spread around him like mysterious black lakes; he guessed they must be parks. From time to time the train jolted and threw out blue flashes of electric sparks. They stopped at little stations—Friedenau and Feuerbachstrasse—the automatic doors opening onto deserted platforms. Finally, as they came into Steglitz the SA man folded his paper and got to his feet. He brushed past Hartmann on his way to the door. He smelled of sweat and beer and leather. He hooked his thumbs into his belt and turned to address Hartmann. His plump, brown-clad body swayed with the train; he reminded Hartmann of a fat chrysalis about to burst.

"Those fellows were disgusting."

"Oh, I don't know. They seemed harmless enough."

"No, should've been locked up."

The doors opened and he stumbled out onto the platform. As the train pulled away Hartmann looked back and saw him bent over, hands on his knees, vomiting.

Out here, the trees grew close to the track. The trunks of silver birches flashed past, luminous in the dark. One might imagine oneself to be in a forest. He rested his cheek against the cool glass of the window and thought of home and boyhood and camping in the summer, of singing and campfires, of the Wandervogel and the Nibelungenbund, of the noble elite and the salvation of the nation. He felt a sudden sense of exhilaration. A few more passengers got off at Botanischer Garten and at last he felt sure he was alone. At the next stop, Lichterfelde West, he was the only person to alight onto the platform until the very last moment when the doors had already started to close and a man in the carriage in front just managed to squeeze through the gap. He glanced briefly over his shoulder as the train pulled away and Hartmann had an impression of a blunt-jawed, brutal face. The Leibstandarte-SS Adolf Hitler—the Führer's bodyguard—had their barracks in Lichterfelde: perhaps he was an officer, off duty. The man bent to tie his shoelaces and Hartmann walked quickly past him, along the platform, up the flight of steps, through the deserted station with its closed ticket office, and out into the street.

He had memorised the route before he left the office—right, right, fourth left—but instinct warned him to wait. He crossed the cobbled square in front of the station and stood in the doorway of a butcher's shop opposite. The station was eccentric. It had been built in the last century to resemble an Italianate villa. He felt as if he were a spy in a foreign country. After half a minute his fellow passenger emerged, hesitated and looked around, as if searching for Hartmann, then turned right and disappeared. Hartmann gave it another five minutes before he set off.

It was a pleasant, leafy, bourgeois suburb—hardly a place in which to plot treason. Most of the inhabitants were already asleep, their shutters closed. A couple of dogs barked as he passed. He wondered why Oster wanted them to meet out here. He walked down Königsberger Strasse and into Goethe Strasse. Number 9 was a plain, double-fronted house—the sort of villa a bank manager might choose to live in, or a headmaster. The lights in the front windows were off and suddenly it occurred to him that he might be walking into a trap. Kordt was a Nazi, after all. He had worked with Ribbentrop for years. But then Hartmann was a Party member himself: if one wanted to rise to a position of any influence, one had to be. He banished his suspicion, opened the little wooden gate, marched up the path to the front door and rang the bell.

A well-educated voice said, "Identify yourself."

"Hartmann. Foreign Ministry."

The door was unlocked. An elderly, bald-headed man of about sixty stood on the threshold. Large round melancholy blue eyes were set deep into his skull. A small duelling scar ran horizontally just below the left corner of his mouth. It was a fine, intelligent face. In his grey suit and blue tie, he might have been a professor. "Beck," he said, and stuck out his hand. He pulled Hartmann into the house with a firm grip, then shut the door and locked it.

My God, thought Hartmann, Ludwig Beck—General Beck—the Chief of the General Staff.

"This way, please." Beck led him down a passage towards a room at the back of the house where half a dozen men were seated. "I presume you know most of these gentlemen."

"Indeed." Hartmann nodded a general greeting. How much the strain had aged them over just the last few months! There was the clerkish Kordt, whose elder brother Theo was the chargé d'affaires at the embassy in London—another member of the opposition—who so hated Ribbentrop he had decided he was willing to risk his neck to stop him; and Colonel Oster, the deputy head of military intel-

ligence, a cavalryman of charm, who was their leader, in so far as
so fissiparous a group could tolerate such a thing; and Hans Bernd
Gisevius and Count von Schulenburg of the Interior Ministry; and
Hans von Dohnányi of the Justice Ministry. The sixth man he didn't
know, but he recognised him. It was the S-Bahn passenger he had
seen earlier tying his shoelaces at the railway station.

Oster noticed his look of surprise. "This is Captain Friedrich
Heinz. I don't expect you know him. He's on my staff at the Abwehr.
He is our 'man of action,'" he added with a smile.

Hartmann didn't doubt it. The Abwehr man had the face of a
boxer who had been in too many fights.

"We've met," said Hartmann, "after a fashion."

He sat down on the sofa. The room was oppressively hot and
cramped. A pair of heavy velvet curtains was drawn across the
window. The bookshelves were full of literature—French as well
as German—and volumes of philosophy. On the table was a jug of
water and some small glasses.

Oster said, "I'm grateful to General Beck for agreeing to see us
tonight. The general would like to say something, I believe."

Beck had seated himself on a hard wooden chair that placed him
slightly higher than the rest of them. "Only Colonel Oster and Herr
Gisevius are aware of what I am about to tell you." His voice was dry,
clipped, precise. "A little under six weeks ago, I resigned as Chief of
the General Staff in protest at the plan to go to war with Czechoslovakia. You won't have heard of my action because I promised the
Führer I wouldn't make it public. I regret agreeing to his request,
but there it is—I gave my word. However, I am still in touch with
my former colleagues in the high command, and I can tell you there
is strong opposition to what is happening—so strong, that I believe
that if Hitler issues the order for mobilisation tomorrow, there is a
good chance the Army will disobey it and move against the regime
instead."

There was a silence. Hartmann could feel his heartbeat accelerating.

Oster said, "Obviously this changes everything. We now have to be prepared to act decisively tomorrow. We may never get a better chance."

Kordt said sceptically, "And how is this 'coup' to happen?"

"With one stroke: the arrest of Hitler."

"The Army will do this?"

"No, we will need to do it."

"But surely only the Army has the strength to accomplish such a task?"

Beck said, "The Wehrmacht's difficulty is that we have sworn an oath of loyalty to the Führer. However, if there were to be some sort of disturbance in the Chancellery, the Army could certainly move in to maintain order. That would not be incompatible with our oath. It's merely that the first move against Hitler could not be ours. It would have to come from others."

Oster said, "I have been analysing this for weeks. It really wouldn't take many men to arrest Hitler, provided we had the advantage of surprise, along with an undertaking that the Army would then protect us from any rescue attempt by the SS. Captain Heinz and I estimate we would need an initial force of about fifty men."

"And where are we to find these fifty men?" asked Kordt.

"We already have them," said Heinz. "Experienced fighters, prepared to move tomorrow."

"Good God!" Kordt stared at him as if he were crazy. "Who are they? Where are they? How are they armed?"

"The Abwehr will issue them with weapons," said Oster. "We are also providing them with safe houses close to Wilhelmstrasse where they can wait until they receive the signal to move."

Heinz said, "They will be in position at dawn tomorrow. Each one of these men is a reliable comrade, known personally to me. Remember, I fought with Kapp in 1920, then with the Stahlhelm."

"It's true—if anyone can pull it off, Heinz can." Hartmann knew Schulenburg only vaguely—a socialist aristocrat who had joined the Party before it came to power, and who had since become disillusioned. Nowadays he was stuck in some low-level police job in the Interior Ministry.

Schulenburg said to Beck, "And you really think, General, that the Army will turn on the Führer, after all he's done for them, and for Germany?"

"I agree that much of what he's achieved in the foreign sphere has been remarkable—the return of the Rhineland, the incorporation of Austria. But the point is, they were bloodless victories. And the return of the Sudetenland could be bloodless, too. Unfortunately, he isn't interested in achieving his aims peacefully anymore. The truth about Hitler, I came to realise over the summer, is that he actually *wants* war with Czechoslovakia. He is under the delusion that he is some kind of military genius, even though he never rose higher than corporal. You fail to understand the man unless you understand that. And on one thing the Army is agreed: war with France and Britain this year would be a disaster for Germany."

Hartmann took his opportunity to speak. "Actually, I can show you the latest proof that Hitler wants war." He reached into his inside pocket and pulled out the text of Hitler's letter to Chamberlain. "This is the Führer's response to the British, sent to London earlier tonight." He handed the telegram to Oster, then sat back and lit a cigarette and watched as the letter was passed around.

Kordt said, "How did you get hold of this?"

"I had to take it from the Reich Chancellery to the British Embassy. I made a copy."

"That was quick work!"

"Well, this settles it, gentlemen," said Oster when he had finished reading. "There's not a hint of compromise anywhere in it."

Beck said, "It's tantamount to a declaration of war."

Oster said, "We need to get it into the hands of the Commander-in-Chief, first thing tomorrow morning. If this doesn't convince him that Hitler isn't bluffing, nothing will. Is it all right for us to keep it, Hartmann, or does it need to go back to the Foreign Ministry?"

Hartmann said, "No, you can show that to the Army."

Dohnányi—a skinny, bespectacled figure, who even in his mid-thirties still looked like a law student—raised his hand. "I have a question for Captain Heinz. Assuming we succeed in arresting Hitler tomorrow, what will we do with him?"

"Kill him," said Heinz.

"No, no, no—I don't agree with that."

"Why not? Do you imagine he'd hesitate for a second to do the same to us?"

"Of course not, but I don't want to stoop to his level of brutality. Besides, killing him would turn him into the greatest martyr in German history. The country would live in his shadow for generations."

"Naturally, we won't *announce* we killed him. We can simply say he died in the fighting."

"That won't fool anyone. The truth will come out—it always does." He appealed to the room. "Gisevius—help me here."

"I don't know what I think." Gisevius was a baby-faced lawyer who had started his career in the Gestapo until he realised the sort of people he was working with. "I suppose the best course would be to put him on trial. We have a file of evidence against him a metre thick."

Beck said, "I agree absolutely. I couldn't be a party to any extra-judicial killing. The fellow should be taken somewhere secure and subjected to a thorough psychiatric examination. Then he can either be locked away in an asylum or made to account for his crimes."

Heinz muttered, "Psychiatric examination!"

Oster said, "Kordt? What's your opinion?"

"The problem with a trial is that it will give him a platform. He would be brilliant in a courtroom. Remember what happened after the Beer Hall Putsch."

"That's true. Hartmann? Your view?"

"If you want my advice, we should kill the whole filthy lot of them—Himmler, Goebbels, Göring—the entire criminal gang." The violence in his voice surprised him. His fists were clenched. He stopped, conscious of Oster staring at him.

"My dear Hartmann—usually so detached and ironical! Who knew you carried such hate?"

Heinz was looking at him with interest for the first time. "You say you were in the Chancellery this evening?"

"That's right."

"Could you make sure you were there tomorrow morning?"

"Perhaps." Hartmann glanced over at Kordt. "Erich, what do you think?"

"I expect we could find some pretext. Why?"

"We need someone on the inside to make sure the doors stay open."

"All right." Hartmann nodded. "I'll try."

"Good."

Dohnányi said, "But what shall we do with Hitler, gentlemen? What is our decision?"

The conspirators looked from one to another. Eventually, Oster said, "This is like arguing about what form of government we should have after the Third Reich. Will it be a monarchy or a democratic republic, or some combination of the two? The fact is, as the proverb says, before you can cook your rabbit you first have to catch it. Our absolute priority has to be stopping this madman from issuing the order for mobilisation tomorrow afternoon. All else must be secondary to that objective. If he surrenders himself into our custody—all well and good, and we'll take him alive. If it looks as though he might get away, I don't think we have any choice except to shoot him. Can we agree on that?"

Hartmann was the first to nod. "I second that." One by one the others followed suit, including eventually Dohnányi, and—finally and most obviously reluctantly—Beck.

"Good," said Oster, with a sigh of relief. "That at least is settled. Tomorrow we strike."

———

They left the house at intervals to avoid attracting attention. Hartmann was the first to go. A brief handshake with each of the others; an exchange of glances; a muttered "Good luck" from Oster; that was all.

The contrast between the violence they were contemplating and the sleeping suburban street was so incongruous that Hartmann had barely gone fifty paces before the entire encounter began to seem like an hallucination. He had to repeat the astonishing truth to himself: By this time tomorrow Hitler could be dead. It was both impossible and yet entirely feasible. The hurling of a bomb, the pulling of a trigger, the slashing of a knife across the tyrant's throat—wasn't this how history was so often made? For a moment he imagined himself as some noble young senator, walking back from Brutus's house on the eve of the Ides of March, down from the Palatine to the Forum Romanum under the same cloudy European sky.

He saw a signpost pointing to the river. On impulse he followed it. He was too restless to think of returning to his apartment. In the middle of the bridge he stopped to light a cigarette. There was no traffic. Beneath him the Spree was greyly luminescent, disappearing into the distance towards the centre of Berlin between dark masses of trees. He set off along the footpath that ran beside it. He couldn't see the water but he could sense its rustling movement, could hear its soft splashes as it encountered rocks and undergrowth. He must have walked for a couple of kilometres, his head full of images of violence and martyrdom, until eventually streetlights appeared ahead. The path ended in a small park with a children's play area— slide, swings, a seesaw, a sandpit. The prosaic sight depressed him. It brought him back to earth. Who was he? Who indeed were Oster, Heinz, Dohnányi, Schulenburg, Kordt and Beck? A handful against millions! They must be mad to think they could bring it off.

On the far side of the park was a main road where the last bus from Steglitz was waiting to depart for the city. He climbed the twisting staircase to the upper deck. A young couple occupied the front seat: his arm around her shoulders, her head resting against his cheek. He sat at the back and watched them. In the cold stale air of the bus he could smell the girl's perfume. The engine whined, the bus swayed. When she started to kiss her boyfriend he looked away. The old longing returned. Ten minutes later, as they came into Schöneberg, he went back down the steps and stood on the platform until he saw a street he recognised. The bus slowed slightly and he jumped off it sideways, his legs absorbing the impact in half a dozen long strides until he was able to bring himself to a halt.

Her apartment block was above an automobile showroom. Behind the plate glass, in the harsh neon light, swastika banners hung from the ceiling between glittering Opels and Mercedes.

The entrance was unlocked. He climbed three floors, past the heavy closed doors of the other apartments. The landings smelled of dried flowers. There must be money somewhere for her to afford all this.

Almost as soon as he rang the bell she let him in. He wondered if she had been waiting for him.

"Frau Winter."

"Herr Hartmann."

She locked the door behind him.

She was wearing a kimono, the belt untied, her toenails painted the same brilliant scarlet as the silk. Her black hair, unpinned now that she was away from the office, fell all the way to the small of her back. The skin of her feet, of her stomach and between her breasts was alabaster-white. As he followed her into the bedroom he could hear a radio in the sitting room, tuned illegally to a foreign station, playing jazz. She slipped off her robe and left it pooled on the carpet, then lay on the bed and watched him undress. When he was naked he moved to switch off the light.

"No. Leave it."

She guided him into her at once. She never wanted them to take their time. It was one of the things he liked about her. Afterwards, as she always did, she went into the kitchen to fetch them a drink, leaving him as usual to stare at the photograph on the nightstand of her dead husband. She never removed it, or laid it flat. Late twenties, infantry captain, handsome in his uniform in the photographer's studio, his gloved hands resting on the hilt of his sword. Hartmann guessed he must be about the same age as him. Was that what this was about? Did she like to imagine it was the ghost of Captain Winter who was fucking her?

She came back into the bedroom naked, two cigarettes between her lips, a glass of whisky in either hand, a large envelope under her arm. She gave him his drink and cigarette, then dropped the envelope onto his chest. He looked down his nose at it without moving.

"What's this?"

"See for yourself."

The bed creaked as she climbed back onto it. She hugged her knees and watched as he opened it. He pulled out the pages and started to read.

"My God . . ." He sat up abruptly.

"You want the English to fight? Show them that."

Day Two

1

It took Legat a few moments to work out where he was.

His narrow mattress was hard; the room was not much larger than the metal bed frame. Regency striped wallpaper. A ceiling that sloped steeply at an angle of nearly forty-five degrees. No window. Instead a skylight directly above his head through which he found himself squinting at low grey cloud. Seagulls whirled across it like litter in the wind. It reminded him of a seaside boardinghouse.

He groped around the bedside table and opened his pocket watch. A quarter to nine. The Prime Minister had kept him up fetching documents for his speech until nearly three. Afterwards he had lain awake for hours. He must have fallen asleep just before dawn. He felt as if someone had rubbed grit in his eyes.

He threw off the sheet and blanket and swung his feet to the floor.

He was wearing a pair of duck-egg blue pyjamas from Gieves & Hawkes that Pamela had given him for his birthday. Over these he pulled a plaid dressing gown. Sponge bag in hand he opened the door and inspected the corridor. There were three bedrooms crammed into the attic of Number 10 for staff who had to be on call throughout the night. As far as he could tell he was the only occupant.

The pale green Ministry of Works linoleum was clammy underfoot. It flowed along the passage and into the bathroom. He pulled the light cord. Again, no window. He had to run the tap for more than a minute before the water turned lukewarm. While he waited he placed a hand on either side of the basin and leaned towards the mirror. Increasingly these days the face he shaved was his father's. A face from a sepia photograph: manly, resolute, oddly innocent. All that was lacking was the large dark moustache. He lathered his face with soap.

Back in his room he put on a clean shirt and threaded his cuff-links. He knotted his purple and dark-blue striped Balliol tie. Behold the Third Secretary! It was five years to the day since he had looked in the back pages of *The Times* and discovered the list of successful candidates in the 1933 Diplomatic Service Entrance Examinations. The names were printed in order of marks achieved: Legat, Reilly, Creswell, Shuckburgh, Gore-Booth, Grey, Malcom, Hogg . . . He had read it several times before it sank in. He had come top. A few lines of newsprint had turned him from an Oxford graduate with a first-class degree in Mods and Greats into a man of the world, an official highflyer. He would be an ambassador certainly; possibly even Per-manent Under-Secretary. Everybody said so. Two days later, still in a state of euphoria, he had proposed to Pamela, and to his amazement she had accepted. If anything, her fantasies had outstripped his own. She would be Lady Legat. She would preside elegantly and effort-lessly over receptions at the Paris embassy in the rue du Faubourg Saint-Honoré . . . They had both behaved like children. It had been madness. And now the world had grown old and ugly around them.

By the time he was fully dressed it was nine o'clock. There were six hours left until Hitler's ultimatum expired.

He went in search of breakfast.

The narrow stairs led down to a landing outside the Prime Minister's flat, and from there to the anteroom next to Chamberlain's study. His intention was to slip out to the Lyons Corner House near Trafalgar Square—he could be there and back in thirty minutes—but before he could reach the main staircase he heard a door open behind him and a woman's voice called out, "Mr. Legat! Good morning!"

He stopped and turned to face her. "Good morning, Mrs. Chamberlain."

Her costume was funereal, charcoal grey and black, with a necklace of large beads of jet. "Did you manage to get some sleep?"

"Yes, thank you."

"Come and have some breakfast."

"I was just about to go out."

"Don't be silly. We always give the duty secretary breakfast." She peered at him myopically. "It's Hugh, isn't it?"

"That's right. But really—"

"Nonsense. There's such a crowd gathering outside already. It will be much easier for you to eat here."

She took his arm and gently tugged him after her. They passed through the state drawing rooms watched by various Whig and Tory statesmen, looking down their noses at them from heavy gilt frames. To his surprise she continued to hold on to him. They might have been fellow guests at a country-house weekend going in to dinner together. "I am so grateful for all that you young men do for my husband." Her tone was confiding. "You have no idea how much you lighten his burden. And don't say you're just doing your job—I know the personal cost of public service."

She opened the door to the dining room. It was not the grand official one but the more intimate, wood-panelled room with a table for twelve. At the far end, reading *The Times*, was the Prime Minister. He looked up at his wife and smiled. "Good morning, my dear." He nodded at Legat. "Good morning." He resumed reading.

Mrs. Chamberlain gestured to a side table where half a dozen dishes with silver covers were being kept warm on a hotplate. "Do please help yourself. Coffee?"

"Thank you."

She handed him a cup and went and sat next to the Prime Minister. Legat lifted the nearest cover. The greasy-sweet smell of the bacon reminded him how hungry he was. He went along the table filling his plate: scrambled eggs, mushrooms, sausages, black pudding. When he sat down, Mrs. Chamberlain smiled at the size of his breakfast. "Are you married, Hugh?"

"Yes, Mrs. Chamberlain."

"Any children?"

"A boy and a girl."

"Exactly the same as us. How old?"

"They're three and two."

"Oh, how wonderful! Ours are much older. Dorothy is twenty-seven—she was recently married. Frank is twenty-four. Do you like this coffee?"

Legat took a sip; it was disgusting. "It's very good, thank you."

"I make it with chicory."

The Prime Minister rustled his paper slightly and grunted. Mrs. Chamberlain fell quiet and poured herself some tea. Legat resumed eating. For several minutes there was silence.

"Ah, now this is interesting!" The Prime Minister suddenly lifted his paper and folded it to the page he had been reading. "Could you make a note of this?" Legat quickly put down his knife and fork and took out his notebook. "I shall need to write a letter to"—he brought the small print up close to his eyes—"a Mr. G. J. Scholey of Thirty-eight Dysart Avenue, Kingston-upon-Thames."

"Yes, Prime Minister." Legat was bewildered.

"He has a letter to the editor printed: *'In the spring of this year I was observing a blackbird with a nest of eggs in a steep bank. Upon my approach each day the sitting bird would allow me to observe her at a few feet distant. And then one morning her familiar figure was missing. On peering over the bank I found her four young chicks cold and lifeless in the nest. A thin trail of blackish breast feathers led me down the bank to a small bush, under which I discovered the mangled remains of my old blackbird. And, intermingled in that trail of blackbird's feathers were a few others—those which could only have come from the breast and flanks of a little owl . . .'"* The Prime Minister tapped the paper with his finger. "I have observed exactly the same behaviour by the little owls at Chequers."

Mrs. Chamberlain said, "Oh, Neville, really! As if Hugh hasn't got enough to do!"

Legat said, "Actually, I believe it was my grandfather on my mother's side who helped introduce the little owl to the British Isles."

"Did he really?" For the first time the Prime Minister looked at him with genuine interest.

"Yes, he brought several pairs back with him from India."

"What year would this have been?"

"I should think about 1880."

"So in barely more than fifty years, this little bird has spread all over southern England! That is something to celebrate."

"Not if you're a blackbird, apparently," said Mrs. Chamberlain. "Do you have time for a walk, Neville?" She looked across the table at Legat. "We always take a walk together after breakfast."

The Prime Minister put down his paper. "Yes, I need some air. But not the park, I'm afraid—not today. There are too many people. It will have to be the garden. Why don't you come with us . . . Hugh?"

He followed the Chamberlains as they descended the grand staircase arm in arm. When they reached the private secretaries' corridor, the Prime Minister turned round to Legat. "Would you mind just checking whether there's been a reply from Rome to my telegram last night?"

"Of course, Prime Minister."

They continued on to the Cabinet Room while Legat ducked into his office. Miss Watson was behind her wall of files.

"Has the Foreign Office messenger been over yet?"

"Not that I've seen."

He checked with Syers, who said, "They don't normally show up till eleven. How was last night?"

"This morning, you mean."

"Christ. How are you feeling?"

"Bloody awful."

"And the PM?"

"Fresh as a daisy."

"Irritating, isn't it? I don't know how he does it."

Cleverly was in his office, dictating a letter to his secretary. Legat put his head round the door. "Excuse me, sir. Has a telegram come in from the Rome embassy this morning? The Prime Minister wants to know."

"I haven't seen anything. Why? What is he expecting?"

"He wrote to Lord Perth late last night."

"About what?"

"Instructing him to ask Mussolini to intervene with Hitler."

Cleverly looked alarmed. "But that wasn't authorised at Cabinet. Does the Foreign Secretary know?"

"I'm not sure."

"Not sure? It's your job to be sure!" He reached for the telephone. Legat took advantage of his distraction to escape.

Inside the Cabinet Room, one of the doors to the terrace was open. The Chamberlains had already descended the steps and were strolling across the lawn. Legat hurried after them.

"No reply from Rome yet, Prime Minister."

"You are sure it was sent?"

"Definitely. I stood in the cipher room and watched it go."

"Well then, we shall just have to be patient."

The Chamberlains resumed their walk. Legat felt awkward. He was conscious of Cleverly standing at his office window, talking on the telephone, watching him. Nevertheless, he fell in behind them. The weather was still mild and gloomy, the big trees turning brown. Drifts of fallen leaves lay across the damp grass and the flower beds. From beyond the high wall came the sound of traffic. The Prime Minister stopped beside a bird table. From his pocket he pulled a piece of toast he had taken from the rack at breakfast. He broke it into pieces and laid them out carefully, then stepped back and folded his arms. He brooded.

"What a day this promises to be," he said quietly. "You know, I would gladly stand up against that wall and be shot if only I could prevent war."

"Neville—really—please don't say such things!" Mrs. Chamberlain looked as if she were about to burst into tears.

The Prime Minister said to Legat, "You were too young to fight in the last war, and I was too old. In some ways that made it worse." He glanced up at the sky. "It was an absolute agony to me to see such suffering and to be so powerless. Three-quarters of a million men killed from this country alone. Imagine it! And it wasn't just they who suffered, but their parents and their wives and children, their families, their friends . . . Afterwards, whenever I saw a war memorial, or visited one of those vast cemeteries in France where so many dear friends are buried, I always vowed that if ever I was in a position to prevent such a catastrophe from happening again, I would do anything—sacrifice anything—to maintain peace. You can understand that?"

"Of course."

"This is sacred to me."

"I understand."

"And it all happened only twenty years ago!" He fixed Legat with a gaze almost fanatical in its intensity. "It's not simply that this country is militarily and psychologically unprepared for war—that can be remedied—we are remedying it. It's rather that I truly fear for the spiritual health of our people if they don't see their leaders doing absolutely everything they can to prevent a second great conflict. Because of one thing I can assure you: if it comes, the next war will be infinitely worse than the last, and they will require great fortitude to survive it."

Suddenly, he turned on his heel and started marching back across the lawn to Number 10. Mrs. Chamberlain stared helplessly at Legat for a moment, then went after him. "Neville!" The energy of the old man was more than merely remarkable, thought Legat: it was disconcerting. The Prime Minister trotted up the dozen steps to the terrace and disappeared into the Cabinet Room. His wife was not far behind.

Legat followed at a distance. On the terrace he stopped. Through the open door he could see the Chamberlains embracing. The Prime Minister was stroking her back in reassurance. After a while he stepped away slightly. He held her by the shoulders and stared at her intently. Legat couldn't see her face. "Go on, Annie," he said gently. He smiled at her, brushed something from her cheek. "We'll be all right." She nodded and left without turning round.

The Prime Minister beckoned Legat into the room. He pulled a chair out from the Cabinet table. "Sit down," he ordered.

Legat sat.

Chamberlain stayed on his feet. He patted his inside pockets, pulled out a cigar case, tipped out a cigar and snipped off the end with his thumb. He struck a match and lit the cigar, sucking at it until it was well alight. With a vigorous shake of his hand he extinguished the match and threw it into an ashtray. "Take this down."

Legat reached for a sheet of headed notepaper, pen and ink.

"To Reich Chancellor Adolf Hitler . . ."

His nib scratched across the paper.

"After reading your letter I feel certain that you can get all essentials without war and without delay." Legat waited. The Prime Minister paced up and down behind him. *"I am ready to come to Berlin myself at once to discuss arrangements for transfer with you and representatives of the Czech Government . . ."* He paused until he saw Legat had caught up. *". . . together with representatives of France and Italy if you desire. I feel convinced that we could reach agreement in a week."*

At the end of the room the door opened and Horace Wilson slipped in. He nodded to the Prime Minister and took a seat in the far corner of the table. Chamberlain resumed.

"I cannot believe that you will take the responsibility of starting a world war which may end civilisation, for the sake of a few days' delay in settling this long-standing problem." He stopped.

Legat glanced round at him. "Is that it, Prime Minister?"

"That's it. Sign it with my name, and have it sent care of Sir Nevile Henderson in Berlin." He turned to Wilson. "All right?"

"Excellent."

Legat began to stand.

Chamberlain said, "Wait. There's another. This one is to Signor Mussolini." He took a few more puffs on his cigar. *"I have today addressed a last appeal to Herr Hitler to abstain from force to settle the Sudeten problem, which, I feel sure, can be settled by a short discussion and will give him the essential territory, population and protection for both Sudetens and Czechs during transfer. I have offered myself to go at once to Berlin to discuss arrangements with German and Czech representatives, and if the Chancellor desires, representatives also of Italy and France."*

Across the table, Legat could see Wilson nodding slowly.

The Prime Minister continued. *"I trust Your Excellency will inform the German Chancellor that you are willing to be represented and urge him to agree to my proposal which will keep all our peoples out of war. I have already guaranteed that Czech promises shall be carried out and feel confident full agreement could be reached in a week."*

Wilson said, "Are you going to inform the Cabinet?"

"No."

"Is that constitutional?"

"I don't know, and frankly at this stage, what does it matter? Either this will work and everyone will be too relieved afterwards to quibble, or it won't and they will be too busy trying on gas masks to care." He said to Legat, "Will you take those over to the Foreign Office and make sure they are dispatched at once?"

"Of course, Prime Minister." He gathered the papers together.

"At any rate," Chamberlain resumed to Wilson, "my conscience will be clear. The world will see I have done everything humanly possible to avoid war. The responsibility from now on rests solely with Hitler."

Legat quietly closed the door.

2

Hartmann sat at his desk and pretended to work. In the open file in front of him was a copy of the Führer's latest telegram to President Roosevelt, dispatched the previous evening. It justified invasion on the grounds that 214,000 Sudeten Germans had so far been forced to flee their homes to escape *the outrageous violence and bloody terror* inflicted on them by the Czechs. *Countless dead, thousands of injured, tens of thousands of detainees and prisoners, desolate villages . . .* How much of this was true? Some of it? None of it? Hartmann had no idea. Truth was like any other material necessary for the making of war: it had to be beaten and bent and cut into the required shape. Nowhere in the telegram was there any hint of compromise.

For the hundredth time he checked his watch. It was three minutes past eleven.

Over by the windows, von Nostitz and von Rantzau were also at their desks. They were staring down into the street as if waiting for something to happen. Neither had uttered more than a dozen words all morning. Nostitz, who worked in the Protocol Department, was a Party member; Rantzau, who had been due to go to the London embassy as Second Secretary until the Sudeten crisis blew up, was not. They weren't such bad fellows, Hartmann thought. He had mixed with their type all his life: patriotic, conservative, clannish. For them, Hitler was like some crude gamekeeper who had mysteriously contrived to take over the running of their family estates: once installed, he had proved an unexpected success, and they had consented to tolerate his occasional bad manners and lapses into violence in return for a quiet life. Now they had discovered they couldn't get rid of him and they looked as if they were starting to regret it. Hartmann briefly considered confiding in them but decided it was too risky.

The shrilling of his telephone made all three men jump. He picked up the receiver. "Hartmann."

"Paul, it's Kordt. Come to my office immediately."

The line went dead. Hartmann hung up.

Rantzau couldn't keep the anxiety out of his voice. "Is something going on?"

"I don't know. I'm wanted over the road."

Hartmann closed the Roosevelt file. Beneath it was the envelope he had been given by Frau Winter. He ought to have hidden it somewhere when he went back to his apartment to change but he couldn't think of any place secure enough. Now he slipped it into an empty folder, unlocked the bottom left-hand drawer of his desk and buried it in a pile of documents. He locked the drawer and stood. It struck him that if things went wrong he might never see his colleagues again. He felt an unexpected rush of affection. *Not such bad fellows . . .* He said, "If I hear anything more, I'll let you know."

He collected his hat and hurried out of the door before his face could betray him or they could ask him more questions.

Although he had been made Foreign Minister in February, Ribbentrop still preferred to operate out of his old headquarters on the opposite side of Wilhelmstrasse, in the massive Prussian Ministry of State building. His staff shared the same floor as the Deputy Führer, Rudolf Hess, and Hartmann was obliged to make his way past half a dozen brown-uniformed Nazi Party officials, huddled in conversation, before he reached Kordt's office. Kordt himself opened the door, beckoned him inside and locked it after him. Normally he had a secretary but she wasn't there. He must have sent her away.

"Oster just came to see me. He says it's happening." The Rhinelander's eyes were blinking rapidly behind his thick glasses. He opened his desk drawer and took out a pair of handguns. "He gave me these."

He laid them on the desk carefully. Hartmann took one. It was the latest Walther—small, only about 15 centimetres long, easy to conceal. He weighed it in his hand, clicked the safety catch off and on. "Loaded?"

Kordt nodded. Suddenly he started giggling like a schoolboy. "I can't believe this is happening. I've never fired a gun in my life. Have you?"

"I've hunted since I was a boy." Hartmann took aim at the filing cabinet. His finger tightened around the trigger. "Rifles, mostly. Shotguns."

"Isn't it the same thing?"

"Not exactly. But the principle is the same. So what's going on?"

"Oster gave your copy of Hitler's reply to Chamberlain to General Halder in Army headquarters this morning."

"Who's Halder?"

"Beck's successor as Chief of the General Staff. Halder was appalled, according to Oster. He's definitely with us—even more opposed to Hitler than Beck."

"He'll order the Army to move?"

Kordt shook his head. "He hasn't the authority. He's in charge of planning, not operations. He's going to talk to Brauchitsch—as Commander-in-Chief, Brauchitsch has the power. Would you mind putting that thing down? You're making me nervous."

Hartmann lowered the gun. "And Brauchitsch is sympathetic?"

"Apparently."

"So what happens now?"

"You're to go over to the Chancellery, exactly as we agreed last night."

"On what pretext?"

"The British Embassy just rang. It seems Chamberlain has written another letter to Hitler—God knows what it says—and Henderson wants an appointment to deliver it by hand to the Führer as soon as possible. The request has to be cleared by Ribbentrop, and he's with the Führer now. I thought you could go over and inform him."

Hartmann considered this. It sounded plausible. "All right." He tried concealing the gun in various pockets. It fitted best inside his double-breasted jacket, on the left, next to his heart. He could draw it with his right hand. When he had fastened the buttons it was hard to tell it was there.

Kordt was watching him with something like horror. He said, "Telephone me the moment you have Ribbentrop's response. I'll come over and join you. For God's sake, remember your job is simply to keep the doors open. Don't get involved in any shooting. That's for Heinz and his men."

"I understand." Hartmann tugged his jacket straight. "Well, then. I'd better go."

Kordt unlocked the door and offered his hand. Hartmann gripped it. His friend's palm was cold with fear. He could feel the tension spreading to him like an infection. He pulled his hand away and stepped out into the corridor. "I'll call you in a few minutes." He said it loudly enough for the Party officials to hear. As he approached, they shifted out of the way to let him pass. He strode to the stairs, descended quickly to the lobby and went out into Wilhelmstrasse.

The fresh air braced him. He walked past the brutalist modern facade of the Propaganda Ministry, waited for a lorry to go by, then crossed the street towards the Chancellery. The forecourt was crowded with twenty or thirty official cars—long black limousines flying swastika pennants; some had SS number plates. It looked as though half the regime had turned up to witness the historic moment when the ultimatum expired. Hartmann showed his identity card to the policeman on the gate and stated his business. He was an official from the Foreign Ministry. He had an urgent message for Herr von Ribbentrop. The mere act of repeating it gave him confidence: it had the merit of being true, after all. The policeman opened the gate. He strode rapidly around the perimeter path of the courtyard to the main entrance. A pair of SS guards blocked his way, then stood aside even before he had finished his explanation.

Inside the crowded lobby he counted three more guards with machine guns. The high double doors to the reception rooms were closed. A tall SS adjutant in a white ceremonial jacket stood in front of them. His face was unnaturally hard and angular. He looked like the male model in the cigarette advertisement in Potsdamer Platz, except with blond hair. Hartmann approached him and saluted.

"*Heil Hitler!*"

"*Heil Hitler!*"

"I have an urgent message for Foreign Minister von Ribbentrop."

"Very well. Give it to me and I'll make sure he gets it."

"I must deliver it personally."

"That is not possible. Foreign Minister von Ribbentrop is with the Führer. No one is to be admitted."

"Those are my orders."

"And those are *my* orders."

Hartmann used his height and three centuries of Junker ancestry. He stepped up close to the adjutant and lowered his voice. "Listen to me very carefully, because this is the most important conversation you will ever have in your life. My mission concerns a personal message from the British Prime Minister to the Führer. You will take me to Herr von Ribbentrop immediately, or I can assure you he will speak to the Reichsführer-SS and you will spend the rest of your career shovelling shit in a cavalry barracks."

The adjutant was defiant for a second or two, then something shifted in his clear blue eyes, and broke. "Very well." He nodded stiffly. "Follow me."

He opened the door onto a crowded salon. A central group of perhaps a dozen men was standing beneath the immense crystal chandelier, with smaller clusters radiating out from this inner core. A lot of uniforms—brown, black, grey, blue—were sprinkled among the civilian suits. There was an incessant, urgent drone of conversation. Here and there, a famous face. Goebbels leaning against the back of a chair, arms folded, brooding, alone. Göring, in powder blue, like a general in an Italian opera, holding court to an attentive circle. As Hartmann threaded his way between them he was conscious of heads turning to follow his progress. His eyes met eager, curious expressions, hungry for news, and he realised that they must know nothing, that they were all just waiting, even the most powerful figures in the Reich.

He followed the adjutant's white jacket through a second set of doors—permanently open, he noticed—and into another huge reception room. The atmosphere here was quieter. Diplomats in frock coats and striped trousers were whispering to one another. He recognised Kirchheim from the French desk of the Foreign Ministry. On the left was a closed door with a guard beside it; in an armchair nearby was SS-Sturmbannführer Sauer. He jumped to his feet as soon as he noticed Hartmann. "What are you doing here?"

"I have a message for the Foreign Minister."

"He's in with the Führer and the French Ambassador. What is it?"

"Kordt says Chamberlain has written the Führer a letter. The British Ambassador wants to deliver it in person as soon as possible."

Sauer absorbed this, nodded. "All right. Wait here."

The adjutant said, "Shall I leave Herr Hartmann with you, Herr Sturmbannführer?"

"Yes, of course."

The adjutant clicked his heels and moved away. Sauer tapped lightly on the door, opened it and disappeared inside. Hartmann looked around the salon. Once again he found himself calculating. One guard here, plus those he had already seen. How many did that make? Six? But Oster surely hadn't anticipated such a congregation of senior Party figures inside the Chancellery. What if they had all brought bodyguards of their own? Göring, as head of the Air Force, would certainly have several.

Sauer reappeared. "Tell Kordt that the Führer will receive Ambassador Henderson at twelve-thirty."

"Of course, Herr Sturmbannführer."

As Hartmann set off back towards the lobby he looked at his watch. It was just after eleven-thirty. What were Heinz and the others doing? If they didn't strike soon, half the Berlin diplomatic corps might be caught in the crossfire.

He opened one of the doors to the lobby and left it ajar. The adjutant was nearby. Hartmann went over to him. "I need to make an urgent call to the Foreign Ministry."

"Yes, Herr Hartmann." He was like some handsome stallion: now that he had been broken, he was entirely pliant. He led Hartmann over to the big desk facing the entrance and gestured to the telephone. "You will be automatically connected to the operator."

"Thank you." Hartmann waited until he had moved away, then picked up the receiver.

A male voice said, "Can I help you?"

Hartmann gave the number of Kordt's direct line and waited for the connection. Through the open door of the entrance he could see the back of one of the SS guards and beyond him a couple of limousines drawn up in the courtyard. Two chauffeurs in SS uniform were leaning against one of the cars, smoking. He guessed they must be armed.

There was a click, half a ringtone, and the phone was answered: "Kordt."

"Erich? It's Paul. A message from the Chancellery: the Führer will see Henderson at twelve-thirty."

"Understood. I'll inform the British Embassy." Kordt's voice was staccato.

"It's busy here—much busier than I expected." He hoped Kordt would detect his warning emphasis.

"I understand. Just stay where you are. I'm coming over."

Kordt rang off. Hartmann kept the receiver pressed to his ear and pretended he was still listening. The door to the salon remained slightly open. It occurred to him that when the attack began, his best tactic would probably be to shoot the adjutant to prevent him closing it. The thought of the blood seeping through that immaculate white jacket gave him a moment of pleasure. The operator said, "Do you wish to make another call?"

"No, thank you."

He replaced the receiver.

Suddenly he was aware of a commotion outside. A man was on the steps demanding loudly to be admitted. The adjutant hurried towards the entrance and Hartmann's hand slipped immediately beneath the fabric of his suit to his inside left pocket. He could feel the gun. There was an exchange on the steps and then a stooped, bespectacled, red-faced figure in a bowler hat pushed his way into the lobby. He was out of breath and elderly. He looked as if he might be about to have a heart attack. Hartmann withdrew his hand at once. He recognised him from the diplomatic circuit: the Italian Ambassador, Attolico. His eye fell on Hartmann. He squinted at him in dim recognition.

"You are from the Foreign Ministry, yes?" His German accent was atrocious.

"Yes, Your Excellency."

"Will you please then tell this fellow I need to see the Führer at once?"

"Of course." To the adjutant Hartmann said, "Leave this with me." He guided Attolico towards the grand salon. The adjutant made no attempt to stop him.

Attolico nodded to a few of the men he recognised—to Goebbels and to Göring—but he did not break his step, even as the conversations paused all around them. They went on into the second reception room. Sauer scrambled to his feet in surprise. Hartmann said, "His Excellency needs to speak with the Führer."

Attolico said, "Tell him I have an urgent message from the Duce."

"Of course, Your Excellency."

After Sauer had vanished into the other room, Attolico remained where he was, staring straight ahead. He was trembling slightly.

Hartmann said, "Would you care to sit, Your Excellency?"

Attolico briefly shook his head.

There was the sound of a door opening. Hartmann turned to look. Sauer emerged first, followed by the Foreign Office interpreter, Paul Schmidt, and then—frowning, his arms crossed over his chest, plainly both mystified and wary of what this sudden arrival might portend—Adolf Hitler.

Legat was in the Garden Room of Number 10, once again standing behind Joan as she finished typing the Prime Minister's speech. It was just after one o'clock. The PM was due to leave for the House of Commons at two.

Unlike his broadcast of the night before, this one was a monster: as long as a Budget statement—forty-two typed pages, more than eight thousand words. No wonder it had taken until the early hours of the morning to complete. Legat reckoned the old man would need the best part of an hour and a half simply to deliver it, even if there were no interruptions.

Today we are faced with a situation which has had no parallel since 1914 . . .

It was so long not by choice but of necessity. Parliament had been in recess for the past two months, and when the House had risen for the summer there had been no Czech crisis, no imminent war, no gas masks or slit trenches. Families had gone on holiday; England had beaten Australia in the Fifth Test at the Oval by an innings and 579 runs; it had been another world. The Prime Minister had a duty to bring the country's elected representatives up to date on all that had happened since July. The telegrams and minutes on which the speech was based, which Legat had compiled for the PM the night before, were at that moment being printed by His Majesty's Stationery Office as a White Paper ("The Czechoslovakian Crisis, Notes of Informal Meetings of Ministers"); it would be released to peers and MPs at the same time as the Prime Minister was speaking. Not every document was to be made public. The Foreign Office and the Cabinet Office had weeded out the more sensitive documents. In particular, the agreement between Chamberlain and the French Prime Minister, Daladier—that even if a war was fought and won, Czechoslovakia in its present form would cease to exist—was to remain classified. As Syers observed, it would be bloody hard to convince people the sacrifice was worth making if *that* became known.

Joan finished typing the final page and pulled it from her machine. Four copies. One top sheet for the Prime Minister plus three flimsy carbons—for the Foreign Office, the Cabinet Office and Number 10. She clipped each of them together and handed them to Legat.

"Thank you, Joan."

"You're welcome."

He lingered for a moment beside her desk. "Joan *what*, might I ask?"

"Just plain Joan will be sufficient, thank you."

He smiled and went upstairs to his office. To his surprise he found the room was occupied. Cleverly was seated at his desk. He couldn't swear to it but it seemed to him that the older man had been going through his drawers.

"Ah, Legat. I was looking for you. Is the PM's speech ready?"

"Yes, sir. It's just been typed up." He showed him the copies.

"In that case, there is something else I need you to do, if you wouldn't mind coming with me."

Legat followed him along the corridor into the Principal Private Secretary's office. He wondered what was coming next. Cleverly pointed to his desk where the telephone receiver lay on the blotter beside its cradle. "We're keeping the line open to the embassy in Berlin. We can't risk losing the connection. I want you to listen out for news at the other end. All right?"

"Of course, sir. What exactly is it I'm listening out for?"

"Hitler has agreed to give Sir Nevile Henderson an audience. He should be back from the Chancellery at any minute, with Hitler's response to the Prime Minister's letter."

Legat drew in his breath. "My goodness, things are getting tight."

"They most certainly are. I'll be with the PM," added Cleverly. "The moment you hear anything, let us know."

"Yes, sir."

Cleverly's office, like Wilson's, had a communicating door with the Cabinet Room. He stepped through it and closed it after him.

Legat sat at the desk. He picked up the receiver and placed it cautiously to his ear. When he was a boy, his father had given him a shell and told him that if he listened hard enough he would be able to hear the sound of the sea. That was what he heard now. How much of it was the hiss of static on the line and how much the sound of his own blood pulsing through his ear it was impossible to tell. He cleared his throat. "Hello? Is anyone there?" He repeated it a couple of times. "Hello . . . ? Hello . . . ?"

It was a task that could have been entrusted to a junior clerk. Presumably that was the point. It was designed to put him in his place.

He glanced out of the window at the deserted garden. A blackbird was hopping around the PM's bird table, pecking at the crumbs. He wedged the heavy Bakelite receiver between his ear and his shoulder, took out his pocket watch, disconnected it from its chain and placed it open on the desk. He started to go through the Prime Minister's speech, checking it for errors.

For His Majesty's Government there were three alternative courses that we might have adopted. Either we could have threatened to go to war with Germany if she attacked Czechoslovakia, or we could have stood aside and allowed matters to take their course, or, finally, we could attempt to find a peaceful settlement by way of mediation . . .

After a while, Legat laid aside the speech and brought the watch up close to his face. The little hand was an elongated diamond shape, the big hand much finer. If one looked closely at it, one could just about see its infinitesimal movement as it worked its way towards the vertical. He imagined the German soldiers in these last few minutes waiting in their barracks for the signal to move out, the troop trains heading towards the Czech border, the panzers trundling down the narrow country roads of Saxony and Bavaria . . .

At 1:42 p.m., a male voice said, "Hello, London."

Legat's heart jumped. "Hello, this is London."

"This is the embassy in Berlin. Just checking the line is still open."

"Yes, it seems to be fine our end. What's happening over there?"

"We're still waiting for the Ambassador to return from the Chancellery. Stand by, please."

The hiss resumed.

The blackbird had disappeared. The garden was deserted. It was starting to spot with rain.

Legat went back to the speech.

In those circumstances I decided that the time had come to put into operation a plan which I had had in my mind for a considerable period as a last resort . . .

As Big Ben struck two o'clock the door opened and the top half of Cleverly's body appeared. "Anything?"

"No, sir."

"The line still working?"

"I believe so."

"We'll give it another five minutes and then the PM will have to go."

The door closed.

At seven minutes past two Legat heard the sound of the telephone being picked up in Berlin. A nasal voice said, "This is Sir Neville Henderson."

"Yes, sir. This is the Prime Minister's Private Secretary." Legat reached for his pen.

"Please tell the Prime Minister that Herr Hitler has received a message from Signor Mussolini, delivered by the Italian Ambassador, assuring him that in the event of conflict Italy will stand by Germany, but asking him to postpone mobilisation for twenty-four hours so that the situation can be reexamined. Please tell the Prime Minister that Herr Hitler has agreed. Have you got all that?"

"Yes, sir. I'll tell him now."

Legat hung up. He finished writing and opened the door to the Cabinet Room. The Prime Minister was sitting next to Wilson. Cleverly was opposite him. As his head swung to face Legat the tendons on his thin neck stood out. He looked like a man about to be hanged, standing on the trapdoor but still hopeful of a reprieve. "Well?"

"Mussolini has sent a message to Hitler: Italy will fulfil its obligations to Germany if it comes to war, but he has asked Hitler to postpone mobilisation for twenty-four hours, and Hitler has agreed."

"Twenty-four hours?" Chamberlain's head drooped in disappointment. "Is that all?"

Wilson said, "It's better than nothing, Prime Minister. It shows he's having to listen to outside opinion at least. This is good news."

"Is it? I feel as though I'm slithering towards a cliff edge and trying to catch hold of every root and branch to stop myself sliding into the abyss. Twenty-four hours!"

Cleverly said, "At least it gives you an ending for your speech."

The Prime Minister tapped his forefingers on the table. Eventually he said to Legat, "You'd better come with me. We can amend the speech in the car."

"I can come if you prefer," said Cleverly.

"No, you'd better wait here in case there are further developments in Berlin."

Wilson said, "It's nearly quarter-past. You need to go. The debate starts in fifteen minutes."

Chamberlain pushed himself up from the table. As Legat followed him, he was conscious of a look of pure loathing from Cleverly.

In the entrance hall, Chamberlain stood under the brass lantern while Wilson helped him on with his overcoat. A dozen members of the Number 10 staff had gathered to see him off. He looked around him. "Is Annie—?"

"She's gone on ahead," said Wilson. "Don't worry, she'll be in the gallery." He brushed a few specks from Chamberlain's collar and gave him his hat. "I'll be there, too." He fished the PM's umbrella from the stand and pressed it into his hand. "Remember: you are prevailing, inch by inch."

The Prime Minister nodded. The porter opened the door. The familiar brilliant white glare briefly silhouetted him and Legat thought how slight a figure he looked, even in his overcoat—rather like a blackbird himself. He doffed his hat, first right, then left, and stepped onto the pavement. There were a few cheers, a little applause. A woman shouted, "God bless you, Mr. Chamberlain!" It sounded as though there was hardly anyone present. But when Legat followed him out into the blinding light and his eyes adjusted he saw that Downing Street was actually filled from end to end with a silent, shuffling multitude so huge that a policeman mounted on a horse had been brought in to escort the car. The Prime Minister climbed into the Austin through the nearside door; his plainclothes detective got in beside the driver. Legat had to squeeze his way round through the crowd to the other side. It was hard to open the door. He slid into the seat beside the Prime Minister. The crush of bodies closed the door after him. Through the windscreen he could see the rear end of the police horse. It moved off slowly, clearing a path for them.

The Prime Minister murmured, "I have never seen anything like this in my life."

Flashbulbs lit the interior. It took them almost a minute to reach the top of Downing Street and turn right into Whitehall. A huge crowd stretched ahead, eight or ten deep on the pavements and gathered around the Cenotaph, which rose from a field of freshly laid flowers. A pair of Chelsea Pensioners in their medals and scarlet uniforms, carrying a wreath of poppies between them, turned to stare at the Prime Minister's car as it drove past.

Legat pulled out his fountain pen and flicked through to the last page of the speech. It was hard to write in the moving car. *Signor Mussolini has informed Herr Hitler that while Italy will fulfil its obligations to Germany, it nevertheless requests that mobilisation be postponed for twenty-four hours. Herr Hitler has agreed.*

He showed it to the Prime Minister, who shook his head. "No, that doesn't go far enough. I must pay some kind of tribute to Musso. We need to keep him on our side." He closed his eyes. "Write this down: *'Whatever views Honourable Members may have had about Signor Mussolini in the past, I believe that everyone will welcome his gesture of being willing to work with us for peace in Europe.'*"

As they entered Parliament Square the car was once again forced to slow to walking pace, then brought to a halt. Mounted police surrounded them. The grey sky, the sombre quiet of the crowd, the red wreaths, the clatter of the horses' hooves—it was like a state funeral, thought Legat, or the two-minute silence on Armistice Day. Finally, the car broke free and they accelerated through the iron gates into New Palace Yard. He glimpsed a policeman saluting. Their tyres thumped over the cobbles. They passed under an arch into Speaker's Court and pulled up beside a Gothic wooden door. The detective jumped out. A few seconds later Chamberlain was across the cobbles and climbing the stone staircase, Legat behind him.

They emerged onto a green-carpeted, wood-panelled corridor directly adjacent to the Commons Chamber. Six hundred MPs were already assembled, waiting for the session to begin. Through the closed doors came a continuous low rumble of conversation. In the outer office of the Prime Minister's suite, the female secretaries stood to attention as the PM entered. Chamberlain marched past them into the conference room, handing his hat and umbrella to Miss Watson. He shrugged off his overcoat. Two men were waiting by the long table: his Parliamentary Private Secretary, Alec Dunglass—the heir to an earldom whose misfortune, or perhaps it was the key to his success, was to look as if he had just stepped out of a novel by P. G. Wodehouse—and the Chief Whip, Captain Margesson.

The Prime Minister said, "I'm so sorry to keep you all waiting. The crowds are quite unbelievable."

Margesson said briskly, "If you're ready, Prime Minister, it's nearly a quarter to three. We should go in right away."

"Very well."

They walked back out of the office and across the corridor towards the doors of the Chamber. The noise grew louder.

The Prime Minister adjusted his cuffs. "What is the mood of the House?"

"Strong support for your action right across the Party—even Winston is subdued. You'll see some contraption beside the Dispatch Box: you can ignore it. The BBC wanted to broadcast your statement but the Labour whips have refused. They say it gives the government an unfair advantage."

Dunglass said, "I've put a little brandy in your water, Prime Minister. It's good for the voice."

"Thank you, Alec." Chamberlain stopped and held out his hand. Legat gave him his copy of the speech. He weighed it in his hand and managed a smile. "I certainly have a lot to get through."

Dunglass pulled the door open. Margesson went in first. He used his shoulders to clear a path through the MPs who were crowded around the Speaker's chair. As the Prime Minister came into the full view of the Chamber the rumble of noise swelled to a deep masculine roar. Legat felt it as something almost visceral—the heat, the colour, the noise—like emerging into a football stadium. He turned right and made his way with Miss Watson to the bench reserved for government officials.

Behind him the Speaker's voice cut through the din. "Order! Order! The House will come to order!"

The Prime Minister was heard in absolute silence. No Member rose to interrupt him as he recounted day by day, sometimes hour by hour, the narrative of the crisis. The only movement came from the House Messengers in their black frock coats and ceremonial chains, endlessly bringing in telegrams and pink telephone-slips recording the messages that were pouring into Westminster.

"So I resolved to go to Germany myself to interview Herr Hitler and find

*out in personal conversation whether there was yet any hope of saving the
peace . . ."*

From his vantage point Legat could see Winston Churchill leaning forward on the Conservative front bench below the gangway,
listening intently, accumulating telegram after telegram which he
held bundled together with a red elastic band. In the gallery, the former prime minister, Stanley Baldwin, rested his arms on the wooden
railing and gazed down at the proceedings like a farmer at market
wearing his Sunday best. Further along, the pale powdered imperial
effigy of Queen Mary, the mother of the King, regarded Chamberlain
without expression. Nearby sat Lord Halifax.

*"I knew very well that in taking such an unprecedented course I was
laying myself open to criticism on the ground that I was detracting from
the dignity of a British Prime Minister, and to disappointment, and perhaps
even resentment, if I failed to bring back a satisfactory agreement. But I felt
that in such a crisis, where the issues at stake were so vital for millions of
human beings, such considerations could not be allowed to count . . ."*

Legat checked the Prime Minister's delivery against his copy of
the speech, marking the few occasions when Chamberlain departed
from the text. The PM's manner was unhurried, forensic, quietly
theatrical—now with his thumbs tucked behind the lapels of his
jacket, now putting on a pair of pince-nez to read from a document,
now removing them to gaze briefly up at the skylight as if seek-
ing inspiration. He described his two visits to Hitler as if he were
a Victorian explorer at the Royal Geographical Society reporting on
his expeditions to meet some savage warlord. *"On 15th September I
made my first flight to Munich. Thence I travelled by train to Herr Hitler's
mountain home at Berchtesgaden . . . On the 22nd I went back to Germany
to Godesberg on the Rhine, where the Chancellor had appointed a meeting
place as being more convenient for me than the remote Berchtesgaden. Once
again I had a very warm welcome in the streets and villages through which
I passed . . ."*

The Prime Minister had been on his feet for more than an hour,
and was just embarking on a description of the events of the last

two days—"*as a last effort to preserve peace I sent Sir Horace Wilson to Berlin*"—when Legat became aware of a disturbance in the Peers' Gallery. Cadogan was standing at the entrance, accompanied by a messenger. He was waving his hand, trying to attract the attention of Lord Halifax. Eventually it was Baldwin who noticed him and who reached round behind the back of Queen Mary and tapped the Foreign Secretary on the shoulder. He pointed to Cadogan, who beckoned urgently to Halifax to come and join him. Halifax rose stiffly, his useless arm dangling at his side, and with much bowing and apology to Her Majesty, made his way to the back of the gallery and disappeared.

"*Yesterday morning Sir Horace Wilson resumed his conversations with Herr Hitler, and finding his views apparently still unchanged, repeated to him in precise terms, on my instructions, that should the forces of France become actively involved in hostilities against Germany, the British Government would feel obliged to support them . . .*"

Legat whispered to Miss Watson, "Would you mind just checking what the PM says against the text?" Without waiting for a reply he handed her the speech.

The tension in the Chamber was tightening sentence by sentence as the Prime Minister's narrative drew closer to the present. The MPs standing between the officials' box were too rapt to take any notice of Legat as he twisted and squeezed his way between them. "Excuse me . . . Sorry . . ."

He reached the space at the back of the Speaker's chair just as Cadogan and Halifax came through the door. Cadogan saw him and waved at him to come over. He said quietly, "We've just received a direct response from Hitler. We need to inform the PM before he finishes speaking." He pressed a note into Legat's hand. "Give this to Alec Dunglass."

It was a single sheet of paper, folded once, with *Prime Minister— urgent* written on the outside.

Legat went back into the Chamber. He could see Dunglass sitting on the second row of benches, immediately behind the Prime Minister's place. There was no way he could reach him directly. He gave the note to the MP at the end of the bench. He was aware of hundreds of MPs opposite and behind watching him, fascinated by what was going on. He whispered to the MP, "Would you mind passing this along to Lord Dunglass?"

He followed its progress as it travelled from hand to hand like a lit fuse until it reached Dunglass, who opened it with his usual slightly goofy expression and read it. Immediately he leaned forward to murmur in the ear of the Chancellor of the Exchequer, who put his hand over his shoulder and took the note.

The Prime Minister had just finished reading out his latest telegrams to Hitler and Mussolini.

"In reply, I am told Signor Mussolini has asked Herr Hitler for extra time to re-examine the situation and endeavour to find a peaceful settlement. Herr Hitler has agreed to postpone mobilisation for twenty-four hours."

For the first time since he started speaking there was a murmur of approval.

"Whatever views Honourable Members may have had about Signor Mussolini in the past, I believe that everyone will welcome his gesture of being willing to work with us for peace in Europe."

More noises of agreement. The Prime Minister paused and suddenly looked to the bench beside him where Sir John Simon was tugging at the bottom of his jacket. He frowned and bent down, took the note and read it. The two men held a whispered conversation. The Chamber was silent, watching. Finally, the Prime Minister straightened and placed the note on the Dispatch Box.

"That is not all. I have something further to say to the House yet. I have now been informed by Herr Hitler that he invites me to meet him at Munich tomorrow morning. He has also invited Signor Mussolini and Monsieur Daladier. Signor Mussolini has accepted and I have no doubt Monsieur Daladier will also accept. I need not say what my answer will be."

The silence lasted a split second longer. Then came a deafening eruption of relief. All around the Chamber, MPs—Labour and Liberals too—rose to their feet applauding and waving their order papers.

Some Conservatives actually stood on their benches to cheer. Even Churchill eventually lumbered to his feet although he looked as sulky as a toddler. On and on it went, minute after minute, as the Prime Minister glanced around, nodding, smiling. He tried to speak but they would not let him. Eventually he managed to wave them back into their places.

"We are all patriots, and there can be no Honourable Member of this House who did not feel his heart leap that the crisis has been once more postponed to give us an opportunity to try what reason and good will and discussion will do to settle a problem which is already within sight of settlement. Mr. Speaker, I cannot say any more. I am sure that the House will be ready to release me now to go and see what I can make of this last effort. Perhaps they may think it will be well, in view of this new development, that this Debate shall stand adjourned for a few days, when perhaps we may meet in happier circumstances."

There was further prolonged acclamation and it was only then, to his embarrassment, that Legat realised he had forgotten his professional neutrality and had been cheering with all the rest.

4

On the principle that the best hiding place is in plain sight, the core group of conspirators met at five o'clock that afternoon in Kordt's office in the Prussian State building: Gisevius and von Schulenburg from the Interior Ministry, Dohnányi from Justice, Colonel Oster of the Abwehr, and Kordt and Hartmann from the Foreign Service.

Six men! Hartmann found it hard to restrain his contempt. Six men to bring down a dictatorship that controlled every aspect of life and society in a country that had swollen to eighty million? He felt naive and humiliated. The whole thing was a joke.

Kordt said, "I propose that if anyone asks us about this meeting, we should tell them it was purely informal, to discuss creating an interdepartmental planning group for the newly liberated Sudeten territories."

Dohnányi nodded. "That has a certain horrible bureaucratic plausibility."

"Naturally, Beck cannot be seen anywhere near us. Nor can Heinz, for that matter."

"'The newly liberated Sudeten territories,'" repeated Gisevius. "Listen to how that sounds. My God, he's going to be more popular than ever."

Schulenburg said, "And why not? First Austria, now the Sudetenland. The Führer has added ten million ethnic Germans to the Reich in less than seven months without needing to fire a shot. Goebbels will say he is our greatest statesman since Bismarck, and perhaps he is." He looked around the room. "Have you considered that, gentlemen? That we may be wrong?"

Nobody responded. Kordt was seated behind his desk. Oster was leaning against it. Gisevius, Schulenburg and Dohnányi occupied the three armchairs. Hartmann was sprawled full length on his back on the sofa, hands folded behind his head, staring at the ceiling. His large feet dangled over the armrest. Eventually he said quietly, "So what happened to the Army, Colonel Oster?"

Oster shifted his backside slightly against the desk. "In the end, everything depended on Brauchitsch. Unfortunately, he was still making up his mind what to do when the Führer issued the order to postpone mobilisation for twenty-four hours."

"And if mobilisation hadn't been postponed—would he have acted then?"

"Beck says that Halder told him he was definitely sympathetic—"

Hartmann interrupted him. "'Beck says . . . Halder told him . . . *sympathetic* . . .'!" He swung his legs to the floor and sat up straight. "Forgive me, gentlemen, but if you ask me, this is just castles in the air. If Brauchitsch had been serious about getting rid of Hitler, he would have gone ahead and done it."

"That's too simplistic. It was always understood that the only circumstances in which the Army would take action would be if they were convinced there was going to be a war against France and Britain."

"Because they thought that Germany would lose?"

"Exactly."

"So let us be clear about the logic of the Army's position. They have no moral objection to Hitler's regime; their opposition is entirely conditional on the country's military prospects?"

"Yes, of course. Is that so shocking? They are soldiers, not clergymen."

"Well, that is very nice for them, I'm sure! No need for conscience there! But you see what it means for the rest of us?" He looked at each of the others in turn. "As far as the Army is concerned, as long as Hitler is winning, he is safe. Only when he starts to lose will they turn against him—by which time it will be too late."

"Keep your voice down," warned Kordt. "Hess's office is just along the corridor."

Oster was visibly controlling his temper. "I am as disappointed as you are, Hartmann. More so, I would imagine. Please don't forget it has taken me months to get the Army even this far. All summer I've been sending messages to London, telling them that if only they would stand firm they could leave the rest to us. Unfortunately, I hadn't reckoned on the cowardice of the British and the French."

Kordt said, "They will pay a terrible price for it in the long run. And so will we."

There was a silence. It still seemed unbelievable to Hartmann that Hitler had swerved away from war at the last minute. He had watched it happen: history made at a distance of five metres. The red-faced, trembling Attolico had stammered out his message loudly enough for everyone nearby to hear, as if he were a herald in a play: "The Duce informs you that whatever you decide, Führer, Fascist Italy stands behind you. But the Duce is of the opinion that it would be wise to accept the British proposal, and begs you to refrain from mobilisation." As Schmidt translated the Italian into German, Hitler's face had betrayed neither anger nor relief, his features as immobile as a bronze bust. "Tell the Duce that I accept his proposal." And with that he had returned to his office.

From the corridor came a burst of raucous laughter. The Party officials were celebrating. Hartmann had narrowly managed to avoid their embraces on the way in. One had a bottle of schnapps he was passing round.

"So what are we to do now?" asked Gisevius. "If we can't make a move without the Army, and if Hartmann's analysis of their attitude is correct, then we are nothing but a group of powerless civilians, doomed to wait and watch until our country is destroyed."

"It seems to me there's only one chance left to us," said Hartmann.

"We need to try to prevent an agreement being signed tomorrow at Munich."

"That's highly unlikely," said Kordt. "It's as good as signed already. Hitler is going to accept what the British and the French have already offered him, which is basically what he asked for in the first place. Therefore, the conference is a ritual. Chamberlain and Daladier will fly in and stand in front of the cameras and say, 'Here you are, dear Führer,' and then they'll fly home again."

"It doesn't have to be like that. Hitler has postponed mobilisation; he hasn't cancelled it."

"Nevertheless, I can assure you that is how it will be."

Hartmann said quietly, "I need to meet with Chamberlain."

"Ha!" Kordt threw up his hands. "Naturally!"

"I am serious."

"Your seriousness is not the issue. In any case, we're past that stage. My brother sat in Halifax's office in the Foreign Office just three weeks ago and warned him explicitly what was coming. It still did no good."

Hartmann said, "Halifax isn't Chamberlain."

Dohnányi said, "But my dear Hartmann, what could you possibly say to him that would make the slightest difference?"

"I'd show him proof."

"Proof of what?"

"Proof that Hitler is bent on a war of conquest, and that this may be the last chance to stop him."

Dohnányi appealed to the others. "This is simply foolish! As if Chamberlain would take any notice of a low-level young person such as Hartmann!"

Hartmann shrugged. He took no offence. "Nevertheless, it's worth a try. Does anyone have an alternative idea?"

Schulenburg said, "Might we also be allowed to see this 'proof'?"

"I would prefer not."

"Why?"

"Because I promised the person who gave it to me I would only show it to the British."

There was some muttering—of protest, scepticism, irritation.

"I must say I find it highly offensive that you won't trust us."

"Do you really, Schulenburg? Well, I'm afraid that can't be helped."

Oster said, "And how do you propose to arrange your own private meeting with the Prime Minister of the United Kingdom?"

"Obviously, as a first step, I would need to be accredited to the conference, as part of the German delegation."

Kordt said, "How is that to happen? And even if you were let in, there's simply no possibility you could get access to Chamberlain alone."

"I believe it could be done."

"Quite impossible! How?"

"I know one of his private secretaries."

The revelation took them by surprise. After a pause, Oster said, "Well, that is something, I suppose, although I am not sure how it helps us."

"It means I must stand a chance of getting through to Chamberlain, or at least of getting my information into his hands." He leaned forward, imploring. "Nothing may come of it, I accept. I understand your scepticism. But surely it is worth one last try? Colonel Oster, you have contacts in Whitehall?"

"Yes."

"Is there time to get a message to them, to ask if this man could fly to Munich as part of Chamberlain's entourage?"

"Possibly. What's his name?"

Hartmann hesitated. Now it came to it, he found it oddly difficult to say it out loud. "Hugh Legat."

Oster produced a small notebook from his breast pocket and wrote it down. "And he works in Downing Street, you say? Will he be expecting to hear from you?"

"Possibly. I've already sent him something anonymously, and I'm fairly sure he will guess it's from me. He knows I'm in the Foreign Ministry."

"How did you get it to him?"

Hartmann turned to Kordt. "Your brother delivered it."

Kordt's mouth flapped open in surprise. "You used Theo behind my back?"

"I wanted to open my own channel of communication—to show him something, to establish I was serious."

"And what was this earlier 'something'? Or is that also secret?"

Hartmann was silent.

Schulenburg said bitterly, "No wonder the English don't take us seriously. We must appear to them to be complete amateurs—each man speaking for himself, no central coordination, no plan for a Germany without Hitler. I've had enough of this, gentlemen."

He pushed himself out of his armchair.

Kordt followed suit. He held out his hands in appeal. "Schulenburg, please—sit down! We've suffered a reverse—we're disappointed—but let's not bicker among ourselves."

Schulenburg grabbed his hat. He pointed it at Hartmann. "You, with your stupid schemes, will get us all hanged!"

He slammed the door behind him.

As the reverberations died away, Dohnányi said, "He's quite right."

"I agree," said Gisevius.

Oster said, "So do I. But we are at an impasse, and on balance I am inclined to support Hartmann's plan—not that I think it will work, but because we have no viable alternative. What do you say, Erich?"

Kordt had lowered himself back into his chair. He looked more like a man in his fifties than his mid-thirties. He took off his spectacles, closed his eyes and massaged his eyelids with his thumb and forefinger. "The Munich conference," he muttered, "is a locomotive that cannot be stopped. In my opinion, it's useless even to try." He put his glasses back on and stared at Hartmann. His eyes were pink with exhaustion. "On the other hand, even if we can't derail it, it would obviously be valuable to our cause to open communication with someone who sees Chamberlain every day. Because of one thing we may be sure: today isn't the end of this process. Given what we know of Hitler, the Sudetenland is only the start. There will be other crises, perhaps fresh opportunities. So let us see what you can do, Paul. But I think at the very least you should tell us what it is you plan to give to the British. You owe us that."

"No. I'm sorry. Perhaps when I return—if I can get agreement from my source—I'll show you then. But for now, for your own sakes as well as theirs, it's probably better if you don't know."

Another silence ensued. Finally, Oster said, "If we are to try to make this happen, we have no more time to lose. I'll go back to Tirpitzufer and try to make contact with the British. Erich, is it possible for you to get Hartmann into the conference?"

"I'm not sure. I can try."

"Couldn't you speak to Ribbentrop?"

"God, no! He's the last man I'd approach. He would be suspicious at once. Our best hope is probably Weizsäcker. He likes to play both ends. I'll go and talk to him." He turned to Hartmann. "You'd better come too."

Oster said, "We should probably leave separately."

"No," said Kordt. "Remember, we've merely held an informal interdepartmental meeting. It will look more natural if we all go out together."

At the door, Oster drew Hartmann to one side. He said in a low voice, so that the others couldn't hear, "You have a weapon, I believe? I should return it to the Abwehr armoury."

Hartmann held his gaze. "I think I would prefer to keep it, if you don't mind."

Hartmann and Kordt left the building together and walked in silence across Wilhelmstrasse towards the Foreign Ministry. The sun was shining; a definite lightness was in the air. One could see it on the faces of the government workers pouring out of the ministries to go home at the end of the day. People were even laughing. It was the first time Hartmann had seen such normality in the streets since the Czech crisis blew up more than two weeks ago.

In the State Secretary's outer office, all three typists, including Frau Winter, were bent over their machines. Kordt had to raise his voice to be heard above the racket. "We need to see Baron von Weizsäcker."

Frau Winter looked up. "He's with the British and French ambassadors."

Kordt said, "Even so, Frau Winter, it's an urgent matter."

She glanced at Hartmann. Her expression was one of complete indifference. He admired her coolness. He had a sudden vision of her naked on the bed waiting for him—her long white limbs, her heavy breasts, her nipples hard—

"Very well."

She tapped lightly on the door to the inner office and went inside. Hartmann heard a clink of glasses, voices and laughter. Less than a minute later Sir Nevile Henderson emerged, a scarlet carnation fresh in his lapel, followed by François-Poncet. The French Ambassador had a small black moustache, waxed upwards at the tips. He looked rakish, amused, like an actor from the Comédie-Française. He was said to be the only member of the diplomatic corps whom Hitler actually liked. The ambassadors nodded amiably at Hartmann, then shook hands with Kordt.

François-Poncet said, "This is a relief, Kordt." He continued to pump Kordt's hand. "A great relief! I was with the Führer moments before he spoke to Attolico. When he returned to the room his exact words to me were, 'Tell your government I have postponed mobilisation for twenty-four hours to meet the wishes of my great Italian ally.' Imagine if the communists had cut the telephone lines from Rome to Berlin that morning—we would all be at war! Instead of which"—he flourished his hand at the room—"we still have a chance."

Kordt bowed slightly. "Your Excellency, it is a great deliverance."

Frau Winter appeared at the door. "The State Secretary is waiting for you."

Hartmann caught her scent as he passed her.

Henderson called after them, "We shall see you in Munich. We haven't finished this thing yet."

Von Weizsäcker had a bottle of Sekt open on his desk. He did not bother with the Hitler salute. "Gentlemen, let us empty the bottle." He poured out three glasses expertly, so that not a drop was lost, and handed one each to Kordt and Hartmann. He raised his glass. "As I said to the ambassadors, I won't propose a toast: I don't want to tempt fate. Let us simply enjoy the moment."

Hartmann sipped politely. The sparkling wine was too sweet and fizzy for his taste, like a child's drink.

"Sit, please." Weizsäcker gestured to a sofa and two armchairs. His dark blue pinstriped suit was beautifully cut. The swastika lapel pin glinted in the late-afternoon sunlight slanting through the high window. He had only joined the Party that year. Now he had an honorary rank in the SS and was Germany's senior diplomat. If he had sold his soul, he had at least got a good price. "What can I do for you, gentlemen?"

Kordt said, "I would like to propose that Hartmann here be accredited to our delegation at the conference tomorrow."

"Why are you asking me? Ask the Minister—you're a member of his office."

"With the greatest respect to the Minister, his automatic response to any suggestion is generally to say 'No' until he can be won round, and in this instance there is no time for the usual process of persuasion."

"And why is it so important that Hartmann goes to Munich?"

"Apart from the fact that his English is impeccable, which will be useful in itself, we believe there is an opportunity for him to cultivate a potentially important contact on Chamberlain's staff."

"Really?" Weizsäcker studied Hartmann with interest. "Who is this person?"

Hartmann said, "He is a diplomat, presently working as one of Chamberlain's private secretaries."

"How do you know him?"

"I was at Oxford with him."

"Is he sympathetic to the new Germany?"

"I doubt it."

"Hostile, then?"

"I should imagine he shares the general attitude of Englishmen of his type."

"That could mean anything." Weizsäcker turned back to Kordt. "How do you know he will even be in Munich?"

"We don't. Colonel Oster of the Abwehr is trying to arrange it."

"Ah. Colonel Oster." Weizsäcker nodded slowly. "Now I understand. *That* sort of contact." He poured himself the last of the Sekt and drank it slowly. Hartmann contemplated his bobbing Adam's apple, the smooth pink cheeks, the fine silver hair that matched his brand-new Party badge. He felt the contempt rise in his throat like gorge. He would take an old Brownshirt with a broken nose any day over this hypocrite. The State Secretary replaced his empty glass on the table. "You want to be careful of Colonel Oster. You might even warn him from me: his activities have not gone entirely unnoticed. Up to now there has been a certain toleration of dissent, so long as it doesn't go too far, but I sense things are starting to change. National Socialism is moving into a new and more vigorous phase."

He went over to his desk, felt around under it and pressed a button. The door opened.

"Frau Winter, would you add Herr von Hartmann's name to the list of those accredited to the conference tomorrow? Put him down as a translator, to assist Dr. Schmidt."

"Yes, sir."

She withdrew. Kordt caught Hartmann's eye and nodded. Both men stood. "Thank you, State Secretary."

"Yes," said Hartmann. "Thank you." He hesitated. "May I ask a question, Herr Baron?"

"What is it?"

"I was wondering what caused the Führer to change his mind. Did he really intend to invade, do you think, or was he bluffing all along?"

"Oh, he wanted to invade, no question of it."

"So why did he call it off?"

"Who can say? No one really knows what's in his mind. I suspect in the end he realised Chamberlain had removed his casus belli: Mussolini's intervention was decisive in that regard. Goebbels put it rather well over lunch, even though he personally favoured invasion: 'One can't wage a world war over points of detail.' The Führer's error was to list specific demands. Once they had mostly been met, he was stranded. I suspect he won't make the same mistake next time."

He shook their hands and closed the door. The remark echoed in Hartmann's mind. *He won't make the same mistake next time.*

Frau Winter said, "Your name will be on the list at the Anhalter Bahnhof, Herr Hartmann. It will be enough if you show your identification at the gate. The special train is scheduled to leave at eight-fifty tonight."

"The train?"

"Yes, the Führer's train."

He was conscious of Kordt waiting for him, of the two other women typing.

Kordt touched his arm. "We'd better hurry. You need to pack."

They went out into the corridor. Hartmann glanced back over his shoulder but she was already seated at her desk, typing. Something about her complete indifference disturbed him. As they walked, he said, "That was easier than I'd expected."

"Yes, our new State Secretary is so delightfully *ambiguous*, isn't he? He manages to be both a pillar of the regime and to indicate his sympathy for the opposition at the same time. Are you going straight to your apartment?"

"Not immediately. I need to pick up something from my office first."

"Of course." Kordt shook his hand. "I'll leave you then. Good luck."

Hartmann's office was deserted. No doubt von Nostitz and von Rantzau were out celebrating somewhere. He sat at his desk and unlocked the drawer. The envelope was where he had left it. He slipped it into his briefcase.

Hartmann's apartment was at the western end of Pariser Strasse, in the fashionable shopping district close to St. Ludwig's Church. Before the war, when his grandfather the old Ambassador had still been alive, the family had owned the whole building. But they had been obliged to split it up and sell it piece by piece to repay the mortgage on the estate near Rostock. Now there was only the second floor left.

He stood at the window with a tumbler of whisky, smoking a cigarette, and watched the last traces of the sun disappear behind the trees of Ludwigkirchplatz. The sky glowed red. The trees looked like the shadows of primitive dancers cavorting around a fire. On the radio, the opening of Beethoven's Coriolan Overture signalled the start of a special news bulletin. The announcer sounded half-crazed with excitement.

"Prompted by the desire to make a last effort to bring about the peaceful cession of the Sudeten German territory to the Reich, the Führer has invited Benito Mussolini, the head of the Italian Government; Neville Chamberlain, the Prime Minister of Great Britain; and Edouard Daladier, the French Prime Minister, to a conference. The statesmen have accepted the invitation. The discussion will take place in Munich tomorrow morning, September 29th . . ."

The communiqué made it seem as if the whole thing had been Hitler's idea. And people would believe it, thought Hartmann, because people believed what they wanted to believe—that was Goebbels's great insight. They no longer had any need to bother themselves with inconvenient truths. He had given them an excuse not to think.

He drank more whisky.

He was still troubled by his encounter in von Weizsäcker's office. The whole thing had been too easy. There had also been something odd about her absolutely determined refusal to meet his eye. He replayed the scene over and over.

Perhaps she had not stolen the documents from von Weizsäcker's safe after all. Perhaps she had merely been given them to pass on to him.

The moment he thought of it, he knew it must be true.

He stubbed out his cigarette and went into the bedroom. On top of the wardrobe was a small suitcase embossed with his initials which he had been given when he was first sent away to school. He flicked open the catches.

Inside were letters, mostly—from his parents and his brothers and sisters, from friends and girlfriends. The Oxford letters were tied together and still in their envelopes: he had liked the English stamps, and to see his name and address written in Hugh's small neat hand. At one period he had written to him once or twice a week. There were photographs, too, including the last photograph of them together, taken in Munich, the date written on the back: 2 July 1932. They were in walking gear—boots, sports jackets, open-necked white shirts—a glimpse of a courtyard in the background. Leyna stood between them, her hands gripping their upper arms. She was so much shorter than he was; it was comical. All three smiling. He remembered she had asked the owner of the inn to take it before they set out for the day. Clipped to it was the cutting from the *Daily Express* he had come across in the summer: *Among the Foreign Office's brightest young stars, now assisting the PM . . .* Judging by the photograph he had hardly changed. But the fashionable woman beside him—his wife, this "Pamela"—she was not at all the sort of girl he had imagined that Hugh would end up with. It occurred to him that if something went wrong and his apartment was searched by the Gestapo, these souvenirs would be incriminating.

He took the Oxford letters over to the fireplace and burned them, one by one, setting fire to the bottom right-hand corner of each with his lighter and dropping it into the grate. He burned the newspaper cutting. He hesitated over the photograph but finally he burned that too, watching it scorch and curl until it was indistinguishable from the other ashes.

It was dark by the time Hartmann arrived at the Anhalter Bahnhof. Outside the pillared entrance to the main concourse police were patrolling with dogs. In his suitcase he had the envelope, in his inside pocket the Walther. He felt his legs begin to weaken.

He braced his shoulders and passed through the grand doors into the smoke and gloom of the glass-roofed station, as high as a Gothic cathedral. Swastika banners, three or four storeys high, descended over every platform. The annunciator board displayed the evening's departures: Leipzig, Frankfurt-am-Main, Dresden, Vienna . . . It was 8:37 p.m. There was no mention of Munich, or a special train. An official of the Reichsbahn, in dark blue uniform and peaked cap, his toothbrush moustache doubtless grown in homage to the Führer, noticed his uncertainty. When Hartmann explained his mission he insisted on escorting him personally: "It will be my honour."

Hartmann spotted the gate before they reached it. Somehow people must have guessed that the Führer would be passing through and a small, respectful crowd of about a hundred had gathered, women mostly. The SS were keeping them at a distance. At the gate itself, two more police dog handlers and SS guards with machine guns were checking passengers. A man who was queuing to board was being ordered to open his suitcase and Hartmann thought, if they frisk me, I'm finished. He thought of turning back and dumping the gun in the toilets. But the Reichsbahn official was ushering him forward and a moment later he found himself face-to-face with one of the sentries.

"*Heil Hitler!*"

"*Heil Hitler.*"

"Name?"

"Hartmann."

The sentry ran his finger down the list of names, flipped one page, then another.

"There's no Hartmann here."

"There." Hartmann pointed to the last page. Unlike the others, which were typed, his name had been added in ink. It looked suspicious.

"Papers?"

He handed over his identity card.

The other sentry said, "Open your suitcase, please."

He balanced it on his knee. His hands were shaking; he was sure his guilt must be obvious. He fumbled with the catches, lifted the lid. The sentry shouldered his machine gun and rummaged through the contents—two shirts, underwear, shaving kit in a leather case. He picked up the envelope, shook it and put it back. He nodded. With his gun barrel he gestured towards the train.

The first sentry returned his ID. "You are in the rear carriage, Herr von Hartmann."

They started to check the man behind. Hartmann walked through onto the platform.

The train was drawn up about twenty metres along the track, on the right-hand side. It was long: he counted seven carriages, all a gleaming, spotless dark green as if freshly painted for the occasion, with a Nazi eagle, wings spread wide, picked out on the bodywork in gold. Every door was guarded by an SS sentry. At the front, a black locomotive gently vented steam; it too was guarded. Hartmann walked slowly towards the rear carriage, took a last look up at the floodlit spars of the roof, the fluttering pigeons, the black sky beyond, then clambered aboard.

It was a sleeper car, the compartments on the left. An SS adjutant, a clipboard in one hand, marched along the corridor, halted and thrust out his arm in the Hitler salute. Hartmann recognised him as the same white-jacketed flunky he had threatened that morning at the Chancellery. He returned the salute with what he hoped was a convincing snap of fanaticism.

"Good evening, Herr von Hartmann. Follow me, please."

They walked to the end of the carriage. The adjutant checked his clipboard and slid open the door of the final compartment. "This is your berth. Refreshments will be served in the dining car once we have left Berlin. You will then be informed of the operations of the Führer-train." He saluted again.

Hartmann stepped into the compartment and closed the door behind him. It was done out in the art deco style favoured by the Führer. Two bunks, upper and lower. Dim yellowish lighting. A smell of wood polish, dusty upholstery, stale air. He threw his suitcase onto the bottom mattress and sat down next to it. The compartment was claustrophobic, like a cell. He wondered whether Oster had managed to make contact with the British. If not, he would have to devise some fallback plan but his nerves were too on edge to think of one at the moment.

Presently he heard shouting in the distance and some cheering. Through the window he saw a man trotting backwards very quickly, holding a camera. A few seconds later a flash lit up the platform and the Führer's party came into view, marching quickly. At the centre was Hitler, wearing a belted brown overcoat, flanked and followed by men in SS black. He passed within three metres of Hartmann, staring straight ahead, his expression one of intense irritation, and disappeared out of sight. His entourage trailed after him—dozens of them, or so it seemed, and then Hartmann heard the compartment door opening. He swung round and there was Sturmbannführer Sauer on the threshold with the SS adjutant. For an instant he thought they had come to arrest him but then Sauer said in a baffled voice, "Hartmann? What are you doing here?"

He stood. "I have been assigned to help Dr. Schmidt with translation."

"Translation will only be required in Munich." Sauer turned to the adjutant. "It's not necessary for this man to be on the Führer's train. Who authorised it?"

The adjutant looked helplessly at his clipboard. "His name was added to the list—"

Suddenly the train lurched forward and stopped abruptly. All three had to grab onto something to maintain their balance. Then very slowly the platform began to slide past the window—empty luggage trolleys, a sign reading BERLIN-ANHALTER.BHF, the line of saluting officials—a procession of images that gradually increased in velocity until the train emerged from the shadows of the station into the wide expanse of the marshalling yard, as vast as a steel prairie in the moonless September night.

5

Cleverly called a meeting of the junior private secretaries in his office at 9 p.m. sharp. They trooped in together—Legat, Syers, Miss Watson—and stood in a line while he perched on the edge of his desk. They were braced for what Syers liked to call his "staff-officer-visits-the-trenches speech."

"Thank you all for your efforts today. I know how hectic it's been. Even so I need to ask everyone to be on parade again tomorrow morning by seven-thirty. I want to be sure we're all here to give the PM a rousing send-off. He'll leave Number Ten for the drive to Heston Aerodrome at seven-forty-five. Two aircraft will be making the trip to Munich." He picked up a sheaf of papers. "It's been decided that on the first plane will be the PM, Sir Horace Wilson, Lord Dunglass and three officials from the Foreign Office—William Strang, Frank Ashton-Gwatkin and Sir William Malkin. We've also been instructed to send someone from the Private Office." He turned to Syers. "Cecil, I'd like it to be you."

Syers's head rocked back slightly in surprise. "Really, sir?" He looked at Legat, who promptly stared at his shoes: he felt nothing but relief.

"I suggest you pack on the assumption you'll be staying for up to three nights—the Germans are arranging hotel rooms. On the second plane will be two detectives for the PM's protection, the PM's doctor, and two girls from the Garden Room. Each plane has space for fourteen passengers, so if one of them develops any mechanical problem, everyone can transfer to the other."

Syers raised his hand. "I appreciate the honour, sir, but wouldn't Hugh be a better choice? His German is ten times better than mine."

"I've made my decision. Legat will stay here with Miss Watson and deal with correspondence. We have telegrams of congratulation to answer from almost every leader in the world, let alone the thousands of letters from members of the public. If we don't make a start on it soon we'll never get on top of it. All right?" He looked along the line. "Good. Thank you all. I'll see you in the morning."

Once they were back in the corridor, Syers beckoned Legat into his office. "I'm so sorry about this, Hugh. It's absolutely bloody ridiculous."

"Really, don't give it another thought. You're senior to me."

"Yes, but you're the German expert—for God's sake, you were in Vienna when I was still in the Dominions Office."

"Honestly, it's fine." Legat was so touched by his concern he felt he should try to alleviate it. "To be perfectly frank, between you and me, I'm relieved not to be going."

"Why on earth wouldn't you want to go? Don't you want to see Hitler in the flesh? Something to tell the grandchildren?"

"Actually, that's just it: I've already seen Hitler in the flesh—in Munich, as a matter of fact, six months before he came to power—and I can assure you, once was quite enough."

"You've never mentioned that before. What happened? Did you go to a Nazi rally?"

"No, I didn't hear him speak." Suddenly Legat wished he'd never brought the subject up, but Syers was so insistent on hearing more he couldn't really leave it at that. "It was only in the street one day—outside his apartment building, to be exact. We ended up being chased off by his Brownshirts." He closed his eyes briefly, as he always did whenever he thought of it. "I'd only just left Oxford, so I suppose I could at least plead youth as an excuse. Anyway, enjoy Munich—assuming you get a chance to see it."

He escaped into the corridor. Syers called after him, "Thanks, Hugh—I'll give your regards to the Führer!"

Back in his own office, Miss Watson was putting on her coat to go home. Nobody knew where she lived. Legat guessed she must be lonely but she rebuffed all invitations. "Oh, there you are," she said irritably. "I was just about to write you a note. Sir Alexander Cadogan's secretary called for you. He wants to see you right away."

Workmen, lit by floodlights, were laying sandbags outside the entrance to the Foreign Office. Legat found the sight mildly disturbing. Apparently nobody had bothered to tell the Ministry of Works that the Sudeten crisis was supposed to be over.

Cadogan's outer office was deserted, the door to his inner sanctum slightly ajar. When Legat knocked, the Permanent Under-Secretary appeared in person, smoking a cigarette. "Ah, Legat. Come in."

He was not alone. Seated on the leather sofa at the far end of the cavernous room was a man of about fifty—saturnine, elegant, with a thick moustache and deep-set staring dark eyes.

Cadogan said, "This is Colonel Menzies." He pronounced the name in the Scottish manner: *Ming-ies.* "I asked him to take a look at the document you brought in last night. You'd better sit down."

A colonel wearing a Savile Row suit in Whitehall, thought Legat. That could only mean the Secret Intelligence Service.

The armchair matched the sofa—hard, brown, scuffed, exquisitely uncomfortable. Cadogan took its twin. He reached up and turned on a tasselled standard lamp. It too looked as if it might have been borrowed from some baronial Scottish castle. A grimy ochre light suffused their corner of the office. "Colonel?"

On the low table in front of Menzies was a thick manila folder. He opened it and took out the document that had been put through Legat's door. "Well, the first thing to say is it's genuine, as far as we can tell." He spoke in a friendly Etonian drawl that immediately put Legat on his guard. "It ties in with everything we've been hearing from various opposition figures in Germany since the beginning of the summer. But this is the first time they've produced actual written evidence. I gather from Alex you have no idea why it should have come to you."

"That's right."

"Well, they are a disparate lot, it must be said. A handful of diplomats, a landowner or two, an industrialist. Half of them don't appear to be aware of the existence of the other half. The only thing they all seem to agree on is they expect the British Empire to go to war to restore the Kaiser, or at any rate his family—which considering we lost the best part of a million men getting rid of the bugger less than twenty years ago betrays a certain political naivety, to put it mildly. They say they have support within the Army but frankly, apart from a few disaffected Prussians at the top, we're not convinced. Your chap, on the other hand, sounds as if he might be a bit more interesting."

"My chap?"

The colonel consulted his folder. "I assume the name Paul von Hartmann is not unknown to you?"

So that was it. It had happened at last. The file looked intimidatingly extensive. Legat could see no point in evasion. "Yes, of course. We were at Balliol together. He was a Rhodes scholar. So you think he is the one who delivered the document?"

"Sent it rather than delivered it—he's in Germany. When did you last see him?"

Legat pretended to think. "Six years ago. The summer of 'thirty-two."

"You've not been in contact since?"

"No."

"Do you mind if I ask why not?"

"No specific reason. We simply drifted apart."

"Whereabouts did you last see him?"

"In Munich."

"Munich, really? Suddenly all roads seem to lead to Munich." The colonel smiled, but his eyes bored into Legat's. "Do you mind if I ask what you were doing there?"

"I was on holiday—a walking holiday in Bavaria, at the end of finals."

"On holiday with von Hartmann?"

"Among others."

"And you haven't communicated since—not even a letter?"

"That's right."

"Well, then—forgive me—it doesn't sound as if you drifted apart so much as had a blazing row."

Legat took his time before replying. "It's true we had some political differences. In Oxford they didn't seem to matter so much. But this was Germany, in July, in the middle of a general election campaign. You couldn't escape politics at that time—especially in Munich."

"So your friend was a Nazi?"

"No, if anything he considered himself a socialist. But he was also a German nationalist—that was what led to the arguments."

Cadogan cut in: "A national socialist, then—but lower case, perhaps, rather than upper? You're smiling? I've said something droll?"

"Forgive me, Sir Alex, but that is what Paul would have called 'a classic piece of English sophistry.' "

For a moment he thought he might have gone too far, but then Cadogan's mouth twitched down slightly, which was his way of registering amusement. "Yes, fair enough, I suppose he would have had a point."

The colonel said, "Did you know that Hartmann had entered the German diplomatic service?"

"I did hear his name mentioned in that connection, by mutual friends from Oxford. I wasn't surprised: it was always his intention. His grandfather was an ambassador under Bismarck."

"Did you also know he'd joined the Nazi Party?"

"No, but again it makes sense, given his belief in a Greater Germany."

"We're sorry to have to ask you all these questions, Legat, but a situation has arisen and we need to understand precisely what sort of relationship you have, or had, with this particular German." The colonel put down the folder and it occurred to Legat that most of it probably had nothing to do with him—that it was merely a trick to fool him into thinking they knew more than they did. "It seems your former friend Hartmann is now working with the opposition to Hitler. His position inside the Foreign Ministry has given him access to secret material which he is willing to share with us—or more specifically, which he is willing to share with *you*. How do you feel about that?"

"Surprised."

"But willing in principle to take matters further?"

"In what sense?"

Cadogan said, "Willing to go to Munich tomorrow and meet with your old friend?"

"Good heavens!" Legat had not been expecting that. "He's going to be in Munich?"

"Apparently, yes."

The colonel said, "One member of the German opposition whom I *do* take seriously has been in touch with us this evening, via a secret channel, to ask if we can arrange for you to travel to Munich as part of the PM's party. In return they will try to make sure Hartmann is included in the German delegation. It appears Hartmann has another document in his possession, more important than the one you received last night. He has some mad notion of handing it to the Prime Minister personally, which obviously cannot be allowed to happen. However, he will give it to you. We'd very much like to know what it is. Therefore, we think you should go and meet him."

Legat stared at him. "I'm utterly astonished."

"It's not without risk," warned Cadogan. "Technically, at least, it will be an act of espionage on foreign soil. We wouldn't want to mislead you about that."

The colonel said, "Yes, but on the other hand, it's hard to believe the Germans would seek to embarrass His Majesty's Government with a spying scandal in the middle of an international conference."

"Are you sure about that?" Cadogan shook his head. "With Hitler, anything is possible. The last thing he wants to do tomorrow is sit down with the PM and Daladier. I suspect he's perfectly capable of seizing on exactly such an incident as an excuse to break off negotiations." He turned to Legat. "So you need to consider it carefully. The stakes are high. And there's another point. We think it best if the Prime Minister knows nothing about this."

"Do you mind if I ask why?"

The colonel said, "Often in these delicate matters it's better for politicians not to know the full details."

"You mean in case something goes wrong?"

"No," said Cadogan. "Rather because the PM is already under the most immense strain, and it's our duty, as public servants, to do everything we can not to add to it."

Legat made one last feeble attempt at escape. "You do know that Oscar Cleverly has already told Cecil Syers that *he* will be travelling to Munich?"

"That's not an issue that need concern you. Leave Cleverly to us."

"Absolutely," said the colonel. "I know Oscar."

Both men fell silent, watching him, and Legat had a peculiar sense of—what was it, he wondered afterwards?—not of déjà vu exactly, but of inevitability: that he had always known Munich was not done with him; that however far he might travel from that place and time he was forever caught in its gravitational pull and would be dragged back towards it eventually.

"Of course," he said. "Of course I'll do it."

By the time he got back to Number 10, Syers had gone for the night. Cleverly was still working—he could see the light under his door and could hear his voice talking on the telephone. He crept past, anxious to avoid the possibility of an encounter, collected his overnight case from the corner of his office and set off to walk home.

Images he had consciously suppressed for half a decade stalked him at every step, memories not so much of Germany but of Oxford. As he walked past the Abbey he sensed again the impossibly tall figure loping at his side through a damp evening along the Turl ("night is the best time for friendship, my dear Hugh"), his profile in the lamplight as he stopped to light a cigarette—beautiful, fanatical, almost cruel—and that astonishing smile after he had exhaled; the swirling skirts of his full coat brushing the cobbles; the curious combination of his manliness—he had seemed so much older and more experienced than the rest of them in the boy-world of Oxford—and yet a self-dramatising defeatism ("my passionate melancholy") that was entirely adolescent, indeed verging on the comic: he had once clambered up onto Magdalen Bridge and threatened to throw himself into the river in despair at what he said was their mad generation until Legat had pointed out that he would only succeed in getting himself wet and possibly catching a chill. He used to complain that he lacked "the one great characteristic of the English, and that is distance—not only from one another but from all experience: I believe it is the secret of the English art of living." Legat could remember every word.

He reached the end of North Street, found his key and let himself into the house. Now that the immediate crisis seemed to be over he had half-expected to find Pamela at home with the children. But when he turned on the light he saw that the place was empty, exactly as he had left it. He set down his suitcase at the bottom of the stairs. Still wearing his coat, he went into the drawing room, picked up the telephone and dialled the operator. It was after ten, an unsociable hour for a call, especially in the English shires, but he thought the circumstances justified it. His father-in-law answered, pedantically reciting his number. Pamela always said he had done something "unspeakably boring" in the City before retiring at fifty and Legat could believe it, although he had been careful never to enquire precisely what it was; he avoided speaking to his in-laws as much as possible. Somehow the conversation always turned to money and his lack of it.

"Hello, sir. It's Hugh. Sorry to ring so late."

"Hugh!" For once the old boy actually sounded glad to hear him. "I must say we've been thinking about you rather a lot today. What a business it's been! Were you very much involved?"

"Oh, only on the margins, you know."

"Well, having been all the way through the last show, I can't tell you the relief at avoiding another." He put his hand over the receiver and Legat heard him call out, "Darling, it's Hugh!" He came back on the line immediately. "You must tell me all about it. Were you in the House when the Prime Minister received the news?"

Legat sat in an armchair and patiently described the events of the day for a couple of minutes, until he felt he had done all that filial politeness required of him. "Anyway, sir, I can give you the full blow-by-blow the next time I see you. I just wanted a quick word with Pamela, if I might."

"Pamela?" The voice on the other end sounded suddenly confused. "Isn't she with you? She left the children with us and drove back to London about four hours ago."

After he had hung up—"Actually, sir, don't worry, I think I can hear her at the door now"—he sat and stared at the telephone for a long while. Occasionally his eyes flickered to the diary that lay beside it—a Smythson featherweight diary, bound in red Morocco, gilt-edged, of the sort he bought her every Christmas. Why did she leave it lying around, except for him to pick it up, to leaf through it with his usual clumsy nervous fingers, to find the date, to read the number, and for once—just this once: the only time he had ever done so—to call it?

It rang a long time before it was answered. A man's voice, vaguely familiar, came on the line—confident, relaxed. "Yep? Hello?"

Legat pressed the receiver very hard against his ear and listened intently. He heard the sound of the sea.

"Hello?" the voice repeated. "Who is this?"

And then in the background, distinctly enough that he suspected she might have intended it to be overheard, the voice of his wife: "Whoever it is, tell them to go away."

Day Three

The Führer's special train was unusually heavy, entirely made of welded steel. It steamed steadily southwards through the night at an average speed of fifty-five kilometres per hour. It did not stop. It did not even slow down. It passed through big cities, such as Leipzig, and smaller country towns and villages, and between them it traversed great stretches of nothingness broken only by the occasional light of an isolated farmhouse.

Sleepless, Hartmann lay in his underclothes on the top bunk, his fingers parting the blind so that he could stare into the darkness. He had the sensation of voyaging in a liner across an ocean of unmeasurable extent. This immensity was what he had never been able to convey to his Oxford friends, whose concept of their own nationality was so nicely bounded by a coast—this hard wide vast landscape, fertile in its genius, limitless in its possibilities, which demanded a constant effort of will and imagination to order into a modern state. It was hard to talk about such feelings without sounding mystical. Even Hugh had not understood. To the English ear one invariably came across as a German nationalist—although what was wrong with that? The corruption of honest patriotism was one of the many things for which Hartmann would never forgive the Austrian corporal.

The sound of Sauer's rhythmic heavy breathing rose through the thin mattress. Before they had even left Berlin's city limits, the Sturmbannführer had pulled rank to insist on having the bottom bunk. Not that Hartmann had objected. It meant he was able to put his belongings into the luggage rack immediately above his head. The wide string mesh bulged under the weight of his suitcase. He had not let it out of his sight.

Soon after 5 a.m. he noticed the sky at its edges beginning to turn an oyster grey. Gradually the dark crests of the wooded pine hills emerged, serrated like saw's teeth against the spreading light, while in the valleys the white mist seemed as solid as a glacier. For the next half-hour he watched as the countryside took on colour—green and yellow meadows, red-roofed villages, white-painted wooden church spires, a turreted castle with blue shutters beside a wide slow river he assumed must be the Danube. When he was sure that sunrise could only be a few minutes away he sat up and cautiously took down his suitcase.

He muffled the noise of the catches one at a time with his hand and opened the lid. He extracted the document and stuffed it under his vest, then he put on a clean white shirt and buttoned it. He took the gun from his jacket and folded his trousers around it. Holding that in one hand, and with his shaving kit tucked under the other arm, he carefully descended the ladder. As Hartmann's bare feet touched the floor of the compartment, Sauer muttered and turned over. His uniform was on a hanger at the end of his bed; he had spent a long time before he went to sleep brushing it and straightening the creases. His boots were perfectly aligned beneath it. Hartmann waited until his breathing had resumed its regular pattern, then slowly lifted the catch and slid open the door.

The corridor was empty. He swayed along it towards the toilet at the back of the carriage. Once inside, he drew the bolt and turned on the light. Like the sleeper compartment it was lined in polished light-coloured wood with modernist fittings made of stainless steel; there were tiny swastikas on the taps. (There was no escaping the Führer's aesthetic, thought Hartmann, not even when one took a shit.) He inspected his face in the mirror above the tiny washbasin. Disgusting. He removed his shirt and lathered his chin. He had to shave with his feet braced wide apart to steady himself against the movement of the train. When he had finished he dried his face, then crouched on his haunches and inspected the wooden panel beneath the sink. He ran his fingers around the back until he found a gap. He pulled and it came away easily, exposing the plumbing. He unwrapped the gun from his trousers, wedged it behind the waste pipe and pushed the panel back into place. Five minutes later he was making his way along the corridor. Beyond the windows an empty autobahn ran beside the railway track, gleaming in the early-morning sunshine.

He slid open the door of his compartment to discover Sauer in his underwear bent over the lower bunk. He had tipped out Hartmann's suitcase and was rummaging through the contents. Hartmann's jacket lay next to it: it looked as though he had checked through that already. He didn't even bother to turn round.

"I'm sorry, Hartmann. It's nothing personal. I'm sure you're a decent fellow. But when a man is this close to the Führer I'm not prepared to take any chances." He stood and gestured to the mess on the mattress. "There you are. You can put it all back now."

"Don't you want to give me a full body search while you're at it?" Hartmann raised his hands.

"That won't be necessary." He clapped Hartmann on the shoulder. "Come on, man—don't look so offended! I've apologised. You know as well as I do the Foreign Ministry is rotten with reaction. What is it that Göring says about you diplomats? That you sharpen your pencils all morning and take tea all afternoon?"

Hartmann pretended to be offended, then nodded curtly. "You're right. I admire your vigilance."

"Excellent. Wait for me while I shave and then we'll go for breakfast."

He picked up his uniform and boots and went out into the corridor.

After he had gone, Hartmann tugged the document out from under his vest. His hands were shaking. He placed it in the suitcase. Surely Sauer wouldn't search it again? Or perhaps he would? He imagined him at that very moment on his knees inspecting behind the washbasin. Hartmann folded his clothes back into the case, closed the catches and heaved it up into the luggage rack. By the time he had finished dressing and had regained his composure there was a clump of boots in the corridor. The door opened and Sauer was back, once more clad in his SS uniform, looking as if he had just stepped off the parade ground. He threw his sponge bag onto his bed. "Let's go."

They had to pass through another sleeper carriage to reach the dining car. The train was all awake by now. Men half-dressed or still in underpants were squeezing past one another in the narrow corridor and queuing outside the toilets. There was a smell of sweat and cigarettes, a changing-room atmosphere, laughter as the train jolted and they were thrown together. Sauer exchanged *Heil*s with a couple of SS comrades. He opened the connecting door and Hartmann followed, stepping over the metal platform that made a junction into the restaurant car. Here it was all much quieter: white linen tablecloths, the smell of coffee, the chink of cutlery on china, a waiter wheeling a trolley laden with food. At the far end of the carriage, an Army general in a field-grey uniform with red collar tabs was talking to a trio of officers. Sauer noticed Hartmann staring at him. "That's General Keitel," he said. "Chief of the Wehrmacht Supreme Command. He's breakfasting with the Führer's military adjutants."

"What's a general doing at a peace conference?"

"Perhaps it may not turn out to be a peace conference." Sauer winked.

They took a nearby table for two. Hartmann sat with his back to the engine. The carriage darkened as they passed beneath a station canopy. On the platform a line of waiting passengers waved. He guessed an announcement must have been made over the loudspeaker that the through train was Hitler's. Enthusiastic faces whirled past the window in a mist of steam.

"If nothing else," continued Sauer, unfolding his napkin, "the presence of General Keitel will remind those elderly gentlemen from London and Paris that a single word from the Führer is all it will require for the Army to cross the Czech frontier."

"I thought Mussolini had put a stop to mobilisation?"

"The Duce will be joining the train for the final part of the journey to Munich. Who knows what will happen when the leaders of fascism confer? Perhaps the Führer will persuade him to change his mind." He beckoned to the waiter to bring them coffee. When he turned back to the table his eyes were shining. "Admit it, Hartmann, whatever happens—isn't there something intensely satisfying, after all those years of national humiliation, in finally making the British and the French dance to our tune?"

"It is certainly an amazing achievement." The man was intoxicated, thought Hartmann: drunk on a little man's dreams of revenge. The waiter arrived with a tray of food and they both filled their plates. He took a bread roll and broke it in half. He found he had no appetite, even though he couldn't remember the last time he had eaten. "May I ask, Sauer, what you did before you joined the Foreign Minister's staff?" He didn't really care; he was just making conversation.

"I worked in the office of the Reichsführer-SS."

"And before that?"

"Before the Party came to power, you mean? I sold automobiles in Essen." He was eating a hard-boiled egg. A piece of yolk was stuck to his chin. Suddenly his face twisted into a sneer. "Oh, I can see what you're thinking, Hartmann. 'What a vulgar fellow! A car salesman! And now he fancies himself as a second Bismarck!' But we have done something your kind never managed. We have made Germany great again."

"Actually," said Hartmann mildly, "I was thinking you have egg on your chin."

Sauer put down his knife and fork and wiped his mouth with his napkin. His face had turned red. It was a mistake to have teased him, thought Hartmann. Sauer would never forgive him. And at some point in the future—maybe later that day, or next month, or next year—revenge would be exacted.

The meal resumed in silence.

"Herr von Hartmann?"

Hartmann looked round. A large man, portly in a double-breasted suit, was looming over him. His domed head was bald, his thin dark hair combed back and plastered into place behind his ears with oil. He was sweating.

"Dr. Schmidt." Hartmann put down his napkin and stood.

"Forgive me for disturbing your meal. Sturmbannführer." The Foreign Ministry's chief interpreter bowed towards Sauer. "We have received the overnight English-language press summary and I wondered if I could trouble you, Hartmann?"

"Of course. Excuse me, Sauer."

Hartmann followed Schmidt the length of the dining car, past General Keitel's table and into the next carriage. Along the left-hand side were desks, typewriters, filing cabinets. On the right, the windows were blacked out; Wehrmacht signals officers wearing headphones faced one another across tables stacked with short-wave radio equipment. It wasn't so much a train as a mobile command post. It struck Hartmann that the original plan must have been for Hitler to travel in it to the Czech frontier.

Schmidt said, "The Führer expects to see a press summary as soon as he gets up. Two pages will be sufficient. Concentrate on the headlines and the editorial view. Get one of the men to type it for you."

He deposited a sheaf of handwritten English transcripts on a desk and hurried away. Hartmann sat. It was a relief to have something to do. He shuffled through the dozens of quotations, pulling out the most interesting, sorting them according to the influence of the publication. He found a pencil and began to write.

The London Times—praises Chamberlain for his "indomitable resolution."

The New York Times—"the sense of relief felt around the world."

The Manchester Guardian—"For the first time in weeks we seem to turn towards the light."

The tone was the same regardless of the political line of the paper. All described the dramatic scene in the House of Commons as Chamberlain read out the Führer's message. (*Within minutes and even seconds the message of hope was being hailed by millions whose lives a moment before seemed to hang upon the pull of a trigger.*) The British Prime Minister was the hero of the world.

When he had finished his translations he was directed by the unit commander to an Army corporal. Hartmann lit a cigarette, stood behind the corporal's shoulder and dictated. The machine was a special typewriter reserved for documents that went direct to the Führer, its typeface almost a centimetre high. His digest came out at exactly two pages.

As the corporal wound it out of the typewriter an SS adjutant appeared at the far end of the carriage. He looked harassed. "Where is the foreign press summary?"

Hartmann waved the pages. "I have it here."

"Thank God! Follow me." As the adjutant opened the door he pointed to Hartmann's cigarette. "No smoking beyond this point."

They entered a vestibule. An SS sentry saluted. The adjutant opened the door onto a panelled conference room with a long polished table and seats for twenty. He indicated that Hartmann should go ahead of him. "Is this your first time?"

"Yes."

"Salute. Look him in the eye. Don't speak unless he speaks to you." They had reached the end of the carriage and passed through into the vestibule of the next. Another sentry. The adjutant patted Hartmann on the back. "You will be fine."

He knocked lightly on the door and opened it. "The foreign press summary, my Führer."

Hartmann walked into the room and raised his arm. *"Heil Hitler."*

He was leaning over a table, his hands bunched into fists, looking down at a set of technical drawings. He turned to glance at Hartmann. He was wearing a pair of steel-rimmed spectacles. He took them off and looked past Hartmann to the adjutant. "Tell Keitel to set up the maps in here." The familiar metallic voice. It was strange to hear it at a conversational level and not ranting over a loudspeaker.

"Yes, my Führer."

He held out his hand for the press summary. "And you are?"

"Hartmann, my Führer."

He took the two sheets and started reading, rocking gently up and down on the balls of his feet. Hartmann had an impression of great energy barely suppressed. After a while he said, contemptuously, "Chamberlain this, Chamberlain that. Chamberlain, Chamberlain . . ." When he reached the bottom of the first page he stopped and flexed his head as if he had a crick in his neck, then read aloud in a tone of intense sarcasm: " '*Mr. Chamberlain's description of his last meeting with Herr Hitler is agreeable proof that his strong candour was rewarded with liking and respect.*' " He turned the page back and forth. "Who wrote this shit?"

"That is an editorial in *The Times* of London, my Führer."

He raised his eyebrows as if he expected nothing else and flicked over to the second page. Hartmann looked briefly around the carriage: a saloon car—armchairs, a sofa, watercolours of pastoral scenes hanging on the light-coloured wood-panelled walls. It occurred to him that the two of them had now been entirely alone for more than a minute. He inspected the fragile head—bent oblivious, reading. If he had known, he would have brought his gun. He imagined feeling for it in his inside pocket, quickly withdrawing it, pointing the barrel, a moment of eye contact perhaps before he squeezed the trigger, a final look and then the explosion of blood and tissue. He would have been reviled until the end of time, and he realised he could never have done it. The insight into his own weakness appalled him.

"So you speak English?" He was still reading.

"Yes, my Führer."

"You have spent time in England?"

"I was at Oxford for two years."

He looked up, stared out of the window. His expression became dreamy. "Oxford is the second-oldest university in Europe, founded in the twelfth century. I have often wondered what it would be like to see it. Heidelberg was founded a century later. Of course, Bologna is the oldest of them all."

The door opened and the adjutant appeared. "General Keitel, my Führer."

Keitel marched in and saluted. Behind him an Army officer carried rolled-up charts. "You wished to have the maps in here, my Führer?"

"Yes, Keitel. Good morning. Set them up on the table. I want to show them to the Duce."

He threw the press summary onto the desk and watched as the maps were unrolled. One was of Czechoslovakia, the other of Germany. On both, the positions of military units were drawn in red. He folded his arms and stared down at them. "Forty divisions to destroy the Czechs—we would have done it in a week. Ten divisions to hold the conquered territory, the remaining thirty transferred to the west to hold the frontier." He rocked up and down again on the balls of his feet. "It would have worked. It could still work. *'Liking and respect!'* That old arsehole! This train is heading in the wrong direction, Keitel!"

"Yes, my Führer."

The adjutant touched Hartmann on the arm and gestured to the door.

As he left the compartment he looked back for a moment. But all attention was now focused on the maps and he saw that his existence had already been forgotten.

2

Legat had spent the night at his club.

He had arrived to discover a backgammon evening in progress. Much strong drink had been taken. Until long after midnight the muffled noises of heavy male conversation and stupid laughter permeated the floorboards of his room. Even so, he preferred it to the silence of North Street where he would only have lain awake listening for the sound of Pamela's key in the latch—assuming, that is, she bothered to come home at all. On previous form it was just as likely she would slink back a day or two later, offering some alibi which they both knew he would never endure the humiliation of checking.

As the hours passed he stared at the pattern of the streetlights on the ceiling and thought about Oxford and Munich and his marriage, trying to disentangle the three. But however much he tried, the images remained entwined and his methodical mind became disordered with fatigue. By morning the skin beneath his eyes was puffy like black crêpe, and in his tiredness he had shaved too closely, so that his cheeks and chin were raw, pricked with tiny pinpoints of blood.

He was too early for breakfast: the tables were still being laid. Outside, the muggy weather had broken and it was drizzling. The air was a moist cool gauze on his face, the traffic just beginning to build from St. James's Street. Wearing his homburg and his Crombie, his suitcase in his hand, he trudged the shiny wet pavements down the slope towards Downing Street. Against the battleship-grey sky the barrage balloons were barely visible, like tiny silvery fish.

There was a small bedraggled crowd in Downing Street. The workmen had finished the wall of sandbags around the Foreign Office entrance. Six black cars were drawn up from Number 10 all the way back beyond Number 11, pointing towards Whitehall, ready to take the Prime Minister's party to Heston Aerodrome.

The policeman saluted.

Inside the lobby, three senior Foreign Office officials stood with their suitcases at their feet, like guests waiting to check out of a hotel. He took them in at a glance: William Strang, the tall, dehydrated, broomsticklike figure who had taken over from Wigram as Head of the Central Department and had already been twice with the Prime Minister to visit Hitler; Sir William Malkin, the Foreign Office's senior Legal Adviser, who had also met Hitler and who looked like a reassuring family solicitor; and the bulky, slope-shouldered Frank Ashton-Gwatkin, Head of Economic Relations, who had spent much of the summer in Czechoslovakia listening to the grievances of the Sudeten Germans, and who was known behind his back, on account of his drooping moustache and lugubrious manner, as the Walrus. Legat thought it a curious trio to send into battle against the Nazis. *What must they make of us?*

Strang said, "I didn't know you were coming to Munich, Legat."

"Neither did I, sir, until late last night." He heard the deference in his tone and felt a flicker of self-contempt—the youthful Third Secretary; the promising high-flyer, always careful never to seem too full of himself.

"Well, I hope you've taken something for travel sickness—in my experience, and I'm beginning to acquire a lot of it, flying can be as rough as a Channel crossing."

"Oh dear, I'm afraid I haven't. Will you excuse me for a moment?"

He walked quickly towards the back of the building and found Syers in his office reading *The Times*. His suitcase was by his desk. He said in a dull voice, "Hello, Hugh."

Legat said, "I really am most awfully sorry, Cecil. I didn't ask to go—I'd honestly prefer to stay behind in London."

Syers made an effort to look unconcerned. "My dear fellow, don't give it a second's thought. I always said it ought to be you, not me. And Yvonne will be relieved."

"Well, it's very decent of you. When did you hear?"

"Cleverly told me ten minutes ago."

"What did he say?"

"He simply said he'd changed his mind. Is there anything more to it than that?"

"Not that I'm aware of." The lie came easily.

Syers took a step closer and peered at him with concern. "I hope you don't mind me asking, but are you all right? You look a little rough."

"I didn't sleep much last night."

"Nervous about flying?"

"Not really."

"Ever been up in a plane before?"

"No."

"Well, if it's any consolation, as I said to Yvonne this morning, being on the same flight as the Prime Minister must be about as safe as one can get."

"That's what I keep telling myself." From the corridor came the sound of voices. Legat smiled and shook hands with Syers. "I'll see you when I get back."

The Prime Minister had descended from his flat and was walking towards the entrance hall along with Mrs. Chamberlain, Horace Wilson, Lord Dunglass and Oscar Cleverly. A pair of detectives followed, carrying the PM's luggage, including the red dispatch boxes containing his official papers. Behind them trailed two Garden Room secretaries—one a middle-aged woman Legat didn't recognise, the other Joan. Cleverly noticed him and waited for him to catch up. They walked together. His mouth was clenched, his voice low and angry. "I've no idea what's going on but I have acceded—with considerable reservations, I might add—to Colonel Menzies's request to allow you to accompany the PM. You'll be in charge of his boxes, as well as dealing with anything else that comes up." He gave him the keys to the dispatch cases. "Make contact with the office as soon as you reach Munich."

"Yes, sir."

"I trust I don't need to emphasise the absolute necessity that you do nothing whatsoever that might imperil the success of this conference?"

"Of course not, sir."

"And when this is all over, you and I will need to have a talk about the future."

"I understand."

They had reached the lobby. The Prime Minister was embracing his wife. The Downing Street staff gave him a discreet round of applause. He broke away, smiled shyly, and raised his hat to them. His complexion was ruddy, his eye bright. There was no hint of tiredness. He looked as if he had just come back from the river for breakfast after landing a good salmon. The porter opened the door and he strode out into the rain. He paused to allow his photograph to be taken and then stepped across the pavement and into the first car, where Horace Wilson was already waiting. His entourage filed out after him. Unconsciously, they had arranged themselves in order of seniority. Legat was the last to leave, carrying the two red boxes and his own suitcase. He gave them to the driver and climbed into the fourth car, next to Alec Dunglass. The doors slammed and the convoy pulled away—out of Downing Street, into Whitehall, around Parliament Square and south along the river.

It was not at all clear to anyone, including Legat, why Dunglass had been included in the party, except that he was a friendly face with a country house in Scotland and extensive fishing rights on the Tweed, and therefore good for the Prime Minister's morale. Miss Watson insisted that beneath his diffident manner lurked one of the cleverest politicians she had ever encountered: "He will be Prime Minister one day, Mr. Legat, mark my words, and you will remember that I was the first to say it." But as Dunglass would in due course inherit his father's title and become the 14th Earl of Home, and as it was inconceivable that in the modern age a premier could sit in the House of Lords, her prediction was dismissed in the Private Office as a *folie d'amour.* He had a very thin, straight smile and a curious, tight-lipped way of speaking, as if he were practising to be a ventriloquist. After a few desultory exchanges about the rain and what the weather might be like in Munich, they lapsed into silence. Then, as they were passing through Hammersmith, he said abruptly, "Did you hear about Winston's remark to the PM at the end of his speech yesterday?"

"No. What was that?"

"He came up to him at the Dispatch Box, while everyone was still cheering, and said, 'I congratulate you on your good fortune. You were very lucky.'" Dunglass shook his head. "I mean, *really!* One can level many charges against Neville—one can argue his policy is entirely wrong—but one can hardly maintain this conference in Munich is a matter of luck: he has worked himself half to death to achieve it." He gave Legat a sidelong look. "I noticed you were joining in the applause yourself."

"I shouldn't have done that. I'm supposed to be neutral. But one rather got carried away by the mood. I should think nine-tenths of the country were relieved."

The thin smile came again. "Yes, even the socialists were on their feet. It seems we are all appeasers now."

They had left central London and were motoring into the suburbs. The dual carriageway was wide and modern, lined by pebbledashed semis with small front gardens and privet hedges, interspersed with light industrial factories. Household names gleamed with grim cheerfulness through the pouring rain—Gillette, Beecham's Powders, Firestone Tyre & Rubber. Chamberlain must have been responsible for a lot of this development, thought Legat, when he was Minister of Housing and then Chancellor of the Exchequer.

The country had come through the Depression and was prosperous again. As they drove through Osterley he noticed that people were starting to wave as they passed—a few at first, mostly mothers taking their children to school, but gradually they became more numerous until, when the convoy slowed to turn off right towards Heston, he saw that drivers had pulled over on both sides of the Great West Road and were standing beside their cars.

"Neville's people," murmured Dunglass without moving his lips.

At the entrance to the aerodrome they came to a halt. Spectators blocked the road. Beyond the chain-link fence and white buildings Legat could see a pair of large planes drawn up on the grass at the edge of the concrete apron, lit by the lights of the newsreel crews, surrounded by a tightly packed crowd of several hundred. Their umbrellas were up. From a distance they looked like a bulbous black fungus. The car moved forward again, past saluting policemen, through the gate, and then in a wide sweep around the back of the terminal and hangar and onto the airfield, where the convoy halted. A policeman opened the rear passenger door of the lead car and the Prime Minister emerged, to cheers.

Dunglass sighed. "Well, I suppose this is it."

He and Legat climbed out. They collected their suitcases and the red boxes—Legat carried one, Dunglass insisted on taking the other—and set off towards the planes. The rain had stopped. The umbrellas were being furled. As they came closer Legat recognised the tall figure of Lord Halifax in his bowler hat and then, to his amazement, Sir John Simon, Sam Hoare and the rest of the Cabinet. He said to Dunglass, "Was this in the schedule?"

"No, it's a surprise. It was the Chancellor's idea. I was sworn to secrecy. It seems that suddenly they all want to share his limelight—even Duff."

The Prime Minister went around shaking hands with his colleagues. The crowd jostled forward, pressing against the line of policemen for a better view—reporters, airport workers in blue and brown overalls, local people, schoolboys, a mother with a baby in her arms. The newsreel cameras swung to follow Chamberlain's progress. He was grinning broadly, waving his hat, childish in his delight. Finally, he stood in front of the cluster of microphones.

"When I was a little boy," he began, and paused as those who were still talking were shushed into silence, "I used to repeat, 'If at first you don't succeed, try, try, try again.' That's what I am doing." He had a small piece of paper in his hand and glanced down at it briefly, reminding himself of the line he had prepared, then looked up again. "When I come back, I hope I may be able to say, as Hotspur says in *Henry IV*: 'Out of this nettle, danger, we pluck this flower, safety.'" He nodded emphatically. The crowd cheered. He smiled and waved his hat again, milking every last drop of acclaim, then turned towards his plane.

Legat moved forward with Dunglass. They gave their suitcases to the aircrew, who were loading the luggage into the belly of the aircraft. Legat kept possession of the red boxes. The Prime Minister shook hands with Halifax and mounted the three metal steps into the back of the plane. He ducked out of sight, then reemerged for one last round of cheering before vanishing for good. Wilson scuttled up next, followed by Strang, Malkin and Ashton-Gwatkin. Legat stood aside to let Dunglass go ahead of him. Close up, the plane seemed smaller and more fragile than it had at a distance. It was only about forty feet long. He thought one had to admire the Prime Minister's nerve: when he had first flown to see Hitler he hadn't even wanted to tell him he was coming until he was in the air, so that the dictator couldn't refuse to meet him. Standing on the bottom step, looking out at the enthusiastic faces, he felt suddenly intrepid himself, a pioneer.

He stooped to pass through the low door.

Inside the cabin were fourteen seats, seven on either side, with an aisle between them and a door at the far end to the cockpit. The nose of the plane was tilted five or six feet higher than the tail; there was a noticeable slope. It felt small and oddly intimate. The Prime Minister was already in his place at the front, on the left, with Wilson to his right. Legat hoisted the red boxes into the wire luggage rack, removed his coat and hat and stowed them alongside. He took the right-hand seat at the back so that he could see the Prime Minister in case he was needed.

A man in a pilot's uniform was the last to board. He locked the door after him and walked to the front of the plane.

"Prime Minister, gentlemen: welcome. My name is Commander Robinson. I am your pilot. This is a Lockheed Electra, operated by British Airways. We shall be flying at an altitude of seven thousand feet, at a maximum speed of two hundred and fifty miles an hour. Our flying time to Munich is approximately three hours. Would you please fasten your safety belts? It may get a little bumpy, so I suggest you keep them fastened unless you need to move around the cabin."

He went into the cockpit and took the seat next to the copilot. Through the open door Legat could see his hand reaching across the instrument panel, flicking switches. One of the engines stuttered into life, then the other. The noise increased. The cabin began to shake. The note seemed to climb a musical scale from bass to treble until it was subsumed into a single deafening sawing noise and the plane lurched forward onto the grass airfield. They bumped their way over the rough ground for a minute or two, raindrops scudding across the windows, then turned and stopped.

Legat fastened his seat belt. He looked across at the terminal building. Beyond it were white factory chimneys. Columns of smoke rose almost vertically. There was not much wind. That must be good. He felt quite calm. *I know that I shall meet my fate / Somewhere among the clouds above* . . . Perhaps Yeats would have been a more appropriate poet for the Prime Minister to quote than Shakespeare.

The engines became much louder and suddenly the Lockheed began to accelerate across the grass. Legat gripped the armrests as the plane raced past the terminal. Yet still they remained firmly earthbound. Then, just as he thought they were bound to crash into the fence at the edge of the airfield, the bottom of his stomach seemed to fall away and the cabin tilted upwards even more sharply, pressing him back in his seat. The propellers clawed at the air, hauling them into the sky. Slowly they banked and the landscape slid past the window—green fields, red roofs, slick grey streets. He looked down at the Great West Road a couple of hundred feet below, at the semidetached houses and the cars still drawn up with their drivers beside them, and he saw that in almost every garden people had come out and were craning their heads to the sky and waving—hundreds of them, waving with both arms crossed above their heads in frantic farewell—and then they juddered up into the base of the low cloud and the scene flickered out of sight.

After a few minutes of climbing steeply through thick grey mist they broke free into a burst of sunshine and blueness more beautiful than anything Legat had imagined. A crystal-white vista of peaks and ravines and waterfalls carved out of cloud stretched into the distance. It reminded him of the Bavarian Alps, but purer and unsullied by humanity. The plane levelled off. He unfastened his seat belt and made his way unsteadily towards the front.

"Excuse me, Prime Minister. I just wanted to let you know I have your boxes whenever you need them."

Chamberlain was staring out of the window. He looked at Legat. His earlier good spirits seemed to have left him. Or perhaps, thought Legat, they had only ever been a show for the crowds and the cameras. "Thank you," he said. "I suppose we had better make a start."

Wilson said, "Why don't you have some breakfast first, PM? Hugh, would you mind asking the pilot?"

Legat put his head into the cockpit. "Sorry to bother you, but where might I find some food?"

"There's a locker at the back, sir."

Legat lingered for a moment, briefly mesmerised once more by the sight of the clouds through the windscreen, then turned back to the cabin. Strang, Malkin, Ashton-Gwatkin, even Dunglass—now they all looked pensive. In the rear of the plane he found the locker. Two wicker hampers stencilled with the name of the Savoy Hotel were crammed full of neatly wrapped and labelled packages: grouse and smoked salmon sandwiches, pâté and caviar, bottles of claret and beer and cider, flasks of tea and coffee. It seemed an inappropriate feast, a picnic for a day at the races. He carried the hampers to the empty seats in the middle of the plane. Dunglass got up to help him distribute it all. The Prime Minister took a cup of tea and refused everything else. He sat very upright, holding his saucer in his left hand, his little finger crooked primly as he sipped. Legat retreated to his seat with coffee and a smoked salmon sandwich.

After a while, Strang went past him to the toilet cubicle. He stopped on his way back, buttoning his flies.

"Everything all right?" The Head of the Central Department was another official who had gone through the war and had retained the habit of talking to his subordinates as if he were inspecting their trench.

"Yes, thank you, sir."

"*'The condemned men ate a hearty breakfast . . .'?*" He folded his tall frame into the seat beside Legat's. He was in his mid-forties but looked sixty. His suit exuded a faint aroma of pipe tobacco. "Do you realise you're the only man on this plane who speaks German?"

"I hadn't thought of that, sir."

Strang gazed out of the window. "Let's hope this landing's better than the last one. There was a rainstorm over Munich. The pilot couldn't see a thing. We ended up being thrown around all over the place. The only person who didn't seem to mind was the PM."

"He's quite a cool customer."

"Isn't he? One never really knows what's going through his mind." He leaned across the aisle and spoke more quietly. "I just wanted to give you a gentle warning, Hugh. You haven't been through this before. There's a chance this whole thing could turn out to be a fiasco. We have no agreed agenda. No preliminary work has been done. There are no official papers. If it breaks down and Hitler grabs the chance to invade Czechoslovakia after all, we could be in the ludicrous position of having the leaders of Britain and France both stranded in Germany on the outbreak of war."

"Surely that's not likely?"

"I was with the PM in Bad Godesberg. We thought we had an agreement then, until Hitler suddenly came up with a new set of demands. It's not like dealing with a normal head of government. He's more like some barbarian chieftain out of a Germanic legend—Ermanaric, Theodoric—with his housecarls gathered around him. They leap up when he comes in and he freezes them with a look, asserts his authority, and then he settles down at a long table to feast with them, and to laugh and boast. Who'd want to be in the PM's shoes, trying to negotiate with such a creature?"

The pilot appeared in the doorway of the cockpit. "Gentlemen, just to let you know—we have crossed the English Channel."

The Prime Minister glanced down the plane and gestured to Legat. "I think we'd better start work on those boxes now."

3

The Führer's train was slowing. After more than twelve hours of relentless forward motion, Hartmann could detect a slight but definite swaying back and forth as the driver gently applied the brakes.

They were in the hilly country an hour south of Munich, not far from where he had gone walking with Hugh and Leyna in the summer of '32. Beyond the windows the woodland had begun to thin, a river glinted silver through the trees, and then an ancient town curved into view on the opposite bank. Gaily painted houses—pale blue, lime green, canary yellow—fronted onto the water. Behind them, a grey stone medieval castle sprawled across a wooded hill. In the distance rose the Alps. Framed by the window, it looked exactly like the Reichsbahn poster for a Tyrolean holiday that had lured them south six years before. Even the half-timbered station they were pulling into was picturesque. The train slowed to walking pace and then, with a slight jolt and a squeak of metal, stopped. It let out an exhausted exhalation of steam.

A sign beside the waiting room announced KUFSTEIN.

Austria, then, thought Hartmann—or rather, what had once been Austria until the Führer got to work on the map.

The platform was deserted. He checked his watch. It was a good watch, a Rolex, given to him by his mother on his twenty-first birthday. With beautiful efficiency they had arrived at 9:30 a.m. precisely. He wondered if the British delegation had taken off yet.

He rose from his table in the communications wagon, walked to the door and lowered the window.

All along the length of the train men were disembarking to stretch their legs. The station itself appeared ghostly in its emptiness. Hartmann guessed it must have been sealed off by the security services. But then something caught his eye: a man's white face staring through a grimy window. He was wearing a Reichsbahn cap. When he realised he had been spotted, he ducked out of sight.

Hartmann jumped down onto the platform and headed straight towards him. He pushed open the door and entered what looked to be the stationmaster's office, stuffy with the burned-out reek of coal and cigarettes. The official was at his desk—lank-haired, forties, pretending to read some papers. As Hartmann approached he scrambled to his feet.

Hartmann said, *"Heil Hitler."*

The man saluted. *"Heil Hitler!"*

"I'm travelling with the Führer. I need to use your telephone."

"Of course, sir. An honour." He pushed it towards Hartmann, who waved his hand imperiously.

"Get me an operator."

"Yes, sir."

When the man gave him the phone, Hartmann said to the operator, "I need to place a call to Berlin. I am with the Führer. It is a matter of the utmost urgency."

"What number in Berlin, sir?"

He gave her Kordt's direct line. She repeated it back to him. "Shall I call you when I have a connection?"

"As soon as possible."

He hung up and lit a cigarette. Through the window he could see activity further up the platform. The locomotive was being uncoupled and was getting up steam again. A group of SS men had gathered around the door of one of the carriages, facing away from the train with their machine guns clasped across their chests. An adjutant opened the door and Hitler appeared. The railway official standing beside Hartmann gasped. The Führer stepped down onto the platform. He was wearing his peaked cap, his belted brown uniform, highly polished jackboots. Behind him was the Reichsführer-SS, Heinrich Himmler. He stood for a moment flexing his shoulders, staring at the Kufstein castle, then set off down the platform in Hartmann's direction, accompanied by Himmler and his SS bodyguard. As he walked he swung his arms back and forth in unison, presumably to stimulate his circulation. There was something about the motion that was disturbing, simian.

The telephone rang. Hartmann picked it up.

"I have your connection, sir."

He heard the number ringing. A woman answered: "Kordt's office."

He turned away from the window. The line was poor. It was hard to hear. He had to put a finger in one ear and shout over the noise of the locomotive. "It's Hartmann. Is Dr. Kordt there?"

"No, Herr Hartmann. Can I help you?"

"Possibly. Do you know if we've received notification from London of who will be in Prime Minister Chamberlain's delegation?"

"Wait, please. I'll check."

The Führer had turned around and was strolling back in the direction he had come. He was talking to Himmler. In the distance Hartmann could hear the whistle of another train approaching from the south.

"Herr Hartmann, I have the list from London."

"Wait." Hartmann clicked his fingers impatiently at the railway official and mimed writing. The man tore his gaze from the window, took a stubby pencil from behind his ear and handed it over. Hartmann sat at the desk and found a scrap of paper. As he wrote each name he recited it back to her to be sure he had heard correctly. "Wilson . . . Strang . . . Malkin . . . Ashton-Gwatkin . . . Dunglass . . . Legat." *Legat*. He grinned. "Excellent. Thank you. Goodbye." He hung up and cheerfully threw the pencil back at the railwayman, who fumbled and just managed to catch it. "The office of the Führer thanks you for your help."

He slipped the list of names into his pocket and went outside into the fresh mountain air. A second train was crawling into the station. A large welcoming party had gathered, with Hitler at its centre. The cab of the oncoming locomotive was decorated with the green, white and red tricolour of Italy. It came to a halt just short of the Führer's train. An SS guard stepped forward smartly and opened a door.

Half a minute later, in a pale grey uniform and peaked cap, Mussolini appeared on the top step. His arm shot out in salute. Hitler's did the same. The Duce descended to the platform. The dictators shook hands—not at all the usual diplomatic formality but a warm and mutual double-clasp. They might almost have been two old lovers, thought Hartmann, the way they were grinning and gazing into one another's eyes. The flashes of the photographers lit up the reunion and suddenly everyone was beaming: Hitler, Mussolini, Himmler, Keitel, and Ciano—the Italian Foreign Minister and Mussolini's son-in-law—who had also emerged from the train with the rest of the delegation, all in uniform. Hitler gestured for the Italians to accompany him. Hartmann realised he had better get out of the way.

He half-turned, just in time to see Sturmbannführer Sauer disappear into the railwayman's office.

Immediately, he swivelled back to his original position, and stood frozen, unsure of what to do. It could hardly be a coincidence, which meant that Sauer must have been watching him all along. Now presumably he was going to question the railway official. Hartmann tried to remember if he had said anything incriminating. Thank God Kordt hadn't been in his office, otherwise he might have been indiscreet.

Barely thirty metres away, Hitler was insisting that Mussolini board the train ahead of him. Mussolini made a remark but Hartmann was too far away to hear it. There was laughter. The Italian swung his muscular body up into the doorway. Hartmann saw Schmidt, the interpreter, watching from the fringes of the group: Mussolini fancied he spoke German well enough not to need the services of a translator and for once Schmidt, normally at the centre of every meeting, looked slightly lost. Hartmann walked towards him. In a quiet voice he said, "Dr. Schmidt?"

Schmidt swung round to see who it was. "Yes, Herr Hartmann?"

"I thought you might like to know I've managed to get hold of the list of Englishmen accompanying Chamberlain." He offered him the scrap of paper with its pencilled scrawl. "I thought you might find it useful."

Schmidt seemed surprised. For a moment Hartmann thought he might demand to know why on earth he should be interested in such a thing. But then he accepted it and scanned it with increasing interest. "Ah, yes. Wilson I know, of course. And Strang and Malkin were both at Godesberg—neither speaks German. The other names are not familiar to me."

He glanced over Hartmann's shoulder. Hartmann turned as well. Sauer was bearing down on them. He wore a look of triumph. He called out even before he reached them, "Dr. Schmidt, excuse me. Did you authorise Herr Hartmann to call Berlin?"

"No." Schmidt looked at Hartmann. "What is this?"

Hartmann said, "I'm sorry, Sauer, I wasn't aware I needed authorisation to make a simple telephone call to the Foreign Ministry."

"Of course you need authorisation! All outside communications from the Führer's train must be cleared in advance!" He said to Schmidt, "May I see that paper?" He took it and ran his finger down the names. He frowned and turned it over. Finally, he returned it. "Again and again I find Herr Hartmann's behaviour suspicious."

Schmidt said mildly, "I really don't think there's much cause for suspicion here, Sturmbannführer Sauer. Surely it's useful to know who's coming from London? The fewer of these British officials who speak German, the more translation will be required."

Sauer muttered, "Even so, it's a breach of security."

From the far end of the platform came the noise of metal clashing against metal. The locomotive that had hauled them from Berlin had been turned around in the marshalling yard and had been backed up to be reconnected to the opposite end of the train.

Hartmann said, "We ought to board or we'll be left behind."

Schmidt patted Sauer's arm. "Well, let us say that I authorise Herr Hartmann's action retrospectively—is that good enough?"

Sauer looked at Hartmann. He nodded curtly. "It will have to be." He turned on his heel and strode away.

Schmidt said, "What a touchy fellow. I take it he's not a friend of yours?"

"Oh, he's not so bad."

They walked towards the train.

Sauer is a terrier, thought Hartmann, and I am his rat. The SS man would never give up. On three occasions he had nearly caught him—in Wilhelmstrasse, on the train, and now here. He would not get away with it a fourth time.

The order of the train was now reversed. The Führer's saloon car was at the rear; the sleeper carriages for his entourage at the front. In the centre were the communications wagon and the dining compartment, which was where Hartmann sat with Schmidt as they rolled north towards Munich. The Berliner had produced a large pipe and made a great business out of keeping it going—tamping down the tobacco with his box of matches, sucking at it, lighting it again, producing alarming spouts of flame. He was clearly nervous. Every time one of the Führer's adjutants passed through he looked up expectantly to see if he was needed. But Hitler and Mussolini appeared to be making themselves understood without him. He seemed put out. "The Duce's German is good, although not as good as he thinks it is. Let's hope they don't start a war by accident!" He thought this was such a good joke he whispered some variation of it whenever an adjutant left the dining car. "No war yet, eh, Hartmann?"

In the middle of the carriage was a table of SS officers at which Himmler was holding court. Sauer was among them. They were drinking mineral water. From his position Hartmann could see only the back of the Reichsführer's shaven neck and his protuberant, rather delicate small pink ears. Plainly he was in excellent spirits. Eruptions of laughter punctuated his monologue. Sauer smiled mechanically with the others but always his gaze reverted to Hartmann.

Schmidt puffed on his pipe. "Mussolini, I must say, is very easy to translate—nothing abstract about him: a down-to-earth practical politician. The same is true of Chamberlain."

"The Führer I would imagine is somewhat different."

Schmidt hesitated, then leaned across the table. "A monologue of twenty minutes is not uncommon. Sometimes even an hour. And then I have to read it all back in another language. If he's in that mood in Munich, we'll be there for days."

"Perhaps the others won't put up with it."

"Chamberlain certainly gets impatient. He's the only man I ever saw interrupt the Führer. This was at their first meeting, at Berchtesgaden. He said, *'If you are so determined to proceed against Czechoslovakia, why did you let me come to Germany in the first place?'* Imagine that! The Führer was speechless. There's no love lost there, I tell you."

Behind him the SS men roared with laughter. Schmidt winced, glanced over his shoulder and settled back in his seat. In a louder voice he said, "It's such a relief to have you with me, Hartmann. Obviously, I'll translate for the Führer and the other leaders, but if you can be on hand to help deal with the rest, that will ease my burden greatly. What languages do you have, apart from English?"

"French. Italian. Some Russian."

"Russian! You won't be requiring that!"

"Nor Czech."

Schmidt raised his eyebrows. "Quite."

The adjutant reentered the carriage and this time he stopped at their table. "Dr. Schmidt, General Keitel is about to make some technical explanations to the Duce, and the Führer wants you to be present."

"Of course." Schmidt quickly knocked the contents of his pipe into the ashtray. In his anxiety he spilled ash across the table. "Sorry, Hartmann." He stood and buttoned his double-breasted jacket and tugged it down over his broad stomach. He jammed the pipe into his pocket. "Do I smell of smoke?" he asked the adjutant. To Hartmann he said, "If he smells smoke, he'll send you out of the room." He pulled out a tin of peppermints and popped a couple into his mouth. "I'll see you later."

After he had gone, Hartmann felt suddenly vulnerable, like a boy who had escaped being bullied only because he had stayed close to his teacher. He rose and made his way towards the front of the carriage. As he passed the SS table, Sauer called out, "Hartmann! Aren't you going to salute the Reichsführer?"

Hartmann was aware of a sudden silence. He stopped, turned, clicked his heels and raised his arm. *"Heil Hitler!"*

Himmler's watery eyes peered up at him from behind his rimless spectacles. The top half of his face was very smooth and pale, but around his lips and his weak chin there was already a five-o'clock shadow. He raised his arm slowly. He smiled. "Don't worry about it, my dear fellow." He flicked his fingers dismissively and lowered his arm.

As Hartmann reached the end of the dining car he heard another outbreak of laughter behind him. He guessed he must be the object of some joke. He felt his face begin to burn with shame. How much he loathed them! He pulled the door open violently and strode through the sleeper carriage. When he reached the front coach he tried the handle of the toilet door. Locked. He put his ear to it and listened but he could hear nothing. He lowered the nearby window and leaned out to get some air. The landscape was flat and monotonous, the fields brown and bare after the harvest. He turned his head into the onrushing air. The cold wind steadied his nerve. In the distance he could see factory chimneys. He guessed they must be nearing Munich.

The toilet door opened. One of the Wehrmacht signals officers emerged. They exchanged nods. Hartmann went inside and drew the bolt. The cubicle stank of human waste. Sodden yellow-stained paper was strewn across the floor. The smell seemed to catch in the back of his throat. He bent over the toilet bowl and retched. His face in the mirror when he stared into it was cadaverous, hollow-eyed. He splashed himself with water, then lowered himself onto his haunches and pulled away the panelling beneath the basin. His fingers felt around the pipework, the wall, the underside of the sink. Someone tried the toilet door. He couldn't find the gun. He panicked. He reached in further, touched it and pulled it out. Now the door handle was being rattled vigorously.

"All right," he called, "I'm finished."

He slipped the Walther into his inside pocket. To cover the sound he made pushing the panel back into position he flushed the toilet again.

He half-expected to find Sauer in the corridor waiting to arrest him. Instead it was one of the Italian delegation in a pale grey fascist uniform. Hartmann returned his salute and lurched off down the passage. Inside his compartment he slid the door shut and hauled down his suitcase. He sat on the edge of the bottom bunk, rested it on his knees and opened it. The document was still inside. He hung his head in relief. He felt his body sway sideways. There was a scrape of metal, a slight shuddering beneath his feet. He looked up. Sunshine was glinting on the backs of houses and apartment buildings. Swastikas hung from some of the windows.

They were coming into Munich.

It was the time of the Oktoberfest, the annual funfair and folk festival, celebrated in these days of national unity under the official slogan *Proud City, Cheerful Country.* And now—behold!—there was another reason to be joyful. With only a few hours' notice, the Party was calling on everyone to welcome the Führer and his distinguished foreign guests.

Citizens of Munich—Get out onto the streets! Starting 10:30 a.m.!

Schools had been closed and workers had been given time off. In the station, posters announced the various hotels where the delegations would be staying and the routes along which the leaders would travel: *Bahnhof—Bayerstrasse—Karlsplatz—(Lenbachplatz—Hotel Regina, Hotel Continental)—Neuhauser Strasse—Kaufingerstrasse—Marienplatz—Dienerstrasse . . .*

The moment he stepped off the train Hartmann could hear the crowd outside the station and the sound of a band playing. Göring was waiting on the platform wearing some elaborate black uniform, presumably of his own design, with broad white piping on the trouser legs and diamond-shaped lapels. Hartmann inwardly cringed at the vulgarity. He waited until the dictators and their entourages had descended from the train and passed him—Mussolini's broad face lit up by a smile, like a child's drawing of a sun—then he followed them across the station concourse.

When they emerged into the cobbled square of Bahnhof Platz the ovation was deafening. It was a hot day, sticky with humidity. People were lining the pavements and cramming the windows of the neighbouring post office building. Hundreds of young children were waving swastika flags. An SS honour guard in white gloves and black coal-scuttle helmets shouldered their rifles. A military band struck up the Italian national anthem. And yet what riveted Hartmann's attention most was the grimness of Hitler's expression. He stood through the anthems and inspected the troops as if this flummery was the very last thing he wanted. Only when two little girls in white dresses were allowed to pass through the line of police and present him and the Duce with flowers did he manage a smile. But as soon as he had given his bouquet to an aide and climbed into his open-topped Mercedes his expression darkened. Mussolini, still grinning, settled down beside him while Göring, Himmler, Keitel, Ciano and the other bigwigs piled into the cars behind. The convoy pulled away into Bayerstrasse. From the street came the sound of more cheering.

The crowd began to disperse. Hartmann looked around.

Beneath the colonnades of the station, a harassed official of the Foreign Ministry was explaining the day's protocol to those who had been left behind. The Führer and the Duce, he announced, reading from a sheet of paper, were presently on their way to the Prinz-Carl-Palais, where the Italians would be staying. The British and the French would be landing in less than an hour: the British would be put up at the Regina Palast Hotel, the French at the Vier Jahreszeiten. While the Duce refreshed himself, the Führer would return by motorcade to the Führerbau to prepare for the conference. The rest of the German delegation should make their way there immediately. For those who desired transport, cars were waiting; otherwise, it was only a short walk. Someone asked where they would be spending the night. The official looked up from his paper and shrugged: he did not know as yet. Perhaps the Bayerischer Hof. Hotel rooms were hard to come by during the Oktoberfest. The whole thing seemed slightly chaotic.

Hartmann chose to walk.

He had always been careful over the past few years to avoid this part of Munich. It was only a ten-minute stroll from the station, along a pleasant tree-lined street—past the Old Botanical Gardens, a girls' school, some academic buildings—to the huge open space of Königsplatz. In his mind he had preferred to preserve it as he remembered it from that summer: a red-and-grey checked blanket spread beneath the trees, Leyna in a white dress with brown bare ankles, a picnic, Hugh reading, the scent of fresh-cut grass drying in the sun . . .

All gone!

The immensity of the vista stopped him in his tracks. He set down his suitcase in shock. It was worse than he had anticipated, worse even than in the newsreels. The park had been eradicated to provide a vast parade ground to stage the spectacles of the Third Reich. In place of the grass were tens of thousands of granite slabs. The trees had become metal flagpoles; from two hung swastikas more than forty metres high. On either side of him was a Temple of Honour, supported by pillars of yellow limestone, each containing eight bronze sarcophagi where the martyrs of the Beer Hall Putsch were now interred. Eternal flames flickered in the hot sunshine, guarded by a pair of SS men standing inhumanly still, their faces sheened with sweat. Beyond the temple to his left was the hideous brutalist facade of the Nazi Party administration building, beyond the temple to his right its near-identical twin, the Führerbau. All was functional white and grey and black, straight lines and sharp edges; even the neoclassical columns of the temples were square.

Outside the Führerbau he could see activity: cars drawing up, guards, flashbulbs, milling crowds. Hartmann saluted the martyred dead as one was obliged by law to do—it was dangerous to disobey: one never knew who might be watching—picked up his suitcase and walked towards the conference.

The Prime Minister had worked throughout the flight and now he was finished. He closed a census report listing every county of Czechoslovakia and the exact proportion of its population that was German-speaking and replaced it in his dispatch case. He screwed the cap back onto his fountain pen and returned it to his inside pocket. Then he lifted the red box from his knees and handed it to Legat, who was waiting in the aisle.

"Thank you, Hugh."

"Prime Minister."

He carried the dispatch box to the back of the plane, locked it and stowed it in the luggage rack, then fastened his seat belt. From the pressure in his ears he guessed they must be descending. All conversation in the cabin had ceased. Each man was peering out of his window, alone with his thoughts. The plane jolted and shuddered in the clouds.

For a long time, they seemed to be diving towards the bottom of a rough sea. It was easy to imagine the vibrations tearing off an engine or a wing. But at last they dropped out of the base of the cloud, the shaking stopped, and a drab olive-green landscape appeared beneath them, scored by the clear white line of an autobahn running as straight as a Roman road between conifer forests and across hills and plains. Legat pressed his face to the glass. It was the first time he had seen Germany in six years. For his Foreign Office entrance examination, he had been required to translate Hauff into English and J. S. Mill into German. He had accomplished both tasks with time to spare. Yet the country itself remained a mystery to him.

They were losing height fast. He had to pinch his nose and swallow hard. The plane banked. In the distance he saw the factory chimneys and church spires of what he presumed must be Munich. They straightened, flew on for a minute or two, passed low above a field dotted with brown cattle. A hedge flashed past, there was a rush of grass, and then—once, twice, three times—they bounced along the ground and braked so hard he felt himself pitched forward against the seat in front. The Lockheed skittered over the airfield, past terminal buildings that looked bigger than at Heston—two or three storeys, with crowds of people packed along the terraces and on the roof. Swastika banners hung from the parapet and fluttered from flagpoles alongside the Union Jack and the French tricolour. Legat thought of Wigram and was glad he was not alive to see it.

The Prime Minister's plane came to a stop at Oberwiesenfeld airport at 11:35 a.m. The engines whined and died. Inside the cabin, after three hours of flight the silence was a noise in itself. Commander Robinson emerged from the cockpit, bent to have a word with the Prime Minister and Wilson, then walked past Legat to the back of the plane, unlocked the door and lowered the steps. Legat felt a blast of warm air, heard German voices. Wilson rose from his seat. "Gentlemen, we should let the Prime Minister disembark first." He helped Chamberlain on with his overcoat and gave him his hat. The Prime Minister came down the slope of the aisle grabbing the headrests of the seats to steady himself. He was staring straight ahead, his jaw jutting, fixed, as if he were biting down on something. Wilson followed him and waited beside Legat while the Prime Minister descended to the concrete apron. He bent to peer out of the window. "My spies tell me you went to see Sir Alexander Cadogan last night." He said it quietly, without turning round. "Oh, God," he added quickly, "there's Ribbentrop."

He ducked through the door after Chamberlain. Behind him,

Strang, Malkin, Ashton-Gwatkin and Dunglass were lining up to disembark. Legat waited until they had passed. Wilson's remark had unsettled him. What did it mean? He wasn't sure. Perhaps Cleverly had said something to him. He stood and put on his coat and hat, reached up to the rack and took down the Prime Minister's red boxes. As he emerged from the plane a military band started playing "God Save the King" and he had to stand awkwardly to attention on the steps. When they had finished that, and just as he was about to move, they embarked on "Deutschland über alles." His gaze wandered across the crowded airfield in search of Hartmann—past the newsreel cameramen and the photographers, the official reception, the SS honour guard, the dozen big Mercedes limousines with swastika pennants drawn up side by side. He couldn't see him. He wondered if he had changed much. The music ended to loud applause from the crowds in the terminal. A chant of "Cham-ber-lain! Chamber-lain!" drifted over the concrete. Ribbentrop gestured to the Prime Minister and the two men walked across the apron to inspect the line of soldiers.

At the foot of the steps, an SS officer with a clipboard asked Legat for his name. He scanned the list. "Ah, yes, you have replaced Herr Syers." He placed a small tick beside it. "You are assigned to the fourth car," he said in German, "with Herr Ashton-Gwatkin. Your luggage will be taken to the hotel. Please." He tried to take the red boxes.

"No, thank you. I need to keep these."

There was a brief tug of war until finally the German let go.

The Mercedes was open-topped. Ashton-Gwatkin was already seated in the back. He wore a heavy overcoat with an astrakhan collar. He was perspiring profusely in the heat. "What an absolute beast," he murmured as the SS man moved away. He turned his hooded eyes on Legat. Legat knew him by reputation only—the most brilliant classicist of his year at Oxford even though he had left without taking a degree, a Japanese scholar, the husband of a ballerina, childless, a poet, a novelist whose lurid bestseller, *Kimono,* had caused such resentment in Tokyo he had had to be recalled—and now an expert on the economy of the Sudetenland!

Legat said, "The PM is hating every minute of this."

Chamberlain was hurrying through his review of the SS formation. He barely bothered to glance at the young men in their black uniforms. He also ignored Ribbentrop, whom he detested. When he realised he was supposed to share the lead car with the German Foreign Minister, he looked around helplessly for Wilson. But there was no escape. The two men settled into the open Mercedes and the cortège moved off, slowly passing along the length of the airport terminal in order that the crowds could cheer Chamberlain, who politely raised his hat in acknowledgement. At the airport gate they turned south towards Munich.

Hartmann had booked their tickets during Hilary term 1932. They had just been to the Cotswolds to visit Legat's mother in her cottage in Stow-on-the-Wold. She hated all Huns on principle; Paul she had adored. When they got back to Balliol that Sunday night, Hartmann had said, "My dear Hugh, as soon as finals are over, allow me to show you some proper countryside for a change—something that is not merely 'pretty.'" He had a girlfriend who lived in Bavaria: they could meet up with her.

It had never occurred to either of them that while life went on in Oxford in the same old way, Hindenburg might dissolve the Reichstag and provoke a general election. They had arrived in Munich on the same summer's day that Hitler had addressed a giant rally outside the city, and however much they had tried to ignore politics and get on with their vacation, there had been no escape, not even in the smallest town. Legat remembered a blur of marches and countermarches, the Storm Battalion versus the Iron Front, demonstrations outside buildings and arguments in cafés, Nazi posters—"Hitler over Germany!" "Germany Awake!"—that were put up by the Brownshirts during the day and torn down by the leftists overnight, a meeting in a park that had ended in a cavalry charge by mounted police. When Leyna had insisted that they go and stand outside Hitler's apartment, and had shouted abuse when he appeared, they had been lucky not to be beaten up themselves. It was a long way from Hauff and J. S. Mill.

Translate into German: "The administration of a joint stock association is, in the main, administration by hired servants . . ."

He stared out of the car. All the way into the centre of the town, along Lerchenauer Strasse and Schleissheimer Strasse, the citizens of Munich lined the streets so that the motorcade seemed to travel behind a bow-wave of applause for the Prime Minister, borne along a surging river of red, white and black flags. Occasionally, when they swerved to take a corner, Legat glimpsed him in the front car, leaning out slightly, his hat permanently in his hand, circling it in the direction of the crowds. Hundreds of arms rose in the fascist salute.

Ten minutes after leaving the airfield, the convoy swept down Brienner Strasse and into Maximiliansplatz. It rounded the square and drew to a halt outside the Regina Palast Hotel. A huge swastika dangled above the portico. Beneath it stood the British Ambassador, Henderson, and Ivone Kirkpatrick, Head of Chancery at the Berlin embassy. Ashton-Gwatkin let out his breath. "I think I could rather get used to that, couldn't you?"

He heaved his ungainly body out of the Mercedes. Ribbentrop was already being driven away. In the public gardens opposite the hotel the crowd was eight or ten deep, held back by a line of Brownshirts. They cheered. The Prime Minister waved. More flashes from the cameras. Henderson ushered him inside. Legat, a red box in either hand, walked quickly after them.

The large, galleried lobby looked as if it hadn't changed much since the Kaiser's day—a stained-glass ceiling, a parquet floor covered in Persian rugs, a plethora of potted palms and armchairs. Several dozen mostly elderly guests were gawping at the sight of Chamberlain. He was standing close to the reception desk in a huddle with Henderson, Kirkpatrick and Wilson. Legat stopped and waited nearby, unsure whether or not to approach them. Suddenly all four turned to look at him. He had the sensation that he was under discussion. A moment later, Wilson was heading across the foyer towards him.

5

The Führerbau was barely a year old, the work of Hitler's favourite architect, the late Professor Troost—so brand-new that the white stone seemed to sparkle in the morning light. On either side of the twin porticoes hung giant flags; the German and the Italian flanked the southern entrance, the British and the French the northern. Above the doors were bronze eagles, wings outstretched, swastikas in their talons. Red carpets had been run out from both sets of doors, down the steps and across the pavement to the kerb. Only the northern entrance was in use. Here an eighteen-man honour guard stood with their rifles presented, alongside a drummer and a bugler. Hartmann passed them unchallenged, climbed the steps and went inside.

Its function was not entirely clear. It was not a government building, or a Party headquarters. Rather, it was a kind of monarch's court, for the enlightenment and entertainment of the emperor's guests. The interior was clad entirely in marble—a dull plum colour for the floors and the two grand staircases, greyish-white for the walls and pillars, although on the upper level the effect of the lighting was to make the stone glow golden. The foyer was crowded with dark suits and uniforms. An anticipatory buzz animated the air, as if a gala performance were about to begin. He spotted a few faces he recognised from the newspapers—a couple of Gauleiters, and Rudolf Hess, the Führer's deputy, with his usual vaguely dreamy expression. He gave his name to the SS guards and was nodded through.

Straight ahead of him was the northern staircase. To his right, the lobby opened to a long, semicircular cloakroom, with two queues. He spotted a gentlemen's lavatory and diverted his course towards that. He locked himself into a cubicle, opened his suitcase, took out the document, unbuttoned his shirt and thrust it under his vest. Then he did up his buttons, sat on the toilet and examined his hands. They were strange to him, cold and shaking slightly. He rubbed them together vigorously, breathed on them, then flushed the lavatory and went back out into the cloakroom. He laid his hat, coat and suitcase on the counter and checked them in.

He climbed the northern staircase to the first-floor gallery. He was starting to understand the layout of the building. Above the first gallery was a second; above that an opaque white glass ceiling flooded the whole space with natural light. It was perfectly symmetrical and logical—impressive, in fact. Waiters passed him carrying trays of food and bottles of beer. For want of a better idea he followed them. Through the nearest of three open doors he saw a large salon with a buffet lunch laid out on white tablecloths. Further along the wide corridor that ran the length of the front of the building was a gallery with armchairs and low tables. Beyond that an SS sentry stood guard in the corridor. He was turning away anyone who tried to approach. Hartmann guessed that must be the room where Hitler was waiting.

"Hartmann!"

He swung round to see von Weizsäcker in the same room as the buffet lunch. He was standing beside the window, talking to Schmidt. He beckoned to Hartmann to join them. The room was panelled in dark wood with carved reliefs of various joyless rural activities. A few adjutants stood around holding whispered conversations. Each time someone came in they stiffened and then relaxed when they saw it wasn't Hitler.

"Schmidt was just telling me of your encounter on the Führer's train with Sturmbannführer Sauer."

"Yes, he seems to have got it into his head that I'm an unreliable element."

"To Sauer we are all unreliable elements!" The State Secretary laughed, then stopped abruptly. "Seriously, Hartmann, try not to antagonise him any further. He has the ear of the Minister and is capable of creating all sorts of trouble."

"I'll do my best."

"But will you? I worry about your 'best.' When this is over, I think perhaps it might be prudent to post you overseas somewhere. Washington, perhaps."

Schmidt said, "How about Australia?"

Weizsäcker laughed again. "An excellent suggestion! Even Party Comrade Sauer can't follow you across the Pacific Ocean!"

From beneath the window came the sound of cheering. The three men looked down into the street. An open Mercedes had just drawn up. Sitting very straight in the back was the British Prime Minister. Next to him was a slight and furtive-looking figure Hartmann didn't recognise.

"And so it begins," said Weizsäcker.

"Who is that with Chamberlain?"

"Sir Horace Wilson. The Führer can't abide him either."

More cars were pulling up behind the Prime Minister's. Hartmann tried to look further along the street but his view was obscured. "Isn't the Führer going to go outside to meet him?"

"I doubt it. The only place the Führer wishes to see that particular old gentleman is in his grave."

Chamberlain climbed out of the car, followed by Wilson. As he set foot on the red carpet there was a drum roll and a fanfare. He touched the brim of his hat in acknowledgement, then passed out of sight. The Mercedes pulled away. Almost immediately, the crowd started cheering again. Another open-topped limousine drew up to take its place. In the back of this were Göring and the French Prime Minister, Daladier. Even at a distance one could sense Daladier's unease. He was hunched down in the car, as though he could pretend he wasn't really there. Göring in contrast looked delighted. Somehow, since leaving the railway station, he had managed to change into a new uniform. This one was snow white. It bulged and strained to contain the rolls of his fat. Beside him, Hartmann heard Weizsäcker suppress a snort of derision. "What on earth is he wearing now?"

Hartmann said, "Perhaps he wanted to make Monsieur Daladier feel at home by dressing as the Michelin Man?"

Weizsäcker wagged his finger at him. "Now that is exactly the sort of remark I was warning you against."

"State Secretary," said Schmidt. He nodded to the doorway where Chamberlain had appeared.

"Your Excellency!" Weizsäcker moved smoothly across the floor with both hands extended.

The British Prime Minister was a smaller figure than Hartmann had expected, round-shouldered, with a tiny head, bushy grey eyebrows and moustache, and slightly protruding teeth. He was wearing a charcoal pinstriped suit with a watch chain across the waistcoat. The delegation filing in after him were equally unprepossessing. Hartmann examined each face as it appeared—this one lugubrious, that avuncular, this austere, another chinless. The hopelessness of his task briefly overwhelmed him. Of Legat there was no sign.

The room was starting to fill. Göring came in through the central door with Daladier and his entourage. Hartmann had read that the French Prime Minister, on account of his stocky muscular frame, was known in Paris as "the Bull of Vaucluse." Now his great block of a head was down and his eyes flicked warily left and right as he was led towards the buffet table. Chamberlain went over to greet him in his schoolboy French: *"Bonjour, Monsieur Premier Ministre. J'espère que vous avez passé un bon voyage . . ."* Göring was filling a plate for himself with a great pile of cold meats, cheeses, pickles, vol-au-vents. While all eyes were on the prime ministers, Hartmann took his chance to slip away.

He walked along the gallery and peered over the stone balustrade to the staircase and the crowded foyer below. He descended to the ground floor, looked into the cloakroom, the lavatory, and went outside, past the drummer and the bugler, down the red carpet and onto the pavement. He even put his hands on his hips and surveyed the crowd. It was no use. Legat was nowhere. The spectators started to applaud again. He looked along the street to see a Mercedes approaching. In the back, their profiles as haughty as those of Roman emperors, were Mussolini and Ciano. A guard opened their door for them and they stepped gracefully onto the pavement, tugging down the jackets of their pale grey uniforms. A gust of wind fluttered the flags. The Army musicians played their fanfare. The Italians strutted into the building. Two more cars with their uniformed entourage drew up behind.

He waited for perhaps half a minute and then followed them back inside. They were standing in the lobby being greeted by Ribbentrop, while behind them, descending the red marble staircase—almost shyly, as it seemed to Hartmann, bare-headed and alone—was Hitler. He was wearing a creased brown double-breasted Party jacket with a swastika armband, a pair of black trousers and scuffed black shoes. He stood on the landing halfway down the stairs, his hands clasped modestly in front of him, waiting for Mussolini to take notice of him. When the Führer's presence was finally pointed out by Ribbentrop, the Duce threw up his hands in a show of delight and swiftly mounted the steps to grasp Hitler's hand. The two dictators turned and began to walk up to the first floor, trailing their retinues.

Hartmann inserted himself at the back.

For the next few minutes he acted as interpreter, facilitating some stilted small talk about their recent experiences of flying between General Keitel and the British diplomat Strang. All the while he was keeping an eye on the room and its entrances. He noticed many things in rapid sequence. The way Chamberlain and Daladier hastened over to greet the fascist leaders. The way whenever Mussolini moved, Hitler moved with him, as if he was nervous of being left on his own in such a large gathering of strangers. He watched Ribbentrop conferring with Ciano—two arrogant, handsome peacocks together—and behind Ribbentrop he saw Sturmbannführer Sauer, who immediately locked eyes on his. Keitel had finished speaking and was waiting for him to translate. He made an effort to remember what had just been said. "General Keitel was recalling the weather when he flew back to Berlin after your last meeting at Godesberg. It was evening and his plane had to make detours around dozens of lightning storms. He says it was an incomparable spectacle at a height of three thousand metres."

"It's curious he should say that," replied Strang, "because tell him we also had a difficult experience . . ."

There was a stir of activity around one of the entrances. Hitler, whose boredom and unease had become increasingly evident, was leaving.

The instant the Führer exited the room, all the Germans moved quickly to follow him. Hartmann walked with Keitel. They went into the corridor and turned right. He was not sure what he was supposed to do. He was conscious of Sauer in the group just ahead of him with Ribbentrop. They passed the long gallery where various lounging SS officers jumped to their feet and saluted as Hitler went by. At the entrance to his office he halted. The effect was comic, like a pile-up of traffic. He wore a look of intense impatience.

"We shall talk in here," he said to Ribbentrop in his harsh voice. "Leaders and one adviser only." His dull blue eyes swept around his entourage. Hartmann, who was standing quite close to him, felt himself briefly come under the heat of his scrutiny. The gaze moved on, stopped and then returned to him. "I need to borrow a watch. Lend me yours, please." He held out his hand.

Hartmann stared at him, momentarily paralysed.

Hitler turned to the others. "He thinks he won't get it back!"

There was a roar of laughter.

"Yes, my Führer." Hartmann's fingers were clumsy as he unfastened the watch and handed it over. He was rewarded with a nod.

"Good. Let us get this business started."

He went into his office. Ribbentrop went after him. Schmidt turned in the doorway. "Hartmann, will you go and tell the others we are ready to begin?"

Hartmann walked back towards the reception room. He rubbed the pale skin on his left wrist where he had worn his watch night and day for the past eight years. It was odd to be without it. And now that man had it. He felt dangerously detached from what was happening, as if he were wandering through a dream. Beside the buffet table, Chamberlain was talking to Mussolini again. As he approached, Hartmann caught the words, "A good day's fishing ..." Mussolini was nodding politely, bored.

Hartmann said, in English, "Excuse me for interrupting, Your Excellencies. The Führer would like to invite you to join him in his study to begin the talks. He suggests leaders and one adviser only."

Mussolini looked around for Ciano, saw him and snapped his fingers. Ciano came to heel immediately. Chamberlain called to Wilson: "Horace, we're going in."

Daladier, watching from a short distance away, turned his melancholy eyes on Hartmann. *"Nous commençons?"* He was standing with a group of French officials. Hartmann recognised the Ambassador, François-Poncet. Daladier glanced about him, frowned. *"Où est Alexis?"* Nobody seemed to know. François-Poncet volunteered to go and find him. *"Peut-être qu'il est en bas."* He hurried out of the room. Daladier looked at Hartmann and shrugged. Occasionally one lost the head of one's Foreign Ministry—what was one to do?

Chamberlain said, "I don't think we should keep Herr Hitler waiting." He moved towards the door. After a brief hesitation the French and Italian delegations followed him. When he reached the corridor he stopped. "Which is the way?" he said to Hartmann.

"Please follow me, Your Excellency."

He led them past the long gallery where the Germans were standing watching. How drab the British and the French looked in their office suits, crumpled after their long journeys, compared to the uniforms of the SS and the Italian fascists. How unvirile; how dowdy and outnumbered.

At the entrance to the Führer's study Hartmann stood aside to let them enter: Chamberlain first, then Mussolini and Daladier, then Ciano and Wilson. The head of the French Foreign Ministry, Léger, was still missing. Hartmann hesitated before he went into the room. He had an impression of largeness, of dark wood and masculinity—a huge globe, a floor-to-ceiling bookcase and a desk at one end; a heavy table in the centre; and at the opposite end, drawn up in a semicircle around a brick-and-stone fireplace, a group of wood-and-wicker armchairs and a sofa. A portrait of Bismarck hung above the chimney piece.

Already seated in the armchair furthest to the left was Hitler, with Schmidt beside him. He indicated with a wave that his guests could sit where they pleased. There was something offhand about the gesture, as if it was all the same to him. Chamberlain claimed the armchair closest to the Führer. Wilson sat to his right. The Italians took the sofa which faced the fireplace. Ribbentrop and Daladier completed the group, leaving an empty chair for Léger.

As he bent to speak quietly to Ribbentrop, Hartmann noticed his watch lying on the low table in front of Hitler.

"Forgive me, Herr Minister, but Monsieur Léger is not yet ready."

Hitler, shifting in his chair with impatience, must have overheard him. He made a dismissive gesture. "Let's start in any case. He can join us later."

Daladier said, "I can't possibly begin without him. Léger knows all the details. I know nothing."

Chamberlain sighed and folded his arms. Schmidt translated his statement into German. Abruptly, Hitler leaned forward and picked up Hartmann's watch. He studied it ostentatiously for a few seconds. "Keitel!" The general, waiting by the door, hastened to his side. Hitler whispered in his ear. Keitel nodded and left the room. The others stared at Hitler, unsure of what was happening.

Ribbentrop said to Hartmann, "Go and see if you can find him."

Hartmann went out into the corridor just in time to see Léger hurrying into view. He was a small man in a black suit with a jet-black moustache and widow's peak. His face was pink from the exertion of running. He looked like a figure made of icing on the top of a wedding cake.

"Mille excuses, mille excuses . . ."

He darted into the Führer's study.

Hartmann had a last glimpse of the four leaders and their advisers, together with Schmidt, seated as still as figures in a photograph, before the SS guard closed the door.

6

The Regina Palast was an immense, monumental grey stone cube of a hotel, built in 1908, with Versailles-style reception rooms, a Turkish bath in the basement and three hundred bedrooms arranged over seven floors, of which the British delegation had been allotted twenty. These ran along the front of the hotel on the third floor with views across the trees of Maximiliansplatz to the distant twin Gothic spires of the Frauenkirche.

After the Prime Minister and his team had left for the start of the conference, Legat spent the next ten minutes walking up and down the dimly lit carpeted corridor in the company of the hotel's assistant manager. He found it hard to hide his frustration. *I might as well have been a bloody hotelier,* he thought. His first task, given to him by Horace Wilson, was to allocate a room to each member of the British party and then to make sure the porters delivered the correct luggage to the right room.

"I'm sorry to be a bore," Wilson had said, "but I'm afraid I'm going to have to ask you to stay in the hotel for the duration of the conference."

"The entire duration?"

"Yes. It seems they're giving us a corridor of rooms to use as our headquarters. Someone needs to get an office set up and running, establish an open line to London, make sure it's permanently manned. You're the obvious choice." The dismay must have shown in Legat's face because he went on smoothly: "I understand it's a disappointment for you not to be at the main show—just as it must have been for poor old Syers to be left behind in London, after his name was in the papers as one of the Prime Minister's party—but it simply can't be helped. So sorry."

For a moment Legat had considered confiding in him why he was in Munich in the first place. But instinct warned him it might only make Wilson even more determined to keep him away from the German delegation. Indeed, there was something about Wilson's manner—a vague hard shape lurking beneath the oily surface—which suggested to him that the Prime Minister's Chief Adviser already had a shrewd idea of what he had come to do.

So all he said was, "Of course, sir. I'll make a start right away."

The suite designated for the Prime Minister included a bedroom with a four-poster bed and a Louis XVI drawing room with gilt chairs and French windows that opened onto a balcony. "It is the finest room in the hotel," the undermanager assured him. The next-best rooms Legat awarded to Wilson, Strang, Malkin, Ashton-Gwatkin and the two diplomats from the Berlin embassy, Henderson and Kirkpatrick. In a spirit of self-sacrifice, his own room and Dunglass's were the smaller ones, on the opposite side of the corridor, and had views of the interior courtyard, as did those of the two detectives, the PM's doctor, Sir Joseph Horner—who had gone immediately to the bar—and the two Garden Room secretaries, Miss Anderson and Miss Sackville. (So that was her name, he thought: Joan Sackville.)

The large double-aspect room in the southeast corner had been set aside as the delegation's office. A tray of open sandwiches and some bottles of mineral water had been provided for lunch. It was here that the two women set up their typewriters—two Imperials and a Remington portable—and unpacked their stationery. Legat put the PM's red boxes on the desk. An old-fashioned telephone was the only means of communication. He asked the hotel operator to book an international call to the switchboard of Number 10, then hung up and paced around the room. After a while, Joan suggested he ought to sit down.

"Sorry. I'm a bit on edge." He sat and poured himself a glass of mineral water. It was warm and tasted vaguely of sulphur. Almost immediately the phone rang. He jumped up to answer it: "Yes?" Over the voice of the hotel operator informing him that he was connected to London he could just make out the exasperated tone of the telephonist in Downing Street repeatedly asking what extension he required. He had to shout to make himself heard. It was another minute before the Principal Private Secretary came on the line.

"Cleverly."

"Sir, it's Legat. We're in Munich."

"Yes, I know. It's running on the news wires." His voice was very faint and hollow. There was a series of faint clicks on the line. That would be the Germans listening, thought Legat. Cleverly said, "It sounds as though you—" The robot-voice was lost in a crackle of static.

"I'm sorry, sir. Could you repeat that?"

"I said, it sounds as though you had quite a reception!"

"We certainly did, sir."

"Where's the PM?"

"He's just left for the conference. I'm at the hotel."

"Good. I want you to stay there and make sure this line stays open."

"With respect, sir, I think I would be more useful if I was actually in the same building as the PM."

"No, absolutely not. Do you hear me? I want—"

Another burst of static, like gunfire. The line went dead. "Hello? Hello?" Legat pressed the lever on the cradle with his finger half a dozen times. "Hello? Damn!" He hung up and regarded the apparatus with hatred.

For the next two hours Legat made repeated attempts to establish a line to London. It proved impossible. Even the number he had been given for the Führerbau was constantly engaged. He started to suspect the Germans were deliberately isolating them—either that, or the regime was not as efficient as it liked to pretend. Throughout all this, in the garden opposite the hotel, the crowd kept growing. There was a holiday atmosphere, the men in leather shorts, the women in floral dresses. Much beer was being drunk. An oom-pah band arrived and began to play the current English hit.

> *"Any time you're Lambeth way,*
> *Any evening, any day,*
> *You'll find us all doin' the Lambeth walk."*

At the end of each chorus, the crowd chanted in a Bavarian accent a ragged and slightly inebriated *"Oy!"*

After a while, Legat covered his ears. "This is surreal."

Joan said, "Oh, I don't know. I think it's rather sweet of them to try to make us feel at home."

He found a tourist guide to the city in the desk drawer. The hotel appeared to be only about half a mile from the Führerbau—left along Max-Joseph-Strasse and up to Karolinenplatz, over the roundabout . . . Assuming he could find Paul quickly enough, he could be there and back in half an hour.

"Are you married, Mr. Legat?"

"I am."

"Any children?"

"Two. What about you?"

She lit a cigarette and regarded him through the smoke with an expression of amusement. "No. No one will have me."

"I find that hard to believe."

"No one will have me whom I want to be had by, if you know what I mean." She started to sing along with the band:

> *"Everything's free and easy,*
> *Do as you darn well pleasey,*
> *Why don't you make your way there,*
> *Go there, stay there . . ."*

Miss Anderson joined in. They had good voices. Legat knew they would think him a stuffed shirt for not taking part—that was what Pamela always called him. But it ran counter to his nature at the best of times to sing, or to dance for that matter, and he hardly thought this was an occasion for levity.

From outside, clearly audible even through the closed windows, came a resounding Germanic *"Oy!"*

At the Führerbau, they waited.

Each delegation had been allotted its own area. The Germans and the Italians shared the long open gallery that was next to the Führer's study; the British and the French occupied the two reception rooms at the far end of the corridor that faced it. Hartmann positioned himself in an armchair in the gallery that afforded him a clear view between the pillars across the wide open space to where the Allied officials sat in silence, reading and smoking. Both had left their doors wide open in case they were needed. He could see them occasionally moving around, casting hopeful, anxious glances towards the big corner study, where the Führer's door remained firmly shut.

Still Legat did not come.

One hour passed, and then another. From time to time, a Nazi chieftain—Göring, Himmler, Hess—wandered by with his attendants, occasionally stopping to exchange a few words with the Germans. The boots of the SS adjutants rang on the marble floor. Messages were whispered. The atmosphere was that of a big hushed institution—a museum perhaps, a library. Everyone watched everyone else.

From time to time, Hartmann reached inside his jacket and touched the metal of the gun, warmed by the heat of his body, then slid his hand down the side of his shirt and felt the outline of the envelope. Somehow he would have to get it into the hands of the British delegation, and sooner rather than later—there was no point in leaving it until a deal was agreed. Legat, it seemed, was out of the picture: why, he did not know. But if not Legat, who? The only Englishman to whom he had spoken was Strang. He had seemed decent enough, albeit as stiff as an old Latin schoolmaster. How was he to make contact with Strang without being seen by Sauer? Every time he looked around, it seemed the SS man was watching him. He suspected he had also alerted some of his comrades.

It would take him less than half a minute to saunter over to the British delegation's room. Unfortunately, he could only do so in full view of the entire assembly. What possible excuse could he contrive? His mind, tired from two nights of little sleep, circled endlessly around the problem without finding a solution. Nevertheless, he decided he would have to try.

At three o'clock he stood to stretch his legs. He walked around the corner, past the Führer's office to the balustrade nearest the British delegation's room. He rested his hands on the cold marble, leaned casually against it and looked down into the lobby. A group of men was standing together at the foot of the second staircase, talking quietly. He guessed they were the drivers. He risked a surreptitious glance at the British.

Suddenly there was a noise behind him. The door to Hitler's study opened and Chamberlain appeared. He looked much grimmer than he had a couple of hours earlier. After him came Wilson, then Daladier and Léger. Daladier, patting his pockets, pulled out a cigarette case. At once, the British and French delegations streamed out from their respective rooms to meet them. As they hurried past him, Hartmann heard Chamberlain call out, "Come on, gentlemen, we're leaving," and the two groups walked along the gallery to the far staircase and began to descend. A minute later, Hitler and Mussolini emerged and stalked off in the same direction, with Ciano trailing behind. Hitler's expression was still one of irritation. He was gesticulating at the Duce, muttering to him angrily, his right hand making sweeping gestures as if he wished to consign the entire business to oblivion. The glorious possibility occurred to Hartmann that perhaps the whole thing had collapsed.

———

Legat was at the desk in the Regina Palast office, sorting through the contents of the red boxes and putting aside the documents annotated by the Prime Minister requiring urgent action, when he heard the crowd begin to cheer again. He got to his feet and looked down into Maximiliansplatz. An open Mercedes had drawn up outside the hotel. Chamberlain was climbing out, accompanied by Wilson. Other cars were arriving behind it. The British delegation appeared on the pavement.

Joan joined him at the window. "Were you expecting them back this early?"

"No. There was nothing scheduled."

He locked the boxes and went out into the corridor. At the far end the lift-bell rang softly. The doors opened and the Prime Minister emerged with Wilson and one of his Scotland Yard detectives.

"Good afternoon, Prime Minister."

"Hello, Hugh." His voice was tired. In the weak electric light, he looked almost spectral. "Where are we based?"

"Your suite is here, sir."

As soon as he crossed the threshold the Prime Minister disappeared into the bathroom. Wilson went over to the window and looked down at the crowd. He, too, seemed exhausted.

"How did it go, sir?"

"It was pretty bloody. Will you tell the others to come in here? Everyone needs to be briefed."

Legat stationed himself in the corridor and diverted the arriving delegates into the room. Within two minutes it was full: Strang, Malkin, Ashton-Gwatkin and Dunglass, together with Henderson and Kirkpatrick from Berlin. Legat went in last. He closed the door behind him, just as the Prime Minister came out of his bedroom. He had changed his collar and washed his face. The hair behind his ears was still damp. He looked altogether brighter. "Gentlemen, please sit down." He took the large armchair facing the room and waited while they all found a seat. "Horace, why don't you put everyone in the picture?"

"Thank you, Prime Minister. Well, the whole thing was somewhat of a Mad Hatter's tea party, as you've probably gathered." He pulled a small notebook from his inside pocket and flattened it out on his knee. "We started with a speech from Hitler, the gist of which was (a) that Czechoslovakia is now a threat to peace in Europe, (b) that a quarter of a million refugees have fled the Sudetenland into Germany in the past few days, and (c) that the whole situation is critical and must be settled by Saturday—either Britain and France and Italy will have to guarantee that the Czechs will start evacuating the disputed territory on that day, or he'll march in and take it. He kept looking at his watch as if he was checking when the twenty-four-hour pause on mobilisation would expire. Overall, I must say my impression is that he's not bluffing and we either sort this thing out today or it's war."

He turned a page.

"Then Mussolini produced a draft agreement in Italian which the Germans have since had translated." He fished around in his other inside pocket and pulled out a few typewritten pages. "Translated into German, that is. As far as we can gather, it's more or less what was proposed before." He threw it onto the coffee table.

Strang said, "Will Hitler accept an international commission to determine which areas are to become German?"

"No, he says there's no time for that—there should be a plebiscite and each district can decide according to a simple majority."

"And what happens to the minority?"

"They will have to evacuate by October the tenth. He also wants us to guarantee that the Czechs won't destroy any of their installations before they leave."

The Prime Minister said, "It's the word 'guarantee' I don't like. How on earth can we guarantee anything unless we know the Czechs will agree?"

"Then surely they need to be at the conference?"

"Exactly the point I made. Unfortunately, this led to the usual vulgar tirade against the Czechs. There was a lot of this—" The Prime Minister smacked his fist into his open palm repeatedly.

Wilson consulted his notes. "To be exact, he said that he had agreed to postpone military action—'*but if those who had urged him to do so were not prepared to take responsibility for Czechoslovakia's compliance, he would have to reconsider.'*"

"Good God!"

Chamberlain said, "Nevertheless, I stood my ground. It's inconceivable that we should guarantee Czech compliance unless the Czechs themselves agree."

Henderson said, "What was the French position on bringing the Czechs into the talks?"

"To begin with Daladier backed me up, but then after about half an hour he changed his tune. What exactly was it he said, Horace?"

Wilson read from his notebook. "*'If the inclusion of a Prague representative would cause difficulties he was ready to forgo this, as it was important that the question should be settled speedily.'*"

"To which I countered that I wasn't insisting that the Czechs should actually take part in the discussions, but at the very least they should be in the next room, so that they could give us the necessary assurances."

Wilson said, "You were very firm, Prime Minister."

"Well, yes, I was. I had to be! Daladier is utterly useless. He gives the impression he's loathing every minute of being here and just wants to sign an agreement and get home to Paris as quickly as possible. Once it became clear we weren't going to get anywhere—in fact, that there was a risk the whole thing might break up in acrimony—I proposed we adjourn for an hour so that we could consult with our respective delegations about Mussolini's draft."

"And the Czechs?"

"Let's wait and see. By the end Hitler had a face like thunder. He's taken Mussolini and Himmler back to his apartment for lunch—I can't say I envy Musso that particular social engagement!" He broke off. He screwed up his face in disgust. "What on earth is *that*?"

Through the closed windows came the thump of the band outside the hotel.

Legat said, "It's 'The Lambeth Walk,' Prime Minister."

In the Führerbau, the German and Italian officials had drifted back towards the room where the buffet lunch had been laid out. The two groups didn't mingle. The Germans felt themselves superior to the Italians. The Italians thought the Germans vulgar. Over by the window, a circle formed around Weizsäcker and Schmidt. Hartmann collected a plate of food and joined them. Weizsäcker was showing round a document, typed in German. He seemed very pleased with himself. It took a moment for Hartmann to grasp that this was some kind of draft agreement, produced at the leaders' meeting by Mussolini. So the talks hadn't broken down after all. He felt his earlier good spirits evaporate. His dismay must have shown on his face, because Sauer said, "There's no need to look quite so miserable about it, Hartmann! At least we have the basis of an agreement."

"I'm not miserable, Herr Sturmbannführer, merely amazed that Dr. Schmidt should have managed to translate it so quickly."

Schmidt laughed and rolled his eyes at his naivety. "My dear Hartmann, I didn't have to translate a thing! That draft was written last night in Berlin. Mussolini pretended it was his own work."

Weizsäcker said, "Do you honestly think we would have left something so important to the Italians?"

The others joined in the laughter. Across the room, a couple of the Italians turned to look at them. Weizsäcker became serious. He put his finger to his lips. "I think we should keep our voices down."

Legat spent the next hour in the office, translating the text of the Italians' draft agreement from German into English. It wasn't very long—less than a thousand words. As he finished each page he gave it to Joan to type. At various points, the members of the British delegation trooped into the office to read over his shoulder.

1. The evacuation will begin on October 1st.
2. The United Kingdom, France and Italy guarantee that the evacuation of the territory shall be completed by October 10th . . .

And so it went on, eight paragraphs in all.

It was Malkin, the Foreign Office lawyer, sitting in an armchair in the corner, reading through the pages and puffing on his pipe, who suggested that "guarantee" should be replaced with "agree"—a clever stroke, seemingly trivial, that completely altered the tenor of the draft. Wilson took it along the corridor to show to the Prime Minister, who was resting in his room. The word came back that Chamberlain agreed. It was Malkin also who pointed out that the whole thrust of the document implied that three powers—Britain, France and Italy—were making concessions to a fourth, Germany: a thrust which gave what he called "an unfortunate impression." He therefore wrote out a preamble to the agreement in his Chancery Lane copperplate:

Germany, the United Kingdom, France and Italy, taking into consideration the agreement, which has been already reached in principle for the cession to Germany of the Sudeten German territory, have agreed on the following terms and conditions governing the said cession and the measures consequent thereon, and by this agreement they each hold themselves responsible for the steps necessary to secure its fulfilment.

The Prime Minister signalled his agreement to that as well. He also asked for the folder containing the 1930 Czech census results that was in his red box. Joan retyped the document from the beginning. Just after 4 p.m. it was finished and the delegation began moving downstairs to their cars. Chamberlain came out from his bedroom into the drawing room, looking tense, nervously smoothing his moustache with his thumb and forefinger. Legat handed him the folder. Wilson muttered, "Perhaps a better quotation from Shakespeare to have used at Heston might have been, '*Once more unto the breach, dear friends.*'" The corners of the Prime Minister's mouth turned down slightly.

His detective said, "Are you ready to go, sir?"

Chamberlain nodded and walked out of the room. As Wilson turned to follow him, Legat decided to make one last appeal. "I really think I would be more useful at the actual conference, sir, rather than hanging around here. There's bound to be further translating to be done."

"Oh, no no—the Ambassador and Kirkpatrick can handle that. You man the fort here. Really, you're doing a splendid job." He patted Legat's arm. "You need to get onto Number Ten straight away and read them the text of our revised draft. Ask them to make sure it's circulated to the Foreign Office. Well—here goes."

He hurried after the Prime Minister. Legat returned to the office, picked up the telephone and once again booked a call to London. This time, to his surprise, it went through.

For Hartmann, the existence of a draft agreement changed everything. Clever minds would now bend themselves to smoothing over points of difference. Iron principles would shimmer and then magically vanish. The most contentious issues of all, on which no accord was possible, would simply be ignored entirely and left to sub-committees to deal with at a later date. He knew how these things worked.

He edged away from the luncheon party, replaced his plate on the buffet table and slipped out of the room. He reckoned he might only have an hour or two at best. He needed to find some secluded space. To his left were a couple of closed doors and beyond them a gap in the wall. He walked towards it: the landing of a service staircase. He looked over his shoulder. No one seemed to have noticed his departure. He side-stepped quickly and began to descend. He passed a chef in kitchen whites climbing the stairs carrying a tray of covered dishes. The man ignored him. He continued on down, past the ground floor, all the way to the basement.

The passage was wide, the walls whitewashed, the floor smooth flagstones, like the cellar of a castle. It appeared to run the entire length of the building. He could smell food cooking nearby, could hear the metallic crashes of a kitchen. He walked on firmly, in the manner of a man who had every right to be wherever he wished. There was a loud murmur of conversation ahead, a clattering of plates and cutlery. He came out into a large cafeteria where several dozen SS guards were having lunch. The air was thick with cigarette smoke and the smell of coffee and beer. A few faces turned to look at him. He nodded. Beyond the cafeteria the passage resumed. He passed a staircase, a guardroom, opened a large metal door and stepped into the heat of the afternoon.

It was the car park at the back of the building. A dozen black Mercedes were drawn up in a line. A couple of the drivers were smoking. Faintly in the distance he heard cheers and shouts of "Sieg Heil!"

He turned around quickly and went back inside. An SS man appeared from the guardroom. "What are you doing?"

"Hurry up, man! Can't you hear the Führer is returning?"

He pushed past him and started climbing the staircase. He trotted up the steps quickly. His heart felt too full for his chest. He was sweating. He passed the ground floor and ascended the next two flights and emerged more or less exactly where he had been standing when the first session of the conference broke up. There was a flurry of activity. Aides were moving hastily into position, straightening their jackets, smoothing down their hair, looking along the corridor. Hitler and Mussolini came into view, walking side by side. Behind them came Himmler and Ciano. It was clear that the luncheon interval had done nothing to improve Hitler's mood. Mussolini stopped to talk to Attolico but Hitler stamped on regardless, followed by the German delegation.

At the entrance to his study he halted and turned to look down the length of the building. Hartmann, no more than ten paces away, saw the irritation in his face. He began to rock up and down on the balls of his feet—that same strange unconscious mannerism Hartmann had witnessed on the train. From outside came a burst of even louder applause, and shortly afterwards Chamberlain appeared at the top of the far staircase, followed by Daladier. They, too, began to confer, standing together beside a pillar. Hitler watched the two democratic leaders for perhaps a minute. Suddenly he wheeled round, located Ribbentrop, and gestured angrily at him to go and fetch them. He disappeared into his study and Hartmann felt a rush of renewed optimism. The professional diplomats might imagine the deal was already done, but nothing could be settled until Hitler willed it, and he still looked as if he would like nothing more than to send them all packing.

It must have been after five when Legat finished dictating the final clause to the stenographer in Downing Street.

"The Czechoslovak Government will, within a period of four weeks from the date of this agreement, release from their military and police forces any Sudeten Germans who may wish to be released, and the Czechoslovak Government will within the same period release Sudeten German prisoners who are serving terms of imprisonment for political offence."

"Have you got all that?"

"Yes, sir."

He tucked the receiver under his chin and began gathering together the pages of the draft. In the distance he heard raised voices. The door had been left half-open. There was some kind of argument going on in the corridor. *"Engländer!"* a man was shouting in a thick accent. *"Ich verlange, mit einem Engländer zu sprechen!"*

Legat exchanged puzzled glances with the two secretaries. He beckoned to Joan to take the telephone, put his hand over the receiver and said to her, "Get them to keep the line open." She nodded and slipped into his place at the desk. He went out into the corridor. At the far end of the passage, near the back of the hotel, a figure was gesticulating, trying to push his way past a group of four men in suits. They kept moving to block his path. "An Englishman! I demand to speak to an Englishman!"

Legat walked towards them. "I am English! Can I help?"

The man called out, "Thank God! I am Dr. Hubert Masarík, *chef de cabinet* of the Foreign Minister of Czechoslovakia! These men are from the Gestapo and they are holding me and my colleague, the Czech Minister in Berlin, Dr. Vojtek Mastny, imprisoned in this room!"

He was about forty, distinguished-looking, in a pale grey suit with a handkerchief in his breast pocket. His long, high-domed head was flushed. At some point his round tortoiseshell spectacles had been knocked awry.

Legat said, "May I ask who is in charge here?"

One of the Gestapo men swung round. He was broad-faced with a hard tight mouth and badly pockmarked cheeks, as if he had suffered smallpox in his youth. He looked ready for a fight. "And who are you?"

"My name is Hugh Legat. I am the Private Secretary to Prime Minister Chamberlain."

The Gestapo officer's attitude changed at once. "There is no question of imprisonment, Herr Legat. We have merely asked these gentlemen to wait in their room for their own security while the conference is in progress."

"But we are supposed to be observers at this conference!" Masarík adjusted his spectacles. "I appeal to the representative of the British Government to allow us to do what we were sent here to do."

"May I?" Legat gestured to be allowed to pass. The three other Gestapo men looked to the officer. He nodded. They stood aside. Legat shook hands with Masarík. "I'm very sorry about this. Where is your colleague?"

He followed Masarík into the bedroom. A professorial figure in his sixties, still wearing his overcoat, was seated on the edge of the bed, holding his hat between his knees. He stood as Legat entered. He looked utterly dejected. "Mastny." He held out his hand.

Masarík said, "We landed from Prague less than an hour ago and were met by these people at the airport. We assumed we were being taken directly to the conference. Instead we have been forced to remain here. It is an outrage!"

The Gestapo man was standing listening in the doorway. "As I have explained, they are not allowed to participate in the conference. My orders are that they are to wait in their hotel room until further instructions have been issued."

"Therefore we are under arrest!"

"Not at all. You are free to return to the airport and fly back to Prague whenever you wish."

Legat said, "May I ask who issued this order?"

The Gestapo officer stuck out his chest. "I believe it comes from the Führer himself."

"An outrage!"

Mastny put his hand on his younger colleague's arm. "Calm yourself, Hubert. I am more used to life in Germany than you are. There is no point in shouting." He turned to Legat. "You are the Private Secretary to Mr. Chamberlain? Perhaps you might speak to the Prime Minister on our behalf, and see if this unfortunate situation can be resolved?"

Legat looked at the two Czechs, and then at the Gestapo man who was standing with his arms folded. "Let me go and see what I can do."

The crowd in the park opposite the hotel was still large. They watched him leave without interest: yet another official in a suit; a nobody. He walked quickly, head down.

Max-Joseph-Strasse was quiet and lined with cherry trees flanked in turn by handsome apartment blocks of red and white stone. There was a smoky mellowness in the air. Pushing through the autumn drifts in the warm late-afternoon light reminded him of Oxford. Two well-dressed elderly women exercised their dogs. A uniformed nanny pushed a pram. It was only after he had been walking for about five minutes—after he had passed the obelisk in the centre of the roundabout and gone a little way towards Königsplatz—that he sensed that at some point, without noticing, he had crossed an invisible frontier into a darker and less familiar world. What he remembered as a park had become a parade ground. In a pagan temple, a black-uniformed soldier stood guard before an eternal flame.

He could tell the Führerbau by the crowd on the granite square in front of it. The building itself was classical, impersonal, of whitish stone: three storeys, with a balcony in the middle of the first where he could imagine Hitler appearing at one of those vast quasireligious spectacles that filled the newsreels. He walked past the hanging flags and the bronze eagles to the edge of the second red carpet. He explained his official status to a sentry and was allowed to pass. An officer in an SS uniform just inside the lobby checked his name on a list.

"Where would I find the British delegation?"

"On the first floor, Herr Legat, in the reception room in the far corner." The adjutant clicked his heels.

Legat climbed the wide red-marble staircase and turned right. He passed an area of low tables and armchairs and suddenly there ahead of him was Hartmann. It took him a few seconds to be sure it was actually him. He was standing, holding a cup and saucer, talking to a silver-haired man in a dark blue suit. His hair had been receding when he was at Oxford but now he was almost entirely bald. His handsome head was cocked, listening to his companion. He looked stooped, strained, weary. Yet for all that something of the old aura still hung around him, even at a distance. He spotted Legat over the other man's shoulder, registered him with a slight widening of his violet eyes and gave a barely perceptible shake of his head. Legat walked on.

Through the open door he could see Strang and Dunglass. The British party looked up as he walked in. They had spread themselves around the large room. Henderson was reading a German newspaper. Kirkpatrick had his legs stretched out and his eyes closed. Malkin had some papers on his lap. Ashton-Gwatkin appeared to be reading a volume of Japanese poetry. Strang said sharply, "Hugh? What are you doing here? I thought you were supposed to stay at the hotel?"

"I was, sir, but something's come up. The Czech delegation have arrived at the Regina Palast and they're being prevented from leaving their room."

"Prevented how?"

"By the Gestapo. They want the Prime Minister to intercede on their behalf."

There were groans from all round the room.

"The Gestapo!"

Ashton-Gwatkin muttered, "Beasts . . ."

Henderson said, "I don't see why they should imagine the PM can do anything about that."

"Even so, it will be hard to make an agreement without them." Strang sucked on the stem of his unlit pipe; it cracked and whistled. "I think you'd better go and soothe them, Frank. You know them better than the rest of us."

Ashton-Gwatkin sighed and closed his book. Legat noticed that Dunglass was craning his neck to peer along the corridor, in the manner of one of those mystified-looking birds he liked to shoot.

Kirkpatrick saw it too. "What is it, Alec? Is something happening?"

"Yes," said Dunglass. As usual he drawled without seeming to move his lips. "Hitler's door is open."

Hartmann thought that the passage of six years had barely changed Legat at all. He might have been crossing the quad at Balliol. There was the same odd combination of age and youth: the thick dark boyish hair flicked back off his forehead and the pale gravity of his expression; the lightness of his movements—he had been a runner at Oxford—encased in those stiff old-fashioned clothes. The sight of him caused Hartmann briefly to lose track of what von Weizsäcker was saying. He failed to notice Schmidt hurrying towards them.

"Herr von Weizsäcker and Signor Attolico"—Schmidt nodded to the State Secretary and beckoned to the Italian Ambassador— "excuse me, gentlemen: the Führer would like you to join the talks."

The men sitting nearest them overheard. Heads turned. Weizsäcker nodded as if he had been expecting this. "Does he want anyone else?"

"Only the British and French ambassadors."

"I'll fetch them," volunteered Hartmann. Without waiting for approval he set off towards the two delegations. He entered the French room first. "Monsieur François-Poncet?" The boulevardier's face with its old-fashioned wax moustache swung round to look at him. "Forgive me, Your Excellency, the leaders would like their ambassadors to join them." Even before François-Poncet was on his feet, Hartmann was striding next door. "Sir Nevile, a request from the Führer's study—would you please be good enough to join the heads of government?"

Strang said, "Only Sir Nevile?"

"Only Sir Nevile."

"At last!" Henderson folded his newspaper and placed it on the table. He stood and checked his buttonhole in the mirror.

Kirkpatrick said, "Good luck."

"Thanks." He sauntered out of the room.

"Does this mean there's been a breakthrough?"

"I fear I am only the messenger, Mr. Strang." Hartmann smiled and bowed slightly. He glanced around. "Are you comfortable in here? Is there anything you need?"

"We're fine, thank you, Herr—" Strang paused.

"Hartmann."

"Herr Hartmann, of course, excuse me." Hartmann waited pointedly and Strang found himself obliged to introduce his colleagues. "This is Lord Dunglass, the Prime Minister's Parliamentary Private Secretary. Sir William Malkin of the Foreign Office. Frank Ashton-Gwatkin, also of the Foreign Office. Ivone Kirkpatrick from the Berlin embassy I expect you know . . ."

"Indeed, Mr. Kirkpatrick. Very good to see you again." Hartmann went round the room shaking hands.

"And this is Hugh Legat, one of the Prime Minister's private secretaries."

"Mr. Legat."

"Herr Hartmann."

Hartmann held on to Legat's hand a fraction longer than he had the others and tugged it gently. "Well, do let me know if I can be of any assistance."

Legat said, "I should get back to the hotel."

"And I suppose I should talk to the poor old Czechos," said Ashton-Gwatkin wearily, "assuming I can find a telephone that works."

The three men went out into the corridor and walked towards Hitler's study. The door had already closed again. Hartmann said, "Let us hope some progress is being made." He stopped. "I shall look forward to seeing you later. If you'll excuse me, gentlemen?" He inclined his head graciously, turned to his left and began to descend the service stairs.

Legat continued on his way with Ashton-Gwatkin for a few more paces, then he, too, halted. "I'm sorry, I've just remembered there's something I need to tell Strang." The ploy seemed so obvious it embarrassed him, but Ashton-Gwatkin merely raised his hand in farewell—"Later, dear boy"—and carried on walking. Legat retraced his steps. Without a backward glance he followed Hartmann down the stairs.

He couldn't see him but he could hear the soles of his shoes ringing on the steps. He expected him to stop at the ground floor; instead the clatter of leather on stone continued for another two flights until Legat found himself emerging on to a basement passage just in time to catch a gleam of daylight to his right and the noise of a door slamming shut.

He preferred not to think of the absurdity of the figure he must cut—the Whitehall civil servant in his dark suit and watch chain hurrying along the subterranean service corridor of the Führer's private palace. If Cleverly could see him he would have a heart attack. *"I trust I don't need to emphasise the absolute necessity that you do nothing whatsoever that might imperil the success of this conference . . . ?"* He passed a guardroom—empty, he was relieved to see—opened the heavy steel door and stepped out into daylight and a courtyard full of black Mercedes. At the far end, Hartmann was waiting. He waved and hurried towards him. But Hartmann immediately set off again, turning right and vanishing from view.

From then on he kept consistently about a hundred yards ahead. He led Legat past the two Temples of Honour with their motionless guards and wavering flames, past another monumental white-stone Nazi building identical to the Führerbau, then out of Königsplatz altogether and into a wide street with big office blocks festooned with swastikas. Legat read their nameplates as he passed: THE OFFICE OF THE DEPUTY FÜHRER, THE REICH CENTRAL OFFICE FOR THE IMPLEMENTATION OF THE FOUR-YEAR PLAN. He glanced over his shoulder. Nobody seemed to be following him. Ahead was an ugly modern building that looked like the entrance to a railway station but advertised itself as "Park-Café." Hartmann went inside. A minute later, Legat did the same.

It was the end of the working day. The bar was crowded, mostly with workers from the nearby government offices to judge by the look of them. There were a lot of brown Party uniforms. He peered around for Hartmann through the clouds of cigarette smoke and saw his bald head in the corner. He was sitting at a table with his back to the room but facing a mirror so that he could watch what was happening. Legat slipped into the seat opposite him. Hartmann's wide mouth split into the familiar vulpine grin. "Well," he said, "here we are again, my friend," and Legat remembered that for Paul there was always amusement to be had in any situation, even this one. Then Hartmann added, more seriously, "Were you followed?"

"I don't know. I don't think so. I'm not exactly used to this sort of thing."

"Welcome to the new Germany, my dear Hugh! You'll find one has to get used to it."

The man at the next table was in an SA uniform. He was reading *Der Stürmer.* A vile caricature of a Jew with the tentacles of an octopus dominated the front page. Legat hoped the noise from the bar was too loud for them to be overheard.

He said quietly, "Is it safe here?"

"No. But safer than staying where we were. We will order two beers. We will pay for them and take them out into the garden. We will continue to speak entirely in German. We are two old friends, meeting after a long interval, with a great deal to catch up on—this much is true. Lies are always best when mostly true." He signalled to the waiter. "Two beers, please."

"You haven't changed much."

"Ah!" Hartmann laughed. "If only you knew!" He pulled out a lighter and a pack of cigarettes, offered one, leaned over and lit Legat's first and then his own. They sat back and smoked in silence for a while. Occasionally Hartmann looked at him and shook his head as if he couldn't believe it.

Legat said, "Won't they be wondering where you are?"

"One or two will no doubt be looking for me." He shrugged. "It can't be helped."

Legat continued to look around the bar. The unfamiliar tobacco was strong. It burned the back of his throat. He felt horribly exposed. "Let's hope they don't finish the talks before we get back."

"I don't think that's likely, do you? Even if there's an agreement, they're sure to be some while yet, settling all the details. And if there isn't an agreement, then it's war . . ." Hartmann flourished his cigarette. "And then you and I and our little meeting will be entirely irrelevant." He regarded Legat through the smoke. His large eyes were more hooded than Legat remembered. "I read that you had married."

"Yes. And you?"

"No."

"What happened to Leyna?" He had promised himself he wouldn't ask. Hartmann's gaze flicked away. His mood changed.

"I'm afraid we no longer speak."

The waiter arrived with their beers. He set them down and moved off to serve another customer. Legat realised he had no German money. Hartmann put a handful of coins on the table. "Have this on me—'my round,' as we used to say." He closed his eyes briefly. "The Cock and Camel. The Crown and Thistle. The Pheasant in St. Giles . . . How are they all? How is everyone? How is Isaiah?"

"It's all still there. Oxford is still there."

"Not for me, alas." He looked maudlin. "Well, I suppose we should transact our business."

The Brownshirt at the next table had paid his bill and was rising to go, leaving his newspaper on the table. Hartmann said, "Excuse me, comrade, but if you've finished with your *Stürmer*, might I take it?"

"My pleasure." The man handed it over, nodded to them affably and left.

"You see?" said Hartmann. "They're quite charming when you get to know them. Bring your beer. We'll go outside." He stubbed out his cigarette.

There were metal tables on a gravel surface beneath bare trees. The sun had gone. It would soon be dusk. The beer garden was as busy as the bar—men in lederhosen, women in dirndls. Hartmann led him over to a small table beside a bed of lavender. Beyond it was a botanical park. The neat paths and flower beds, the specimens of trees, seemed familiar. Legat said, "Haven't we been here before?"

"Yes, we sat over there and had an argument. You accused me of being a Nazi at heart."

"Did I? I'm sorry. Sometimes, to an outsider, German nationalism didn't sound that much different to Nazism."

Hartmann flicked his hand. "Let's not get into all that. There isn't time." He pulled out a chair. The steel legs scraped on the gravel.

They sat. Legat refused another cigarette. Hartmann lit one for himself. "So. Let me go straight to the point of it. I would like you to arrange for me to meet with Chamberlain."

Legat sighed. "They told me in London that was what you wanted. I'm sorry, Paul, it's just not possible."

"But you are his secretary. Secretaries arrange meetings."

"I'm the most junior of his secretaries. I fetch and carry. He'd no more listen to me than he would to that waiter over there. And besides, isn't it rather too late for meetings?"

Hartmann shook his head. "Right now, at this very moment, it is still not too late. It will only be too late after your Prime Minister has signed this agreement."

Legat cupped the beer glass in his hands and bowed his head. He remembered this absurd stubbornness, this refusal to abandon a chain of reasoning even when demonstrably it had started from a false premise. They might have been arguing in the taproom of the Eagle and Child. "Paul, I promise you, there's nothing you can say to him that he hasn't considered already. If you're going to warn him that Hitler's a bad man—save your breath. He knows it."

"Then why is he making this deal with him?"

"For all the reasons of which you're aware. Because on this issue Germany has a strong case, and the fact that it's being put by Hitler doesn't make it any weaker." He remembered now why he had accused Hartmann of being a Nazi: his main objection to Hitler always seemed to be snobbish—that he was a vulgar Austrian corporal—rather than ideological. "I must say you've changed your tune! Weren't you always going on about the injustices of the Versailles Treaty? Appeasement is simply an attempt to redress those same wrongs."

"Yes, and I stand by every word!" Hartmann leaned across the table and continued in an urgent whisper. "And there is a part of me—yes, my dear Hugh, I admit it—that rejoices that you and the French have finally had to come crawling on your hands and knees to put it right. The trouble is, you've left it too late! Overturning

Versailles—that's nothing to Hitler anymore. That's just the prelude for what is to come."

"And this is what you want to tell the Prime Minister?"

"Yes, and not just tell him—I want to show him proof. I have it here." He patted his chest. "You look amused?"

"No, not amused—I just think you're naive. If only things were that simple!"

"They are simple. If Chamberlain refuses tonight to continue to negotiate under duress, then Hitler will invade Czechoslovakia tomorrow. And the moment he issues that order, everything will change, and we in the opposition, in the Army and elsewhere, will take care of Hitler."

Legat folded his arms and shook his head. "It is at this point that I'm afraid you lose me. You want my country to go to war to prevent three million Germans joining Germany, on the off chance that you and your friends can then get rid of Hitler? Well, I have to say, from what I've seen today, he looks pretty well entrenched to me."

He stopped himself from going on, although there was plenty more he could have said. He could have asked whether it was true that Hartmann and his friends—as their emissaries in London had made clear over the summer—intended to hang on to Austria and the Sudetenland even if Hitler was deposed, and if it was also true that their aim was to restore the Kaiser, in which case what should he whisper to his father the next time he visited him, lying in an ocean of white stone crosses in a war cemetery in Flanders? He felt a spasm of irritation. *Let's just sign the bloody agreement, get back on the plane, fly out of here and leave them to get on with it.*

The electric lamps were coming on—strings of pretty yellow Chinese lanterns suspended between ornate wrought-iron poles. They glowed in the gathering dusk.

Hartmann said, "So you will not help me?"

"If you're asking me to arrange a private meeting with the Prime Minister, then I have to say no—it is impossible. On the other hand, if there's some proof of Hitler's ambitions that we ought to be aware of, then yes, if you give it to me now, I'll undertake to make sure he sees it."

"Before he signs any agreement in Munich?"

Legat hesitated. "If there's an opportunity, yes."

"Will you give me your word that you'll try?"

"Yes."

Hartmann stared at Legat for several seconds. Finally, he picked up *Der Stürmer* from the table. It was a tabloid, easy to hold in one hand. He shielded himself with it. With the other hand he began unfastening the buttons of his shirt. Legat twisted on the hard metal chair and looked around the beer garden. Everyone seemed preoccupied with their own amusement. But in the undergrowth around them any number of eyes could be watching. Hartmann folded the paper and slid it back across the table to Legat.

He said, "I should go now. You stay and finish your beer. It would be best from now on if we did not acknowledge one another."

"I understand."

Hartmann stood. It was suddenly important to Legat that things were not left like this. He stood as well. "I do appreciate—we all appreciate—the risks that you and your colleagues are taking. If things become dangerous and you need to leave Germany, I can promise you that you will be well looked after."

"I am not a traitor. I will never leave Germany."

"I know. But the offer is there."

They shook hands.

"Finish your drink, Hugh."

Hartmann turned and walked across the gravel towards the café, his tall figure moving awkwardly between the tables and chairs. There was a brief glow from the interior as he opened the door, then it closed and he was gone.

8

Legat sat motionless, watching the moths dancing around the garden lights. The smell of lavender was strong in the warm night air. After a while, cautiously, with the tip of his thumb and forefinger, he opened the newspaper. Inside, next to a story about Aryan maidens being raped by Jews, lay a plain manila envelope. Judging by its weight it contained perhaps two dozen sheets of paper. He refolded *Der Stürmer*, waited another five minutes, then rose to his feet.

He wove between the tables of beer drinkers, through the smoky bar, out of the door on its opposite side and into the street. In the big office blocks of the Deputy Führer and the Four-Year Plan the windows gleamed. He had an impression of activity, of urgent purposeful preparation. He pressed on towards Königsplatz. As he approached the building that housed the administration of the Nazi Party, a group of uniformed officials came out onto the pavement. After he had skirted them he heard one say, *"Das kann nur ein Engländer sein!"* "That can only be an Englishman!" There was laughter. On the granite parade ground, a pair of swastika banners, six storeys high, was lit by spotlights. He could see the Führerbau directly ahead. He wondered if he should return to the conference. Given what he was carrying it was surely too risky. He turned right between the Temples of Honour. A few minutes later he was pushing through the revolving door into the Regina Palast. In the lobby a string quartet played *Tales from the Vienna Woods*.

On the first-floor corridor he ran into Ashton-Gwatkin. He

stopped beneath one of the dim candelabra. "Hello, Hugh. What have you been up to?"

"Just running errands."

"I know! Isn't it awful? Nothing works. The phones are hopeless." The Walrus's heavy features were more than usually lugubrious. "I've just been in with the Czechos."

"How are they taking it?"

"As one would expect. They think the whole business stinks. I'm sure we would too, in their place. But what can one do? The situation isn't improved by the fact that the Germans still won't let them leave their room."

"Are you heading back to the conference?"

"Apparently I'm wanted. I have a car downstairs." He moved on, stopped, turned. "Incidentally, that fellow Hartmann we met earlier—wasn't he a Rhodes scholar? At our college?"

Legat saw no point in denying it. "That's right, yes."

"I thought the name was familiar. What year did they start it up again after the war? Twenty-eight?"

"Twenty-nine."

"So he must have been there in your day. Surely you knew him?"

"I did."

"But you pretended not to?"

"Obviously he doesn't want to shout about it, so I thought it wiser not to let on."

The Walrus nodded. "Quite right. This whole place is absolutely crawling with Gestapo."

He continued onwards in his stately fashion. Legat went into the corner office. Joan and Miss Anderson were sitting at the table, playing cards. He said, "Have London been on?"

Joan played a card. "Quite often, actually."

"What did you tell them?"

"That you were away from the office having to deal with the Czechs."

"You're an angel."

"I know. What on earth are you reading?"

"Sorry." He transferred the newspaper to his other hand. "It's some ghastly anti-Jew rag. I'm looking for a place to chuck it."

"Give it to me. I'll get rid of it for you."

"It's all right, thanks."

"Don't be silly. Let me take it." She held out her hand.

"Actually, I wouldn't want you to see it."

He could feel himself turning red. What a hopeless spy he was! She was looking at him as if he was very odd.

He went back out into the corridor. At the far end of the passage the two Gestapo men had found a pair of chairs and were sitting outside the Czech delegation's room. He turned left, searched his pockets for his key and opened the door to his own room. It was in darkness. Through the large window he could see lights in the rooms on the opposite side of the courtyard. Inside, several people were moving around, preparing to go out for dinner; in one a man seemed to be staring directly at him. He drew the curtains and turned on the bedside lamp. His suitcase had been brought up by a porter and placed on the small table. He threw the newspaper onto the bed, went into the bathroom, ran the cold tap and splashed his face. He felt shaky. He couldn't get the image of Hartmann out of his mind, especially his expression at the end. His eyes had seemed to stare out at him from across some vast gulf that had widened the longer they talked. He dried himself and returned to the bedroom. He locked the door. He took off his jacket and draped it over the back of the chair, picked up the newspaper, sat at the desk and turned on the green-shaded reading lamp. Finally, he opened the envelope and pulled out the pages.

The document was typed in the same large letters as the one he had received in London. The German was a hybrid of the Hitlerian and the bureaucratic, not easy to translate at first, but after a while he started to get the hang of it.

TOP SECRET
Memorandum
Berlin, 10 November 1937

Minutes of a Conference in the Reich Chancellery, Berlin,
5 November 1937 from 4:15 to 8:30 p.m.

PRESENT:

The Führer and Chancellor
Field Marshal von Blomberg, War Minister
Colonel General Baron von Fritsch, Commander-in-Chief, Army
Admiral Dr. H. C. Raeder, Commander-in-Chief, Navy
Colonel General Göring, Commander-in-Chief, Luftwaffe
Baron von Neurath, Foreign Minister
Colonel Hossbach, military adjutant to the Führer

The Führer began by stating that the subject of the present conference was of such importance that its discussion would, in
other countries, certainly be a matter for a full Cabinet meeting,
but he—the Führer—had rejected the idea of making it a subject
of discussion before the wider circle of the Reich Cabinet precisely because of the importance of the matter. His exposition
to follow was the fruit of thorough deliberation and the experiences of his four and a half years of power. He wished to explain
to the gentlemen present his basic ideas concerning the opportunities for the development of our position in the field of foreign affairs and its requirements, and he asked, in the interests
of a long-term German policy, that his exposition be regarded,
in the event of his death, as his last will and testament.

The Führer then continued:

The aim of German policy was to make secure and to preserve the racial community and to enlarge it. It was therefore
a question of space. The German racial community comprised
over 85 million people and, because of their number and the

narrow limits of habitable space in Europe, constituted a tightly packed racial core such as was not to be met in any other country and such as implied the right to a greater living space than in the case of other peoples—

Legat stopped reading and looked round. Behind him on the bedside table the telephone was ringing.

At the Führerbau things were finally beginning to happen. The door to Hitler's study was now permanently open. Hartmann watched Ashton-Gwatkin come out, followed by Malkin. François-Poncet and Attolico went in to replace them. In the gallery, around the low tables, in the pools of light from the standard lamps, armchairs had been pulled together; officials were bent over papers. He saw Erich Kordt in the centre of one group: he must have travelled down from Berlin during the afternoon. The exception to all this activity was Daladier. He seemed to have withdrawn from the proceedings entirely and was sitting alone in a corner, smoking a cigarette; on the table in front of him was a bottle of beer and a glass. The only person Hartmann couldn't see was Sauer. Where was he? He found his absence ominous.

He circled the first floor, trying to spot him. In the large room next to the French delegation's quarters, the armchairs and sofas had been pushed against the walls and a makeshift office had been set up, with typewriters and extra telephones. Next to that was the banqueting hall. Through the open door he saw a long, white-clothed table with places laid for sixty. Waiters hurried in and out carrying plates and bottles; a florist was arranging an elaborate centrepiece. Clearly a feast was in the offing. A celebration presumably, which meant they must be close to an agreement and he was nearly out of time. All his hopes now rested on Legat. But what realistic hope was there? None, he thought bitterly.

As he completed his circuit and returned to the gallery, Kordt called out to him. "Hartmann, good evening!" He rose. He was holding a sheaf of papers. "I have need of your skills. Would you mind?" He gestured with his head to a quiet corner where there was an empty table. As they sat, he said in a low voice, "Well, what happened? Did you make contact with your friend?"

"Yes."

"And?"

"He has promised to speak to Chamberlain."

"Well, he had better be quick about it. We are almost there."

Hartmann was appalled. "How can that be? I thought the conference was scheduled to last at least another day."

"It was. But I would say that in the person of the Right Honourable Neville Chamberlain, the Führer has finally met a negotiator even more obdurate than himself. The old gentleman has lured him into a morass of detail and he simply can't stand it any longer. All unresolved issues are therefore to be settled after the conference by an international commission of the four powers. In this way, each side can claim victory."

Hartmann swore and bowed his head. Kordt patted his knee. "Cheer up, my dear fellow. I feel as sick about it as you do. But we will regroup and one day we will try again. In the meantime, I advise you to look a little less funereal. The Führer's genius is about to bring three million of our fellow countrymen into the Reich without the firing of a shot. Your long face is inappropriate, and will not go unnoticed.

"Now," he said, raising his voice and becoming businesslike, "I have documents that need to be translated from English into German." He searched through his bundle of documents and pulled out several pages. In a sarcastic tone he read out the heading. " '*Annexes and supplementary declarations relating to minorities and the composition of the international commission.*' It seems our British friends are the only nation keener on paperwork than our own."

Legat picked up the telephone cautiously. "Hello?"

"Hugh?"

"Yes?"

"It's Alec Dunglass."

"Alec!" Legat was relieved. "What's going on?"

"It rather looks as though we have a deal."

"Good Lord. That was quick."

"Hitler's invited us all to some ghastly Teutonic banquet while the documents are prepared for signature but the PM thinks it will convey the wrong impression. Could you organise dinner for us at the hotel? We should be away from here by nine."

"Of course."

"Thanks so much."

Dunglass hung up.

A deal? Legat had thought the talks would grind on into the weekend. He took out his watch. It was just after 8:20. He went back to the desk, propped his head between his hands and resumed reading, but much more quickly now, turning each page as soon as he had the gist of it. The Führer's case was densely argued. It began with his analysis of Germany's increasing need for food, acknowledged the unsustainability of its economy at the present pace of rearmament and warned of the Third Reich's vulnerability to international trade sanctions and disruption of supply.

The only remedy, and one which might appear to us as visionary, lay in the acquisition of greater living space . . .

The space necessary to ensure it can only be sought in Europe . . .

It is not a matter of acquiring population but of gaining space for agricultural use . . .

Germany's problem could only be solved by means of force . . .

If the Führer was still living, it was his unalterable resolve to solve Germany's problem of space at the latest by 1943–45 . . .

Legat flicked back to the first page. *5 November 1937.* Less than eleven months ago.

> The incorporation of Austria and Czechoslovakia within Germany would provide, from the politico-military point of view, a substantial advantage, because it would mean shorter and better frontiers, the freeing of forces for other purposes, and the possibility of creating new units up to a level of about twelve divisions, that is, one new division per million inhabitants.

The second part of the memorandum recorded the ensuing discussion. It was clear, reading between the lines, that the two senior military commanders, Blomberg and Fritsch, and the Foreign Minister, Neurath, had all expressed alarm about the practicability of Hitler's strategy: the French Army was too strong, the Czech border defences were too formidable, Germany's motorised divisions were too weak . . .

All three, Legat realised, had since been removed from their positions and had been replaced by Keitel, Brauchitsch and Ribbentrop.

He pushed back his chair. Hartmann was right. The Prime Minister absolutely ought to be aware of this before he signed any agreement.

He stuffed the memorandum back into its envelope.

In the corner office, he said to Joan, "Would you do me a favour? The PM and the others will be on their way back in about half an hour. Could you see if the hotel could rustle up some supper for everyone?"

"All right, I'll see what I can do. Anything else?"

"Yes, could you get a message to Sir Alexander Cadogan at the Foreign Office? Just tell him I have it."

"You have what?"

"No need to say any more. He'll understand."

"Where are you off to now?"

Legat was unlocking one of the red dispatch boxes. "I'm going to head back to the conference for a minute. There's a document I think the PM ought to see."

He half-walked, half-ran along the corridor. He didn't wait for the lift but instead trotted down the stairs, marched across the lobby and plunged into the Munich evening.

Hartmann was translating the "Supplementary Declaration" from English into German—*all questions which may arise out of the transfer of the territory shall be considered as coming within the terms of reference of the international commission*—when he glanced up and saw Legat striding purposefully towards the room where the British delegation was based. He was carrying a small red case.

The room was empty apart from Dunglass. He stared at Legat in surprise. "I thought I told you we were coming back to the hotel?"

"Something's come up. I need to have a quick word with the PM."

"Well, you can try, but he's still in with the other leaders."

"Where is he?"

Dunglass raised his eyebrows slightly—the closest he came to expressing strong emotion—and pointed to the door at the end of the corridor. It looked like the entrance to a hive—men hovering around it, going in and coming out.

"Thanks."

Legat set off. No one tried to stop him.

The four Heads of Government here present agree that the international commission provided for in the agreement signed by them today shall consist of the Secretary of State in the German Foreign Office, the British, French and Italian Ambassadors accredited to Berlin, and a representative to be nominated by the Government of Czechoslovakia.

Even while his pen moved across the paper, Hartmann's eyes were following Legat as he entered Hitler's study.

The room was large—perhaps fifty feet long—crowded, stuffy. The tall windows were all closed. There was a faint sour odour of male sweat. The Prime Minister was on the sofa in front of the fireplace, talking to Mussolini. Legat could see Wilson in the corner by the window with Sir Nevile Henderson. And at the far end, beside a giant globe, with his arms folded, leaning against the edge of a desk, listening to Ribbentrop and wearing an expression of utter boredom, he could see Hitler. After their first meeting Chamberlain had described him to the Cabinet as "the commonest little dog you ever saw." The Cabinet Secretary had cleaned this up in the minutes to read "there was nothing out of the common about his features." Legat had thought it snobbish at the time but now he could see what the Prime Minister had meant. It was almost compelling how nondescript he was—more so even than when he had glimpsed him in the street six years earlier. He looked like a lodger who always kept himself to himself, or a nightwatchman who disappeared in the morning as soon as the day shift arrived. He found it hard to drag his gaze away and, when he did, he realised that the gathering was breaking up. People were moving towards the door. Chamberlain was already on his feet.

He made haste to intercept him. "Excuse me, Prime Minister."

"Yes?" The Prime Minister turned round.

"I wondered if I could trouble you for a moment?"

Chamberlain glanced at him and then at the red box. "No," he said irritably. "Not now."

He walked out of the room. Almost at once Legat felt someone come up behind him and grip his elbow. Wilson's voice was a warm breath in his ear.

"Hugh? What on earth are you doing here?"

The other delegates continued to leave, stepping around them to get to the door.

"I'm sorry, sir. Lord Dunglass told me there was an agreement so I came to see if I could be of any assistance." He lifted the red box. "Carrying papers back to the hotel and so forth."

"Is that so?" Wilson looked sceptical. "Well, you could have saved yourself the journey. The deed is done."

Hartmann watched them emerge from the study—Chamberlain first, with Henderson, and then the French diplomats: Rochat, Clapier, François-Poncet . . . Léger peeled away from the others and went over to fetch Daladier, still sitting in the corner with his beer. The French Prime Minister slowly got to his feet. Then Legat came out with Wilson, who was holding his elbow like a plainclothes detective who had made an arrest. They passed within a few paces of him. Legat glanced briefly in Hartmann's direction but did not acknowledge him. After a few minutes Hitler appeared with Mussolini, followed by Ciano and Ribbentrop. They walked off in the direction of the big dining room.

Hartmann tried to interpret the meaning of the little pantomime he had just witnessed: Legat presumably had read the memorandum, had brought it to the Führerbau and had tried to speak to Chamberlain about it but had arrived too late. That seemed the most logical explanation.

An adjutant came over and collected his translations. Then suddenly Kordt was bearing down upon him, waving him urgently to his feet. "Hartmann, come with us. Hurry up and straighten your tie. We've been asked to join the Führer for dinner."

"Really, Kordt? How appalling. I never dine with people I hardly know."

"It isn't optional. These are Weizsäcker's orders: the British and the French won't eat with the Führer and so it is necessary for us to make up the numbers. Come." He held out his hand.

Reluctantly Hartmann rose and together they walked around the first floor towards the other side of the building. He said, "Are the British and the French coming back tonight?"

"Yes, after dinner, to sign the agreement."

So it was not entirely done yet, thought Hartmann, although the chances of disruption were so tiny he rather despised himself for even considering them. Nevertheless, he managed to force a more neutral expression onto his face as he entered the room.

Hitler was seated in the centre of the immense table with his back to the windows. Mussolini and Ciano were on either side, Weizsäcker and Ribbentrop directly across from him. His guests were being served wine; he had a bottle of mineral water. As Hartmann crossed the long, panelled salon he noted those he recognised—Göring, Himmler, Hess, Keitel, Attolico—perhaps sixteen men in all. No sign of Sauer.

It was far too small a group for such a big space; the atmosphere was awkward. Waiters were clearing away the settings from either end of the table. Hartmann took a chair on the opposite side to Hitler, as far away from him as he could get, next to the Italian, Anfuso, who was head of the Foreign Ministry in Rome. Even so, he was close enough to the Führer to be able to observe him quite plainly—moodily picking at a roll and making little attempt at conversation. He looked as if he was brooding on this snub from the British and the French. The silence seemed to infect those around him. Even Göring was muted. Only when bread soup was served did the Führer appear to brighten somewhat. He sipped at it and then dabbed his moustache with his napkin.

"Duce," he began, "do you not agree that one may observe the decay of a race in the faces of its leaders?" The remark was ostensibly a question, and in theory directed at Mussolini, but posed in a voice sufficiently loud to carry across the table, and in a tone that implied no answer was required. Other conversations fell silent. He sipped a little more soup. "Daladier to some extent I exempt from this rule.

The French are undoubtedly decadent—Léger is from Martinique and plainly has Negroid ancestry—but Daladier's appearance possesses character. He was an old soldier, just like you and I, Duce. Daladier—yes, one can get on with him well enough. He sees things as they are and draws the proper conclusions."

Mussolini said, "He just wanted to drink his beer and let his advisers get on with it."

Hitler seemed not to have heard him. "But Chamberlain!" He pronounced the name with sarcastic distaste, extending the vowels so that it sounded like an obscenity. "This 'Chamberlain' haggles over every village and petty interest like a market stallkeeper! Do you know, gentlemen, he wanted assurances that the Czech farmers expelled from the Sudetenland would be permitted to take their pigs and cows with them? Can you imagine the bourgeois triviality of a mind that can be bothered with such details? He demanded indemnities for every public building!"

Mussolini cut in, "I enjoyed François-Poncet's remark: 'What? Even the public lavatories?' "

There was laughter around the table.

Hitler was not to be deflected: "Chamberlain! He was even worse than the Czechs would have been! What has he got to lose in Bohemia? What's it to do with him? He asked me if I liked to fish at weekends. I never have weekends—and I hate fishing!"

More laughter. Ciano said, "Do you know what they call him in Paris? 'J'aime Berlin!' "

Hitler scowled at him. He was clearly annoyed at these interruptions. Mussolini gave his son-in-law a reproving look. The smile shrank on Ciano's full lips. The Führer resumed. "It's time Britain learned she has no right to play governess to Europe. If she can't stop interfering, then in the long run war cannot be avoided. And I'll fight that war as long as you and I are still young, Duce, because this war will be a gigantic test of strength for our two countries, and it will call for men in the prime of life at the head of their respective governments—not these decadent pinheaded old women and Negroes!"

There was much applause and banging of the table. Hartmann glanced across at Kordt but he was examining his soup plate. Suddenly he could take it no longer. As the waiters surrounded the table to clear away the first course he laid down his napkin and pushed back his chair. He had hoped he might be able to sidle away unnoticed but just as he was rising to his feet Hitler glanced along the table and noticed him. A puzzled look crossed his face. How dare someone leave when he was speaking?

Hartmann paused in mid-crouch. "My Führer, excuse me. I am needed to help with the translation of the agreement."

A finger was raised. "One moment." Hitler leaned back in his seat and summoned a white-jacketed SS adjutant who stepped smartly to his side. Hartmann slowly straightened. He was aware of all eyes on him. Mussolini, Göring, Himmler—all seemed faintly amused by his predicament. Only Kordt looked rigid with horror. The adjutant began moving around the table towards him. After what seemed to him a long time but in reality must have been only a matter of seconds the adjutant reached Hartmann and presented him with his watch. As Hartmann left the room he heard the familiar voice rasping behind him. "I never forget a personal obligation. For Germany I am prepared to be dishonest a thousand times; for myself—never."

9

Legat had been sent on ahead in the first car by Wilson to make sure the Prime Minister's dinner arrangements were all in hand. He had spoken to the manager, who had assured him a private room had been made ready on the ground floor. Now he waited by the entrance of the Regina Palast for the return of the rest of the British delegation. He felt he had made the most appalling fool of himself. Wilson had been perfectly civil about it but that was almost the worst thing. He could imagine "words being had" when they returned to London: a brief conversation between Cleverly and Cadogan, a discreet summons to the Principal Private Secretary's office, a posting to somewhere less high-pressure, a legation perhaps. And yet stubbornly he remained certain his duty was clear. Chamberlain should be made aware of the existence of the memorandum before the agreement was signed.

The convoy of Mercedes limousines roared into Maximilians-platz to even louder cheers from the crowd opposite. If anything, the numbers and the excitement seemed to be growing in anticipation of the announcement of a deal. As the Prime Minister, accompanied by Dunglass, entered through the revolving door, the hotel guests, many in evening dress, stood and applauded him across the lobby while the string quartet played "For He's a Jolly Good Fellow." Chamberlain nodded to left and right and smiled, but the moment he reached the sanctuary of the dining room he flopped down into the large gilt chair at the head of the central table and asked in a hoarse voice for a whisky and soda.

Legat set down the red box and went over to the tray of bottles arranged on one of the side tables. The walls were mirrored panes, Versailles-style, with electric candles in sconces. As he squirted the soda into the tumbler he was able to keep an eye on Chamberlain in his seat beneath the chandelier. The Prime Minister's chin slowly tilted forward onto his chest.

Dunglass put his finger to his lips and the others came in quietly—Wilson, Strang, Ashton-Gwatkin, Henderson, Kirkpatrick. Only Malkin had not returned to the hotel: he had stayed behind to oversee the final drafting. They tiptoed around the Prime Minister, speaking in whispers. The Scotland Yard detective closed the door and stationed himself outside. Wilson came over to Legat. He nodded towards Chamberlain and said quietly, "He's in his seventieth year, been up for fifteen hours, flown six hundred miles and endured two negotiating sessions with Adolf Hitler. I think he's entitled to feel tired, don't you?" He sounded protective. He took the whisky and soda and placed it gently in front of the Prime Minister. Chamberlain opened his eyes and peered around him in surprise, then sat up straight in his chair.

"Thank you, Horace." He reached for the glass. "Well, that was pretty good hell, I must say."

"Still, it's done, and I don't think anyone could have handled it better."

Henderson said, "Oceans of ink will flow in criticism of your actions, Prime Minister. But millions of mothers will be blessing your name tonight for having saved their sons from the horror of war."

Dunglass said quietly, "Hear, hear."

"You're very kind." The Prime Minister finished his whisky and soda and held out his glass for a refill. He was visibly reviving, like a drooping flower given fresh water. Colour infused his gaunt grey cheeks. Legat fixed him a fresh drink, then stepped out of the room to see what had become of their food. A few guests loitered outside. They tried to peer round him to get a glimpse of Chamberlain. Approaching across the lobby was a line of waiters bearing silver-covered dishes like trophies above their heads.

Dinner was chanterelle soup followed by veal and noodles. At first the conversation was constrained by the presence of the waiters until Wilson asked Legat to tell them to leave. But as soon as the door had closed, and the Prime Minister had started to ask if there was any news from London, Kirkpatrick pointed at the ceiling. "Excuse me, sir, before you go on, I think it would be wise to assume every word we utter is being overheard."

"I don't care if it is. I'm not going to say anything behind Hitler's back I haven't said to his face." He laid down his knife and fork. "Has anyone spoken to Edward or Cadogan?"

Henderson said, "I spoke to the Foreign Secretary. He was most encouraged by the news."

Wilson said, "What we require, Prime Minister, if I may say so, is a point-by-point list of all the concessions you have succeeded in wringing out of the Germans, compared with what they were demanding before we came to Munich. That will be very useful for dealing with any criticism when we get back to London."

Strang said, with a trace of scepticism, "So there have been concessions?"

"Oh, indeed, and they are not negligible. A phased occupation by October the tenth rather than invasion on the first. An orderly evacuation of the Czech minority under international supervision. A mechanism for settling any disputes that may arise."

"I wonder if the Czechs will see it like that."

"The Czechs," murmured Chamberlain. He had lit a cigar and pushed back his chair. "We have rather forgotten about the Czechs." He turned to Legat. "Where are they now?"

"Still in their room, Prime Minister, as far as I know."

"You see—now why does Hitler have to treat them like that? It's so impolite. It's so *unnecessary,* as much as anything else."

Henderson said, "You have prevented him from bombing them, Prime Minister, which is what he most wanted to do. Therefore, all he can do now is inflict petty humiliations upon them. They should be grateful they are not confined to an air-raid shelter."

"But suppose, after the way they've been treated, they reject the agreement? Then we shall all be in the most frightful mess."

A brief silence fell over the room.

Wilson said grimly, "Leave the Czechs to me. I shall explain the realities of the situation. Meanwhile, you should go and rest before the signing ceremony: I expect there will be photographers. Hugh, will you go and fetch the Czechs?"

"Of course, Sir Horace."

Legat put down his napkin. His meal was entirely untouched.

Hartmann closed the door of the banqueting hall and stopped to fasten his watch. It was twenty minutes to ten. From the office along the corridor came the faint sound of typing; a telephone rang.

Again he took the service stairs, descending all the way to the basement. He turned right along the passage, past the noisy kitchens and through the smoky, steamy cafeteria filled as usual with soldiers and drivers. He went past the guardroom and out into the courtyard. He lit a cigarette. The cars were mostly unattended, parked bumper to bumper; the keys were in the ignitions. It crossed his mind to borrow one but he decided against it: better to take his chances on foot. The clouds were low, holding in the heat of the day. The sky was feverish with the reflected light from the spotlights trained on the swastikas in Königsplatz. He could hear the noise of the crowd.

He set off towards the street. He had an uneasy sense that he was being watched or followed. But when he looked back all he could see were the gleaming rows of black limousines and the massive shape of the Führerbau looming above them. The lights were burning in the tall windows. He could clearly make out the banqueting hall because of the figures of the waiters passing back and forth, where no doubt Hitler was continuing to expatiate on the degeneracy of the democracies.

Legat had braced himself for an argument with the Gestapo men guarding the Czech delegation. But when he explained, in his stiff German, that the British Prime Minister wished to brief the representatives of the Czech Government on the progress of the talks, he was told that this was permissible, providing the gentlemen did not attempt to leave the hotel.

He knocked on the door. It was opened by Masarík, the Foreign Ministry official from Prague. He was in his shirtsleeves. So too was the older man, Mastny, the Czech Minister in Berlin. The room was full of cigarette smoke even though the window had been thrown wide open. On the bed was a chess set: a game was in progress. Mastny was sitting on the edge of the mattress, one leg folded across the other, his chin resting in the palm of his hand, studying the position of the pieces. On the desk were the remains of a meal. Masarík saw Legat glance at it. "Oh yes," he said scathingly, "you may inform the Red Cross that the prisoners have been fed."

"Sir Horace Wilson would like to talk to you."

"Only Wilson? What about the Prime Minister?"

"He is busy, I'm afraid."

Masarík said something to Mastny in Czech. Mastny shrugged and made a brief reply. They started putting on their jackets. Mastny said, "It will be exercise, at least. We have been held in here for nearly five hours."

"I'm sorry for the whole situation. The Prime Minister has been doing everything he can."

He led them out into the corridor. The Gestapo men followed close behind. He decided to conduct them round to the rear of the hotel and down the back stairs: he didn't want them accidentally running into the Prime Minister. It was shabbier at the back than the front. The Czechs, alert for any fresh slight, noticed immediately. Masarík laughed. "They are making us use the servants' entrance, Vojtek!" Legat winced. He was glad he had his back to them. The whole business was becoming increasingly embarrassing. The logic of the British position was in theory impeccable. But it was one thing to adjust lines on a map in Downing Street, another to come to Germany and do it face-to-face. He thought of the memorandum lying downstairs in the Prime Minister's red box: *The incorporation of Austria and Czechoslovakia within Germany would provide, from the politico-military point of view, a substantial advantage, because it would mean shorter and better frontiers, the freeing of forces for other purposes . . .*

The private dining room was empty apart from Wilson and Ashton-Gwatkin and a couple of waiters clearing away the dirty plates. Wilson was smoking a cigarette—a thing Legat had never seen him do before. When Ashton-Gwatkin introduced him to the Czechs he transferred the cigarette to his left hand and showered ash onto the carpet. "Let's sit down, shall we?" The waiters left. Ashton-Gwatkin handed him a small rolled-up map. Wilson brushed a few fragments of food from the tablecloth and spread it out. Legat stood behind him.

"Well, gentlemen, this is the best we were able to do for you."

The territories that were to be transferred to Germany were marked in red. The eastern half of the country was mostly unscathed; in the western half, however, three large chunks along the border around the cities of Eger, Aussig and Troppau had been excised, like bites from a piece of meat. An area to the south, adjacent to what had once been Austria, was shaded a lighter pink: its fate, Wilson explained, was to be settled by plebiscite.

At first the Czechs seemed too stunned to speak. Then Masarík burst out: "You have given the Germans everything they asked for!"

"We have only agreed to the transfer of those areas where a majority of the population is German."

"But with them go all our border fortifications—it renders our country indefensible."

"I'm afraid you shouldn't have built your fortifications in areas which were bound to be disputed once Germany was back on her feet."

Wilson lit another cigarette. Legat noticed that his hand was shaking slightly. It was a brutal business, even for him.

Mastny pointed to the map. "Here, at the narrowest point, Czechoslovakia will only be forty-five miles across. The Germans will be able to cut our country in half within a day."

"I am not responsible for the realities of geography, Your Excellency."

"Yes, of course, I understand that. However, the government of France assured us that after any agreement our borders would still be defensible—that geographic, economic and political realities, as well as race, would be taken into consideration."

Wilson spread his hands. "What can I say? Hitler takes the view that this has been the original sin with Czechoslovakia from the start—that yours is an economic and political unit and not a nation. Race for him is the sine qua non. He is unyielding on the point."

"I am sure he would yield if the British and French stood firm."

Wilson smiled and shook his head. "You were not in the room, Mr. Mastny. Believe me, he *hates* the fact that he's even having to negotiate on this issue *at all.*"

"It is not a negotiation. It is a capitulation."

"I disagree. This is the best deal we're going to get. Ninety percent of your country will remain intact and you will not be invaded. Now I suggest you talk to your government in Prague and advise them to accept it."

Masarík said, "And if we refuse?"

Wilson sighed. He turned to Ashton-Gwatkin. "Why don't you spell it out, Frank? I don't seem to be getting through."

"If you refuse," said Ashton-Gwatkin slowly, "then you will have to settle your affairs with the Germans absolutely on your own. That is the reality. Perhaps the French may tell you this more gently but you can take it from us that they share our views. They are disinterested."

The Czechs looked at one another. They seemed to have run out of things to say. Finally, Mastny gestured to the map. "May we take this?"

Wilson said, "Of course." He carefully rolled it up and handed it over. "Hugh, will you show our friends back to their room, and ask if they might be allowed to use the telephone?"

Legat picked up the Prime Minister's red box and opened the door. In the corridor the two Gestapo men were waiting. He stood aside to let the Czechs pass. Wilson called after them, "I shall make sure the Prime Minister sees you personally to explain everything once the agreement is signed."

Legat barely heard him. Across the lobby, beyond the potted palms, standing by the reception desk and talking to the concierge, was the unmistakable tall figure of Paul Hartmann.

It took Legat a few seconds to recover his equilibrium. He said to the senior of the Gestapo men, "It is imperative that Herr Masarík and Dr. Mastny are allowed to speak to their government in Prague as soon as possible. I trust I can rely on you to see that this is done." Without waiting for a reply he set off across the foyer towards Hartmann. Hartmann saw him coming. But instead of indicating some discreet corner where they might talk, as Legat had expected him to do, he advanced towards him.

"Have you read it?"

"Yes."

"Have you spoken to Chamberlain?"

"Keep your voice down. No, not yet."

"Then I must do it immediately. He is on the third floor, yes?" He moved towards the stairs.

"Paul, for God's sake, don't be stupid!" Legat hurried after him. At the bottom of the staircase he caught his arm. He was smaller than Hartmann, and the German was determined, but at that instant his desperation made him the stronger, and he stopped him. "Wait a minute. There's no point in being a bloody fool." He spoke quietly.

He was aware of people looking at them. "We need to talk about this."

Hartmann turned to address him. "I will not have it on my conscience that I did nothing."

"I understand entirely. I feel the same way. I've already tried to raise it with him once and I promise you I'll try again."

"Then let us do it together now."

"No."

"Why not?"

Legat hesitated.

Hartmann said, "You see? You have no answer!" He brought his face very close to Legat's. "Or are you worried it will damage your career?"

He began to climb the stairs. After a moment, Legat followed him. The jibe had stung. Why? Because it had an element of truth? He tried to work out where everyone was. Wilson and Ashton-Gwatkin were still in the dining room, although they would no doubt be leaving at any minute. Malkin was at the conference. The others were probably in their rooms, or in the office trying to talk to London. The Prime Minister was supposed to be resting. It might just be possible.

"All right," he said. "Let me see what I can do."

Hartmann's face broke into the familiar wide smile. At Oxford someone once said you could warm your hands at it. "You are a good man, Hugh."

They climbed the stairs to the third floor. Halfway along the corridor the Scotland Yard detective was in his usual position, stationed outside the Prime Minister's suite. Legat was regretting his decision already. He said, "I warn you—he is old and obstinate and exhausted, and pretty close to the end of his tether. If he does agree to see you, don't for God's sake give him a moral lecture. Just give him the facts. Wait here."

He nodded to the policeman and knocked on the door. In his anxiety he realised he was twisting his hands together. He thrust them into his pockets. The door was opened by the Prime Minister's doctor, Sir Joseph Horner of University College Hospital. He was holding a black rubber bulb attached to a rubber tube with a pressure gauge. Behind him, Legat could see Chamberlain, without his jacket, his right shirt sleeve rolled above his elbow.

Legat said, "I'm very sorry, Prime Minister. I can come back later."

"No, come in. I was just having my blood pressure checked. We've finished, haven't we?"

"Indeed, Prime Minister."

Horner began packing his stethoscope and sphygmomanometer into his Gladstone bag. Legat had never seen Chamberlain without his jacket before. His arm was surprisingly muscular. He rolled down his sleeve and fastened his cuff. "So, Hugh?"

Legat placed the red box on the desk and unlocked it. He waited until Chamberlain had put his jacket back on and Horner had left the room with a grave "Good night, Prime Minister."

"We have come into possession of a document which I think is significant." He handed Chamberlain the memorandum.

The Prime Minister gave him a puzzled look. He put on his spectacles and flicked through the pages. "What is it?"

"It appears to be the minute of a meeting Hitler held with his senior military commanders last November, in which he explicitly commits himself to war."

"And how has it come to us?"

"A friend of mine—a German diplomat—gave it to me this evening in strict confidence."

"Really? Why does he wish us to have it?"

"I think perhaps he should explain that himself. He's waiting outside."

"He's *here*?" The Prime Minister glanced up sharply. "Does Sir Horace know about this, or Strang?"

"No, sir. Nobody knows."

"I'm astonished to hear it. This is not how these matters are supposed to be handled." He was frowning. "You are aware of the chain of command? You are exceeding your authority, young man."

"I understand that, sir. But it seemed to me important. He is risk-ing his life and he asked to see you alone."

"I shouldn't have anything to do with it. This really is most improper." He took off his spectacles and gazed into the middle dis-tance. He tapped his foot a couple of times in irritation. "Very well," he said. "Bring him in. But five minutes—no longer."

Legat went to the door, opened it and beckoned to Hartmann, who was waiting at the end of the corridor. He said to the detective, "It's all right, I know him," then stood aside to let Hartmann enter. "Five minutes," he whispered. He closed the door. "Prime Minister, this is Paul von Hartmann of the German Foreign Ministry."

Chamberlain shook his hand briefly, as if prolonged contact might be contaminating. "Good evening." He gestured towards a seat. "Make it quick."

Hartmann remained standing. "I won't sit, Prime Minister, as I don't wish to take up any more of your time than is necessary. I thank you for seeing me."

"I am not sure it is very wise, for either of us. But you'd better get on with it."

"That document in your hands is conclusive proof that when Hitler claims to have 'no further territorial demands in Europe' he is lying. On the contrary: he plans a war of conquest to gain living space for the German people. This war will be launched at a minimum within the next five years. The incorporation of Austria and Czechoslova-kia is merely the first step. Those who expressed reservations—the commanders of the Army and the Foreign Minister—have all been replaced. I bring this information to you in good faith, and at grave risk to myself, because I wish to urge you—even at this eleventh hour—not to sign the agreement tonight. It will make Hitler's posi-tion in Germany unassailable. Whereas, if Britain and France were to stand firm, I am certain the Army would move against him in order to prevent a disastrous war."

Chamberlain crossed his arms and regarded him for a few mo-ments. "Young man, I applaud your courage and your sincerity, but

I'm afraid you need to learn a few lessons in political reality. It is simply impossible to expect the peoples of Britain and France to take up arms to deny the right of self-determination to ethnic Germans who are trapped in a foreign country they wish to leave. Against that single reality, all else fails. As for what Hitler dreams of doing in the next five years—well, we shall have to wait and see. He's been making these threats ever since *Mein Kampf*. My objective is clear: to avert war in the short term, and then to try to build a lasting peace for the future—one month at a time, one day at a time, if needs be. The worst act I could possibly commit for the future of mankind would be to walk away from this conference tonight.

"Now," he went on, folding up the memorandum, "I advise you to take this document, which is the property of your government, and return it to wherever it came from."

He tried to pass it over but Hartmann refused to take it. He put his hands behind his back and shook his head. "No, Prime Minister. Keep it. Have your experts study it. *That* is the political reality."

Chamberlain drew back. "Now you are being impertinent."

"I have no wish to be offensive, but I came to speak frankly, and I have done so. I believe that what is being done here will one day come to be seen as infamous. Well, that is my five minutes, I suppose." And to Legat's astonishment, he smiled—but a terrible smile, full of agony and despair. "Thank you for your time, Prime Minister." He bowed. "I didn't have much hope for anything better. Hugh."

He nodded at Legat, turned smartly, like a soldier on a parade ground, and walked out of the room, closing the door carefully.

Chamberlain glared after him for a few moments, then turned on Legat. "Get rid of this at once." He thrust the memorandum into his hands. His voice was cold, hard, precise: on the edge of a fury that was all the more alarming for being so tightly controlled. "I simply cannot allow myself to be distracted by what may or may not have been said at a private meeting a year ago. The situation is entirely altered since last November."

"Yes, Prime Minister."

"We will not speak of this again."

"No, sir."

Legat moved to collect the red box from the desk but Chamberlain stopped him. "Leave it. Go." And when he reached the door, the Prime Minister added, "I have to say I am extremely disappointed in you."

The chilly words were pronounced like a professional death sentence. Legat went out quietly into the corridor, a highflyer in the British civil service no longer.

10

Hartmann was certain from the moment he left the hotel that he was being followed. He had an animal's sixth sense—a kind of prickling along his spine—of being stalked by a predator. But there were too many people around for him to be able to recognise his pursuer. The small park opposite the Regina Palast was spilling over with the Oktoberfest crowd. The night was warm enough for the women still to be wearing dresses with bare arms. A lot of the men were drunk. In Karolinenplatz, an impromptu folk choir had formed beneath the obelisk and a red-faced man with a chamois plume in his hat was waving his hands wildly in an attempt to conduct them.

He walked quickly. The fools, he thought. They imagined they were celebrating peace. They had no idea what their beloved Führer had planned for them. When a couple of young women on Brienner Strasse suddenly blocked his path and invited him to join them he pushed his way past them without a word. They jeered at his back. He put his head down. *Fools.* And the greatest fool of all was Chamberlain. He stopped beneath a bare tree to light a cigarette and discreetly checked the road behind him. He allowed himself a certain bitter satisfaction—when all was said and done, he had at least got in to deliver his warning to the British Prime Minister. That was something! He could still see the affronted expression on that narrow provincial face when he had refused to take back the memorandum. Poor Hugh, standing next to him, had looked stricken. Perhaps he had ruined his career? Too bad. It could not be helped. But still he felt a pang of guilt.

He glanced over his shoulder again. A figure was approaching. Despite the heat he was wearing a belted brown raincoat. As he passed, Hartmann had a glimpse of a badly pockmarked cheek. Gestapo, he thought. They had their own smell. And they were like rats: if there was one, there would be more. He waited until the man had reached the edge of Königsplatz and had passed out of sight beyond one of the Temples of Honour, then he threw away his cigarette and set off in the direction of the Führerbau.

The crowd here was much larger—several thousand at least—but more sober, as befitted their proximity to the spiritual heart of the Reich. Hartmann climbed the red-carpeted steps and went into the foyer. As it had been in the morning, it was packed with Nazi worthies. The din of braying voices echoed off the marble. He searched the porcine faces of the old comrades, and the smoother educated countenances of those who had joined the Party since 1933, until he thought he saw the pockmarks of his pursuer. But when he moved towards him, the Gestapo man vanished into the cloakroom. The sheer clumsiness of it infuriated him as much as anything else. He went to the foot of the staircase and waited. Sure enough, after a couple of minutes, the black-uniformed figure of Sauer came through the door. Hartmann moved to block his path.

"Good evening, Herr Sturmbannführer."

Sauer nodded warily. "Hartmann."

"I have missed you for most of the day."

"Indeed?"

"You know, I have the strangest feeling? Perhaps you can set my mind at rest? I have a sense that you've been following me."

For a moment Sauer looked taken aback. Then outrage flashed across his face. "You have some nerve, Hartmann!"

"Well? Have you?"

"Yes, since you raise the matter—I have been investigating your activities."

"That is not a very comradely thing to do."

"I have every justification. As a result, I now know all about you and your English friend."

"I presume you mean Herr Legat?"

"Legat—yes. Legat!"

Hartmann said calmly, "We were at Oxford together."

"I know that. From 1930 until 1932. I have spoken to the personnel department of the Foreign Ministry. I have also contacted our embassy in London, who were able to establish that Legat and you were actually in the same college."

"If you'd asked me I could have saved you the trouble. It amounts to nothing."

"If that was all there was, I might agree. But I have also discovered that Herr Legat was not on the original list of British delegates that was telegraphed to Berlin last night. His name was only added this morning. A colleague of his, a Herr Syers, was supposed to be coming."

Hartmann tried not to show his alarm. "I fail to see the significance."

"Your behaviour at the station in Kufstein—telephoning Berlin to discover who would be coming from London: it struck me at the time as suspicious. Why would you be so concerned? Why were you even on board the Führer's train in the first place? I now believe it was because you had requested that Legat should come to Munich, and you wanted to make sure that he was on Chamberlain's plane."

"You overestimate my influence, Herr Sturmbannführer."

"I am not suggesting you arranged it personally—some member of your group would have made the request on your behalf. Oh yes, don't look surprised—we are aware of what is going on. We are not the fools you take us for."

"I should hope not."

"And now you have been observed leaving the Führerbau by a back entrance in order to walk to the hotel of the British delegation, where I saw you in the lobby with my own eyes, in conversation with Herr Legat, before disappearing together upstairs. The whole thing stinks of treachery."

"Two old friends happen to meet after a long interval. They take advantage of a lull in official business to renew their acquaintance. Where is the evidence of treachery? You are embarrassing yourself, Herr Sturmbannführer."

"The English are inherently hostile to the Reich. Unauthorised contacts between officials are highly suspicious."

"I have been doing nothing more than the Führer has been doing with Herr Chamberlain all afternoon—finding areas of common ground."

For a moment it occurred to Hartmann that Sauer was about to hit him. "We'll see whether you're so sure of yourself after I have brought the matter to the attention of the Foreign Minister."

"Hartmann!"

The shout carried clearly over the hubbub in the foyer. Both men looked around to see where it was coming from.

"Hartmann!"

He glanced up. Schmidt was leaning over the balustrade, gesturing for him to join him.

"Excuse me, Sturmbannführer. I'll wait to hear from you and the Minister."

"You will—you can be sure of it."

Hartmann began to climb the stairs. His legs felt weak. He ran his hand up the cold marble banister, glad of its support. He had been careless. The former automobile salesman from Essen was proving a dogged adversary, and no fool. There must be so many pieces of circumstantial evidence he had left behind him—unguarded conversations, meetings that might have been observed. And his relationship with Frau Winter—how many people in Wilhelmstrasse had guessed at that? He wondered how robustly he would withstand interrogation. One never knew.

Schmidt was waiting for him on the first floor. He looked crumpled. The effort of interpreting between four different languages, and of simply maintaining order long enough for his translations to be heard, had obviously drained him. He said, testily, "I have been looking for you. Where have you been?"

"The British raised a query about one of the translations. I went to their hotel to sort it out with them directly."

Another lie that could easily come back to trap him. But for now it seemed to satisfy Schmidt. He nodded. "Good. The agreements are still being typed. When the delegations return for the signing, you will have to be on hand to translate."

"Of course."

"Also, first thing tomorrow morning, you will be needed back here to prepare the English-language press summary for the Führer. The telegrams will be collated in the office. You will need to get some sleep if you can. There is a room for you at the Vier Jahreszeiten."

Hartmann could not hide his alarm. "Now that we're no longer on the train I thought the summary would be handled by the press department?"

"Normally, yes. So you should be honoured. The Führer himself has requested that you should do it. You seem to have made an impression. He called you 'the young man with the watch.'"

In the lobby of the Regina Palast, the Prime Minister's party was queuing to file out through the revolving door. Chamberlain was already on the pavement: Legat could hear the crowd in the park cheering him. Strang said, "I haven't seen you for a while. I was starting to think you'd decided to sit this one out."

"No, sir. My apologies."

"Not that I'd have blamed you. I wouldn't have minded missing it myself."

They went out into the tumult of the night—the revving engines of the big Mercedes, car doors slamming along the length of the convoy, shouts, white flashbulbs, red brake lights and yellow headlights. Somewhere in the darkness a whistle blew.

For more than an hour, Legat had been expecting the blow to fall. He had sat in the corner office, dictating to a clerk in the Foreign Office the latest amendments to the agreement, his ears cocked for voices in the corridor, waiting for the summons, the dressing down, the dismissal. Nothing. Now Wilson was settling the Prime Minister into the back of the first car. When he had finished he swung round. He noticed Legat. This must be it, thought Legat, and he braced himself, but Wilson merely grinned. "Hello, Hugh. Coming to witness history being made?"

"Yes, Sir Horace. If that's all right."

"Of course it's all right."

Legat watched him move quickly round to the other side of the car. His friendliness was bewildering.

Strang said, "Come on, Hugh. Look lively! Why don't you ride with me?"

They climbed into the third Mercedes. Henderson and Kirkpatrick were in the car in front; Ashton-Gwatkin and Dunglass at the rear. When they pulled away and cornered sharply with a soft squeal of tyres Legat noticed that Strang didn't sway with the motion of the car but remained stiff and immobile. He was hating every moment. The convoy accelerated along Max-Joseph-Strasse and across Karolinenplatz, the wind hard in their faces. Legat wondered if he would see Hartmann at the Führerbau. He didn't resent him for embarrassing him in front of the Prime Minister. It had been a futile gesture, of course, but then they were trapped in an era when futile gestures were all that were available. Paul had got it right that night when he had stood on the parapet of Magdalen Bridge: *"Ours is a mad generation . . ."* Their destinies had been mapped from the moment they met.

The convoy came into Königsplatz. It looked even more pagan in the darkness, its giant symbols and eternal flames and floodlit white buildings glittering around a vast expanse of black granite like the temple complex of some lost civilisation. By the time their car drew to a halt the Prime Minister was already out of his Mercedes and halfway up the steps to the Führerbau. He was in such a hurry that for once he didn't stop to acknowledge the large crowd even though they were chanting his name. They carried on cheering after he had disappeared inside. Strang said, "What an astonishing reception he gets, wherever he goes in Germany. It was exactly the same in Godesberg. I'm beginning to think that if he could stand for election, he'd give Hitler a run for his money." An SS man stepped up and opened the door. Strang shuddered slightly. "Well, let's get it over with."

The foyer was packed and brilliantly lit. Adjutants in white jackets circulated with trays of drinks. Strang went off to find Malkin. Left to himself, Legat wandered round, holding a glass of mineral water, keeping an eye out for Hartmann. He saw Dunglass making his way towards him.

"Hello, Alec."

"Hugh. Some of our press chaps outside are complaining. Apparently no one from a British paper is to be allowed in to take a picture of the actual signing. I was wondering if you could possibly ask if something might be done about it?"

"I can try."

"Could you? Best to keep them happy."

He disappeared into the crowd. Legat handed his glass to a waiter and began to climb the stairs. He paused halfway up and gazed around the balustraded gallery, unsure who he should approach. One of the uniformed figures, an officer of the SS, detached himself from the rest and descended to meet him. "Good evening. You look lost." He spoke in German. There was a strange dead-fish quality about his pale blue eyes. "Can I help you?"

"Good evening. Thank you, yes. I wanted to talk to someone about the press arrangements for the signing of the agreement."

"Of course. Come with me, please." He gestured for Legat to walk with him up to the first floor. "There is an official of the Foreign Ministry who is doing much of the liaison work with our British guests." He led him around to the seating area at the front of the building where Hartmann was standing beside one of the pillars. "You know Herr Hartmann, perhaps?"

Legat pretended not to have heard.

"Herr Legat?" repeated the SS man. His voice was louder, less friendly. "I asked you a question: do you know Herr Hartmann?"

"I don't believe—"

Hartmann cut in. "My dear Hugh, I think that Sturmbannführer Sauer is having a little joke with you. He knows perfectly well that we're old friends and that I came to see you in your hotel this evening. He knows it because he and his friends in the Gestapo followed me there."

Legat managed to smile. "Well, there is your answer. We've known one another for many years. Why do you ask? Is there a problem?"

Sauer said, "You replaced a colleague on Herr Chamberlain's plane at the last minute, I believe?"

"That's right."

"Might I ask why?"

"Because I speak better German than he does."

"But surely that was known from the start?"

"Everything was a bit last-minute."

"And there are people from your embassy in Berlin who can act as translators."

Hartmann said, "Really, Sauer, I don't think you have the right to cross-examine a man who is a guest in our country."

Sauer ignored him. "And before today you and Hartmann last met when, may I ask?"

"Six years ago. Not that it's any of your business."

"Good." Sauer nodded. Suddenly his confidence seemed to be running out. "Well, I shall leave you to talk. No doubt Hartmann will tell you everything you want to know." He clicked his heels, bowed slightly and walked away.

Legat said, "That was ominous."

"Oh, take no notice of him. He is determined to expose me. He will keep digging until he finds something, but he hasn't got anything yet. Now we must assume we are being watched, so we must play our parts. What is it you want to know?"

"Can the British press send in a photographer to record the signing? Who should I ask?"

"Don't bother. It has already been decided. The only still camera permitted in the room will belong to the Führer's personal photographer, Hoffmann, whose assistant, Fräulein Braun, so rumour has it, our not-so-celibate Leader is fucking." He put his hand on Legat's shoulder and said quietly, "I apologise if my actions tonight embarrassed you."

"Think nothing of it. I'm only sorry it wasn't more fruitful." He touched the front of his inside pocket, where the memorandum was folded into three. "What would you like me to do with—?"

"Keep it. Hide it in your room. Take it back with you to London and make sure it reaches a more responsive audience." Hartmann squeezed his shoulder and released it. "Now for both our sakes we should stop talking, and move apart. I'm afraid it would be better if we did not speak again."

Another hour dragged by.

Legat waited in the British delegation's room with the others while the documents were finalised. Nobody spoke much. He kept to himself in the corner. He found to his surprise that he could contemplate the imminent wreckage of his career with equanimity. No doubt this was the anaesthetic of tiredness: he was sure that when he got back to London he would feel differently. But for now he was sanguine. He tried to imagine telling Pamela that her dreams of becoming the chatelaine of the Paris embassy were no longer feasible. Perhaps he would leave the diplomatic service altogether. Her father had once offered to help find him "a nice little berth in the City"—maybe he should take him up on it? It would solve their financial worries, at least until war came.

It was half-past midnight when Dunglass finally put his head round the door.

"The agreement's about to be signed. The PM wants everyone to be there."

Legat would have preferred not to attend. But there was no escape. He rose wearily from his chair and walked with his colleagues along the corridor towards Hitler's study. At the door of the big office a crowd of minor players—aides, adjutants, civil servants, Nazi Party officials—had gathered. They parted to let them through. Inside, the heavy green velvet curtains had all been drawn but the windows must have been opened because Legat could hear the movement of the crowd outside quite distinctly, like a gently moving sea, occasionally ruffled by eddies of shouts and singing.

The room was packed. At the opposite end, standing around the desk, were Hitler, Göring, Himmler, Hess, Ribbentrop, Mussolini and Ciano. They were studying a map—not seriously, it seemed to him, but for the benefit of a photographer using a handheld newsreel camera. He filmed them first from one side and then scampered round to do the same from the front, while Chamberlain and Daladier watched the proceedings from the hearth. All eyes were on Hitler. He was the only one talking. Occasionally he pointed and made sweeping gestures. Finally, he folded his arms and stepped back and the filming ended. There was no sound-recording equipment, Legat noticed. It was like watching the making of some strange silent movie.

He glanced at Chamberlain. The Prime Minister seemed to have been waiting for this opportunity. He left Wilson and went forward and spoke to Hitler, who listened to the translation, nodded vigorously a couple of times. Legat heard the famous harsh voice: "*Ja, ja.*" The exchange lasted less than a minute. The Prime Minister returned to the fireplace. He looked pleased with himself. For an instant his gaze rested on Legat, then almost immediately switched away to Mussolini, who had come over to talk to him. Göring waddled around, rubbing his hands. Himmler's round rimless spectacles flashed in the light of the chandelier like two blind disks.

After another minute or two, a small procession of officials entered, carrying the various documents that made up the agreement. At the back of the group was Hartmann. Legat noticed how carefully he avoided looking at anyone. The map was rolled up and removed from the desk and the papers were laid out. The photographer, a thickset man of about fifty with wavy grey hair—Hoffmann, presumably—gestured for the leaders to stand together. They grouped themselves awkwardly with their backs to the fireplace: Chamberlain on the left in his pinstriped suit, with his watch chain and high-winged collar like a waxwork in a museum of Victoriana; Daladier next to him, mournful, also pinstriped but smaller and with a protruding stomach; then Hitler, impassive, pasty-faced and dead-eyed, with his hands folded together over his crotch; and at the end, Mussolini, a brooding expression on his large fleshy face. The silence was palpable, as if nobody wished to be there, like guests at an arranged wedding. The moment the photograph was taken the group broke up.

Ribbentrop indicated the desk. Hitler went over to it. A young SS adjutant handed him a pair of spectacles. They changed his face in an instant, made him look fussy and pedantic. He peered down at the document. The adjutant gave him a pen. He dipped it into the inkstand, examined the nib, frowned, straightened and pointed irritably. The inkstand was empty. There was an uneasy shifting in the room. Göring rubbed his hands together and laughed. One of the officials pulled out his own fountain pen and gave it to Hitler. Again, he bent forward and studied the paper carefully, then very quickly scribbled his signature. One aide rolled a curved blotter over the wet ink, then a second lifted away the document and a third slid another sheet of paper in front of Hitler. He scribbled again. The same procedure was repeated. It went on for several minutes, twenty times in all—a copy of the main agreement for each of the four powers, along with the various annexes and supplementary declarations—the fruit of some of the most creative legal brains in Europe, which had enabled them to slide over matters of contention, postpone them for later haggling, and reach a settlement in less than twelve hours.

When Hitler had finished, he tossed the fountain pen casually onto the desk and turned away. Chamberlain was the next to step up to the desk. He too put on a pair of spectacles—which he was as reluctant as the Führer to be seen wearing in public—took out his pen, and scrutinised what he was about to sign. His jaw worked slightly back and forth and then carefully he wrote out his name. From outside came a burst of cheering, as if the crowd knew what was happening at that moment. Chamberlain was too absorbed to react. But Hitler grimaced and gestured to the window and an adjutant parted the curtains and closed the sash. In the shadows at the back of the study Hartmann watched it all without seeing, his long face blank and ashy with exhaustion—like a ghost, thought Legat, like a man already dead.

Day Four

Dani Rome

In his bedroom in the Regina Palast Hotel, Hugh Legat was asleep.

He was splayed out on his back, fully clothed and unconscious, his head lolling to one side, like a drowned man fished out of the sea. The light was still on in the bathroom; the door was slightly ajar; the room was cast in a pale bluish light. At one time there had been voices in the corridor outside—he had recognised Strang, then Ashton-Gwatkin—and footsteps. But the Prime Minister had at last gone to bed and gradually these extraneous sounds had ceased, and now there was only the rhythm of his breathing and his occasional muttered cry. He dreamed that he was flying.

He was too deeply asleep to hear the noise of his door handle being tried. What woke him was the tapping. It was soft at first, more like a scratching of fingernails on wood, and when he opened his eyes he assumed it was one of the children trying to clamber into their bed after a nightmare. But then he saw the unfamiliar room and he remembered where he was. He squinted at the luminous hands on the hotel's alarm clock. Half-past three.

The noise came again.

He reached out and turned on the bedside lamp. The memorandum lay on the nightstand. He rolled off the bed, opened the drawer of the desk and inserted it into the hotel's guide to Munich. The floor creaked as he crossed to the door. He touched the handle but at the last moment some instinct warned him not to turn it.

"Who's there?"

"It's Paul."

The German loomed on the threshold, absurd in his conspicuousness. Legat pulled him into the room and glanced quickly up and down the corridor. Nobody was stirring. The duty detective must be spending the night in the Prime Minister's sitting room. He closed the door. Hartmann was going around the bedroom collecting Legat's overcoat, his hat, his shoes. "Put these on."

"What on earth for?"

"Quickly. I want to show you something."

"Are you mad? At this hour?"

"It's the only time we have."

Legat was still half asleep. He rubbed his face and shook his head in an effort to fully wake himself. "What is it you want me to see?"

"If I tell you that, you won't come." In his determination he seemed almost demented. He held out the shoes. "Please."

"Paul, this is dangerous."

Hartmann gave a short bark of laughter. "Do you think you have to point that out to *me*?" He threw the shoes onto the bed. "I shall be at the back of the hotel. I shall wait for you outside. If you're not there in ten minutes, I shall know you're not coming."

After he had gone, Legat paced up and down his small room for a minute. The situation was so preposterous he could almost believe he had dreamed the whole thing. He sat on the edge of the mattress and picked up his shoes. He had been too tired to take them off properly before he went to sleep. Now he found he couldn't unpick the laces, even with his teeth. He had to stand and kick his toes into the shoes and lever in his heels with his fingers. He felt angry. He was also—he would admit it to himself—frightened. He put on his hat and draped his coat over his arm. He went out into the corridor and locked the door behind him, turned left and walked quickly around the corner towards the rear staircase. At the bottom he passed the entrance to the Turkish baths. A moist aroma of steam and sweet oils briefly released memories of the gentlemen's clubs of Pall Mall and then he was out through the glass doors and into the small street at the back of the hotel.

Hartmann was smoking a cigarette, leaning against the bodywork of one of the open-topped black Mercedes they had been driving around in all day. The engine was ticking over. He grinned when he saw Legat, dropped the cigarette into the gutter and ground it out with the toe of his shoe. He opened the front passenger door, like a chauffeur. A minute later they were driving down a wide boulevard of shops and apartment blocks. The breeze was still warm. A swastika pennant fluttered on the bonnet. Hartmann didn't speak. He was concentrating on the road. His face in profile, with its high forehead and Roman nose, was imperious. Every few seconds he checked the mirrors. His anxiety transferred itself to Legat. "Is there anyone behind us?"

"I don't think so. Will you look?"

Legat twisted round in his seat. The road was empty. A gibbous moon had come up and the tarmac was like a canal, flat and silvery. A few of the shop windows were lit. He had no idea of the direction they were travelling. He turned back to the windscreen. The car was slowing for an intersection. A couple of patrolling policemen in their bucket-shaped helmets stood on the corner. Their heads followed the Mercedes as it approached. When they saw the official pennant they saluted. Hartmann looked at Legat and laughed at the absurdity of it, showed his large teeth, and for a second time it struck Legat that he was not entirely sane.

"How did you get hold of the car?"

"I gave the driver a hundred marks to borrow it. I said I needed it to meet a girl."

The city centre had dwindled into suburbs and factories. Across the dark fields Legat could see the fires of furnaces and chimneys— scarlet, yellow, white. For a while a railway track ran along the centre of the autobahn. Then the road narrowed and they were in open country. It reminded Legat of the drive from Oxford up to Woodstock, and the pub they used to go to there—what was it?—the Black Prince. After ten minutes, he could no longer keep his alarm to himself. "Is it much further? I'll need to get back to the hotel soon. The PM is an early riser."

"It's not that far. Don't worry. I'll get you back before morning."

They passed through a small Bavarian town, entirely shuttered and asleep, and presently entered the outskirts of a second. This too appeared entirely normal—whitewashed, half-timbered walls, steep red-tiled roofs, a butcher's shop, an inn, a garage. Then Legat caught sight of a place-name—DACHAU—and he knew why he had been brought out here. He felt obscurely disappointed. So this was it? Hartmann drove carefully through the empty streets until they were on the edge of the town. He pulled up at the side of the road, turned off the engine and doused the headlights. To the right was woodland. The concentration camp was on the left, clearly visible against the moonlit sky—a high barbed-wire fence stretching as far as Legat could see, with watchtowers, and behind them the low outlines of barracks. The barking of guard dogs carried on the still air. A searchlight mounted on one of the towers prodded ceaselessly across a vast parade ground. It was the immensity of it that was most shocking: a captive town within a town.

Hartmann was studying him. "You know what this is, I take it?"

"Of course. It's been reported often enough in the press. There have been regular demonstrations against the Nazi repressions in London."

"You didn't join them, I suppose?"

"You know very well I couldn't. I'm a civil servant. We're politically neutral."

"Naturally."

"Oh, for Christ's sake, Paul—don't be so bloody naive!" It was the obviousness of it that he found most insulting. "Stalin has vastly bigger camps, where people are treated even worse. Do you want us to go to war with the Soviet Union as well?"

"I merely point out that some of the people transferred into Germany by the agreement today may well end up in here by the end of the year."

"Yes, and no doubt they would have ended up here in any case—assuming they hadn't been killed in the bombing."

"Not if Hitler had been deposed."

"*If!* It's always *if*!"

Their raised voices had been noticed. Beyond the wire, a guard with an Alsatian dog on a short leash started shouting at them. The probing finger of the searchlight swung across the parade ground, over the fence and onto the road. It advanced towards them. Suddenly the car was filled with brilliant blinding light. Hartmann swore. He switched on the engine and found reverse gear. He looked over his shoulder, one hand on the steering wheel, and they backed away at speed, swerving from side to side down the middle of the road until they reached a side street. He put the Mercedes into first gear, swung the wheel and they made a U-turn, sending up a spurt of dust and smoking rubber. The acceleration as they pulled away threw Legat back in his seat. When he checked behind them the searchlight was still weaving back and forth across the road, blindly searching. He said furiously, "That was a bloody stupid thing to do. Can you imagine the row if a British diplomat was arrested out here? I want to go back to Munich—now." Hartmann continued to stare ahead and didn't answer. "Did you really drag me all the way out here just to make a point?"

"No. It happened to be on the way."

"On the way to what?"

"Leyna."

So then, at last: Leyna.

She had wanted to set eyes on Hitler—not to hear him speak: she declared herself a communist; that would have been unthinkable—but just to see him in the flesh, this half-sinister, half-comical brawler and dreamer, whose Party only four years earlier had come ninth in the elections with less than three percent of the vote, but who now was on the brink of becoming Chancellor. Most nights during the campaign, after addressing one of his huge rallies, he returned to the city. Everybody knew the address of his apartment. Her proposal was that they should go and stand outside it in the hope that they might catch a glimpse of him.

Hartmann had been against it from the start. He had called it a waste of a good day, a trivial bourgeois diversion ("Isn't that what you people call it?") to focus upon an individual rather than upon the social forces that had created him. But there was more to his reluctance than that, Legat had realised afterwards: Hartmann knew what she was like, the sort of recklessness of which she was capable. She had appealed to Legat to use his casting vote in her favour, and of course he had done so—partly because he was curious to see Hitler himself, but chiefly because he was half in love with her: a fact of which all three were aware. They treated it as a joke, himself included. He was so much less experienced and worldly than Hartmann, still a virgin at twenty-one.

And so, after their picnic on the grass in Königsplatz, they had set off.

It was the first week of July, just after midday, very hot. She was wearing one of Hartmann's white shirts with the sleeves rolled up, a pair of shorts and walking boots. Her limbs were brown from the sun. It was more than a mile away, through the centre of the city. The buildings shimmered like fantasies in the haze of heat. As they passed the southern end of the Englischer Garten, Hartmann had suggested they go swimming in the Eisbach instead. Legat had been tempted but Leyna would not be put off. On they went.

The apartment was at the top of a hill, facing onto Prinzregentenplatz, a busy, drearily impressive half-cobbled square through which trams ran. By the time they reached it they were sweating and bad-tempered. Hartmann was hanging back in a sulk and Leyna had decided to goad him further by pretending to flirt with Legat. The building in which Hitler lived was a luxurious, turn-of-the-century block with a hint of a French château about its design. Outside it a gang of about a dozen stormtroopers was loitering, closing off that portion of the pavement, obliging pedestrians to step into the road and walk around the Führer's six-wheeled Mercedes which was drawn up waiting for him. Across the street, no more than twenty yards away, a small crowd of curious spectators had gathered. So, he was in residence, Legat remembered thinking—and not only that: it looked as though he was about to leave.

He asked, "Which is his apartment?"

"Second floor." She pointed. A balcony ran between two bays with French windows. It was solid, heavy masonry. "Sometimes he comes out to show himself to the crowd. Of course, this is the place where his niece was shot last year." As she delivered the last sentence she raised her voice slightly. A couple of people turned to look at her. "Well, they lived together, didn't they? What do you think, Pauli? Geli Raubal—did she kill herself or was she bumped off because of the scandal?" When Hartmann didn't reply she said to Legat, "The poor kid was only twenty-three. Everyone knew her uncle was fucking her."

A middle-aged woman standing nearby turned and glared at her. "You should shut your filthy mouth."

Across the street, the Brownshirts were coming to attention, forming themselves into an honour guard between the door of the apartment building and the car. The crowd shuffled forward. The door opened. Hitler appeared. He was wearing a dark blue double-breasted suit. (Later, Legat decided he must have been on his way to lunch.) Some of the onlookers cheered and clapped. Leyna cupped her hands to her mouth and yelled, "Niece-fucker!"

Hitler glanced over at the small throng. He must have heard—the stormtroopers certainly had: their heads had all swung in their direction—but just to make sure, she repeated it. "You fucked your niece, you murderer!" His face was expressionless. As he climbed into his car a couple of the SA men broke ranks and started coming towards her. They had short truncheons. Hartmann grabbed Leyna's arm and pulled her after him. The woman who had told her to shut her filthy mouth tried to block their path. Legat pushed her out of the way. A man—a big fellow, her husband presumably—swung a punch and caught Legat just below the eye. The three of them ran out of the square and down a leafy residential road.

Hartmann and Leyna were in front. Legat could hear the boots of the Brownshirts thumping on the cobbles very close behind. His eye was stinging and already beginning to close. His lungs were searing as if they had been pumped full of liquid ice. He remembered feeling both terrified and entirely calm. When a side road appeared to the right, and Hartmann and Leyna ran straight past it, he swung down it, between big villas with front gardens, and presently he became aware that the stormtroopers were no longer pursuing him. He was alone. He leaned on a small wooden gate to recover his breath, gasping and laughing. He felt almost ecstatically happy, as if he had taken a drug.

Later, when he got back to their hostel, he found Leyna sitting in the courtyard with her back to the wall. Her face was turned to the sun. She opened her eyes and scrambled to her feet as soon as she saw him and hugged him. How was he? He was fine: better than fine, actually. Where was Paul? She didn't know—once the fascists had given up the chase and they were safe he had shouted at her and she had shouted back and then he had walked off. She inspected his eye and insisted on taking him upstairs to his bedroom. While he lay on the bed she soaked a hand towel in the basin and folded it into a compress. She sat on the mattress beside him and held it to his eye. Her hip was pressed against him. He could feel the hardness of her muscle beneath her flesh. He had never felt more alive. He reached his hand up behind her head and laced her hair between his fingers and pulled her face down to his and kissed her. She resisted for a moment, then kissed him back and swung astride him, unbuttoning her shirt.

Hartmann didn't come back all that night. The next morning, Legat had left his share of the bill on the dresser and slipped away.

Within an hour he was on the earliest train out of the city. And that had been the only great adventure in the carefully planned life of Hugh Alexander Legat, ex–Balliol College, Oxford, and Third Secretary in His Majesty's Diplomatic Service, until this night.

They motored on in silence along the narrow country roads for the best part of an hour. It was colder now. Legat kept his hands in his coat pockets. He wondered about where he was being taken, what he should say when he arrived. To this day he had no idea whether Hartmann knew about his act of betrayal. He had always assumed he must have done: why else would he never have got in touch in all the years since? He had also written to Leyna—two letters full of love and remorse and pompous moral lectures; in retrospect he was glad they had both been returned unopened.

Finally, they turned off onto a long drive. The headlights picked out neatly trimmed grass verges and low iron railings. Ahead was the shape of a large house—a manor house, it would have been in England—with outbuildings. In a small round window beneath the eaves a solitary light was burning. They passed through an arched gateway and pulled up on a cobbled forecourt. Hartmann switched off the engine.

"Wait here."

Legat watched him walk towards the door. The front of the house was covered by ivy. In the moonlight he could now see that the upper windows were barred. He had a sudden presentiment of horror. Hartmann must have rung a bell. A minute later, a light went on above the door. It was opened from the inside—a cautious crack at first, and then wider, so that Legat could see a young woman in a nurse's uniform. Hartmann said something to her, gestured to the car. She leaned around him to look. There was a discussion. Hartmann raised his hands a couple of times, making some point or other. At last she nodded. Hartmann touched her on the arm and beckoned to Legat to join them.

The hall smelled of overcooked food and disinfectant. Legat registered the details as he passed them: the carved Madonna above the door, the noticeboard covered in green baize and studded with pins but with no notices, the wheelchair at the bottom of the staircase, a pair of crutches beside it. He followed Hartmann and the nurse up to the first floor and a little way along a passage. The nurse had a large bunch of keys attached to her belt. She selected one, unlocked a door. They waited while she went inside. Legat looked at Hartmann, hoping for an explanation, but he wouldn't meet his eye. The nurse reappeared. "She's awake."

It was a small room. The iron bedstead took up most of it. Her head was propped up on the pillow, a thick white nightgown buttoned to her throat. Legat would never have recognised her. Her hair was cut mannishly short, her face was much fatter, her skin waxy. But it was the lack of animation in her features, in her dark brown eyes especially, which rendered her a stranger. Hartmann went forward and took her hand and kissed her forehead. He whispered something to her. She gave no sign of having heard. He said, "Hugh, why don't you come in and say hello?"

With an effort Legat walked to the side of the bed and took her other hand. It was plump, cool, unresponsive. "Hello, Leyna."

Her head turned slightly. She looked up at him. For an instant her eyes narrowed a fraction and it seemed to him that perhaps something moved there. But afterwards he was fairly sure he had imagined it.

On the drive back to Munich Hartmann asked Legat to light him a cigarette. He lit it, placed it between Hartmann's lips, then took one for himself. His hand was trembling. "Are you going to tell me what happened to her?"

Another silence. Eventually Hartmann said, "I can tell you as much as I know, which isn't much—we split up after Munich, as you might expect, and I lost touch with her. She was too much for me. Apparently, she went back to Berlin and started working for the communists more seriously. They had a newspaper—*Die Rote Fahne*—she was part of that. After the Nazis came to power, they banned it, but it carried on publishing underground. As I understand it, she was caught in a raid in 'thirty-five and sent to Moringen, the women's camp. She was married by then, to a fellow communist."

"What happened to her husband?"

"Dead. Killed fighting in Spain." He said it flatly. "After that, they let her out. Of course, she went straight back to the comrades. They caught her again. Only this time they discovered she was Jewish and they were rougher—as you can see."

Legat felt sick. He crushed the cigarette between his fingers and threw it out of the car.

"Her mother got in touch with me. She lives not far from here. She's a widow, used to be a teacher, no money. She'd heard I'd joined the Party, wanted to see if I could use my influence to get her proper treatment. I did what I could, but it was hopeless—her brain was much too badly damaged. All I could do was pay for the nursing home. It's not a bad place. Because of my position, they've agreed to overlook the fact that she is a Jewess."

"That's decent of you."

"'Decent'?" Hartmann laughed and shook his head. "Hardly!"

They drove on for a while without speaking. Legat said, "They must have beaten her terribly."

"They said she fell out of a third-floor window. I'm sure she did. But not before they'd carved a Star of David into her back. Could I have another cigarette?" Legat lit one for him. "This is the thing, Hugh. This is what we could never grasp in Oxford—because it's beyond reason; it's not rational." He waved the cigarette as he spoke, his right hand on the wheel, his eyes fixed on the road ahead. "This is what I have learned these past six years, as opposed to what is taught in Oxford: the power of *un*reason. Everyone said—by everyone I mean people like me—we all said, 'Oh, he's a terrible fellow, Hitler, but he's not necessarily all bad. Look at his achievements. Put aside this awful medieval anti-Jew stuff: it will pass.' But the point is, it won't pass. You can't isolate it from the rest. It's there in the mix. And if the anti-Semitism is evil, it's all evil. Because if they're capable of that, they're capable of anything." He took his eyes off the road just long enough to look at Legat. His eyes were wet. "Do you see what I mean?"

"Yes," said Legat, "I do see. I see now exactly what you mean."

After that, they didn't speak for half an hour.

It was starting to get light. There was traffic at last—a bus, a flatbed truck piled high with scrap metal. Along the railway track in the centre of the autobahn the first train of the morning was moving towards the city. They overtook it. Legat could see passengers reading newspapers announcing the agreement.

He said, "So what will you do?"

Hartmann was so absorbed in his thoughts he seemed at first not to have heard the question. "I don't know." He shrugged. "Carry on, presumably. I imagine this is how it must feel to realise one has an incurable disease: one knows the end is coming, but even so one can't do anything except keep on getting up each day. This morning, for example, I have to prepare a foreign press summary. I may well be required to present it to Hitler personally. I'm told he may have taken a shine to me! Can you believe it?"

"It could be useful, couldn't it—to your cause?"

"Could it? This is my dilemma. Am I right to continue to work for the regime, in the hope that one day I can do some small thing to help sabotage it from within? Or should I simply blow my brains out?"

"Come on, Paul! This is too melodramatic. The former, it has to be."

"Of course, what I really ought to do is blow *his* brains out. But everything I am prevents me, and besides, the one sure consequence would be a bloodbath—certainly all my family would be destroyed.

So in the end one goes on in hope. What a terrible thing hope is! We would all be much better off without it. There is an Oxford paradox to end with." He had started checking the mirror again. "Now I should drop you a few hundred metres away from your hotel, if you don't mind, in case Sturmbannführer Sauer is watching. Can you find your way from here? This is the opposite end of the botanical garden we talked in yesterday."

He pulled up outside a grand official building—a law court, by the look of it, festooned with swastikas. At the far end of the street Legat could see the twin domed towers of the Frauenkirche. Hartmann said, "Farewell, my dear Hugh. All is good between us. Whatever happens we shall have the consolation of knowing that we tried."

Legat climbed out of the Mercedes. He closed the door behind him and turned to say goodbye but it was too late. Hartmann was already moving off into the early-morning traffic.

He walked back towards his hotel in a trance.

At the busy intersection between the botanical garden and Maximiliansplatz he stepped off the kerb without looking. The blast of a car horn and a scream of brakes shattered his reverie. He jumped back and raised his hands in apology. The driver swore and accelerated away. Legat leaned against a lamppost and lowered his head and wept.

By the time he reached the Regina Palast five minutes later the big hotel was coming awake. He paused just inside the entrance, took out his handkerchief, blew his nose and dabbed at his eyes. Cautiously he scanned the lobby. Guests were making their way down the stairs to the dining room; he could hear the clatter of breakfast being served. At the reception desk a family waited to check out. When he was sure there was no member of the British delegation to be seen he launched himself across the foyer towards the elevators. He summoned a car. His aim was simply to get back to his hotel room without being noticed. But when the doors opened he found himself confronted by the dandyish figure of Sir Nevile Henderson. The Ambassador had his usual carnation buttonhole in place, the inevitable jade cigarette holder between his lips. He was carrying an elegant calfskin portmanteau. His face registered surprise.

"Good morning, Legat. I see you've been out and about."

"Yes, Sir Nevile. I felt the need for some fresh air."

"Well, you need to get upstairs, quickly—the Prime Minister's asking for you. Ashton-Gwatkin's already on his way to Prague with the Czechs and I'm off to catch a plane with von Weizsäcker to Berlin."

"Thank you for the warning, sir. Have a good trip."

He pressed the button for the third floor. In the elevator mirror he performed a brief inspection: unshaven, crumpled, red-eyed. No wonder Henderson had been taken aback—he looked as if he'd spent the night on the tiles. He took off his hat and coat. The bell pinged, he squared his shoulders and emerged into the corridor. Outside the Prime Minister's suite, the Scotland Yard detective had resumed his former position. He raised his eyebrows at Legat in a look of amused complicity, knocked on the door and opened it.

"Found him, sir."

"Good. Send him in."

Chamberlain was wearing a plaid dressing gown. His thin bare feet protruded beneath a pair of striped pyjama bottoms. His unbrushed hair was tufted, like the plumage of a grizzled bird. He was smoking a cigar. In his left hand he clutched a sheaf of papers. He said, "Where's that copy of *The Times* with Herr Hitler's speech in it?"

"I believe it's in your box, Prime Minister."

"Find it for me, would you, there's a good fellow?"

Legat put down his hat and coat on the nearest chair and took out his keys. The old man seemed full of that same purposeful energy Legat had noticed in the garden of Number 10. Nobody looking at him would dream he had barely slept. He unlocked the box and sorted through the files until he found his copy of Tuesday's paper, the one he had been reading at the Ritz while he was waiting for Pamela. The Prime Minister took it out of his hands and carried it over to the desk. He spread it out, put on his spectacles and peered down at it. Without turning round he said, "I had a word with Hitler last night, and asked if I might come and see him this morning before flying back to London."

Legat gaped at the Prime Minister's back. "And did he agree, sir?"

"I like to think I've learned how to handle him. I deliberately put him on the spot. He couldn't really refuse." His head was nodding slowly as he ran his eye up and down the columns of type. "I must say, that was a quite remarkably rude young man you brought to see me last night."

Here it came, thought Legat. He braced himself. "Yes, I'm sorry about that, sir. I take full responsibility."

"Have you told anyone about it?"

"No."

"Good. Neither have I." The Prime Minister took off his spectacles, folded the paper and handed it back to Legat. "I want you to take this to Strang and ask him to turn Herr Hitler's speech into a statement of intent. Two or three paragraphs should be sufficient."

Legat's brain was normally sharp; not now. "I'm sorry, sir. I don't quite follow . . ."

"On Monday night," said Chamberlain patiently, "in Berlin, Herr Hitler made a public declaration of his desire for a permanent peace between Germany and Great Britain once the Sudeten issue was settled. I would like his undertaking redrafted in the form of a joint statement on future Anglo-German relations to which we can both put our names this morning. Off you go."

Legat closed the door quietly behind him. A joint statement? He had never heard of such a thing. Strang's room, if he remembered rightly, was three along from the Prime Minister's. He knocked but there was no reply. He tried again, more loudly. After a while he heard someone coughing and Strang opened the door. He was wearing a vest and long cotton underpants. Without his owlish spectacles his face was ten years younger. "Good heavens, Hugh. Is everything all right?"

"I have a message from the Prime Minister. He wants you to draft a statement."

"A statement? About what?" Strang yawned and put his hand to his mouth. "Excuse me. It took me a while to get off to sleep. You'd better come in."

The room was in darkness. Strang padded across to the window and pulled back the curtains. His sitting room was much smaller than the Prime Minister's. Through the connecting door Legat could see his unmade bed. Strang collected his spectacles from the nightstand and carefully put them on. He came back into the sitting room.

"Tell me this again."

"The Prime Minister is going to have another meeting with Hitler this morning."

"What?"

"Apparently, he asked him last night, and Hitler agreed."

"Does anyone else know about this? The Foreign Secretary? The Cabinet?"

"I don't know. I don't think so."

"Good God!"

"He wants to get Hitler to sign some kind of joint statement based on the speech he made in Berlin on Monday night." He gave Strang the newspaper.

"Is this his underlining?"

"No, it's mine."

Strang was so disconcerted he seemed until that moment to have entirely forgotten he was only wearing his underwear. He glanced down at his bare feet in surprise. "I suppose I ought to get dressed. Could you see if you could get us some coffee? And you'd better fetch Malkin."

"What about Sir Horace Wilson?"

Strang hesitated. "Yes, I think so, don't you? Especially if he doesn't know anything about it, either." He suddenly put his hands on either side of his head and stared at Legat, his neat diplomatist's mind plainly appalled at this departure from orthodoxy. "What is he playing at? He seems to regard the foreign policy of the British Empire as his personal fiefdom. What an extraordinary business!"

———

Hartmann parked the Mercedes at the back of the Führerbau and left the key in the ignition. He moved stiffly. His night of driving had left him dangerously exhausted. And this, he knew, was a day, above all others, when he would need to keep his wits about him. But he was glad to have done it. He might never get another chance to see her.

The rear entrance was unlocked and unguarded. Wearily he climbed the service stairs to the first floor. A team of cleaners in Army uniforms was sweeping the marble floors, emptying the ashtrays into paper sacks, collecting the dirty champagne flutes and beer bottles. He made his way to the conference office. Two young SS adjutants were sprawled in armchairs, smoking, boots on the coffee table, flirting with a red-headed secretary who was on one of the sofas, her elegant legs tucked under her.

Hartmann saluted. "*Heil Hitler!* I am Hartmann from the Foreign Ministry. I have to prepare the English-language press summary for the Führer."

At the mention of the Führer, the two adjutants quickly stubbed out their cigarettes, stood and returned his salute. One of them pointed to the desk in the corner. "The material is there waiting for you, Herr Hartmann. *The New York Times* has just been telegraphed from Berlin."

The sheaf of telegrams, as thick as his thumb, was in a wire basket. "Is there any chance of some coffee?"

"Of course, Herr Hartmann."

He sat and pulled the basket towards him. *The New York Times* was on the top.

The war for which Europe had been feverishly preparing was averted early this morning when the leading statesmen of Britain, France, Germany and Italy, meeting in Munich, reached an agreement to allow Reich troops to occupy predominantly German portions of Czechoslovakia's Sudetenland progressively over a ten-day period beginning tomorrow. Most of Chancellor Hitler's demands were met. Prime Minister Chamberlain, whose peace efforts were finally crowned with success, received the loudest applause of Munich's crowds.

Beneath it was another story: CHAMBERLAIN HERO OF MUNICH CROWDS:

There were real cheers, like the kind one hears in an American football stadium, whenever the slim, black-coated Chamberlain, with a smile and a careful walk, came out.

Hartmann thought it was exactly the sort of detail that would make Hitler furious. He took out his pen. He would put it first.

Strang, shaved and fully dressed, was seated at the desk in his hotel sitting room, writing in his small neat hand on a sheet of Regina Palast notepaper. A litter of discarded drafts surrounded his feet. Malkin, a pad of paper on his knee, had pulled up a chair and was looking over his shoulder. Wilson sat on the end of the bed studying the text of Hitler's speech in *The Times*. Legat was pouring coffee.

It was obvious by his initial, startled reaction that Wilson had not known what was in the Prime Minister's mind either. But by now he had recovered his usual equilibrium, and was attempting to make it sound as if the whole thing had been his idea.

Wilson tapped his finger on the newsprint. "This is the crucial passage, surely, where Hitler talks about the Anglo-German Naval Agreement: *'I voluntarily renounced ever again entering upon a naval armaments competition in order to give the British Empire a feeling of security . . . Such an agreement is only morally justified if both nations promise one another solemnly never again to want to wage war against one another. Germany has this will.'*"

Strang grimaced. Legat knew what he was thinking. In the Foreign Office they had come to the view that the 1935 Anglo-German Naval Agreement—in which Germany undertook never to build a fleet greater in size than 35 percent of the Royal Navy—had been a mistake. Strang said, "Don't let's revisit the Anglo-German Naval Agreement, Sir Horace, whatever else we do."

"Why not?"

"Because it's pretty clear Hitler took it as a nod and a wink that in return for his letting us have a Navy three times the size of Germany's, we would let him have a free hand in Eastern Europe. That was when the rot started." He jotted down a sentence. "I suggest we leave that out and just take the second part of his statement and tie it specifically to the deal over the Sudetenland. So it would read: *'We regard the agreement signed last night as symbolic of the desire of our two peoples never to go to war with one another again.'* "

Malkin, the Foreign Office lawyer, sucked his breath through his teeth. "I do hope the Prime Minister realises this has no legal force whatsoever. It's a declaration of goodwill, nothing more."

Wilson said sharply, "Of course he'll be aware of that. He's not a fool."

Strang resumed writing. After a couple of minutes, he held up a sheet of paper. "All right, I've done my best. Why don't you take it to him, Hugh, and see what he thinks?"

Legat went out into the corridor. Apart from the detective outside Chamberlain's suite the only other person was a stout middle-aged chambermaid wheeling her trolley full of cleaning equipment and fresh toiletries. He nodded to her as he passed and knocked on the Prime Minister's door.

"Come!"

A table for two had been laid in the centre of the drawing room. Chamberlain was having breakfast. He was dressed in his usual suit and high-winged collar. Opposite him was Lord Dunglass. The Prime Minister was buttering a piece of toast.

"Excuse me, sir. Mr. Strang has written a draft."

"Let me see."

Chamberlain put down his toast, donned his spectacles and studied the document. Legat risked a glance at Dunglass, who widened his eyes slightly. Legat couldn't read what he was signalling—amusement, concern, a warning; perhaps it was all three. Chamberlain frowned. "Would you go and fetch Strang, please?"

Legat returned to Strang's room. "He wants to see you."

"Is something the matter?"

"He didn't say."

Malkin said, "Perhaps we all ought to go." They were as nervous as schoolboys summoned to see the headmaster. "Would you care to come with us, Sir Horace?"

"If you like." Wilson looked dubious. "Although I'd caution you against trying to change his mind. Once he's set on a course, he'll never change it."

Legat followed the three men into the Prime Minister's suite. Chamberlain said coldly, "Mr. Strang, you've left out the Anglo-German Naval Agreement. Why?"

"I'm not sure it's a thing to be proud of."

"On the contrary, it's exactly the type of agreement we should now try to reach with Germany." Chamberlain took out his pen and amended the draft. "Also, I see you've put my name before his. That will never do. It should be the other way round: *'We, the German Führer and Chancellor and the British Prime Minister, have had a further meeting today . . .'* He circled the titles and drew an arrow. "I want him to sign it first, so that the onus appears to be slightly more on him."

Wilson cleared his throat. "What if he refuses, Prime Minister?"

"Why should he? These are his own public undertakings. If he declines to put his name to them he will only demonstrate that they were hollow all along."

Malkin said, "Even if he signs, it doesn't mean he's obliged to stick by any of them."

"The significance is intended to be symbolic, not legally binding." Chamberlain pushed back his chair and glanced around at the officials. He was clearly irritated by their failure to share his vision. "Gentlemen, we have to rise to the level of events. Last night's agreement settles one local area of dispute only. We may be sure there will be others. I want him to commit himself now to peace and a process of consultation."

There was a silence.

Strang tried again. "But shouldn't we at least tell the French that you're planning to seek this direct agreement with Hitler? After all, Daladier's still in Munich—his hotel is nearby."

"I see no reason at all for saying anything whatsoever to the French. This is entirely between Hitler and me."

He returned his attention to the draft. His pen made short, neat movements, deleting some words, inserting others. When he had finished, he handed it to Legat. "Have it typed. Two copies: one for him and one for me. I have arranged to see the Chancellor at eleven. Make sure a car is available."

"Yes, Prime Minister. This will be to go to the Führerbau, presumably?"

"No. I suggested we should have a private talk, man to man, no officials—I particularly didn't want Ribbentrop anywhere near it—therefore he has invited me to his apartment."

"No officials?" repeated Wilson, shocked. "Not even me?"

"Not even you, Horace."

"But you can't go and see Hitler entirely alone!"

"In that case, I'll just take Alec. He has no official standing."

"Exactly." Dunglass gave one of his lipless smiles. "I'm a nobody."

After Hartmann had finished writing the press digest it had been typed up by the pretty young redhead on the Führer's special large-print machine. Four pages in all—a unanimous exclamation from around the world of relief that war had been averted, of hope that peace could now be made permanent and of praise for Neville Chamberlain. In the latter regard, *The Times* of London was, as usual, the most effusive: *Considering that, if the negotiations had failed and war had broken out, Great Britain and Germany would inevitably have been the protagonists on opposite sides, the cheering and the "heils" to the man whose action throughout the crisis has been single-mindedly and unchallengeably pacific must have seemed to have a clear intention.*

Checking through the pages, Hartmann was forced to concede that there was some truth in this. In the heart of the Third Reich—in the very cradle of National Socialism—a British prime minister had managed to engineer what was, in effect, a daylong demonstration for peace. That was quite an achievement. For the first time, Hartmann was almost prepared to allow himself a flicker of hope. Perhaps the Führer would be denied his war of conquest after all? He refolded the summary and wondered what he was supposed to do with it. He was too tired to go in search of someone who might know. The secretary had gone back to her flirtation with the two SS adjutants. Their inconsequential babble about movie stars and sportsmen was soothing. He felt his eyelids begin to droop. Soon he was asleep in the armchair.

He was woken by a hand roughly shaking his shoulder. Schmidt was bending over him. The Ministry's chief translator was red-faced, in his usual state of nervous agitation. "My God, Hartmann, what do you think you're doing? Where's the press digest?"

"It's here. It's finished."

"That's something! Heavens, look at the state you're in! Well, it can't be helped. We need to get a move on."

Hartmann hauled himself to his feet. Schmidt was already heading towards the door. He followed him out onto the first-floor landing and down the marble staircase. The building was empty and echoing, like a mausoleum. He wanted to ask where they were going but Schmidt was in too much of a hurry. Outside, soldiers were rolling up the red carpet. The French tricolour had already been taken down. A workman atop a ladder was just releasing the last corner of the Union Jack. It fell behind them softly like a shroud.

He climbed into the back of the limousine next to Schmidt, who had opened a black leather folder and was leafing through his notes.

He said, "Weizsäcker and Kordt have flown back to Berlin, so it's all down to you and me now. It seems like there may be trouble in Wilhelmstrasse, did you hear?"

A prickle of alarm. "No. What?"

"Weizsäcker's assistant, Frau Winter—do you know who I mean? Apparently she was picked up by the Gestapo last night."

The car swept around Karolinenplatz. Hartmann sat numb. It wasn't until they were passing the long pillared facade of the House of German Art at the bottom of Prinzregentenstrasse that the appalling realisation came to him of where he was being taken.

Carrying out the Prime Minister's instructions kept Legat busy for more than an hour.

He gave the draft declaration to Miss Anderson to type. He rescheduled their flight back to London from late morning to early afternoon. He spoke to the Protocol Department of the German Foreign Ministry to arrange transport to the Führer's apartment and afterwards to the airport. He called Oscar Cleverly in Number 10 to inform him what was happening. The Principal Private Secretary was in a great good humour. "The atmosphere here could not be more positive. The press is in ecstasies. What time will you be back?"

"Late afternoon, I should think. The PM is going to have a further private talk with Hitler this morning."

"A *further* talk? Does Halifax know?"

"I think Strang is briefing Cadogan now. The point is, he's not taking any officials with him."

"What? Good grief! What are they going to talk about?"

Legat, as ever conscious that the line was probably tapped, said guardedly, "Anglo-German relations, sir. I shall have to leave it there."

He hung up and briefly closed his eyes. He rubbed his hand across his bristled chin. It was almost thirty hours since he had shaved. The office was quiet. Strang and Malkin were speaking to London on the telephones in their rooms. Joan had gone off with Wilson, who had some letters he wished to dictate. Miss Anderson had taken the typed drafts for approval by the Prime Minister.

He walked along the corridor to his room. According to the alarm clock it was a little after 10:30 a.m. The maid had already been in. The curtains were open. The bed had been smoothed. He went into the bathroom, undressed and ran the shower. He turned his face to the jet of hot water and let it massage him for half a minute, and then his scalp and his shoulders. He soaped himself and rinsed away the suds and by the time he stepped out of the cubicle he felt restored. He wiped a porthole in the mirror and shaved, quickly rather than carefully, skirting around a place where he had cut himself the previous morning.

It was only after he had turned off the taps and was drying himself that he heard a noise from the bedroom. It was indistinct—he couldn't tell whether it came from a floorboard or a piece of furniture. He stopped and listened. He wrapped a towel around his waist and went into the other room just in time to see the door being closed, very carefully and quietly.

He threw himself across the room and flung it open. A man was walking away at speed along the corridor. Legat called after him—"Hey!"—but he carried on walking and turned the corner. Legat tried to run after him but it was hard to move quickly with both hands holding on to the towel. By the time he reached the corner the man was vanishing towards the rear staircase. Halfway along the corridor he gave up the chase. He cursed himself. A terrible thought came to his mind. He walked back quickly towards his room. Malkin was just emerging from the office. He drew back in surprise.

"Good Lord, Legat!"

"Sorry, sir."

Legat sidestepped him, went into his room and closed the door.

The wardrobe was open. His suitcase was upended on the bed. The desk drawer had been pulled out completely and the book of tourist information was facedown, open. For a few seconds he stared at it stupidly. The cover showed the hotel lit up at night. *Willkom-men in München!* He picked it up, flicked through it, turned it upside down and shook it. Nothing. He felt a terrible hollowing panic fill in his stomach.

He had been unforgivably careless. Fatally careless.

The towel dropped to the floor. Naked, he went over to the bed-side table and picked up the telephone. How could he find Hart-mann? He tried to think. Hadn't he said something about preparing a foreign press summary for Hitler?

The operator said, "Can I help you, Herr Legat?"

"No. Thank you."

He replaced the receiver.

As fast as he could he dressed. A fresh shirt. His Balliol tie. Once again he found himself kicking on his shoes as he walked. He slipped on his jacket and went back out into the passage. He realised his hair was wet. He plastered it down as best he could, nodded to the detec-tive and knocked on the Prime Minister's door.

"Come!"

Chamberlain was with Wilson, Strang and Dunglass. He was wearing his spectacles, studying the two copies of the draft declara-tion. He glanced briefly at Legat. "Yes?"

Legat said, "Forgive me, Prime Minister, but I'd like to make a suggestion with regard to your visit to Hitler."

"What?"

"That I should accompany you."

"No, that's quite impossible. I thought I made it clear—no officials."

"I am not proposing myself as an official, sir, but as a translator. I'm the only one of us who speaks German. I can make sure that your words are being accurately reported to Hitler, and his to you."

Chamberlain frowned. "I hardly think that's necessary. Dr. Schmidt is very professional."

He returned to his perusal of the document and that might have been that, but Wilson spoke. "With respect, Prime Minister—

remember what happened at Berchtesgaden, when Ribbentrop refused to give us a copy of Schmidt's notes of your first long private conversation with Hitler? To this day we don't have a full record. It would have been a great help to us if there had been a British translator present."

Strang nodded in agreement. "That's certainly true."

Chamberlain could be peevish when he felt he was being pressured. "But it would threaten to change the whole tenor of the meeting! I want him to feel this is very much a personal conversation." He slipped the two copies of the declaration into his inside pocket. Wilson looked at Legat and shrugged slightly: he had tried. A noise came from beyond the window. Chamberlain's brow creased in puzzlement. "What is that sound?"

Strang pulled back the curtain fractionally. "There is a huge crowd in the street, Prime Minister. They're calling for you."

"Not again!"

Wilson said, "You should go out onto the balcony and wave to them."

Chamberlain smiled. "I don't think so."

"You must! Hugh, open the window, will you?"

Legat undid the catch. In the garden opposite the hotel and in both directions along the street the crowd was even greater than it had been on the previous day. As the spectators noticed the French windows opening they began to roar, and when Legat stood back to allow Chamberlain to step onto the small balcony the din became tremendous. Chamberlain bowed modestly three or four times in each direction, and waved. They started to chant his name.

In the hotel suite, the four men listened.

Strang said quietly, "Perhaps he's right—perhaps this is the one moment when Hitler can be persuaded by sheer force of popular opinion to moderate his behaviour."

"You can't accuse the PM of lacking imagination," said Wilson, "or courage. Even so, with great respect to Alec, I'd be happier if one of us was in there with him."

After a couple of minutes, Chamberlain came back into the room. The adulation seemed to have energised him. His face glowed. His eyes were unnaturally bright. "How very humbling. You see, gentlemen, it is the same in every country—ordinary people the world over want nothing more than to live their lives in peace, to cherish their children and their families, and to enjoy the fruits that nature, art and science have to offer them. *That* is what I wish to say to Hitler." He brooded for a moment, then turned to Wilson. "Do you really think we can't trust Schmidt?"

"It's not Schmidt who concerns me, Prime Minister. It's Ribbentrop."

Chamberlain thought it over. "Oh, very well," he said at last. "But be discreet," he warned Legat. "Don't take notes—I only want you to intervene if my meaning is not being properly rendered. And make sure you keep out of his line of sight."

Prinzregentenplatz had scarcely changed in the six years since Hartmann had last seen it. As they came up the hill and rounded the bend his eyes went immediately to the spot in the northeast corner where he had stood with Hugh and Leyna—on the pavement beneath a large white-stone apartment building with a high red-slate roof. A similar-sized crowd had gathered in the same place today, hoping for a glimpse of the Leader.

The Mercedes drew up outside Number 16. A pair of SS sentries guarded the entrance. Seeing them, Hartmann realised he was still carrying his gun. He had grown so used to its snug weight, he kept forgetting he even had it. He ought to have dumped it during the night. If they had picked up Frau Winter he must surely be next. He wondered where they had arrested her—at the office, or in her apartment—and how they were treating her. As he climbed out of the car after Schmidt he could feel the sweat trickling beneath his shirt. The guards recognised Schmidt and waved him through and Hartmann slipped in after him. He was not even asked his name.

They passed another pair of SS men in the concierge's office and climbed the communal staircase—stone at first, that became polished wood. The walls were tiled an institutional grey and green, as in a metro system. There were dim electric lamps but the light came mostly from the landing windows that looked out onto a small rear garden of fir and silver birch trees. They clumped up noisily, past apartments on the ground and first floors. It was said by the Propaganda Ministry that the Führer still had the same neighbours as he did before he became Chancellor: proof that at heart he remained a simple member of the *Volk*. Perhaps it was true, thought Hartmann, in which case what strange goings-on these people must have seen over the past few years, from the death of Hitler's niece in 1931 to yesterday's lunchtime visit by Mussolini. They continued to climb. He felt trapped, as if he were being drawn relentlessly by some dark magnetic force. He slowed his pace.

"Come on," said Schmidt. "Keep up!"

On the second floor, nothing distinguished the apartment's solid double door from the others. Schmidt knocked and they were admitted by an SS adjutant into a long, narrow vestibule. It stretched away on either side, parquet-floored, with rugs, paintings, sculptures. The atmosphere was silent, unhomely, unlived-in. The adjutant invited them to sit. "The Führer is not yet ready." He moved away.

Schmidt whispered confidingly, "He keeps late hours. Often he doesn't emerge from his bedroom until noon."

"You mean we may have to sit here for another *hour*?"

"Not today. Chamberlain is due at eleven."

Hartmann gave him a look of surprise. It was the first he knew that Hitler was meeting the British Prime Minister.

It took Chamberlain's car several minutes to break free from the clutching hands of the crowd around the front of the hotel. The Prime Minister rode in the back with Dunglass, Legat sat up front next to the driver. Behind them was a second Mercedes carrying the Prime Minister's two bodyguards. They made a partial circuit of the square and then sped off across Odeonsplatz into a district of elaborate royal palaces and grand public buildings that Legat vaguely remembered from 1932. He studied Chamberlain in the wing mirror, gazing rigidly ahead. People were shouting his name, waving at him. He sped on, oblivious. No longer the dry-as-dust administrator of popular legend, he had become a seer—a Messiah of Peace, robed in the drab costume of an elderly accountant.

They drove onto a bridge with a stone balustrade. The river was wide and green, the strip of trees along the embankment an advancing line of fire: red, gold, orange. The sun lit the gilded figure of the Angel of Peace leaning forward on top of her high stone column. Beyond the monument the road looped through a park. Emerging, they began to climb the slope of Prinzregentenstrasse. Legat had always pictured it as steep, in the way that one misremembers scenes from childhood, but now in a powerful car it seemed no more than a gentle incline. They passed a theatre on the right and suddenly they were in the space in front of Hitler's apartment, and this at least was exactly as he had carried it in his mind, right down to the crowd on the pavement who recognised Chamberlain and started to cheer. Again, the Prime Minister, in his mystic state, didn't even glance across at them. The guards saluted and an adjutant stepped forward to open the car door.

Legat let himself out and followed Chamberlain and Dunglass through the entrance and up the steps into the gloomy interior.

The adjutant ushered the Prime Minister into a small caged elevator and pressed the button, but it failed to move. He tried for another half-minute, his handsome young face turning blotchy with embarrassment. Finally, he had to pull open the gate and indicate they should proceed on foot. Legat fell in beside Dunglass as they climbed the stairs behind Chamberlain. Dunglass whispered, "No ink last night, hardly any telephones that work. I don't think these chaps are quite as efficient as they like to make out."

Legat was praying that Hartmann would be there. He was not sure what he could offer God in return, but it would be something, he promised Him—a different life, a fresh start, a gesture equal to the age. They arrived at the second floor. The adjutant opened the door to the apartment, and there—*mirabile dictu*—was Hartmann, sitting with his long legs stretched out. Beside him Legat recognised Hitler's translator. They both stood when they saw Chamberlain. Hartmann stared at Legat but there was no opportunity for anything more than a glance to pass between them: the adjutant was insisting Legat follow Chamberlain and Dunglass across the hall and into the room opposite. He told Schmidt to come, too. Hartmann made a move to accompany them but the adjutant shook his head. "Not you. Wait here."

For a few seconds Hartmann stood alone in the empty lobby. Legat's brief glance had been full of warning. Something else must have happened. He wondered if he should slip away while he still had the chance. Then he heard a door open to his right and he turned to see Hitler emerging from a room at the far end of the corridor. He was smoothing his hair and straightening his brown Party jacket, checking his armband—fussy, last-minute adjustments, like an actor preparing to go on stage. Hartmann jumped to his feet and saluted. *"Heil Hitler!"*

Hitler looked at him and raised his hand in absentminded acknowledgement but gave no sign of recognition. He stepped into the room in which the others were waiting and the door was closed behind him.

Afterwards, Legat would be able to claim—not boast: that was never his style—that he had been in the same room as Hitler on three separate occasions, twice at the Führerbau and once in his apartment. But, like most of the British eyewitnesses at Munich, he was never able to provide anything more than the most commonplace description—Hitler looked as he looked in the photographs and the newsreels, except in colour, and the main shock of the encounter lay simply in finding oneself in proximity to a world-famous phenomenon, like seeing the Empire State Building or Red Square for the first time. One detail stuck in his mind, though. Hitler smelled strongly of sweat—he had detected it in his study and caught a whiff of it now as he passed. He had the body odour of a frontline soldier or a workman who had not bathed or changed his shirt for a week. He was yet again in a dour mood and made no attempt to hide it. He stalked in, greeted Chamberlain, ignored everyone else, then went and sat in the furthest corner of the room and waited for his visitor to join him.

The Prime Minister took the armchair to his right. Schmidt sat on his left. The adjutant stationed himself by the door. It was a big room, running almost the entire length of the apartment, looking out onto the street, and furnished in modern style, like a salon aboard a luxury liner. There was a library alcove at the far end, crammed with books, where Hitler and Chamberlain were sitting; an area of sofas and chairs in the middle, where Legat and Dunglass had perched themselves; and a dining table at the opposite end. Legat was close enough to hear what was said but far enough distant not to impinge on the conversation. However, because Hitler was in the corner, it was impossible for him to obey the Prime Minister's instruction and entirely escape the dictator's eye line, and from time to time he noticed those strangely opaque blue eyes flicker in his direction, as if he was trying to work out why these two strangers were present in his flat. There was no offer of refreshment.

Chamberlain cleared his throat. "First of all, I would like to thank you, Chancellor, for inviting me to your home and for agreeing to hold one final conversation before I return to London."

Schmidt translated faithfully. Hitler was sitting slightly propped forward by a cushion. He listened, nodded politely. "*Ja.*"

"I thought we might briefly discuss some areas of mutual interest between our two countries on which we might be able to cooperate in the future."

More nodding. "*Ja.*"

The Prime Minister reached into his jacket pocket and took out a small notepad. From his inside pocket he produced his fountain pen. Hitler watched him warily. Chamberlain opened the first page. "Perhaps we might begin with this terrible civil war in Spain . . ."

Almost all the talking was done by Chamberlain: Spain, Eastern Europe, trade, disarmament—he ticked off the list of topics he wished to raise and to each Hitler responded briefly, without being drawn into detail. "That is a matter of vital interest to Germany" was the most he would say. Or, "Our experts have made a study of the subject." He fidgeted in his chair, folded and refolded his arms, looked over at his adjutant. Legat thought he was like a householder who had agreed in a moment of weakness to let a salesman or a religious proselytiser over the threshold, bitterly regretted it, and was looking for an opportunity to get rid of him. Legat himself kept glancing at the door, trying to calculate how he might be able to escape long enough to whisper a warning to Hartmann.

Even Chamberlain seemed to detect that his audience was becoming distracted. He said, "I realise how busy you are. I mustn't detain you further. What I wish to say in conclusion is this. As I left London yesterday morning, women and children and even babies were being fitted with masks to protect them against the horrors of poison gas. I hope, Herr Chancellor, that you and I can agree that modern warfare, the brunt of which will be directed as never before against ordinary civilians, is abhorrent to all civilised nations."

"*Ja, ja.*"

"I believe it would be a pity if my visit passed off with nothing more than the settlement of the Czech question. In that spirit, I have drafted a short statement putting on record our mutual desire to establish a new era in Anglo-German relations that may bring stability to the whole of Europe. I would like us both to sign it."

Schmidt translated. When he came to the word "statement" Legat saw Hitler dart a look of suspicion at Chamberlain. The Prime Minister drew the two copies from his inside pocket. He handed one to Schmidt. "Perhaps you would be kind enough to translate this for the Chancellor."

Schmidt glanced at it, and then began to read it out in German, carefully emphasising every word.

" 'We, the German Führer and Chancellor and the British Prime Minister, have had a further meeting today and are agreed in recognising that the question of Anglo-German relations is of the first importance for the two countries and for Europe.'"

Hitler nodded slowly. *"Ja."*

"'We regard the agreement signed last night and the Anglo-German Naval Agreement as symbolic of the desire of our two peoples never to go to war with one another again.'"

At that, Hitler cocked his head slightly to one side. Clearly, he had recognised his own words. A slight frown appeared. Schmidt waited to be told to go on but Hitler said nothing. In the end, the translator continued of his own accord.

"'We are resolved that the method of consultation shall be the method adopted to deal with any other questions that may concern our two countries, and we are determined to continue our efforts to remove possible sources of difference and thus to contribute to assure the peace of Europe.'"

For several seconds after Schmidt had finished, Hitler didn't move. Legat could see his gaze travelling round the room. A process of calculation was evidently under way. Presumably, it was hard for him to refuse to sign sentiments which he had himself expressed in public. Yet it was also obvious that he resented it—resented this fussy old English gentleman tricking his way into his home and presenting him with this démarche. He suspected a trap. The English were cunning, after all. On the other hand, if he signed it, at least the meeting would be over and Chamberlain would clear out. And in the end it *was* only a scrap of paper, the expression of a pious hope, without any legal consequence. What did it matter?

This—or at any rate something like it—was what Legat afterwards surmised must have gone through the dictator's mind.

"Ja, ich werde es unterschreiben."

"The Führer says yes, he will sign it."

Chamberlain smiled with relief. Hitler clicked his fingers at the adjutant, who hastened towards him, pulling out a pen. Dunglass stood to get a clearer view. Legat saw his chance and walked over to the door.

Hartmann had sat for ten minutes in the deserted vestibule. The press summary lay on the chair beside him. To his left he could hear the faint sounds of plates clattering, a woman's voice, a door opening and closing. That, he guessed, must be the service area—the kitchen, cloakroom, servants' quarters. The Führer's bedroom must therefore be to the right—the place he had emerged from. The door to the room where Chamberlain and Hitler were meeting was closed; he could hear nothing through the thick wood. Hanging next to it was a watercolour of the Vienna State Opera House—technically proficient, but stilted and soulless. He suspected it must be Hitler's own work. He rose and crossed the parquet floor to examine it. Yes, there were his initials in the bottom right-hand corner. Pretending to study the picture more closely, he glanced towards the Führer's bedroom in the shadows at the end of the passage. There was a room adjoining it, only four or five paces away. Curiosity overcame him. He looked towards the kitchen to check he was unobserved, then casually crossed to it and opened the door.

It was a small bedroom looking out onto the trees in the back garden. The Venetian blind was half down. There was a strong sickly-sweet scent of both dried and fresh flowers and of dark cinnamon-like perfumes that had dehydrated in their bottles. On the dressing table were a vase of withered roses and a bowl of yellow and purple free-sias. Draped across the bed was a simple white cotton nightdress like the one Leyna had been wearing. He walked to the end of the bed and opened the door to a bathroom. He could see, through the open door opposite to Hitler's bedroom, a jacket hanging on the back of a chair. As he retreated he took a closer look at the dressing table. A framed black-and-white photograph of a dog. A pile of notepaper with *Angela Raubal* in the top-left corner. A copy of the fashion magazine *Die Dame.* He checked the date: September 1931.

Leyna had been right. Once one saw it, one could not doubt it. The proximity of the room to Hitler's, the unnatural stifling closeness, the shared bathroom, the way it had been left as a shrine, like an Egyptian burial chamber—

Behind him he heard a noise. He stepped back quickly and closed the door. Legat was emerging from the drawing room. After glancing over his shoulder he said in a quick, quiet voice, "I'm afraid I have bad news—the Gestapo have the document."

It took Hartmann a moment to adjust his mind. He looked past Legat to the open doorway but couldn't see anyone. He whispered, "When?"

"Less than an hour ago. They searched my room while I was showering."

"You're sure it's definitely gone?"

"No question of it. Paul, I'm so very sorry—"

Hartmann held up his hand to silence him. He needed to think. "If it's less than an hour, they must be looking for me. I—"

He stopped himself. The adjutant had appeared behind Legat. He emerged from the drawing room, followed by Chamberlain and Hitler. After them came Schmidt and Dunglass. The Prime Minister was holding two small pieces of paper. He gave one to Hitler. "This is for you, Herr Chancellor."

Hitler handed it immediately to the adjutant. Now that his visitors were leaving he seemed more relaxed. *"Doktor Schmidt begleitet Sie zu Ihrem Hotel. Ich wünsche Ihnen einen angenehmen Flug."*

Schmidt said, "I will escort you back to your hotel, Prime Minister. The Führer wishes you a pleasant flight."

"Thank you." Chamberlain shook hands with Hitler. He looked as if he would like to make a further short speech but decided against it. The adjutant opened the front door and the Prime Minister went out onto the landing with Schmidt. Dunglass said, with an edge of sarcasm, "Coming, Hugh?"

Legat knew he would never see Hartmann again. But there was nothing he could say. He nodded to him and went out after the others.

Once the door had closed, Hitler stood staring at it for several seconds. He was rubbing the palm of his right hand with his left thumb—an unconscious action: round and round, as if he had sprained it. Finally, he noticed the press summary lying on the chair. He turned to Hartmann. "Is that what the foreign press are saying?"

Hartmann said, "Yes, my Führer."

"Bring it in here."

Hartmann had been hoping to slip away. Instead he found himself following Hitler into the drawing room. The adjutant was straightening the furniture, smoothing the cushions. Hartmann handed over the press summary. Hitler fished in his breast pocket for his spectacles. From the street below came the sound of cheering. Glasses in one hand, he glanced at the window, then went over to it. He pulled back the edge of the net curtain and stared down at the crowd. He shook his head. "How can one make war with such a people?" Hartmann crossed to a different window. The crowd had grown much larger in the last half-hour, once word had got out that Chamberlain was in the building. Several hundred people were lining the opposite pavement. The men were waving their hats, the women stretching out their arms. The angle made it impossible to see the Prime Minister's car but one could tell its progress by the way people's heads turned to follow it as he drove away.

Hitler dropped the curtain. "The German population has allowed itself to be duped—and by Chamberlain of all people!" He shook out his spectacles and put them on one-handed. He began scanning the press summary.

Hartmann was about to move away from the window when his eye was caught by fresh activity in the street. A big Mercedes limousine roared into view and pulled up sharply opposite. Hartmann could make out Ribbentrop, and beside him Sauer. Plainly in a hurry, they jumped out and began crossing the road, looking right and left, even before their escort—a second Mercedes, carrying a quartet of SS men—had come to a stop. As Sauer waited for a truck to pass, he stared up at the apartment. Instinctively Hartmann drew back to avoid being seen.

Hitler was flicking through the summary. In a mocking voice he read out the headline in *The New York Times*—CHAMBERLAIN HERO OF MUNICH CROWDS!—and then another sentence: *The cheers for Hitler were mechanical and polite. But for Chamberlain they were ecstatic.*

In the vestibule, the entry bell rang. The adjutant left the room. Hitler threw the document onto the sofa and went over to his desk. For a second time Hartmann was left alone with him. He heard voices in the lobby. He slipped his hand inside his jacket. His fingertips touched metal. But then immediately he withdrew it. It was absurd. He was about to be arrested. Yet *still* he could not act. And if he couldn't do it, who would? In that moment, in a flash of clarity, he saw that nobody—not him, not the Army, not a lone assassin— that no German would disrupt their common destiny until it was fulfilled.

The door opened and Ribbentrop came in. Sauer was behind him. They stopped and saluted. Sauer gave Hartmann a look of violent hatred. Hartmann felt a roaring in his ears. He readied himself. Ribbentrop, however, seemed the more nervous. "My Führer, I am told you have just seen Chamberlain."

"He asked for a private meeting last night. I couldn't see the harm in it."

"May I ask what he wanted?"

"For me to sign a piece of paper." Hitler picked it up from the desk and gave it to the Foreign Minister. "He seemed such a harmless old gentleman. I thought it would be rude to refuse."

Ribbentrop's face appeared to tauten as he read it. Of course, the Führer could not have made an error. It would be unthinkable even to suggest it. But Hartmann could sense a change of atmosphere in the room. Eventually, Hitler said irritably, "Oh, don't take it all so seriously! That piece of paper is of no further significance whatsoever. The problem is here—with the German people."

He turned his back on them and bent to examine the papers on his desk.

Hartmann saw his chance. With a slight bow first to the Foreign Minister and then to Sauer he withdrew towards the door. Neither attempted to stop him. A minute later he was out on the street.

The Lockheed Electra was bucketing through the low cloud that covered the English Channel. Beyond the windows there was nothing to be seen except an infinity of grey.

Legat sat in the same rear seat he had occupied on the flight to Munich, his chin in his hand, staring out at nothing. The Prime Minister was at the front with Wilson. Strang and Malkin were in the middle. Only Ashton-Gwatkin was missing: he was still in Prague, selling the agreement to the Czechs. The atmosphere on board was exhausted, melancholy. Malkin and Dunglass were asleep. There was a hamper of food in the locker behind Legat's seat, provided by the Regina Palast Hotel, but when Chamberlain had been told it was a present from the Germans he had given orders it was not to be touched. It didn't matter. Nobody was hungry.

Once again Legat could tell by the pressure in his ears when they were starting to descend. He took out his watch. It was just after five. Wilson leaned out of his seat. "Hugh!" He gestured to him to come forward. "Gentlemen, could we talk?"

Legat walked unsteadily to the front of the plane. Strang and Malkin shifted into the seats behind the Prime Minister. He and Dunglass had to stand with their backs to the cockpit. The plane lurched and they knocked into one another. Wilson said, "I've been speaking to Commander Robinson. We should be on the ground in about half an hour. Apparently, there's quite a crowd waiting for us, as you might imagine. The King has sent the Lord Chamberlain to conduct the PM directly to Buckingham Palace so that Their Majesties can convey their thanks in person. There will be a meeting of the Cabinet as soon as we get back to Downing Street."

The Prime Minister said, "Obviously, I shall have to make a statement to the cameras."

Strang cleared his throat. "May I say, Prime Minister, that I would urge you to treat any undertaking given by Hitler with the utmost caution? The actual agreement over the Sudetenland is one thing—most people will understand the reasons for that. But this other document . . ." His voice trailed off.

He was seated directly behind Chamberlain. His long face was anguished. The Prime Minister had to turn his head slightly to reply to him, and Legat registered again how stubborn he was in profile. "I understand the Foreign Office point of view, William. I know Cadogan, for example, believes we should treat appeasement simply as a regrettable necessity—make it clear we have no practical alternative as things stand, use it purely as an opportunity to buy time and announce a massive programme of rearmament. Well, we *are* rearming massively—next year alone we shall devote more than half of all government expenditure to arms." And now he spoke to them all—perhaps particularly to Legat, although he could never afterwards be sure. "I am not a pacifist. The main lesson I have learned in my dealings with Hitler is that one simply can't play poker with a gangster if one has no cards in one's hand. But if I speak in such terms when we land that will simply give him the excuse to continue his belligerence. Whereas if he keeps his word—and I happen to believe he will—we will avoid war."

Strang persisted. "But what if he breaks his word?"

"If he breaks it—well, then the world will see him for what he is. No one then can be in any doubt. It will unite the country and rally the Dominions in a way they simply are not at present. Who knows?" He permitted himself a slight smile. "Perhaps it will even bring the Americans in on our side." He patted his pocket. "Therefore, I intend to give this joint declaration the maximum publicity as soon as we land in London."

It was 5:38 p.m. when the Prime Minister's plane finally broke through the clouds and appeared above Heston Aerodrome. As the ground flickered into view, Legat could see the traffic along the Great West Road. Cars were halted for more than a mile in either direction. It had been raining heavily. Headlights reflected off the wet tarmac. A vast swarm of people, thousands upon thousands of them, was clustered at the airport gates. The Lockheed roared low over the terminal building, dropping fast. He gripped the armrests. The wheels bounced on the grass runway a couple of times, then settled, and they lurched over the airfield at a hundred miles an hour, sending up a spray of water on either side, then braking sharply, before turning onto the concrete apron.

The scene beyond the window in the autumn gloom was chaotic—cameramen and newspaper reporters, airport workers, policemen, scores of Eton schoolboys bizarre in their formal dress, Cabinet ministers, MPs, diplomats, members of the public and the House of Lords, the Lord Mayor of London in his ceremonial chain. Even at a distance Legat could make out the immensely tall figure of Lord Halifax in his bowler hat standing like Don Quixote beside the diminutive Sancho Panza of Sir Alexander Cadogan. Syers was with them. Their umbrellas were furled. It must have stopped raining. There was only one car, a big old-fashioned Rolls-Royce, flying the royal standard. A man in overalls guided them onto their stand and signalled that the pilot should cut the engines. The propellers stuttered to a stop.

The cockpit door opened. As before, when they landed in Munich, Commander Robinson stopped to exchange a few words with the Prime Minister, then came down the sloping aisle and opened the rear door. This time the gust of air that blew into the cabin was English, cold and wet. Legat stayed in his seat as the Prime Minister went past. His jaw was clenched with tension. How odd that a man so fundamentally shy should thrust himself into public life and fight his way to the top! The breeze caught the door, flapping it shut, and Chamberlain had to fend it off with his elbow. He bent out his head and descended into a terrific din of clapping and cheering and shouting that seemed almost hysterical. Wilson stood in the aisle and held back the others until the Prime Minister had cleared the bottom of the steps: the moment of glory must be the chief's alone. Only after Chamberlain had started moving along the receiving line, shaking hands, did Wilson venture out after him, followed by Strang, Malkin and Dunglass.

Legat was the last to leave. The steps were slippery. The pilot caught his arm to steady him. In the damp blue twilight, the lights of the newsreel cameras were a brilliant white, like frozen lighting. Chamberlain finished greeting the dignitaries and turned to stand in front of a bank of a dozen microphones, crested with the names of their respective organisations: BBC, Movietone, CBS, Pathé. Legat could not see his face, only his narrow back and sloping shoulders silhouetted against the glare. He waited for the cheering to subside. His voice carried thin and clear in the wind.

"There are only two things I want to say. First of all, I received a tremendous number of letters during all these anxious days—and so has my wife—letters of support and approval and gratitude; and I cannot tell you what an encouragement that has been to me. I want to thank the British people for what they have done."

The crowd cheered again. Someone shouted, "What *you* have done!" Another called out, "Good old Chamberlain!"

"Next I want to say that the settlement of the Czechoslovakian problem which has now been achieved is, in my view, only the prelude to a larger settlement in which all Europe may find peace. This morning I had another talk with the German Chancellor, Herr Hitler, and here is the paper which bears his name upon it as well as mine . . ." He held it aloft, flapping in the breeze. "Some of you perhaps have already heard what it contains, but I would just like to read it to you . . ."

He was too vain to put on his spectacles. He had to hold it at arm's length to make it out. And that was Legat's lasting image of the famous moment—carried burned into the retina of his memory until the day of his death, many years later, as an honoured public servant—the jagged black figure at the centre of a great bright light, his arm stretched out, like a man who had thrown himself onto an electrified fence.

The second Lockheed came in to land just as the Prime Minister was being driven away in the King's Rolls-Royce. As Chamberlain reached the airport gates the distant applause of the well-wishers merged with the roar of aircraft engines. Syers said, "My goodness, would you listen to that! The roads are blocked all the way into central London."

"You'd think we'd just won a war rather than avoided one."

"There were thousands gathering in the Mall when we left. Apparently, the King and Queen intend to take him out on to the balcony. Here, let me carry that." He lifted one of the red boxes out of the aircraft hold. "So, how was it?"

"Pretty ghastly, to be honest."

They walked together across the apron towards the British Airways terminal. When they had gone about halfway, the newsreel lights were abruptly extinguished. In the sudden murk the crowd gave a good-humoured collective groan. They began to drift towards the exit. Syers said, "There's a bus to ferry us all back to Downing Street. God knows how long it will take."

Inside the packed terminal, the Italian and French ambassadors were talking to the Lord Chancellor and the Minister of War. Syers went off to see about the bus. Legat stayed behind to guard the red boxes. Exhausted, he sat down on a bench beneath a poster advertising flights to Stockholm. There was a telephone box by the customs desk. He wondered if he should call Pamela to let her know he had landed, but the thought of her voice and her inevitable questions depressed him. Through the large plate-glass window, he could see the straggle of passengers from the second Lockheed coming into the terminal. Sir Joseph Horner was between the two detectives. Joan was walking with Miss Anderson. She was carrying a suitcase in one hand and a portable typewriter in the other. She headed in his direction the moment she saw him.

"Mr. Legat!"

"Really, Joan, do call me Hugh, for goodness' sake."

"Hugh, then." She sat down next to him and lit a cigarette. "Well, that was thrilling."

"Was it?"

"Yes, I'd say it was." She turned to face him and looked him up and down. Her gaze was frank. "I wanted to catch you before we left Munich but you'd already taken off. I have a tiny confession to make."

"And what is that?" She was very pretty. But he wasn't in the mood for a flirtation.

She leaned in conspiratorially. "Between you and me, Hugh, I am not altogether what I seem."

"No?"

"No. In fact, I am something of a guardian angel."

Now she was starting to get on his nerves. He looked around the terminal. The ambassadors were still talking to the ministers. Syers was in the telephone box, presumably trying to track down their bus. He said wearily, "What on earth are you talking about?"

She hauled her suitcase up onto her lap. "Colonel Menzies is my uncle—well, the father of a second cousin, to be more precise about it—and he likes to give me the odd errand to run. The truth is, the reason I was sent to Munich, apart from my typing skills, which are exemplary, was to watch over *you*." She snapped the catches, opened the lid and from beneath her neatly folded underwear extracted the memorandum. It was still in its original envelope. "I took it from your room last night, for safekeeping, after you went off with your friend. And really, Hugh—I like your name, by the way: it suits you—really, Hugh, *thank God I did*."

The fact of his continuing freedom was miraculous to Hartmann. That afternoon, as he left the Führerbau to be driven to the airport, and later as he sat on board the Junkers passenger plane that had been chartered by the Foreign Ministry to fly them home, and especially that evening when he landed at Tempelhof—at each stage of his journey back to Berlin he expected to be arrested. But there was to be no hand on his arm, no sudden confrontation by men in plain clothes, no "Herr Hartmann, will you come with us?" Instead he walked unmolested through the terminal building to the taxi rank.

The city was full of Friday-night revellers, enjoying the unexpected peace. He no longer felt the same contempt for them he had in Munich. Each raised glass, each smile, each arm around a lover he now saw as a gesture against the regime.

The bell inside her apartment rang unanswered for a long time. He was on the point of giving up. But then he heard the sound of the lock turning and the door opened and there she was.

Later that night, she said, "They will hang you one day—you know that, don't you?"

They were lying at opposite ends of the bath, facing one another. She had lit a candle. Through the open door came the sound of an illegal foreign radio station, playing jazz.

"What makes you say that?"

"Because they told me so, just before they let me go. 'Stay away from him, Frau Winter—that is our advice to you. We know his type. He may think he's got away with it today, but we will catch him out eventually.' They were perfectly polite about it."

"What did you say?"

"I thanked them for the warning."

He laughed and stretched out his absurdly long legs. Water slopped onto the floor. He could feel her skin smooth against his. She was right. They were right. They would hang him one day—on 20 August 1944, to be exact, in Plötzensee Prison, at the end of a length of piano wire: he could sense his destiny even if he could not be exact about it—but there was life to be lived before then, and a battle to fight, and a cause that was worth dying for.

Legat was finally sent home a little after 10 p.m. Cleverly had told him there was no need for him to wait until the end of the Cabinet meeting: Syers would handle the boxes; he should take the weekend off.

He walked from Number 10 through streets that were filled with people celebrating. Fireworks were being set off here and there across the city. The flashes of rockets lit the sky.

The upstairs windows were in darkness. The children must be asleep. He turned his key in the lock and set down his suitcase in the hall. He could see the light on in the sitting room. Pamela put aside her book as soon as he came in. "Darling!" She jumped up and threw her arms around him. For more than a minute they didn't speak. Finally, she broke away and cupped his face in her hands. Her eyes searched his. She said, "I have missed you so much."

"How are you? How are the children?"

"Better for having you home."

She started to unbutton his coat. He caught her hands. "No, don't. I'm not staying."

She took a step backwards. "You have to go back to work?" It was not a criticism; it sounded more like a hope.

"No, it's not work. I'll just go up and see the children."

The house was so small they shared a room. John had a bed. Diana was still in a cot. He never ceased to wonder at the quality of the silence when the children were asleep. By the glow of the landing light they lay, unmoving in the semi-darkness, their mouths slightly open. He touched their hair. He wanted to kiss them but didn't dare in case he woke them. From the top of the chest of drawers the eyepieces of their gas masks watched him. Gently, he closed the door.

Pamela had her back to him when he went down into the sitting room. She turned, dry-eyed. Emotional scenes were never her style. He was thankful for that. She said calmly, "How long will you be gone?"

"I'll just stay at the club. I'll come back in the morning. We can talk then."

"I can change, you know. If you want me to."

"Everything has to change, Pamela. You, me, everything. I've been thinking I might resign from the service."

"And do what?"

"You won't laugh?"

"Try me."

"I thought on the flight back that I might join the RAF."

"But I just heard Chamberlain on the wireless telling the crowd in Downing Street it was peace for our time."

"He shouldn't have done that. He regretted it the moment he said it." According to Dunglass, Mrs. Chamberlain had talked him into it: she was the one person he never could refuse.

"So you still think there'll be a war?"

"I'm sure of it."

"Then what has this all been about—all this hope, this celebration?"

"It's simply relief. And I don't blame people for it. When I look at the children, I feel it myself. But all that's happened really is that a tripwire has been laid down for the future. And Hitler will cross it, sooner or later." He kissed her cheek. "I'll see you in the morning."

She didn't reply. He picked up his suitcase and went out into the night. Someone in Smith Square was letting off rockets. In the gardens he could hear cries of delight. The old buildings gleamed fitfully in the cascades of falling sparks and then returned to darkness.

ACKNOWLEDGEMENTS

This novel is the culmination of a fascination with the Munich Agreement that dates back more than thirty years, and I would like to thank Denys Blakeway, the producer with whom I made a BBC television documentary, *God Bless You, Mr. Chamberlain*, to mark the fiftieth anniversary of the conference in 1988. We have maintained a mild mutual obsession with the subject ever since.

In Germany, my friends at Heyne Verlag, Patrick Niemeyer and Doris Schuck, helped arrange my research in Munich. I am especially grateful to Dr. Alexander Krause for his expert guided tour of what was once the Führerbau and is now the Faculty of Music and Theatre (of which he is Chancellor), and to the Bavarian Interior Ministry for allowing me to visit Hitler's old apartment in Prinzregentenplatz, now used as a police headquarters.

In Britain, my thanks go to Stephen Parkinson, Political Secretary at 10 Downing Street, and to Professor Patrick Salmon, Chief Historian at the Foreign and Commonwealth Office.

I was fortunate, yet again, to benefit from the advice and support of four shrewd "first readers." To my editor at Hutchinson in London, Jocasta Hamilton; and at Knopf in New York, Sonny Mehta; to my German translator, Wolfgang Müller; and to my wife, Gill Hornby, my deepest thanks, as always.

I would also like to acknowledge my debt to the following works: John Charmley, *Chamberlain and the Lost Peace*; Jock Colville, *The Fringes of Power: Downing Street Diaries, 1939–1955*; David Dilks (editor), *The Diaries of Sir Alexander Cadogan*; Max Domarus, *Hit-*

ACKNOWLEDGEMENTS

ler: *Speeches and Proclamations, 1935–1938*; David Dutton, *Neville Chamberlain*; David Faber, *Munich, 1938: Appeasement and World War II*; Keith Feiling, *The Life of Neville Chamberlain*; Joachim Fest, *Albert Speer: Conversations with Hitler's Architect*; Joachim Fest, *Plotting Hitler's Death: The German Resistance to Hitler, 1933–1945*; Hans Bernd Gisevius, *To the Bitter End*; Paul Gore-Booth, *With Great Truth and Respect*; Sheila Grant Duff, *The Parting of the Ways*; Ronald Hayman, *Hitler and Geli*; Nevile Henderson, *Failure of a Mission*; Peter Hoffmann, *German Resistance to Hitler*; Peter Hoffmann, *The History of the German Resistance, 1933–1945*; Peter Hoffmann, *Hitler's Personal Security*; Heinz Höhne, *Canaris*; Lord Home, *The Way the Wind Blows*; David Irving, *The War Path*; Otto John, *Twice Through the Lines*; *The Memoirs of Field Marshal Keitel*; Ian Kershaw, *Making Friends with Hitler: Lord Londonderry and Britain's Road to War*; Ivone Kirkpatrick, *The Inner Circle*; Alexander Krause, *No. 12 Arcisstrasse*; Klemens von Klemperer (editor), *A Noble Combat: The Letters of Sheila Grant Duff and Adam von Trott zu Solz, 1932–1939*; Valentine Lawford, *Bound for Diplomacy*; Giles MacDonogh, *1938: Hitler's Gamble*; Giles MacDonogh, *A Good German: Adam von Trott zu Solz*; Andreas Mayor (translator), *Ciano's Diary, 1937–1938*; Harold Nicolson, *Diaries and Letters, 1930–1939*; John Julius Norwich (editor), *The Duff Cooper Diaries*; NS-Dokumentationszentrum, München, *Munich and National Socialism*; Richard Ollard (editor), *The Diaries of A. L. Rowse*; Richard Overy, with Andrew Wheatcroft, *The Road to War*; David Reynolds, *Summits: Six Meetings That Shaped the Twentieth Century*; Robert Rhodes James (editor), *Chips: The Diaries of Sir Henry Channon*; Andrew Roberts, *"The Holy Fox": A Biography of Lord Halifax*; Paul Schmidt, *Hitler's Interpreter*; Robert Self, *Neville Chamberlain*; Robert Self (editor), *The Neville Chamberlain Diary Letters*, Volume Four; William L. Shirer, *Berlin Diary*; Reinhard Spitzy, *How We Squandered the Reich*; Lord Strang, *Home and Abroad*; Despina Stratigakos, *Hitler at Home*; Christopher Sykes, *Troubled Loyalty: A Biography of Adam von Trott*; A. J. P. Taylor, *The Origins of the Second World War*; Telford Taylor, *Munich: The Price of Peace*; D. R. Thorpe, *Alec Douglas-*

ACKNOWLEDGEMENTS

Home; Daniel Todman, *Britain's War: Into Battle, 1937–1941;* Gerhard L. Weinberg, *The Foreign Policy of Hitler's Germany, 1937–1939;* Ernst von Weizsäcker, *Memoirs;* Sir John Wheeler-Bennett, *The Nemesis of Power: The German Army in Politics, 1918–1945;* Stefan Zweig, *The World of Yesterday: Memoirs of a European.*